# FIFTEEN LIVES OF HARRY AUGUST

PRAISE FOR *THE FIRST FIFTEEN LIVES OF HARRY AUGUST*

"Beautifully written and structured . . . a remarkable book" *Booklist*

"I don't say this lightly, but *The First Fifteen Lives of Harry August* is one of the top ten books I've ever read"
James Dashner, bestselling author of *The Maze Runner*

"A masterful literary thriller . . . *The First Fifteen Lives of Harry August* is absolutely worth tracking down, and throwing yourself into. All the best fiction gives you the thrill of imagining yourself living other lives, but few books do such a great job of giving you so many of them"
*io9.com*

"The writing is impeccable . . . Plus Harry is a fascinating main character . . . And if his next fifteen lives are half as eventful, we look forward to the sequel" *Heat*

"An astonishing re-invention of the time-travel narrative. Bold, magical and masterful" M. R. Carey, author of *The Girl with all the Gifts*

"A truly extraordinary novel: an impeccable portrait of a friendship tortured by time in which masterful character and fantastic narrative come together to tremendous effect" *Tor.com*

"A brave, genre-defying novel, which is mind-blowing in its originality and bold concept . . . Stunning" *Novelicious*

"A thoughtful and considered time-travel novel, shocking twists and, most important of all, a beautiful character. Harry August will break

your heart fifteen times.' Jared Shurin

# THE FIRST
# FIFTEEN
# LIVES OF
# HARRY AUGUST

## CLAIRE NORTH

www.orbitbooks.net

ORBIT

First published in Great Britain in 2014 by Orbit
This paperback edition first published in 2014 by Orbit

A CIP catalogue record for this book
is available from the British Library.

HB ISBN 978-0-356-50258-8

Typeset in Bembo by M Rules
Printed and bound in Great Britain by
Clays Ltd, St Ives plc

Papers used by Orbit are from well-managed forests
and other responsible sources.

MIX
Paper from
responsible sources
FSC® C104740

Orbit
An imprint of
Little, Brown Book Group
100 Victoria Embankment
London EC4Y 0DY

An Hachette UK Company
www.hachette.co.uk

www.orbitbooks.net

# Introduction

I am writing this for you.
   My enemy.
   My friend.
   You know, already, you must know.
   You have lost.

# Chapter 1

The second cataclysm began in my eleventh life, in 1996. I was dying my usual death, slipping away in a warm morphine haze, which she interrupted like an ice cube down my spine.

She was seven, I was seventy-eight. She had straight blonde hair worn in a long pigtail down her back, I had bright white hair, or at least the remnants of the same. I wore a hospital gown designed for sterile humility; she, bright-blue school uniform and a felt cap. She perched on the side of my bed, her feet dangling off it, and peered into my eyes. She examined the heart monitor plugged into my chest, observed where I'd disconnected the alarm, felt for my pulse, and said, "I nearly missed you, Dr August."

Her German was Berlin high, but she could have addressed me in any language of the world and still passed for respectable. She scratched at the back of her left leg, where her white knee-length socks had begun to itch from the rain outside. While scratching she said, "I need to send a message back through time. If time can be said to be important here. As you're conveniently dying, I ask you to relay it to the Clubs of your origin, as it has been passed down to me."

1

I tried to speak, but the words tumbled together on my tongue, and I said nothing.

"The world is ending," she said. "The message has come down from child to adult, child to adult, passed back down the generations from a thousand years forward in time. The world is ending and we cannot prevent it. So now it's up to you."

I found that Thai was the only language which wanted to pass my lips in any coherent form, and the only word which I seemed capable of forming was, why?

Not, I hasten to add, why was the world ending?

Why did it matter?

She smiled, and understood my meaning without needing it to be said. She leaned in close and murmured in my ear, "The world is ending, as it always must. But the end of the world is getting faster."

That was the beginning of the end.

# Chapter 2

Let us begin at the beginning.

The Club, the cataclysm, my eleventh life and the deaths which followed – none peaceful – all are meaningless, a flash of violence that bursts and withers away, retribution without cause, until you understand where it all began.

My name is Harry August.

My father is Rory Edmond Hulne, my mother Elizabeth Leadmill, though I was not to know any of this until well until my third life.

I do not know whether to say that my father raped my mother or not. The law would have some difficulty in assessing the case; the jury could perhaps be swayed by a clever individual one way or the other. I am told that she did not scream, did not fight, didn't even say no when he came to her in the kitchen on the night of my conception, and in twenty-five inglorious minutes of passion – in that anger and jealousy and rage are passions of their kind – took revenge on his faithless wife by means of the kitchen girl. In this regard my mother was not forced, but then, as a girl of some twenty years old, living and working in my father's house, dependent for her future on his money and his family's goodwill, I would argue that she was given no chance to resist, coerced by her situation as much as by any blade held to the throat.

By the time my mother's pregnancy began to show, my father had returned to active duty in France, where he was to serve out the rest of the First World War as a largely undistinguished major in the Scots Guards. In a conflict where whole regiments could be wiped out in a single day, undistinguished was a rather enviable obtainment. It was therefore left to my paternal grandmother, Constance Hulne, to expel my mother from her home without a reference in the autumn of 1918. The man who was to become my adopted father – and yet a truer parent to me than any bio-logical relation – took my mother to the local market on the back of his pony cart and left her there with some few shillings in her purse and a recommendation to seek the help of other distressed ladies of the county. A cousin, Alistair, who shared a mere one eighth of my mother's genetic material but whose surplus of wealth more than made up for a deficit of familial connections, gave my mother work on the floor of his Edinburgh paper mill; however, as she grew larger and increasingly unable to carry out her duties, she was quietly moved on by a junior official some three rungs away from the responsible party. In desperation, she wrote to my biological father, but the note was intercepted by my shrewd grandmother, who destroyed it before he could read my mother's plea, and so, on New Year's Eve 1918, my mother spent her last few pennies on the slow train from Edinburgh Waverley to Newcastle and, some ten miles north of Berwick-upon-Tweed, went into labour.

A trade unionist by the name of Douglas Crannich and his wife, Prudence, were the only two people present at my birth, in the ladies' washroom of the station. I am told that the stationmaster stood outside the door to prevent any innocent women coming inside, his hands clasped behind his back and his cap, crowned with snow, pulled down over his eyes in a manner I have always im-agined as being rather hooded and malign. There were no doctors at the infirmary at this late hour and on this festive day, and the medic took over three hours to arrive. He came too late. The blood was already crystallising on the floor and Prudence Crannich was holding me in her arms at his arrival. My mother was dead. I have only the report of Douglas for the circumstances of her demise, but I believe she haemorrhaged out, and is buried in a grave marked "Lisa, d. 1 January 1919 – Angels Guide Her Into Light". Mrs Crannich, when the undertaker asked her what should be on the stone, realised that she had never known my mother's full name.

Some debate ensued about what to do with me, this suddenly orphaned child. I believe Mrs Crannich was sorely tempted to keep me for her own, but finances and practicality informed against this decision, as did Douglas Crannich's firm and literal interpretation of the law and rather more personal understanding of propriety. The child had a father, he exclaimed, and the father had a right to the child. This matter would have been rather moot, were it not that my mother was carrying about her person the address of my soon-to-be adopted father, Patrick August, presumably with the intention of enlisting his help in seeing my biological father, Rory Hulne. Enquiries were made as to whether this man, Patrick, could be my father, which caused quite a stir in the village as Patrick had been long married, childlessly, to my adopted mother, Harriet August, and a barren marriage in a border village, where the notion of the condom was regarded as taboo well into the 1970s, was always a topic of furious debate. The matter was so shocking that it very quickly made its way to the manor house itself, Hulne Hall, wherein resided my grandmother Constance, my two aunts Victoria and Alexandra, my cousin Clement, and Lydia, the unhappy wife of my father. I believe my grandmother immediately suspected whose child I was and the circumstances of my situation, but refused to take responsibility for me. It was Alexandra, my younger aunt, who showed a presence of mind and a compassion that the rest of her kin lacked, and seeing that suspicion would fairly quickly turn to her family once the truth of my dead mother's identity was revealed, approached Patrick and Harriet August with this offer – that if

5

they were to adopt the child, and raise it as their own, the papers formally signed and witnessed by the Hulne family itself to quiet all rumours of an illegitimate affair, for no one carried authority like the inhabitants of Hulne Hall – then she would personally see to it that they received a monthly amount of money for their pains and to support the child, and that on his growing up she would ensure that his prospects were suitable – not excessive, mind, but neither the sorry situation of a bastard.

Patrick and Harriet debated a while, then accepted. I was raised as their child, as Harry August, and it wasn't until my second life that I began to understand where I was from, and what I was.

# Chapter 3

It is said that there are three stages of life for those of us who live our lives in circles. These are rejection, exploration and acceptance.

As categories go, they are rather glib, and contain within them many different layers disguised behind these wider words. Rejection, for example, can be subdivided into various clichéd reactions, like so: suicide, despondency, madness, hysteria, isolation and self-destruction. I, like nearly all kalachakra, experienced most of these at some stage in my early lives, and their recollection lingers within me like a virus still twisted into my stomach wall.

For my part, the transition to acceptance was unremarkably difficult.

The first life I lived was undistinguished. Like all young men, I was called to fight in the Second World War, where I was a thoroughly undistinguished infantryman. Yet if my wartime contribution was meagre, my life after the conflict hardly added to a sense of significance. I returned to Hulne House after the war, to take over the position which had been held by Patrick, tending to the grounds around the estate. Like my adopted father, I had been raised to love the land, the smell of it after rain and the sudden fizzing in the air when all the seeds of the gorse spilt at once into the sky, and if I felt in any way isolated from the rest of society, it was merely as the absence of a brother might be to an only child. an idea of loneliness without the relevant experience to make it real.

When Patrick died, my position was formalised, though by then, the Hulnes' wealth was almost entirely extinguished through squander and inertia. In 1964 the property was bought by the National Trust, and I with it, and I spent the latter part of my years directing ramblers through the overgrown moors that surrounded the house, watching as the walls of the manor itself slowly sank deeper into the wet black mud.

I died in 1989 as the Berlin Wall fell, alone in a hospital in Newcastle, a divorcee with no children and a state pension who, even on his deathbed, believed himself to be the son of the long-departed Patrick and Harriet August, and who died eventually from the disease that has been the bane of my lives – multiple myelomas which spread throughout the body until the body itself simply ceases to function.

Naturally my reaction to being born again precisely where I had begun – in the women's restroom of Berwick-upon-Tweed station, on New Year's Day 1919, with all the memories of my life that had gone before, induced its own rather clichéd madness in me. As the full powers of my adult consciousness returned to my child's body, I fell first into a confusion, then an agony, then a doubt, then a despair, than a screaming, then a shrieking, and finally, aged seven years old, I was committed to St Margot's Asylum for Unfortunates, where I frankly believed myself to belong, and within six months of my confinement succeeded in throwing myself out of a window on the third floor.

Retrospectively, I realise that three floors are frequently not high enough to guarantee the quick, relatively painless death that such circumstances warrant, and I might easily have snapped every bone in my lower body and yet retained my consciousness intact. Thankfully, I landed on my head, and that was that.

# Chapter 4

There is a moment when the moor comes to life. I wish you could see it, but somehow whenever I have been with you on our walks through the countryside, we have missed those few precious hours of revelation. Instead, the skies have been the slate-grey of the stones beneath them, or drought turns the land to dust-brown thorns, or once it snowed so hard that the kitchen door was barred shut from the outside, and I had to climb out of the window to shovel us a path to freedom, and on one trip in 1949 it rained continually, I believe, for five days without end. You never saw it for those few hours after rain, when all is purple and yellow and smells of black, rich soil.

Your deduction, made early on in our friendship, that I was born in the north of England, for all of my pretentions and mannerisms acquired over many lives, was entirely correct, and my adopted father, Patrick August, never let me forget it. He was the sole groundsman on the Hulne estate, and had been so for as long as he had lived. So had his father before him, and his father before him, as far back as 1834, when the newly rich Hulne family bought the land to sculpt their ideal, upper-class dream. They planted trees, drove roads through the moor, built ridiculous towers and arches – folly by name and folly by nature – which by the time of my birth had sunk into moss-crawled decline. Not for them the grubby scrubland that framed the estate, with its rock teeth and sticky gums of earthen flesh. Previous, energetic generations of the family had kept sheep, or perhaps it would be fairer to say that the sheep had kept themselves, on the wide places beneath the stone walls, but the twentieth century had not been kind to the fortunes of the Hulnes, and now the land, though still theirs, was left untended, wild – the perfect place for a boy to run free while his parents were about their chores. Curiously enough, living my childhood again I found myself far less adventurous. Holes and crags that I had climbed along and leaped in my first life, to my more conservative elder brain suddenly seemed places of danger, and I wore my child's body as an old woman might wear a skinny bikini bought for her by a fragile friend.

Having failed so spectacularly to end the cycle of my days by suicide, I resolved on my third life to instead pursue the answers that seemed so far away. It is some small mercy, I believe, that our memories return to us slowly as we progress through childhood, so that the recollection of having thrown myself to my death came, as it were, like a gently gathering cold, arriving with no sense of surprise, merely an acceptance that this thing was, and had achieved nothing.

My first life, for all it lacked any real direction, had about it a kind of happiness, if ignorance is innocence, and loneliness is a separation of care. But my new life, with its knowledge of all that had come before, could not be lived the same. It wasn't merely awareness of events yet to come, but rather a new perception of the truths around me, which, being a child raised to them in my first life, I had not even considered to be lies. Now a boy again and temporarily at least in command of my full adult faculties, I perceived the truths which are so often acted out in front of a child's sight in the belief that a child cannot comprehend them. I believe that my adopted father and mother came to love me – she far sooner than he – but for Patrick August I was never flesh of his flesh until my adopted mother died.

There is a medical study in this phenomenon, but my adopted mother never quite dies upon the same day in each life she lives. The cause – unless external factors intervene violently first – is always the same. Around my sixth birthday she begins to cough, and by my seventh her coughing is bloody. My parents cannot afford the doctor's fees, but my aunt Alexandra finally furnishes the coin for my mother to go to the hospital in Newcastle and receive a diagnosis of lung cancer. (I believe it to be non-small-cell carcinomas confined primarily to the left lung; frustratingly treatable some forty years after my mother's diagnosis but utterly beyond the realms of science at the time.) Tobacco and laudanum are prescribed, and death swiftly follows in 1927. At her death my father falls into a silence and walks upon the hills, sometimes not to be seen for many days. I tend to myself perfectly competently and now, in expectation of my mother's death, stockpile some food to see me through his long absences. On his return, he remains silent and unapproachable, and though he does not rise to any approaches from my infant self with anger, that is largely because he does not rise at all. In my first life I did not understand his grief nor how it manifested, for I myself was grieving with the blind wordlessness of a child who needed help, which he did not provide. In my second life my mother's death happened while I was still under the asylum roof and I was too concerned with my own madness to process it, but in my third it came as a slow-moving train towards a man tied to the tracks; inevitable, unstoppable, seen far off in the night and the imagination of the thing, for me, almost worse than the event. I knew what was to come, and somehow when it came, it was a relief, an ending of expectation, and so a lesser event.

In my third life my mother's impending death also gave me something of an occupation. The prevention of it, or at least the management of it, concerned me profoundly. As I had no explanation for my situation save that, perhaps, some Old Testament god was acting out a curse upon me, I genuinely felt that by performing acts of charity, or attempting to affect the major events of my life, I might break this cycle of death-birth-death that had apparently come upon me. Having committed no crimes that I knew of which needed redeeming, and with no major events in my life to undo, I latched on to the welfare of Harriet as my first and most obvious crusade, and embarked on it with all the wit my five-year-old mind (pushing ninety-seven) could muster.

I used my ministrations as an excuse to avoid the tedium of school, and my father was too preoccupied to see what I did; instead I tended to her and learned as I had never learned before how my mother lived when my father was away. I suppose you could call it a chance to get to know, as an adult, a woman I had only briefly known as a child. It was in this capacity that I first began to suspect that I was not my father's son.

The Hulne family as a whole attended my adopted mother's funeral, when she finally died in that third life. My father said few words, and I stood by him, a seven-year-old boy dressed in borrowed black trousers and jacket from Clement Hulne, the cousin three years my senior who had tried in my previous life to bully me, when he remembered that I was there to bully. Constance Hulne, leaning heavily on a walking stick with an ivory handle carved in the shape of an elephant's head, spoke a few words about Harriet's loyalty, strength and the family she left behind. Alexandra Hulne told me that I must be brave; Victoria Hulne bent down and pinched my cheeks, inducing in me a strange childish urge to bite the black-gloved fingers that had violated my face. Rory Hulne said nothing and stared at me. He had stared once before, the first time I had stood here in borrowed clothes burying my mother, but I, consumed with grief that had no means of expression, hadn't comprehended the intensity of his gaze. Now I met his eyes and for the first time saw the mirror of my own, of what I would become.

You have not known me in all the stages of my life, so let me describe them here.

As a child I am born with almost red hair, which fades over time to what the charitable would describe as auburn, and which is more fairly carrot. The colour of my hair comes from my real mother's family, as does a genetic predisposition towards good teeth and long-sightedness. I am a small child, a little shorter than average and skinny, though that is as much from a poor diet as any genetic inclination. My growth spurt begins when I turn eleven, and continues until the age of fifteen, when I can, thankfully, get away with pretending to be a boyish eighteen and thus skip three tedious years until manhood.

As a young man, I used to sport a rather ragged beard in the manner of my adopted father, Patrick; it doesn't suit and in its untended state I can often come to look like a set of sensory organs lost in a raspberry bush. Once this revelation was made I began to shave regularly, and in doing so revealed the face of my true father. We share the same pale grey eyes, the same small ears, lightly curling hair and a nose which, along with a tendency to bone disease in old age, is probably the least welcome genetic heritage of all. It is not that my nose is especially large – it is not; but it is undeniably upturned in a manner that would not be ill-suited to the pixie king, and where it should be angularly delineated from my face, rather it seems to blend into my skin like a thing moulded from clay, not bone. People are too polite to comment, but the merest sight of it has on several occasions reduced honest infants from neater genetic lines to tears. In old age my hair turns white, in what feels like an instantaneous flash; this event can be brought on by stress earlier than its norm, and cannot be prevented by any cure, medicinal or psychological. I require glasses for reading by the age of fifty-one; distressingly my fifties fall in the 1970s, a poor decade for fashion, but like nearly all I return to the fashions I was comfortable with as a youth and choose rather demure spectacles in an antique style. With these balanced across my too-close eyes I look every bit the ageing academic as I examine myself in the bathroom mirror; it is a face which, by the time we buried Harriet for the third time, I had had nearly a hundred years to become acquainted with. It was the face of Rory Edmond Hulne, staring at me from across the casket of the woman who could not have been my mother.

13

# Chapter 5

I am of a good age to be enlisted at the outbreak of the Second World War, and yet for my first few lives managed somehow to avoid all the dramatic moments of conflict which I would later read about from the comfort of the 1980s. In my first life I enlisted of my own volition, genuinely believing the three great fallacies of the time – that the war would be brief, that the war would be patriotic and that the war would advance me in my skills. I missed being embarked for France by four days, and felt deeply disappointed in myself that I had not been evacuated from Dunkirk, which at the time seemed like a very triumphant defeat. Indeed, the first year of my war seemed to be spent on perpetual training exercises, first on the beaches as the nation – myself included – waited for an invasion that didn't come, then in the mountains of Scotland as the government began to toy with retribution. Indeed, I spent so much time training for an invasion of Norway that by the time it was finally decided that the exercise would be futile, I and my unit were accounted of such little use in desert warfare that we were held back from the initial embarkation to the Mediterranean theatre until we could be retrained or something else worked out useful for us to do. In this sense, I suppose I achieved one of my ambitions, as with no one seeming to want us to fight, I found myself with nothing better to do than study and learn. A medic in our unit was an objector who had found his conscience in the works of Engels and the poetry of Wilfred Owen, and who all the men in the unit, myself included, considered a weak-chinned toff until the day he stood up to the sergeant, who had enjoyed his power too long and too much, and in front of all the men lambasted him as the slobbering perversion of a childhood bully that he was. The medic's name was Valkeith, and he received three days' confinement for his outburst and the respect of all. His learning, previously a source of much derision, now became something of an object of pride, and though he was still cursed as a weak-chinned toff, now he was *our* weak-chinned toff, and from his mind I began to learn some of the mysteries of science, philosophy and romantic poetry, none of which I would admit to at the time. He died three minutes and fifty seconds after we set foot on the beaches of Normandy, from a shrapnel wound which tore open his gut. He was the only one of our unit who died that day, for we were far from the action and the gun which fired the fatal shot was taken two minutes later.

In my first life I killed three men. They were all together, all of them at once, in a tank retreating in a village in northern France. We'd been told that the village was already liberated, that there would be no resistance, but there it was, sat between the bakery and the church like a horsefly on a slice of melon. We'd been so relaxed we didn't even notice it until the barrel swung round towards us like the eye of a muddy crocodile and its jaws released the shell that killed two of us outright and young Tommy Kenah three days later in his hospital bed. I remember my actions with the same clarity with which I recall all else, and they were these: to drop my rifle, to unsling my bag and to run, never ceasing in my shout, down the middle of the street, still screaming at the tank that had killed my friends. I hadn't done the strap up on my helmet and it fell off my head some ten yards from the front of the tank. I could hear men moving around inside that beast as I approached, see faces darting through the slits in the armour as

15

they tried to swing the gun round towards me or get on to the machine guns, but I was already there. The main gun was hot – even from a foot away I could feel its warmth on my face. I dropped a grenade through the open front hatch. I could hear them shouting, scrambling around inside, trying to get it, but in that confined space they only made it worse. I remember my actions, but not my thoughts. Later the captain said that the tank must have got lost: their friends had turned left, and they'd turned right, and that was why they'd killed three of us and been killed in return. I was given a medal, which I sold in 1961 when I needed to pay for a new boiler, and I felt a great relief once it was gone.

That was my first war. I did not volunteer for my second. I knew it likely that I would soon be conscripted so chose to rely on skills learned in my first life to keep myself alive. In my third life I joined the RAF as a ground mechanic and ran for the shelter faster than any other man in my squad when the sirens went, until finally Hitler began to bomb London and I knew I could begin to relax. It was a good place to be for the first few years. The men who died nearly all died in the air, out of sight and out of mind. The pilots did not really interact with us grease men, and I found it all too easy to consider the plane my only care, and the man who flew it merely another mechanical part to be ignored and overcome. Then the Americans came, and we began bombing Germany, and many more men died in the air, where I only needed to lament the loss of their machines, but more began coming back, shot through with shrapnel, their blood on the floor just thick enough to retain the shape of the footprints that had scrambled through it. I wondered what I could do differently, with my knowledge of what was to come, and concluded that it was nothing. I knew that the Allies would win, but had never studied the Second World War in any academic detail; my knowledge was entirely personal, a thing lived rather than information to be shared. The most I could do was warn a man in Scotland by the name of Valkeith to stay in the boat two minutes longer on the beach of Normandy, or whisper to Private Kenah that there would be a tank in the village of Gennimont which had turned right instead of left and was waiting between the bakery and the church to end his days. But I had no strategic information to impart, no learning or knowledge other than a declaration that Citroën would make elegant unreliable cars and one day people would look back at the division of Europe and wonder why.

Having reasoned myself so eloquently into this position, I continued once again to have a thoroughly unremarkable war. I oiled the landing gear of the planes which would destroy Dresden; I heard rumours of boffins attempting to design a jet engine and how the engineers derided the notion; I listened for the moment that the engines of the V1s stopped, and for a brief period for the silence of a V2 that had already fallen, and when VE day came I got horrendously drunk on brandy, which I don't particularly like, with a Canadian and two Welshmen who I'd met only two days before and who I never saw again.

And I learned. This time I learned. I learned of engines and machines, of men and strategies, of the RAF and the Luftwaffe. I studied bomb patterns, observed where the missiles had fallen so that next time – for I felt 60 per cent confident that there would be a next time, all this again – I would have something more useful to serve myself with, and potentially others, than a few personal recollections about the quality of tinned ham in France.

As it was, the same knowledge which protected me from the world was in later times also to put me in great danger and, by this route, indirectly introduce me to the Cronus Club, and the Cronus Club to me.

# Chapter 6

His name was Franklin Phearson.

He was the second spy I ever met in my life, and he was hungry for knowledge.

He came to me in my fourth life, in 1968.

I was working as a doctor in Glasgow, and my wife had left me. I was fifty years old and I was a broken man. Her name was Jenny and I loved her and told her everything. She was a surgeon, one of the first female surgeons on the ward; I was a neurologist with a reputation for unorthodox and occasionally unethical – though legal – research. She believed in God. I did not. Much must be said of my third life, but for now let me say simply that my third death, alone in a hospital in Japan, had convinced me of the truth of nothingness. I had lived and I had died, and not Allah, Jehovah, Krishna, Buddha, nor the spirits of my ancestors had descended to take away my fear, but rather I had been born again exactly where I had begun, back in the snow, back in England, back in the past where it had all begun.

My loss of faith was not revelatory, nor intensely distressing. It was a prolonged growth of resignation, one which the events of my life had only reinforced, until I was forced to conclude that any conversations I had with a deity were entirely one way. My death and subsequent rebirth back where I had begun rounded the argument off with a sort of weary inevitability, and I viewed it with all the disappointment and detachment of a scientist whose test tubes had failed to precipitate.

I had spent an entire life praying for a miracle, and none had come. And now I looked at the stuffy chapel of my ancestors and saw vanity and greed, heard the call to prayer and thought of power, smelled incense and wondered at the waste of it all.

In my fourth life I turned away from God and sought out science for an explanation. I studied as no man has studied before – physics, biology, philosophy – and at the last fought with every tool at my disposal to become the poorest boy in Edinburgh university, graduating top of my class as a doctor. Jenny was drawn to my ambition, and I to hers, for the ignorant had snickered the first time she took up a scalpel, until they saw the precision of her cuts and the confidence with which she wielded a blade. We'd been together for ten years in unfashionable but politically pointed sin, before marrying in 1963 in that swell of relief that followed the Cuban Missile Crisis; and it had rained, and she had laughed and said we both deserved it, and I had been in love.

So in love that one night, for no very special reason, and without much very special thought, I told her everything.

I said, "My name is Harry August. My father is Rory Edmond Hulne, my mother died before I was born. This is my fourth life. I have lived and I have died many times before now, but it is always the same life."

She punched me in the chest playfully and told me to stop being daft.

I said, "In a matter of weeks a scandal is going to break in the US which will topple President Nixon. Capital punishment will be abolished in England, and Black September terrorists will open fire in Athens airport."

She said, "You should be on the news, you should."

Three weeks later Watergate broke. It broke gently at first, aides

19

sacked across the sea. By the time capital punishment had been abolished, President Nixon was in front of Congressional hearings, and when Black September terrorists gunned down travellers in Athens airport, it was obvious to all that Nixon was on the way out.

Jenny sat on the end of the bed, shoulders bowed and head low. I waited. It was an expectation that had been four lifetimes in the making. She had a bony back and a warm belly, hair cut deliberately short to challenge the conceptions of her surgeon colleagues, and a soft face that loved to laugh when no one was looking. She said, "How did you know – all of this – how did you know it would happen?"

"I told you," I replied. "This is the fourth time I've lived it, and I have an excellent memory."

"What does that mean, the fourth time? How is it possible, the fourth time?"

"I don't know. I became a doctor to try and find out. I've run experiments on myself, studied my blood, my body, my brain, tried to see if there is something in me which . . . isn't right. But I was wrong. It's not a medical problem, or if it is, I don't yet know how to find the answer. I would have left this job long ago, tried something new, but I met you. I have for ever, but I want you now."

"How old are you?" she demanded.

"I'm fifty-four. I'm two hundred and six."

"I can't . . . I can't believe what you're saying. I can't believe that you believe."

"I'm sorry."

"Are you a spy?"

"No."

"Are you ill?"

"No. Not by any handbook definition."

"Then why?"

"Why what?"

"Why would you say these things?"

"It's the truth. I want to tell you the truth."

She crawled on to the bed next to me, took my face into my hands, stared deeply into my eyes. "Harry," she said, and there was fear in her voice, "I need you to tell me. Do you mean what you are saying?"

"Yes," I replied, and the relief of it nearly burst me open from the inside out. "Yes, I do."

She left me that night, pulling her coat on over her shift and slipping into a pair of wellington boots. She went to stay with her mother, who lived in Northferry, just beyond Dundee, and left me a note on the table saying she needed time. I gave her a day then called; her mother told me to stay away. I gave it another day and called again, begging Jenny to ring me. On the third day, when I rang the phone had been disconnected. Jenny had taken the car, so I caught the train to Dundee and a taxi the rest of the way. The weather was beautiful, the sea perfectly still against the shore, the sun low and pink and too interested in the moment to want to set. Jenny's mother's cottage was a little white thing with a child-sized front door set back from the edge of a charcoal cliff. When I knocked, her mother, a woman perfectly designed to fit through that implausibly low door, answered and held it open on the chain.

"She can't see you," she blurted. "I'm sorry, but you have to go away."

"I need to see her," I begged. "I need to see my wife."

"You have to leave now, Dr August," she exclaimed. "I'm sorry it's this way, but you clearly need help." She closed the door sharply, the latch clicking behind the creaking white wood. I stayed there and hammered on the door, then on the windows, pressing my face against the glass. They turned off the lights inside so I wouldn't know where they were, or perhaps hoping I'd get bored and go away. The sun set and I sat on the porch and wept and called out for Jenny, begged her to speak to me, until finally her mother phoned the police and they did the talking instead. I was put in a cell with a man brought in for burglary. He laughed at me and I throttled him to within a few heartbeats from death. Then they put me in a solitary cell and left me there for a day, until at last a doctor came to see me and asked how I was feeling. He

21

listened to my chest, which I pointed out in my calmest possible voice was hardly a rational approach to diagnosing mental illness.

"Do you consider yourself mentally ill?" he asked quickly.

"No," I snapped. "I can just recognise a bad doctor."

They must have rushed the paperwork through, because I was taken to the asylum the very next day. I laughed when I saw it. The name on the door was St Margot's Asylum. Someone had scrubbed out "for Unfortunates", leaving an ugly grammatical gap. It was the hospital I had thrown myself from in my second life, at the age of seven years old.

# Chapter 7

Mental health professionals are, by the 1990s, expected to themselves seek regular counselling and observation for emotional and
mental well-being. I tried being a psychologist once, but found the
problems I had to diagnose either overwhelming or too subjective
as to bear consideration, and the tools at my command either
childish or overblown. In short, I did not have the temperament
for it, and when I was committed to St Margot's Asylum for the
second time in my existence, albeit the first time in this life, I felt
a mixture of fury and pride that my sanity, cultivated despite severe
provocation, could be so misunderstood by the ignorant mortals
around me.

Mental health professionals of the 1960s make their 1990s
counterparts look like Mozarts trampling upon Salieri's lesser
work. I suppose I should consider myself fortunate that some of
the more experimental techniques of the 1960s had not yet made
their way to cosmopolitan Northumbria. I was not tested on
with LSD or Ecstasy nor invited to discuss my sexuality, as our
one and only psychiatrist, Dr Abel, regarded Freud as unsanitary.
The first to discover this was the Twitch, an unfortunate woman
whose real name was Lucy, whose Tourette's syndrome was

treated by a mixture of apathy and brutality. If our warders had a notion of habit-breaking therapy, they acted upon it by hitting Lucy across the side of her head with the palms of their hands whenever she twitched or grunted, and if she became louder as a consequence – as frequently happened when provoked – two of them would sit on top of her, one on her legs, one on her chest, until she nearly passed out beneath them. The one time I attempted to intervene, I received the same treatment and lay pinned beneath Ugly Bill, the head day-shift nurse and sometime jailbird, to the vociferous approval of Clara Watkins and Newbie, who'd worked there for six months and still hadn't said his name. Newbie stood on my wrists, mostly to show willing, while Ugly Bill explained to me that I was being very naughty and disruptive, and just because I thought I was a doctor didn't mean I knew anything. I cried with impotence and frustration, and he slapped me, which gave me cause to rage and through which rage I tried to control my tears, converting self-pity into fury, but I could not do it.

"Penis!" the Twitch shouted at our once-weekly group session. "Penis penis penis!"

Dr Abel, his tiny moustache quivering like a frightened mouse on his top lip, clicked his pen closed. "Now, Lucy ... "

"Come on, give it to me, give it to me, come on, come on, come on!" she screamed.

I watched the progress of the flush through Dr Abel's cheeks. It was a fascinating luminescence, almost visible on a capillary-by-capillary basis, and I briefly wondered if the spread of his blush was representative of the speed of his blood flow through the shallow dermis, in which case he should seriously consider more exercise and a good massage. His moustache had ceased being fashionable the day after Hitler invaded Czechoslovakia, and the only thing I ever heard him say which made any sense was, "Dr August, there is no greater isolation a man may experience than to be lonely in a crowd. He may nod, and smile, and say the right thing, but even by this pretence his soul is pushed further away from the kinship of men."

I asked him what fortune cookie he'd got that from, and he looked bewildered and asked me what fortune cookies were, and if you made them with ginger.

"Give it to me, give it to me!" screamed the Twitch.

"This is unproductive," he quavered, at which point Lucy pulled up her overall to show us her oversized knickers and started to dance, causing Simon, who was at the low point of his bipolar mania, to weep, which set off Margaret rocking, which caused Ugly Bill to storm into the room, stick in hand and straitjacket already on the way, while Dr Abel, the tips of his ears burning like brake lights, scurried away.

Once a month we were permitted visitors, and no one came.

Simon said it was for the best, that he didn't want to be seen like this, that he was ashamed.

Margaret screamed and tore at the walls until her nails were bloody, and had to be taken back to her room and sedated.

Lucy, the spittle rolling down her face, said it wasn't us who should be ashamed but them. She didn't say who they were, and nor did she need to, for she was simply right.

After two months I was ready to leave.

"I see now," I explained calmly, sitting in front of Dr Abel's desk, "that I suffered a mental breakdown. Obviously I need counselling, but I can only express my deep and personal gratitude to you for having helped me overcome this issue."

"Dr August," explained Dr Abel, lining up his pen with the top edge of his writing pad, "I think what you suffered was rather more than just a breakdown. You suffered a complete delusionary episode, indicative, I believe, of more complex psychological issues."

I looked at Dr Abel as though for the first time and wondered just what his measure of success was. Not necessarily a cure, I decided, so long as the treatment was interesting. "What do you suggest?" I asked.

"I'd like to keep you here a while longer," he replied. "There are some fascinating medications coming out which I believe would be exactly what you need . . ."

"Medications?"

"Some very promising developments have been made with the phenothiazines—"

"That's an insect poison."

"No – no, Dr August, no. I understand your concern as a physician but I assure you, when I say phenothiazines what I'm talking about are its derivatives . . . "

"I think I'd like a second opinion, Dr Abel."

He hesitated, and I saw pride flare at the onset of possible conflict. "I am a fully qualified psychiatrist, Dr August."

"Then as a fully qualified psychiatrist, you know how important it is to have a patient's trust in any treatment process."

"Yes," he admitted grudgingly. "But I am the only qualified physician on this ward . . . "

"That's not true. I'm qualified."

"Dr August," he said with a shimmering smile, "you're ill. You are in no fit state to practise, least of all on yourself."

"I want you to call my wife," I replied firmly. "She has a legal say in what you do to me. I refuse to take phenothiazines, and if you are going to force me to take them, then you have to get permission from next of kin. She is my next of kin."

"As I understand it, Dr August, she is partially responsible for suggesting your confinement and care."

"She knows good medicine from bad," I corrected. "Call her."

"I'll consider it."

"Don't consider it, Dr Abel," I replied. "Just do it."

To this day I don't know if he called her.

Personally, I doubt it.

When they gave me the first dose of the drug, they tried to do it discreetly. They sent Clara Watkins, who looked so innocent and had such a malicious pleasure in her job, with a tray containing the usual pills – which I palmed – and a needle.

"Now now, Harry," she chided when she saw my face. "This is good for you."

"What is it?" I demanded, already suspecting.

26

"It's medicine!" she sang out brightly. "You love to take your medicine, don't you?"

Ugly Bill was at the back of the room, his eyes fixed on me. His presence confirmed my suspicions – he was already waiting to strike. I said, "I demand to see a legal consent form, signed by my next of kin."

"You just do that," she said, grabbing at my sleeve, which I pulled away.

"I demand a lawyer, fair representation."

"This ain't no prison, Harry!" she replied brightly, waggling her eyebrows at Ugly Bill. "There's no lawyers here."

"I have a right to a second opinion!"

"Dr Abel is just doing what's best for you Why be difficult about that? Now, Harry ... "

At these words Ugly Bill grabbed me in a bear hug from behind and, not for the first time, I wondered why in over two hundred years I'd never got round to learning some form of martial art. He was an ex-con who found being a nurse at an asylum just like prison but better. He worked out in the private garden of the house, an hour every day, and took steroids that caused his brow to perpetually glisten with sweat and, I suspected, a shrinking in his testicles that he compensated for by taking more exercise and of course, more steroids. Whatever the state of his gonads, his arms were thicker than my thighs, and wrapped themselves around me tight enough to pull me from my chair, feet kicking uselessly at nothing.

"No," I begged. "Please don't do this please please don't ... "

Clara slapped the skin on my elbow to bring a reddish flush to the surface and then managed to miss the vein entirely. I kicked and Ugly Bill squeezed harder so that heat rose to my eyes and wool filled my brain. I felt the needle go in, but not come out, and then they dropped me to the floor and told me to be,

"Not so silly, Harry! Why do you always have to be so silly about things what are good for you?"

They left me there, sat on my own sprawling knees, waiting for it to happen. My mind raced as I tried to think of an easily

27

available chemical antidote to the poison currently slipping through my system, but I had only been a doctor in one life and hadn't yet had time to investigate these modern drugs. I crawled across the floor on my hands and knees to the water jug and drank the whole thing down, then lay on my back in the middle of the room and tried to slow my breathing, slow my pulse and respiration, in a futile attempt to limit the circulation of the drug. It occurred to me that I should make some attempt to monitor my own symptoms so I swivelled round on the floor to keep the clock in sight, noting the time. After ten minutes I felt a little light-headed, but that passed. After fifteen I realised that my feet were on the other side of the world, that someone had sawed me in half but left the nerves still attached, even though the bones were broken and now my feet belonged to someone else. I knew that this could not possibly be so, and yet processed the fact that it quite clearly was with a resignation that dared not fight the simple truth of my predicament.

The Twitch came and stood over me and said,

"Whatcha doing?"

I didn't think she needed an answer, so didn't give one.

There was saliva rolling down one side of my face. I rather enjoyed it, the coldness of the spit on the hotness of my skin.

"Whatcha doing whatcha doing whatcha doing?" she shrieked, and I wondered if they'd heard of adrenergic agonists in Northumbria, or if they were a thing that was yet to come.

She shook me and then went away but was clearly still leaving something behind because I kept on shaking, head banging against the floor, and I knew I had wetted myself but that was OK too, interesting and different like the saliva, the way it was all the same temperature as me until it dried and began to sting, and besides that was a long way away and then Ugly Bill was there and his face had been destroyed. It had been broken against the ceiling above my head like a ripe tomato, the skull smashed in and only a nose, two eyes and leering mouth left in the swimming remnants of blood and dripping brain that surrounded it, and as he leaned over me, bits of his cerebellum dripped round his cheek and rolled to

28

the corner of his mouth and formed a tear of grey-pink matter that hung off his bottom lip and then fell, like mashed apple from a baby's spoon, straight on to my face, and I screamed and screamed and screamed until he strangled me and I didn't scream any more.

Naturally, by this point I'd lost track of time, and thus the diagnostic purpose of the exercise was rather left behind.

# Chapter 8

Jenny visited.

They tied me to the bed and shot me through with a sedative when she came.

I tried to speak, to tell her what they were doing, but I couldn't.

She wept.

She washed my face, and held my hand, and wept.

She was still wearing her wedding ring.

At the door she spoke with Dr Abel and he said he was concerned about my deterioration and was considering a new kind of drug.

I called out for her and made no sound.

She kept her back turned to me when they locked the door.

Then Dr Abel was sitting too close to me, the tip of his pen resting on his lower lip, and he said, "Tell it to me again, Harry?"

There was an urgency in his voice, more than just the fascination with his own treatments.

"End of the oil embargo," I heard someone reply. "Carnation revolution in Portugal, government overthrown. Discovery of the terracotta army. India gets the nuclear bomb. West Germany wins the World Cup."

Ugly Bill was sitting in an orange haze. He said, "Not so smart now not so smart are you so smart so smart you think you're so smart but you're not so smart here you're not so smart smart is nothing smart is shit I'm smart I'm smart I'm the smart one here . . . "

He leaned in close to dribble on my face. I bit his nose hard enough to hear the cartilage crack and found it very, very funny.

Then there was a voice, a stranger's voice, cultured and mildly American.

"Oh no no no no no," it said. "This won't do at all."

# Chapter 9

Jenny.

She has a Glaswegian accent that her mother tried to educate out of her and failed. Her mother believed in getting on, her father believed in staying behind, and as a result they both remained exactly where they'd always been until the day after Jenny's eighteenth birthday, when they finally separated, never to see each other again.

I met her again, in my seventh life.

It was at a research conference in Edinburgh. My badge proclaimed, "Professor H. August, University College London" and hers, "Dr J. Munroe, Surgeon". I sat three rows behind her through an incredibly tedious lecture on the interaction of calcium ions in the periphery nervous system and watched the back of her neck, fascinated. I hadn't seen her face and couldn't be sure, but I knew. In the evening there were drinks and a meal of overcooked chicken and mashed potatoes with soggy peas. There was a band playing medium misses of the 1950s. I waited until the two men she was with grew drunk enough to dance, leaving her alone with the unclean plates and ruffled tablecloth. I sat down next to her and held out my hand.

"Harry," I explained.

"Professor August?" she corrected, reading my badge.

"Dr Munroe," I replied. "We've met before."

"Have we? I can't quite ... "

"You studied medicine at Edinburgh University, and lived for the first year of your time in a small house in Stockbridge with four boys who were all frightened of you. You babysat for your next-door neighbour's twins to make a few more pennies, and decided that you had to be a surgeon after seeing a still-beating heart working away on the operating table."

"That's right," she murmured, turning her body a little further in the chair to look at me. "But I'm sorry, I still don't remember who you are."

"That's OK," I replied. "I was another one of the boys too scared to talk to you. Will you dance?"

"What?"

"Will you dance with me?"

"I ... Oh God, are you trying a line with me? Is that what this is?"

"I am a happily married man," I lied, "with family in London and no ill intentions towards you. I admire your work and dislike seeing a woman left alone. If it will make you happier, as we dance we can discuss the latest developments in imaging technology and whether genetic predisposition or developmental sensory stimuli are more important in the growth of neuron pathways during childhood and pre-teens. Dance with me?"

She hesitated. Her fingers rolled the wedding ring round and round her finger, three diamonds on gold, gaudier than what I'd bought her in another life, a life that had died a long time ago. She looked towards the dance floor, saw safety in numbers and heard the band begin another tune designed to maintain strict social boundaries.

"All right," she said and took my hand. "I hope you've got your biochemical credentials polished."

We danced.

I asked if it was hard, being the first woman in her department.

She laughed and said that only idiots judged her for being a woman – and she judged them for being idiots. "The benefit being," she explained, "that I can be both a woman and a fucking brilliant surgeon, but they'll always only be idiots."

I asked if she was lonely.

"No," she said after a moment. She was not. She had peers she liked, colleagues she respected, family, friends.

She had two children.

Jenny had always wanted children.

I wondered if she'd like to have an affair with me.

She asked when I stopped being afraid of her, to get so lippy on the dance floor.

I said it was a lifetime ago, but she was still beautiful and I knew all her secrets.

"Did you not hear the part about my friends, colleagues, family, kids?"

Yes, I'd heard all of it, and all of it weighed with me when I spoke to her, cried out to walk away, leave her alone, for her life was complete and needed no more complexity. How much greater, I said, must the attraction I felt towards her be, that I could know all this and still whisper sweet allurements in her ear?

"Allurements? Is that what you call it?"

Run away with me, I said, just for a night. The world will turn, and all things will end, and people forget.

For a moment she looked tempted, and then her husband came along and took her hand, and he was loyal and loving and completely sane and what she wanted, and her temptation wasn't so much about me, as about the adventure.

Would I have done things differently, had I known what was to befall Jenny Munroe?

Perhaps not.

Time, it transpires, is not so good at telling after all.

# Chapter 10

Back in the insanity, back in the broken place.

Franklin Phearson, in my fourth life, came to me in the hospital to wean me off one set of drugs, not for my benefit, but for his. His was the voice which stood over me as I lay motionless in my hospital bed and proclaimed, "What have you been giving this man? You said he'd be lucid."

His was the hand that steadied the stretcher as they pulled me out of the front door and into the waiting unmarked ambulance.

His were the hard soles on leather shoes which clacked on the marble steps of the grand hotel, empty for the season, the staff sent home, where eventually they deposited me in a bed of feathers and burgundy blankets, to dream and puke my way towards some kind of salvation.

Going cold turkey from any drug is unpleasant; from anti-psychotics it is a mixed blessing. Certainly I desired death, and they strapped me down to prevent my achieving it. Certainly I knew that all was lost and I with it, that I was cursed and there was no escape, and I longed to lose my mind entirely and push out my eyes and live in madness. And certainly I do not, even now, even with my memory, recall the very worst of those times, but rather remember it all as if it happened to another man. And certainly I know I have the capacity within me to be all of that again, to feel all of that again, and know that, while the door may currently be locked, there is a black pit in the bottom of my soul that has no limit to its falling. They say that the mind cannot remember pain; I say it barely matters, for even if the physical sensation is lost, our recollection of the terror that surrounds it is perfect. I do not want to die at this present moment, though the circumstances of this present writing will dictate my course. I remember that I have wanted it, and it was real.

There was no moment of light, no waking from a darkness to find myself cured in that place. Rather there was a slow shuffling towards comprehension, a few hours of reconciliation followed by a sleep, followed by a waking which stayed awake a little longer. There was a slow restoration of human dignity: clean clothes, my hands freed at last, the scars around my wrists and ankles cleaned of crispy blood. I was permitted to feed myself, first under supervision in my bed, then under supervision by the window, then under supervision down the stairs, and at last on the patio that looked across a croquet lawn and towards a rolling green garden, where the supervision tried to pretend it was simply a friend. I was permitted to clean myself, all sharp objects removed from the bathroom and guards outside, but I barely cared and sat in the shower until my skin was a crinkled raisin and the boiler upstairs began to shudder with distress. A scraggly beard had been growing on my chin, and they brought in a barber who tutted and twitched and splattered me with Italian oils and told me in the loud voice reserved for children,

"Your face is your fortune! Don't spend it all at once!"

Franklin Phearson had been a face on the edge of all this, by whose aloofness I could only assume he was in charge. He sat two tables away from me as I ate, was at the end of the corridor when I left the bathroom and was, I concluded, the man responsible for the two-way mirror in my bedroom, which provided constant monitoring of my room and was only revealed by the slow whirr of the surveillance camera lens as it adjusted its focus.

Then one breakfast he sat with me, no longer apart, and said, "You're looking much better."

I drank my tea carefully, as I drank all things carefully in that place, little sips to test for toxins, and replied, "I feel better. Thank you."

"It may please you to know that Dr Abel has been fired."

He said it so easily, newspaper folded on his lap, eyes half-running over the crossword clues, that I didn't fully grasp his meaning at the first rendition. But the words had been spoken, so I said again, as a neutral child had once spoken to my father, "Thank you."

"I applaud his intentions," went on Phearson, "but his methods were unsound. Would you like to see your wife?"

I counted silently to ten before I dared give an answer. "Yes. Very much."

"She's very distraught. She doesn't know where you are, thinks you've run away. You can write to her. Put her mind at ease."

"I'd like that."

"There will be financial compensation for her. Maybe a trial for Dr Abel. Maybe a petition, who knows?"

"I just want to see her again," I replied.

"Soon," he replied. "We'll aim to take up as little of your time as possible."

"Who are you?"

He threw the newspaper aside at this with a sudden energy, as if he'd been pent up waiting for that question. "Franklin Phearson, sir," he replied, thrusting out a flat pink hand. "An honour to make your acquaintance at last, Dr August."

I looked at the hand and didn't shake it. He retreated it with a little flap, as if it had never been intended for shaking at all but was rather an exercise in muscle relaxation. The newspaper was retrieved from the tabletop and flicked open to the domestic news, which promised strike action yet to come. I ran my spoon over the surface of my cereal and watched the milk ripple beneath it.

"So," he said at last, "you know the future."

I put my spoon down carefully on the side of my bowl, wiped my lips, folded my hands and sat back in my chair.

37

He wasn't looking at me, eyes fixed on the newspaper.

"No," I replied. "It was a psychotic episode."

"Some break."

"I was ill. I need help."

"Yeap," he sang out, snapping the pages of his newspaper taut with a merry flick of the wrist. "That's bu-ll-shit." He enjoyed the word so much it brought a quiver of a smile to the corners of his lips, and he seemed almost to consider saying it again, just to savour the experience.

"Who are you?" I asked.

"Franklin Phearson, sir. I said."

"Who do you represent?"

"Why can't I represent myself?"

"But you don't."

"I represent a number of interested agencies, organisations, nations, parties – whatever you want to call them. The good guys, basically. You want to help the good guys, don't you?"

"And how would I help, if I could?"

"Like I said, Dr August, you know the future."

A silence brushed between us like a cobweb in a gloomy house. He no longer pretended to read his newspaper, and I unashamedly studied his face. At length I said, "There are some obvious questions I need to ask. I suspect I know the answers, but as we are being so frank with each other ..."

"Of course. This should be an honest relationship."

"If I was to attempt to leave, would I be allowed?"

He grinned. "Well, that's an interesting one. Permit me to answer with a question of my own: if you were to leave, where the hell do you think you could go?"

I ran my tongue round the inside of my mouth, feeling healing scars and fresh tears in the soft skin of my cheeks and lips. Then, "If I had this knowledge – which I don't – what use would you make of it?"

"That kinda depends on what it is. If you tell me that the West will come out of this conflict triumphant, that good wins and the bad fall beneath the righteous sword, then hell, I'll be the first guy to buy you a bottle of champagne and a slap-up feast at the brasserie of your choosing. If, on the other hand, you happen to know the dates of massacres, of wars and battles, of men murdered and crimes committed, well then, sir – I cannot tell a lie – we may have to be in conversation a little while longer."

"You seem very ready to believe that I do know something of the future, whereas everyone – including my wife – believes it to be a delusion."

He sighed and folded his newspaper away entirely, as if even the option of pretence were no longer of any interest to him. "Dr August," he replied, leaning across the table towards me, hands folded beneath his chin, "let me ask you something, in this spirit of free and frank conversation. Have you in all your travels – your many, many travels – heard of the Cronus Club?"

"No," I replied honestly. "I haven't. What is it?"

"A myth. One of those wry footnotes academics put at the bottom of a text to liven up a particularly dull passage, a kind of 'incidentally, some say this and isn't that quaint' fairy tale shoved into the small print at the back of an unread tome."

"And what does this small print say?"

"It says ... " he replied, letting out a huff of breath with the weary resignation of the regular storyteller. "It says that there are people, living among us, who do not die. It says that they are born, and they live, and they die and they live again, the same life, a thousand times. And these people, being as they are infinitely old and infinitely wise, get together sometimes – no one really knows where – and have ... Well, it depends on which text you're read-ing what they have. Some say conspiratorial meetings in white robes, others go for orgies at which the next generation of their kin are created. I don't believe in either, because the Klan has really dented the white-robe fashion down South, and orgies are every-one's first bet."

"And this is the Cronus Club?"

"Yes, sir," he replied brightly. "Like the Illuminati without the glamour, or the Masons without the cufflinks, a self-perpetuating society spread across the ages for the infinite and the timeless. I had to investigate it because someone said the Russians were, and from what I can tell it's a fantasy created by a very bored mind, but then . . . then someone like you comes along, Dr August, and that really throws off my paperwork."

"You think that because my delusions correspond to an old wives' tale there must be something to it?"

"God no, not at all! I think that because your delusions correspond to the truth, there must be something in it. And so," a flash of a grin as he leaned back easily into his chair, "here we are."

Time is not wisdom; wisdom is not intellect. I am still capable of being overwhelmed; he overwhelmed me.

"May I have some time to think about it?" I asked.

"Sure thing. You sleep on it, Dr August. Let me know what you think tomorrow morning. Do you play croquet?"

"No."

"There's a beautiful lawn if you want to try."

# Chapter 11

A moment to consider memory.

The kalachakra, the ouroborans, those of us who loop perpetually through the same course of historical events, though our lives within may change – in short, the members of the Cronus Club – forget. Some see this forgetting as a gift, a chance to rediscover things which have already been experienced, to retain some wonder at the universe. A sense of déjà vu haunts the oldest members of the Club, who know that they have seen this all before but can't quite remember when. For others, the imperfect memory of our kin is viewed as proof that we are, for our condition, still human. Our bodies age and experience pain as humans do, and when we die future generations may come and find the place where we are buried and dig up our rotting corpses and say, yes, here indeed is the departed flesh of Harry August, though where his mind has fled to who can say? The implications for reality of this revelation are too numerous to discuss here, but always and again we return to the mind – the *mind* is what takes the journey through time while the flesh decays. We are no more and no less than minds, and it is human for the mind to be imperfect and to forget. So no one can remember who founded the Cronus Club, though everyone has played their part; perhaps even the ouroboran who made that first choice can no longer remember his part in it and wonders with everyone else. When we die it is as if the world resets, and only memory remains as evidence of the deeds we have done, no more and no less.

I remember everything, and sometimes with that intensity when it is not so much recollection as reliving. Even as I address you now I can recall the sun setting on the hills and the brownish smoke from Phearson's pipe as he sat on the patio beneath my window, looking towards the untouched croquet lawn. I cannot re-create the exact pattern of my thoughts, in that they had no words, no constructed thing on which to grapple; but I can tell you the moment I reached my decision, where I sat and what I saw. I was sitting on the bed, and I saw a picture of rustic farm-houses painted in greens and greys, with a spaniel barking outside, its legs ungainly and rabbit-like as it bounded in the air.

I said, "Yes, but I have a condition."

"What would you like?"

"I want to know everything you do about the Cronus Club."

Phearson only thought for a moment. Then, "OK."

So began my first – and nearly only – tampering with the course of temporal events. I began generally, broad strokes. Phearson was delighted to hear about the fall of the Soviet Union, but his delight was tempered with suspicion, in the manner of a man who couldn't quite believe that I wasn't inventing platitudes to appease his aspirations. He demanded details – details – and as I told him of perestroika and glasnost, the fall of the Berlin Wall, of the opening of Austria's borders, the death of Ceauşescu, he continually handed notes to his assistants to check the names I named, to see if there really was a Gorbachev in the Kremlin and to assess if he really could be such a powerful ally in the destruction of his own nation's glory.

His interests weren't purely political. Science and economics were his mid-afternoon distractions, presented as light entertainment between the serious political interrogations. My interests did

42

not aid him. I knew that the mobile phone was coming and that a mysterious force called the Internet was gathering strength but couldn't tell him how or who had invented it as such things had never been of any great interest to me. Domestic politics held almost no interest for him, but his questions adapted to the answers I gave, growing more specific even as I strove to keep it as general as I could. After his initial doubts that the future could indeed be so rosy, he began to embrace the finer details, pressing ever closer for newspaper headlines half-seen on a tabloid board, or recollections of a journey on a train from Kyoto in 1981.

"My God, sir," he exclaimed. "You are either the world's greatest liar or you have one hell of a memory."

"My memory," I replied, "is perfect. I remember everything from when I first had the consciousness to understand that this was recollection. I cannot remember being born; perhaps the brain is simply not developed enough to understand the event. But I remember dying. I remember the moment when it stops."

"What's it like?" asked Phearson, eyes gleaming with a personal enthusiasm I hadn't yet seen in his work.

"The stopping is fine. Nothing. A stop. The getting there is difficult."

"Did you see anything?"

"No."

"Nothing?"

"Nothing more or less than the natural function of a decaying mind."

"Maybe it doesn't count for you."

"'Doesn't count'? You think that my death isn't . . . " I checked myself, looked away. "I suppose I haven't got anything to compare it with, have I?" I didn't add that neither had he.

I told no lies but couldn't quite satisfy him.

"But how does the invasion of Afghanistan happen? There's no one there to fight!"

His ignorance of the past was almost as profound as his ignorance of the future but at least had the advantage of being

43

independently corroborated. I told him to study the Great Game, to research the Pashtun, look at a map. I could give him dates and places, I explained, but the understanding – that'd have to be his own.

And in my spare time I studied. Phearson was, it seemed, as good as his word. I read about the Cronus Club.

There was very little indeed. If it hadn't tallied so closely with my experience, I would have considered the entire thing a hoax. A reference to a society in Athens in AD 56, renowned for their learned discourse and exclusivity, the mystery surrounding their nature leading to their expulsion four years later, which, the recorder noted, they took with remarkable good grace and care-less ease, unbothered by the events of the time. A diarist noting two years before the sack of Rome that a building on the corner of his street dedicated to the cult of Cronus had emptied, the very finely dressed ladies and gentlemen who went there moving on with a warning that soon things would not be worth their staying, and lo, the barbarians came. In India a man accused of murder denying the crime and slitting his own throat in his cell, saying before he died that it was a tedious shame but that like the snake he would swallow his own tail and be born again. A group renowned for their secretive ways leaving Nanjing in 1935 and one, a lady known for her wealth – no one knew how she had acquired it – warning her favourite maid to leave the city and remove her family far afield, giving her coin to do it and proph-esying a war in which everything would burn. Some called them prophets; the more superstitious named them demons. Whatever the truth, wherever they went, the Cronus Club seemed to have a twin knack for avoiding trouble and staying out of sight.

In a sense, Phearson's file on the Cronus Club was his own undoing. For, reading it, for the very first time I began to consider the question of time.

# Chapter 12

I have already mentioned some of the stages which we go through when attempting to understand what we are. In my second life I, in a rather clichéd display, killed myself to make it cease, and in my third life I sought an answer from God.

I have said that I went to some pains to find very dull, safe positions during the Second World War. What I have not stated is that the war also offered an opportunity to learn some more about the limits of my present learning. Thus, from a Jamaican engineer by the questionable name of Friday Boy, I heard about the souls of the dead and the angry ghosts that stay behind when they are not honoured. From a very earnest American officer called Walter S. Brody came the mysteries of Baptism, Anabaptism, Mormonism and Lutheranism laid out with the conclusion, "My ma was all of them at some time, and what she learned is that the best way to talk to God is by yourself."

A Sudanese soldier who had hauled baggage for Rommel's retreating tanks in Tunisia before escaping – or perhaps being captured, the rumour was never clarified – showed me the way to Mecca. He told me how to recite the words, "I bear witness that there is no God but Allah, and I bear witness that Mohammad is

God's servant and his messenger," first in English, then broken Arabic, and finally Acholi, which he proudly declared was a language like no other and he, being Muslim and Acholi, was a man like no other. I recited this last several times to try and get the intonation right, and when he was satisfied he slapped me on the back and proclaimed, "There! Maybe you won't have to burn in hellfire after all!"

I think it was this soldier, more than the others, who encouraged me to travel. He told fantastical and, as it frequently turned out, entirely fictional tales of glorious lands beyond the Mediterranean Sea, of mysteries and answers waiting in the sands. When the war ended I found the first ship I could to these lands that so many Englishmen were leaving and, drunk on the times, stumbled through various misdeeds and adventures with a blind ignorance worthy of the youth I appeared to wear. In Egypt I became passionately convinced of the truth of Allah's word, until one day I was cornered in an alley in Cairo and beaten senseless by three of my brothers from the mosque. They pulled my beard out and shaved my head with dull knives, spat in my face and tore at my ill-fitting white robes, which I had acquired with the zealousness of the convert, proclaiming that I was a Jewish spy – albeit a ginger one – an imperialist, a communist, a fascist, a Zionist and above all else, not one of them. I spent four days in hospital and on my discharge went to my mullah for comfort. He politely poured me tea in a glass tulip cup and asked me how I felt about my calling.

I left the next day.

In the newly founded state of Israel I toyed for a while with Judaism, but for all my war-wounded credentials in the cause of Hebrew espionage, I was clearly not about to belong, and my status as an ex-soldier of the hated British did me few enough services. I saw men and women with camp tattoos still blue on their skins, who fell to their knees beneath the Wailing Wall and wept with relief to see its sun-drenched stones, and knew that I was not a part of their universe.

A Catholic priest on top of Mount Sinai greeted me when I

46

climbed it in search of a god to answer my prayers. I knelt at his feet and kissed his hand and said his being there was a sign, a sign that there was a god who had a purpose for me, and I told him my story. Then he knelt at my feet and kissed my hand and said I was a sign, a sign from God that there was a purpose to his life after all, and that in me his faith was renewed, and he became so earnest in his declarations of my wonder that I began to doubt it myself. He said he would take me to Rome to meet the Pope, that I would have a life of meditation and prayer to fathom the mysteries of my existence, and three days later I woke to find him on the floor of my room, naked except for a string of beads, kneeling and kissing my hand as I slept. He said I was a messenger and apologised that he had ever harboured any doubts, and I sneaked out of the back window and down the garden wall just before sunrise.

I headed to India, having heard tales of mysticism and philosophies which might perhaps succeed in explaining my situation where Western theology had failed. I arrived in 1953, securing a job easily as a mechanic for an endlessly failing succession of commercial airlines. Their failure rarely affected me; I could leave work on a Monday employed by one man only to come in for work on a Tuesday to find my old contract destroyed and a new, perfect copy waiting to be signed, all clauses exactly the same except for the date and name of employer. India was settling down from its partition and I was in the south, away from the worst of the bloodshed that had stained her independence. Nehru was prime minister and I found myself madly in love, first with an actress whose eyes seemed to look at me and only me from the silver screen, and then with a look-alike girl who sold fruit at the airport and hadn't a word of any significance, who I idolised abjectly and courted disastrously. It has been observed among even the oldest of our kind that a certain biological incentive drives us, regardless of the ages of our mind. As a child I had felt only a biological incentive to grow and be intellectually despondent at the same. As a teenager I had fought depression with occupation and the conspiracies of the Hulne household. Now as a man in the prime of life, the urge was upon me more than ever before to go out into the world and challenge it like a bullfighter in the ring. I travelled in search of answers, argued with men who argued back, loved from the pit of my soul and was rejected to the bottom of my heart, and idolised Meena Kumari, Bollywood goddess, as a symbol of perfection though I spoke not a word of Hindi when first I saw her films.

Answers failed to arise from either love or God. I spoke of resurrection and reincarnation with the Brahmins, and they told me that if I lived a good and pure life, I could return as something greater than myself.

"And what about myself? Can I return as me?"

This question caused quite a stir among the wise men of Hinduism to whom I put it. I like to think that I introduced the first inklings of relativistic physics into their discourse, as academics sat up earnestly debating the question of whether resurrection needed to be temporarily linear in nature. Finally the answer came back from one wise man with a big belly and very neat eating habits who proclaimed,

"Don't be ridiculous, English! You get better or you get worse, but all things change!"

This answer gave me little satisfaction and, with my savings from ten years repairing the same jet with a weekly different name, I moved on. China was hardly welcoming, and my timing was poor in terms of visiting Tibet, so I headed south, dodging around Vietnam, Thailand, Myanmar and Nepal, judging my moves on the basis of where the Americans would not be invading, or a civil war was not imminently going to break out. I shaved my head and ate only vegetables, learned to pray out loud with impossible words and asked every permutation of every Buddha, from the one Gautama to his ten thousand aspects, why I was what I was, and whether this death would be my last. I acquired something of a reputation, the Englishman who knew the discourse of all faiths, who could argue with any monk or imam, padre or priest on any philosophical topic they could raise as long as it pertained to the immortal soul. In 1969 I was visited by a cheerful man with round glasses who sat cross-legged from me in my hut and proclaimed, "Good evening, revered sir. My name is Shen. I am with a concerned institution, and I am here to ask you what your intentions are."

I was living in Bangkok at the time, having discovered that no amount of purity of prayer could alleviate the misery of tropical moulds growing in the folds of your skin during a wet jungle life. The newspapers carried stories of the government's greatness in big, bold letters, and whispers of communist guerrillas in the hills in far smaller letters of sombre black. I did not know if I believed that the eightfold path would bring me enlightenment, but I knew that I was getting too old to believe anything else so divided my time between fixing cars in my orange robes and meditating on what I would do if I could not die.

Mr Shen, face like a polished conker and blue shirt sticky with sweat down the back and beneath his arms, pushed his glasses a little higher up his face and added, "Are you here to engage in counter-revolutionary activities?"

I had gone through a phase of cultivating wise mystic answers, but frankly one gets too old for such things, so blurted, "Are you with the Chinese security services?"

"Of course, revered sir," he intoned, bowing from his seated pose, hands together, in the custom that is respectful for Thais addressing a teacher. "We have very little interest in this country, but it has been suggested by some that you are in fact a Western imperialist agent intending to ally with such counter-revolutionary forces as bourgeois separatist the Dalai Lama, and that your temple is a hub of capitalist subversion created to strike at the heart of our glorious people."

He spoke all this so pleasantly that I was forced to ask, "Isn't that bad?"

"Of course it's bad, revered sir! It would be the kind of subversive activity that would prompt retaliation from my government, though of course," a flash of bright, cheerful smile, "you would naturally be protected by your imperialist allies, and there would doubtless be repercussions."

"Oh!" I exclaimed, realisation dawning. "You're threatening to kill me?"

"I would hate to go so far, revered sir, not least as I personally believe that you are merely an eccentric Englishman looking for an easy time."

"How would you kill me?" I asked. "Would it be quick?"

"I would hope so, yes! Unlike your propaganda, we are not barbarians."

"Would I have to know about it? If you were to, say, kill me painlessly in my sleep, would that be an option?"

A look of consternation flashed across Shen's face as he considered this. "I imagine it would be politic for everyone involved if we could make your death seem both painless and natural. Your being awake would doubtless lead to a struggle and signs of self-defence, which would be unacceptable in a monk, even an imperialist pig monk. You're ... *not* an imperialist pig, are you?"

"I am English," I pointed out.

"There are good English communists."

"I'm not communist."

Shen chewed his lower lip uncertainly, eyes darting round the edge of the room as if he half expected to find a crack in the bamboo walls through which a rifle might appear. Then, in a rather more hushed voice, "I am hoping you aren't an imperialist agent, revered sir," he murmured. "I was asked to compile the case file against you and I couldn't find any evidence that you were more or less than a harmless madman with old-fashioned beliefs. It would be a poor reflection on my paperwork if you were to turn out to be a spy."

"I'm definitely not a spy," I assured him.

He looked relieved. "Thank you, sir," he exclaimed, wiping his forehead with his sleeve and then hastily bobbing an apology for this act of sweaty disrespect. "It did seem very unlikely, but you have to be thorough, times being as they are."

"May I interest you in tea?" I suggested.

"No, thank you. I can't be seen fraternising unnecessarily with the enemy."

"I thought you said I wasn't the enemy."

"You're ideologically corrupt," he corrected, "but harmless."

50

So saying, and still bowing profusely, he made to leave.

"Mr Shen," I called after him. He paused in the door, his face with the strained expression of a man who sincerely hopes that his desk is not about to become busier. "I cannot die," I explained politely. "I am born, and I live, and I die, and I live again, but it is the same life. Has your government got any information on this which may be of use to me?"

He smiled, genuine relief flooding his features. "No, revered sir. Thank you for your cooperation." Then, an afterthought, "Good luck with all that."

He let himself out.

He was the first spy I have ever met, and Franklin Phearson was the second. Of the two, I think I preferred Shen.

# Chapter 13

Some seventy or so years later, Phearson sat across the table from me in that manor house in Northumbria and grew angry as I said, "Complexity should be your excuse for inaction. The complexity of events, the complexity of time – what good is this knowledge to you?"

It was raining outside, a hard, relentless downpour that had come after two days of stifling heat, an unclenching from the sky. Phearson had gone to London; on his return, he had brought more questions and a less yielding attitude.

"You're holding back!" he belted. "You say all these things will happen, but you don't say how. You talk of computers and telephones and the goddamn end of the Cold War but you don't give us shit on how any of it works. We're the good guys – we're here to make things better, do you see? A better world!"

When angry a blue vein like a writhing snake stood out on his left temple, and his face, rather than growing red, grew greyish pale. I considered his accusations and felt a not inconsiderable part of them to be baseless. I was no historian; the events of the future had unfolded as actions in the present with little time for retrospective analysis or contemplation, but rather as news stories told on the TV in sixty-second chunks. I could no further explain the functioning of the home computer than I could balance a kipper on the end of my nose.

And yes, I was holding back – not on all things, but on some. I had read about the Cronus Club, and the primary lesson I had learned was that it was a place of silence. If its members were like me, if they knew the future, at least as it pertained to their personal lifelines, then they had the power to affect it outright. Yet they chose not to do so. And why?

"Complexity," I repeated firmly. "You and I are merely individuals. We cannot control massive socio-economic events. You may try to tamper, but to alter even one event, even in the smallest possible way, will invalidate every other event that I have ever described. I can tell you that the trade unions will suffer under Thatcher, but in truth I cannot pin down the economic forces behind this phenomenon, or explain in a glib few words why society permits its industries to be destroyed. I can't tell you what is in the minds of the people who dance at the fall of the Berlin Wall, or exactly who will stand up in Afghanistan and say, 'Today is a good day for jihad.' And what good is my information to you, if acting on a single piece of it destroys the whole?"

"Names, places!" he exclaimed. "Give me names, give me places!"

"Why?" I asked. "Will you assassinate Yasser Arafat? Will you execute children for crimes they haven't committed yet, arm the Taliban in advance?"

"That's a policy decision, these are all policy decisions . . ."

"You're making your decisions based on crimes which haven't been committed yet!"

He threw his arms wide in a great gesture of frustration. "Humanity is evolving, Harry!" he exclaimed. "The world is changing! In the last two hundred years humanity has changed in ways more radical than it achieved in the last two thousand! The rate of evolution is accelerating, as a species and as a civilisation. It's our job, the job of good men, good men and good women, to oversee this process, to guide it so that we don't have any more fuck-ups and disasters! You want another Second World War? Another Holocaust? We can change things, make them better."

"You regard yourself as fit to oversee the future?"

"Goddamn it, yes!" he roared. "Because I'm a fucking defender of democracy! Because I'm a fucking liberal-minded believer in freedom, because I'm a fucking good guy with a good heart and damn it because someone has to!"

I sat back in my chair. The rain was slicing in sideways, pounding against the glass. There were fresh flowers on the table, cold coffee in my cup. "I'm sorry, Mr Phearson," I said at last. "I don't know what it is you want me to tell you."

He shuffled round quickly on to a chair, pulled it closer to me, dropping his voice to an almost conspiratorial level, hands pressed down in a might-be apology. "Why don't we win in Vietnam? What are we doing wrong?"

I groaned, pressing my palms against my skull. "You're not wanted! The Vietnamese don't want you, the Chinese don't want you, your own people don't want you in Vietnam! There's no winning a war no one wants to fight!"

"What if we dropped the bomb? One bomb, Hanoi, a clean sweep?"

"I don't know because it never happened, and it never happened because it's obscene!" I shouted. "You don't want knowledge, you want affirmation, and I . . . " I stood suddenly, as surprised to find myself standing as anyone else in the room. " . . . I can't give you that," I concluded. "I'm sorry. I thought when I agreed to this that you were . . . that you wanted something else. I think I was wrong. I need . . . to think."

Silence between us.

In Chinese, asthma is described as the panting of an animal, its breath heavy with illness. Phearson's body was statue-still, his hands carved to civilised containment, his suit straight, his face empty, but his breath was all animal bursting up from within his chest. "What is the point of you?" he asked, and the words were shaped by years of polite upbringing, careful self-control, and the breath that drove it wanted to rip my throat out with bare teeth and swallow blood. "You think this doesn't matter, Dr August? You think you die and that's it? The world resets, bang!" A slam of his hand into the table, hard enough to make china cups bounce in porcelain saucers. "Us little men with little lives are dead and gone, and all this –" he didn't need to move, didn't need to do more than flick his eyes around the room "– was just a dream. Are you God, Dr August? Are you the only living creature that matters? Do you think, because you remember it, that your pain is bigger and more important? Do you think, because you experience it, that your life is the only life that gets counted? Do you?"

He didn't shout, didn't raise his voice, but the animal breath came fast even as his fingers tightened against their own instinct to tear. I found I had nothing. No words, no ideas, no justification, no rebuke. He stood suddenly, sharply, a breaking of a sort, though of what I didn't dare say, the vein on his temple writhing busily beneath his skin. "OK." He panted the word out. "OK, Dr August. OK. We've both got a little tired, a little frustrated ... Maybe we need a break. Why don't we take the rest of the day off and you can think about it, OK? OK," he decided before I could answer. "That's a plan. Great. I'll see you tomorrow."

So saying, he strode from the room without another word and without looking back.

# Chapter 14

I had to leave.

The feeling had been growing upon me for a while, and now it reached its ultimate proof. I could see no good outcome of remaining and had to go. It would not be as simple as walking out of the front door, but then sometimes the best escape plans are the simplest.

Why, in all my years in the east, had I not bothered to learn even a little kung fu?

The question seemed ridiculous now as I sat in my room and waited for dusk. There were guards – not dressed as guards clearly, but in my time I had learned enough of the rhythms of that place to recognise no fewer than five men on duty at any given moment, loitering quietly in the background waiting for a command. At seven every evening they swapped shifts, and the new team was usually still digesting its evening meal. That made them sloppy, slower and a little too relaxed. The land beyond my window was a mix of gorse and heather, and the milkman when he made his delivery had the thick accent of the North. I didn't need much more than that. I had been a groundsman raised in these parts; I had lived and died by this soil in my first life and knew how to survive on a moor. Phearson, for all his resources and his men, struck me as a city boy not used to the wild hunt. All I needed was to get beyond the walls.

As the land began to turn to a faded grey and 7 p.m. approached, I gathered up what resources I could. A kitchen knife I had stolen from dinner, a metal cup and a small metal plate purloined from the kitchen, a box of matches, bar of soap, toothbrush, toothpaste and a couple of candles. Phearson had been careful: there was little else readily available to an eager thief. He had given me paper to write down my recollections; on it I wrote two letters ready for my departing. I wrapped everything in my blanket and tied it to my back with strips of the sheet from my bed. At five minutes past seven, as the last light began to fade across the moor, I eased open my bedroom door, feeling every bit a ridiculous child, and headed downstairs.

There would be guards on the main and kitchen doors, but several slept on site and no one bothered to guard the bedrooms of the guards themselves. I found a heavy-duty coat and several pairs of socks in one of them, and a few precious shillings on the dresser, then headed towards the rear of the house to where a window opened on to a low coal-shed roof. I eased myself out feet first, balancing precariously on the edge, then dropped with a metal thud that rattled me to my very bones, and waited for retribution.

No retribution came, so I slipped further down, easing on to the gravel path that snaked around the house. To run was to declare my escape, so I walked at an easy swagger as I had heard the guards do, heart racing with every step, until I was finally behind the yew hedges and ready to run, which at last I did.

I was out of shape, having never been in much of a shape to get out of, and my confinement had hardly aided the process. But I wasn't hugely burdened, and an odd exhilaration, a recollection of the sounds and smells of childhood and the moor, a liberation in the length of my own stride, powered me on. There was a wall all around the grounds, which I had noticed on my supervised walks in the garden, but it was a wall designed more for keeping strangers out than prisoners in, and it was a minimal challenge to find an old oak tree whose lowest branch dangled over the yellow brick like a pirate's gangplank. I climbed up, fingers brushing aside insects feeding on rotting wood, slipped along the branch as I had so many times as a boy, and dropped down the other side. And, like that, I was free.

If it had been that simple.

I had a plan, within which there were other plans which could end a number of different ways, depending on how the overall plan proceeded. I considered the prospect of my recapture to be highly likely, in light of how inexperienced I was at evading authorities and how much of myself I had given away, but the intermediate time was mine.

Whatever happened, I needed to find where I was, to determine how hard the rest of my scheme would be. A tatty road ran between great banks of untamed trees; I followed it to the west, hiding in the forest at the sound of the three cars that passed by in all the hours of my walking. Creatures rustled in the woods beside me, wondering what I was doing; it would have been romantic to say an owl hooted, but it had more common sense and kept clear of me as I passed. I estimated that, at the outside, I would have three hours before the alarm was raised back in the house. It could be a lot less, if I was unlucky.

A T-junction stood just beyond a stream crowned with a tiny brick bridge. It offered two choices – Hoxley in five miles, or West Hill in seven. I chose Hoxley, knowing it to be the more obvious decision but also the fastest, and set out parallel to the road. My forest covering quickly gave way to more open fields framed with low stone walls; I hopped on to the muddy side of these and ducked down behind whenever I heard the rumble of an engine, no matter how far off. The moon was half full – optimum in terms of providing just enough light to see, but not so much to expose me. The air, so hot in the day, now turned cold enough for my breath to steam. The ground was still muddy from the rain, my trousers splattered and my socks soaked through to a ubiquitous squelch. I found the North Star, Orion's Belt, Cassiopeia and the Great Bear. Cassiopeia was high, the Bear was low, which made the first car that tore by me at the speed of urgency a little past midnight. I had got lucky: they'd taken several hours to notice my absence and now they had little choice but to drive around the countryside with headlights on full in search of me while I could navigate by starlight.

Hoxley was a little stone village on the edge of a little stone hill where once they'd mined and now they declined. I crept in sideways between the houses, down the little back streets that ran out at fields and fences. Though it could not have held more than four hundred souls, Hoxley had a war memorial in a tiny centre square, bearing the lists of names of those who'd died in two wars. A silver car was parked beside it, lights on, a figure lost inside. It had stopped by the one pub and clearly disturbed the landlord, who stood in the doorway arguing with a second man, indignant at his night being broken. I crawled away from the square up what had to be called the High Street, with its one little grocer selling fresh tomatoes and lamb, and the post office, proudly painted in chipped bright red. Now I knew where it was, I slunk again to the edge of town and crawled between the loose planks of a lopsided barn, to hide among the rusted wheelbarrow, bundled stacks of hay and dusty chicken feathers lost in a fight.

I did not sleep, and that was not a problem.

# Chapter 15

I had timed sunrise during my stay at the house and knew exactly when it came.

I waited what I estimated to be an hour after before crawling out of my den, and was the first, mud-stained, feather-brushed man to walk up to Hoxley post office even as the postmistress, a sour woman with a flushed round face, unlocked the door. With the shillings I had stolen from my guards I bought two envelopes and a couple of stamps, and pressed my letters into her hand.

"You're very kind," I said in my best Scottish accent, and she raised her eyebrows to hear a stranger.

It was a poor attempt at disguise, but if my would-be captors were to ask, I wished to confuse the matter of my presence there as far as possible. I watched her slip my two letters into her bag and left.

The day was hot, bright and beautiful.

Rather reluctantly, I abandoned my stolen coat, which had done sterling service in the coldest parts of the night. It was, I felt, too easily recognisable and marked too heavily with my night's trudging. Without it, underneath, I was an almost respectable, if rather muddy gentleman.

The silver car I had seen in the night was prowling the edge of Hoxley. I ducked down behind a tenement wall smelling of soap and the outdoor privy that it protected as the over-expensive, over-fuelled vehicle rumbled by. The time had come to strike out overland again, away from the daylight danger of the roads.

I headed north, on a largely arbitrary whim, and for a few brief hours felt liberated by the daylight and the warmth, until thirst, hunger and the fuzzy quality of my own teeth began to distract annoyingly. I looked for a dip in the land, or a place where trees grew despite human carving, and by these signs found my way to a shallow stream aspiring to be a river, slippy fat round rocks pressed along its bed. I washed my face, my hands, my neck, and drank deep. I brushed my teeth and watched the white foam of my spit drift busily downstream. I counted the pennies I had left from my night's theft, and wondered how far to the next town and how heavily patrolled it would be. I was too old to set snares for rabbits, so I gathered up my goods and walked on.

I reached the next village in the early afternoon.

Phearson's men stood out like flies crawling in the wild horse's eye. There was a baker, the smell of yeast almost unbearable. I watched for Phearson's men to move on, then strode confidently in and declared, this time in my most received pronunciation, "A loaf and any butter you may have, please."

The baker moved with glacial speed as he considered the question of butter. "Well, sir," he concluded at last, "will lard do you now?"

Lard would do me fine, as long as it came soon.

"You not from here, sir?" he asked.

No, I wasn't from here; I was out walking and needed to join my friends.

"Beautiful weather for it, sir."

Yes, wasn't it just. Let's hope it holds.

"Would it be your friends what came into town this morning, sir? They said they were looking for someone?"

He talked so slowly, so amiably, that it was almost tragic to perceive the sound of suspicion, the quiet accusation in his voice.

Did they look like they were here for the hunting?

No, no, they didn't.

Ah well then. They couldn't be my friends. Thank you for the bread, thank you for the lard and now—

"Harry!" Phearson too, it turned out, could do RP when he needed to. I stood frozen in the door, bread under one arm, bundle of lard half-unwrapped and ready to smear. Phearson walked right up to me and threw his arms around me with gigantic affection. "I was so worried we were going to miss you!" he exclaimed, voice bouncing hugely down the quiet stone street. "Thank God you made it in time."

His car was parked not twenty yards away, a roaring beast in a fairy-tale forest. The rear passenger door was already open, one of my anonymous guards – quite possibly the one I'd stolen the coat from – holding it open. I looked at it, looked at Phearson, and then, not feeling particularly confident about the gesture but feeling it needed to be made, dropped the bread and hit him as hard as I could in the face with the sharp end of my elbow.

I am pleased to say something went crack, and when I drew my arm back, there were flecks of blood staining the sleeve.

Regrettably I got no more than ten yards before the baker, moving with surprising speed for such a sedentary man, took me down with a well-placed rugby tackle and sat on my head.

# Chapter 16

Drugs.

More drugs.

They strapped me to my bed, just like Dr Abel had, but unlike Dr Abel they didn't have the medical instruments so fell back on a mixture of ties and belts. They didn't beat me more than was necessary to achieve submission, merely enough to make it clear that submission was the only option. Then Phearson said, "I'm really sorry it came to this, Harry, I really am. I hoped you would understand."

Scopolamine made me laugh; temazepam made me sleep. They tried sodium amytal and I couldn't stop crying, though I didn't feel very sad. They misjudged the first dose of barbiturates and my heart nearly popped out of my ears. They modified the dose and Phearson sat as I drooled nonsensical nothings.

He said, "We don't want to hurt you, Harry. Christ, I'm not that guy, I'm just not; I'm one of the good guys. I'm a good guy trying to do the best. We don't want to hurt you, but you gotta understand this is bigger than you or me, much, much bigger."

Then they brought up the jump leads from the garage down-stairs and he pressed his face close to mine and said, "Harry, don't make me do it. Come on, we can do this. We can make things better, you and me. We can make this world a better place!"

When I didn't answer, they pumped me full of antipsychotics and stuck the leads into a socket on the wall. But one of the guys got it wrong and touched the wrong bit, and shocked himself, yowling like a cartoon character and jumping a foot in the air. They had to take him downstairs to put ice on his hand and didn't try anything else electric that night.

"Come on, Harry," whispered Phearson. "Do the right thing. Make a difference, damn it! Make a difference!"

I laughed and rode on the warmth of the temazepam wave.

# Chapter 17

Complexity should be your excuse for inaction.

This was ever the mantra of the Cronus Club, and I say it to you now. It is not noble, it is not bold, it is not righteous, it is not ambitious, but when you are dabbling with the sweep of history, with time itself, it is a sacred vow which should be pinned above every Cronus Clubhouse door. I had said as much to Phearson, and he could not understand.

I have said before of the passage of our lives, that there are three stages. Rejection of what we are, I think I had fairly well covered by the time Phearson came to pump me full of psychotropic hallucinogens. My situation held me a long way from acceptance, but I believe I was, in my own way, attempting to explore my nature to the best of my abilities. In my third life I tried God; in my fourth biology. My fifth we shall return to, but in my sixth life I attempted to explore the mysteries of what we are, albeit rather late in the day, through physics.

You have to understand that I was a boy in the 1930s. Not merely a boy, but a child growing up the bastard son of a man who had about as much interest in scientific development as I could muster in the pedigree of his favourite horses. I had no notion of the revolution that was overtaking scientific thought, of relativity and nuclear physics, of Einstein, Bohr, Planck, Hubble and Heisenberg. I had some loose concept of the notion that the world was round and an apple that falls from the tree will descend towards the mass below, but for many centuries of my early lives time itself was a concept as linear and uninteresting as a metal ruler in a builder's yard. It took me to the 1990s to begin to understand the concepts of the 1930s, and how they impacted not merely on the world around me, but possibly the very question of who and what I was.

In my sixth life I had my first doctorate by the age of twenty-three – not because I was especially talented in the realms of science, but because I was able to skip so much of the tedious general knowledge phase of my education and jump straight into the areas that interested me. I was invited to work on the Manhattan Project, the youngest member of the team, and agonised for many long nights about whether to accept. Ethics were of no concern – the bomb would be built and the bomb would be dropped, regardless of my personal feelings. Rather the project offered an exciting opportunity to meet some of the greatest minds of the day, locked together in the same room. In the end, the idea of being locked, and of my background being explored too deeply, combined with a reluctance to expose myself to unnecessary danger in those days when radiation was poorly controlled and criticality not yet understood, held me back, and I worked the most part of the war developing surprisingly plausible hypotheses on Nazi technology, ranging from bomb mechanisms and rocket engines, through to heavy water and their own nuclear reactor plant.

I met Vincent in late 1945. The war was won, but rationing still cast its pall over my dinner table. It is petty, I know, to still find oneself frustrated by how bland the food is for so much of my early life, or how long it takes for central heating to become ubiquitous. I was a lecturer at Cambridge, and was in bitter competition for a professorship that I was far too young to take and which I deserved to a far higher degree than my fifty-three-year-old rival,

P. L. George, a man distinguished mainly for the complexities of his mathematical errors. I would not get the professorship in the end; my unfashionable dedication to the notion of the Big Bang over steady state and my unreasonable insistences on the nature of wave-particle duality, combined with my highly unfashionable youth, made me less than popular at the high table. Indeed, I was justly rebuked for my views on both, since to a large degree they were formed on the basis of evidence which hadn't yet been uncovered, and required technology which had not yet been invented to justify.

It was, in fact, this very same fallacy that brought Vincent to my door.

"Dr August," he said firmly, "I wish to discuss the multiverse."

As opening statements go, this was rather unexpected, and I was painfully aware that every second Vincent stood in my doorway was another in which the warmth of my carefully nurtured fire would be expended in true entropic principle for no one else to enjoy. Seeing, however, that he was not about to move, and in light of the thickening snow falling outside, I invited him in, though I was hardly in the mood.

Vincent Rankis. The first time we met, he was young, barely eighteen years old, but already he had the physicality of the perpetually middle-aged. Somehow, despite rationing, he was chubby without being fat, rounded without being particularly overweight, though he would never be described as muscle-bound. His mouse-brown hair was already thinning at the crown, the promise of a bald patch to come, and a pair of grey-green eyes looked out from within a face moulded by a busy sculptor from rather wet clay. His trouser legs were even then rolled up in a manner designed to disencourage social enquiry, and he wore a tweed jacket that I was never to see him out of regardless of the time of year. His claims that the jacket would last a thousand years I can perhaps tolerate; his insistence that the rolled trousers were in aid of cycling I would rebuff, as nothing wheeled was getting through the blocked Cambridge streets on that night. He sat down in the more tattered armchair by the fire with a great huff of effort, and before I had even settled opposite him, attempting to drag my brain out of silent warmth and back into the realms of modern science, he exclaimed,

"To permit the philosophers to apply their banal arguments to the theory of the multiverse is to undermine the integrity of modern scientific theory."

I reached for the nearest glass and bottle of Scotch, buying time to answer. The teacher within me was tempted to play devil's advocate; the teacher lost.

"Yes," I said. "I agree."

"A multiverse has no relevance to individual responsibility for action; it merely extends into a rather simplified paradigm the Newtonian concept that for every action there is an opposite action, and the concept that where there can be no state of absolute rest there cannot be understanding of a particle's nature without changing the thing observed!"

He seemed very indignant on the subject so once again, I said, "Yes."

His eyebrows waggled furiously. He had an uncanny knack of talking with his eyebrows and chin, while the rest of him remained to a good degree static. "Then why did you waste fifteen pages of your last paper discussing the ethical implications of a quantum theory?!"

I sipped my drink and waited for the eyebrows to descend to their natural – but not absolute – state of rest. "Your name," I said at last, "is Vincent Rankis, and I am only aware of this fact because when the beadle challenged you for cutting the corner of the grass you gave him this same name while informing him that in this changing society his role would soon be not merely redundant, but mocked by the imminently approaching future generations. You were wearing that very same olive shirt, if I recall, and I—"

"Blue shirt, grey socks, dress robe, heading at high speed towards the gate in a manner which I can only assume meant you were late for a lecture, it being five minutes to the hour and most of your lectures occurring more than ten minutes away."

I looked at Vincent once again, and this time made conscious note of all the characteristics I had already unconsciously perceived. Then, "Very well, Vincent, let's discuss ethical musings and the scientific method—"

"One is subjective, the other valid."

"If your view is so absolute, I hardly see what good my view will serve."

A flicker of a smile occurred in the corner of his mouth, and he had the grace to look, briefly, ashamed. "Forgive me," he said at last. "I may have had a little something to drink on my way over here. I know I can come across as . . . firm."

"A man travels back in time . . . " I began, and at Vincent's immediate flinch of distaste I raised my hand and said placatingly, "Hypothetically speaking, a thought experiment if you like. A man travels back in time and sees the events of the past unfolding like a future before his eyes. He steps out of his time machine —"

"Immediately altering the past!"

"— and his very first act is to post his younger self the winning riders at Newmarket. Result?"

"Paradox," declared Vincent firmly. "He has no memory of having been posted these numbers; he never won at Newmarket. If he had, he may not have built the time machine and gone back in time to post the numbers to himself to begin with — logical impossibility."

"Result?"

"Impossibility!"

"Indulge the hypothesis."

He huffed furiously, then exclaimed, "Three possible outcomes! One: at the very instant that he makes the decision to send himself the winning numbers, he remembers receiving them and his personal timeline changes, thus he self-perpetuates his own existence as without the winning numbers he could not have built his time machine. Paradox within that being that nothing can come from nothing, and his initiative, his causal event, is in fact an effect, effect preceding cause, but I don't suppose we're dealing with logic in this scenario. Two: the whole universe collapses. Rather melodramatic, I know, but if we consider time as a scalar concept with no negative value then I really see no other way, which seems a shame if all we're discussing here is a little bet at Newmarket. Three: at the very instant he makes the decision to send himself the numbers, a parallel universe is created. In his universe, his linear timeline, he returns home having not won anything at Newmarket in his life, while in a parallel universe his younger self is rather surprised to discover that he's a millionaire and carries on quite happily thank you. Implications?"

"I have no idea," I replied brightly. "I merely wished to see if you were capable of lateral thinking."

He gave another great huff of exasperation and stared fuming into the fire. Then, "I enjoyed your paper. Ignoring the wishy-washy, namby-pamby philosophical stuff, which, I personally thought, verged on the almost theological, I thought your paper was marginally more interesting than the usual journal matter. That's what I wished to say."

"I am honoured. But if your complaint is that ethics have no place in pure science, I'm afraid I must be forced to disagree with you."

"Of course they don't! Pure science is no more and no less than the logical process of deduction and experimentation upon observable events. It has no good or bad about it, merely right or wrong in a strictly mathematical definition. What people do with that science is cause for ethical debate, but it is not for the true scientist to concern themselves with that. Leave it to the politicians and philosophers."

"Would you shoot Hitler?" I asked.

He scowled. "I thought we had just determined a likelihood of the universe being destroyed by such temporal tampering."

"We also posited a parallel universe which you might be able to save from the trials of war," I replied. "We even hypothesised a world in which you yourself could experience the joy of said peace, paradox being left aside."

He drummed his fingers along the edge of his chair then blurted, "There are socio-economic forces that must be considered too. Was Hitler the sole cause of war? I would argue no."

"But the direction the war took . . . ?"

"But there's the thing!" he exclaimed, the eyebrows back into full swing. "If I make the decision to shoot Hitler, how do I not know that someone less willing to fight in Russia in the dead of winter, or to besiege cities with minimal strategic value at the cost of hundreds of thousands of men, or start bombing London and not her airfields – how do I know that this other, saner warmonger will not emerge from the conditions already in place?"

"You argue complexity as an excuse for inaction?"

"I argue . . . I argue . . ." He groaned, throwing his hands off the arms of his chair in frustration. "I argue that it is precisely these hypothetical dabblings with philosophy that undermined the otherwise sound integrity of your paper!"

He fell silent and I, already tired before he came, enjoyed it a while. He stared into the fire and looked for all the world like he had been in my armchair his whole life, as much a piece of furniture as it. "Would you like a drink?" I asked at last.

"What are you drinking?"

"Scotch."

"I've already had a bit much . . . "

"I won't tell the beadle."

A brief hesitation then, "Thank you."

I poured him a glass, and as he took it I said, "So tell me, Mr Rankis, what brings you to our hallowed halls?"

"Answers," he replied firmly. "Measurable, objective. What lies beneath this reality, what is going on in the world we cannot perceive, deeper than protons and neutrons, bigger than galaxies and suns. If time is relative then light speed has become the measuring stick of the universe, but is that all time is? An inconstant factor in the equations of speed?"

"And here I thought the young were only interested in sex and music."

He grinned, the first genuine flash of humour I'd seen. Then, "I hear you're up for a professorship."

"I won't get it."

71

"Of course not," he answered amiably. "You're far too young. It wouldn't be just."

"Thank you for your vote of confidence."

"You can't say you're not expecting to achieve a thing, then express resentment that others agree with you."

"You're right, it is irrational. You seem very ... forthright ... for an undergraduate."

He shrugged. "I can't waste time with being young, there's far too much to do which society will not permit to the under-thirties."

His words produced an instant and inevitable tug within me; I had spent twenty-five tedious years living them. "You're interested in time?"

"Complexity and simplicity," he replied. "Time was simple, is simple. We can divide it into simple parts, measure it, arrange dinner by it, drink whisky to its passage. We can mathematically deploy it, use it to express ideas about the observable universe, and yet if asked to explain it in simple language to a child – in simple language which is not deceit, of course – we are powerless. The most it ever seems we know how to do with time is to waste it."

So saying, he raised his glass in salute to me, and drank it down, though I found suddenly that I was not in a drinking mood.

# Chapter 18

Complexity should be your excuse for inaction.

I should have screamed it at Phearson, should have nailed his ears to the Clubhouse door and made him listen to the stories of disaster and mayhem unleashed down the generations recorded at the Cronus Club. As it was, I could not have known just how accurate my assessment of his tampering could be; nor predicted how far he would go to get more answers from me than I considered it safe to give.

When, in that fourth life, Phearson and his men finally tortured me for my knowledge of things to come, they began uncertainly. They were perfectly prepared to use extreme violence to obtain their results, but they were afraid of damaging the goods in question. I was unique, a once-in-a-lifetime catch, my potential still unknown and unexplored, and to inflict any permanent physical, or worse mental, damage would be an unforgivable sin. Realising this, I screamed the louder, and coughed and foamed and writhed in my own piss and blood. They were so alarmed by this that, briefly, they backed off until Phearson came close again and whispered, "We're doing this for the world, Harry. We're doing this for the future."

Then they started again.

At the end of the second day, they dragged me into the shower and turned it on cold. I sat in the tray while they ran the water over me, and wondered if the glass shower screen could be broken with a punch, and how long it would take me to find a piece with which I could slit my wrists.

On the third day they were a little more confident. The willingness of one inspired the other, a team-player mentality settling in as they tried not to let each other down. Phearson was careful never to be in the room when they went about their work, but always left a few minutes before, and returned a few minutes after. There was a rose-red sunset playing across my ceiling that third night. The others went out and he sat down by my bed and held my hand and said, "Jesus, Harry, I'm so sorry. I'm so sorry that you're doing this. I wish I could make it stop."

I hated him and started to cry, and pressed my face into his hand and knelt at his feet and wept.

# Chapter 19

I had written two letters.

*Dear Jenny,*

*I love you. I feel there should be more than this, more that should be said, but now I come to write to you, I find it is simply this. That there are no more words beyond these, that there is no truth greater, or simpler, or truer. I love you. I am so sorry that I have made you afraid, and so sorry for all that was said, and done, and which must be said, and done. I do not know if my deeds have consequences beyond this life, but if you should live on without me, do not blame yourself for what you shall hear, but live long, and happy, and free. I love you. That is all.*

*Harry*

I put the address of a friend on the envelope in case her mail was being monitored. The second letter was addressed to Dr S. Ballad, neurologist, occasional academic rival, sometime drinking partner and, in a way which neither of us had ever really felt a need to express, a reliable friend. It said:

*Dear Simon,*

*You will have heard things about me in recent months which will have led you to doubt and question. This letter will only deepen those doubts and questions, and for that I must apologise. I cannot here go into my situation, nor even the details of what I now need, for this is nothing if not a letter requesting a favour. Forgive me asking you to do this with so little to go on, but for our friendship, for the respect that is between us and for the hope of better times yet to come, please indulge my request. Below is a notice which I need posted in the personal section of the major newspapers. The posts must be on the same day, at the same time. The day itself is immaterial, save that it must be soon. If I get the chance, I will refund you the cost and do whatever it is I can to repay you for your courtesy and time.*

*Looking at this letter you will doubt if you can do this. You will question my motives and your own responsibility towards me. I do not think that I can, with these few words, persuade you of a position you do not already hold. I can only hope, therefore, that the mutual bond which exists between us, and the guarantee I put in this letter of my good intentions and the entirely positive outcome of this deed, will be enough. If they are not, then I do not know what will come of me, and so I can only beg you, as I have never asked any such thing before, to honour this request.*

*Give my love to your family, and best wishes to yourself, and know I remain,*
*Your friend,*

*Harry*

Beneath the letter was the text of the notice itself:

*Cronus Club.*
*I am Harry August.*
*On 26 April 1986 reactor four went into meltdown.*
*Help me.*

The notice was printed in the personal columns of the *Guardian* and *The Times* on 28 September 1973 and expunged from all records three days later.

# Chapter 20

Phearson broke me.

Back again, back to my fourth life, and always we seem to return here, even when I try not to, back to kneeling at his feet, sobbing into his hand, begging him to make it stop, please, please God, make it stop.

He broke me.

I was broken, and it was a relief.

I became an automaton, reciting newspaper headlines and stories I had seen, word by word, day by day, reaching back across the lives which had gone before. Sometimes I'd drift into the languages of my travels, mixing reports of massacres and rulers overthrown with the sayings of the Buddha or little pieces of Shinto dogma. Phearson never stopped or corrected me, but sat back while the tape recorder clicked on, two great fat wheels spinning, which seemed to require changing every twenty minutes. He had mastered carrot and stick: always he stood by me for the carrot and was never there at the stick, so that in my mind, though I knew this was precisely what he aimed to achieve, Phearson became something of a golden angel, bringing with him warmth and relief from pain. I told him everything: my perfect memory now become a perfect curse until, three days later, she came.

I sensed, somewhere through the drugs and the exhaustion, her arrival as a commotion in the hall. Then an imperious voice rang out, "For goodness' sake!"

I was in the smaller of the two lounges, sitting hunched by the tape recorder as I always was, intoning dull recollections of the assassination attempt on President Reagan. She burst into the room in a flurry of long, almost medieval sleeves, her curly grey hair bouncing on her head like a creature living unto its own laws, the rouge on her face pressed deep into the canyons of her skin, her heavily ringed fingers flashing as she twisted them in the air. "You!" she barked at Phearson, who instinctively switched off the record. "Out!"

"Who the hell are— "

She cut him off with a single imperious gesture of her wrist, snapping, "Call your control, you ghastly little man. Dear me, what have you been doing? Don't you realise how useless this all is now?" He opened his mouth to speak and again was stopped short. "Buzz buzz buzz, trot off, make your telephone calls!"

Perhaps seeing that reasonable communication was not a likely outcome here, a scowl spread across his face and he strode from the room, slamming the door petulantly behind him. The woman sat down opposite me, and rather distractedly prodded a few buttons on the tape machine, chuckling at its size and response. I kept my eyes down on the floor, the fixed hunch of all frightened men awaiting retribution, unable to hope.

"Well, what a terrible little pickle," she said at last. "You look quite the state. I'm Virginia, if you're wondering – which I can see you are. Yes you are, aren't you?"

She addressed me as one might speak to a frightened kitten, and the surprise more than anything else made me glance up towards her, taking in a brief impression of beaded bracelets and giant necklace that hung down almost to her navel. She leaned forward on her cupped hands, looked me in the eye and held the gaze.

"Cronus Club," she said at last. "I am Harry August. On 26 April 1986 reactor four went into meltdown. Help me."

I caught my breath. She had seen my ad – but so could Phearson if he'd bothered to look. So could anyone who read the personal pages of whichever newspaper Simon had printed my message in. Help or retribution? Salvation or a trap?

Either way, did I care?

"You have caused us such a problem," she sighed. "It's not your fault of course, lambkin. I mean – look at you, of course, entirely understandable, such a shame! Now, when it's all over you will be wanting post-traumatic stress counselling, although I understand how difficult these things will be to come by. You look ... fifty, maybe? Which means you must have been born in the twenties – ghastly, so many Freudians in the twenties, so much wanting to sleep with your mother. There's this wonderful little chap in Finchley though, very good, very understanding, no rubbish about cigars. Failing that, I always find local priests are handy, as long as you go to them in the form of a confessional. Scares the buggery out of them sometimes too! Now absolutely don't, *don't.*" She stabbed the table with her index finger, the little joint at the end bending backwards with the force of her determination. "Don't tell yourself that just because you've been around a bit you're not in a terrible state. You are absolutely in a terrible state, Harry dear, and the silent, noble number won't get you anywhere."

Now I couldn't look away from her. Was this face – this old made-up face beneath its bouncing mass of sprayed hair – salvation? Was this woman with her great dangling purple sleeves and chiffon cardigan, with her clattering pendants and expanding belly, a creature of the mysterious Cronus Club? I found it hard enough to think, let alone apply higher reason to the problem.

"There's no joining fee," she explained as if reading my thoughts, "but you are rather expected to chip in for the next generation, good form and all that. Only one rule set in stone – you can do whatever you like so long as you don't bugger it up for the next lot. So no nuking New York, please, or shooting Roosevelt, even if for experimental purposes. We just can't handle the hassle. I'm going to assume you're interested," she added to my silence, "in which case I really feel we should have another meeting."

She leaned across the table. I thought she was giving me a business card, but when her hand lifted there was instead a small penknife folded into a wooden handle. Her eyes glinted and her voice was low. "How would . . . 2 p.m., Trafalgar Square, July 1st 1940 work for you?"

I looked from the knife, to her and back again. She understood and stood up, still smiling. "I personally favour the thigh," she explained. "A bath helps, but one must make do, mustn't one? Tra-la, Dr August, so long and all that!"

So saying, she sauntered merrily away.

I cut open my femoral artery that very same night, and bled out in under four minutes. Regrettably, there wasn't an easily available bath to use at the time, but after the first sixty seconds I didn't really notice the pain and rather savoured the mess.

# Chapter 21

Death holds no fear for us.

It is rebirth where the terror lies. Rebirth, and the lingering fear that no matter how much our bodies are renewed, our minds cannot be saved.

I was in my third life when I realised my illegitimacy, standing above the coffin of Harriet August, staring into the face of my father – my biological father – on the other side of the soil.

There was no outrage or indignation. I felt, perhaps out of grief as much as rational reasoning, gratitude to Harriet and Patrick for raising me, even as the revelation settled on my soul that I could not be blood of their blood. I studied my biological father coolly, as one might study any sample which one suspects of being a placebo rather than the cure. I wondered not why or how, but what. What if he was like me?

I must admit, my scrutiny was hardly informative. With Harriet dead and my adopted father retreating ever deeper into his lone-liness and grief, I increasingly took over his duties, forsaking school altogether to become the all-purpose boy of the estate. The Great Depression was coming upon us and the Hulne family had not been wise in its investments. My grandmother Constance had a level fiscal head on her shoulders, but also a great pride which resulted in a conflict of interests. She hoarded coin on fuel and repairs to the grounds, pinched at every penny and derided any and all expense, yet would every year throw a feast for all relatives and distant friends of the Hulnes to come and hunt on the lands, which single event would easily consume two times the expenditure she had saved. Of my aunts, Alexandra married a pleasant if essentially bland civil servant, and her sister Victoria continued in a lifestyle of excess and scandal which my grandmother simply refused to acknowledge. The frost between my biological father and his wife kept both of them from any great expense. She wasted most of her time in London, an activity permitted on the basis that it was her own money or the money of her family that she wasted; he spent most of his days in the countryside or dabbling, unwisely, in local politics, and when the two shared a house or a bed they did so with the same stiff efficiency and impassioned rigour of my grandmother's yearly feast. In this way the family declined, first by vacancies in the household not being filled, and then by servants being laid off altogether. My adopted father was kept on as much for pity for his position as the services he rendered the family; also, I began to realise, for a certain debt owed by the Hulnes to the Augusts for a child raised without complaint.

I earned my keep, as I had in my first life, and was in fact of rather more use now that I had so many years to draw upon. I knew the land almost better than my father, and had over the years also acquired skills such as fixing an engine, patching a pipe, tracing a faulty cable back to its home, which seemed at the time marvellously advanced technological skills, especially for a teenage boy. I went out of my way to ensure that I was everywhere and nowhere, indispensible and unseen, as much to avoid the monotony of my life as to observe what I now understood to be my biological family. My grandmother studied the art of ignoring me; Aunt Alexandra was rarely in the house to perceive me; Victoria ignored me without having to try; and my father Rory stared until he was caught staring, though whether it was curiosity or guilt which motivated his gaze I was at a loss to say.

I looked at this man, stiffly dressed and stiffer born, a moustache sitting on his top lip like an old family pet, which he cared for secretly in a little green net, and I wondered if he was like me. When they fired the butler and I became a cheaper form of house servant, I would stand behind his chair at the head of the table and watch him cut his overcooked chicken into smaller and smaller pieces, never touching them until every last piece was square. I observed the one ritual kiss on the cheek he gave his wife when she arrived, and the one ritual kiss he gave her on the other cheek when she departed the day after, her wardrobe renewed for a trip back to town. I heard Aunt Victoria whisper when the weather was cold that she had just the thing for the pain in his hip, where in the war he'd been briefly grazed and which his mind had confounded to a greater thing, an injury I hardly begrudged for I too had fought in a war and knew the power of such things. Aunt Victoria knew a funny little man in Alnwick, who knew another excellent man in Leeds, who received regular shipments from Liverpool of a new-fangled thing, diacetylmorphine, just the stuff, just what he needed. I watched through the door the first time my father took it, and saw him shake and twitch and then grow still, the spit running down the side of his face from his open jaw and pooling just in front of his ear. Then my aunt caught me peeping and screamed that I was a foolish ignorant boy, and hit me with the back of her hand and slammed the door.

The police arrested her little man in Alnwick three days later. They received an anonymous letter written in a brisk, unstately hand. They were only to receive one other letter in the same hand, from the same anonymous source, who warned that Mr Traynor, the bauxite man, liked to touch boys, and that enclosed was the testimony of Boy H confirming the same. Experts, had they been called, might have noted a marked similarity between the adult's hand and the boy's. As it was, the bite marks on the thumb of Mr Traynor when he was taken into questioning were confirmed as a child's and, though no more notes were forthcoming, it was suggested that he move swiftly on.

In my first life my biological father – even if he showed interest in me which I did not perceive – almost never went so far as to express it to me outright. In my second life I was too busy committing suicide to deal with any external affairs, but in my third there was enough deviation in my behaviour to induce a deviation in his. Unlikely as it is in light of my future careers, we found ourselves most united in our attendance at church. The Hulnes were Catholic, and their hereditary shame at the same had in recent years translated into a sort of decisive pride. A chapel had been built and maintained at their cost and for their benefit, which locals attended with very little interest in its denomination but for the advantages of proximity. The parson was a rather too irreverent man by the name of the Reverend Shaeffer, who had forgone his rigid Huguenot upbringing for the more spectacular joys of Catholicism and all its perks. This lent a certain glee to all his duties, as if, freed from the burden of habitually wearing black, he had resolved instead to always wear purple. Neither I nor my father went when we felt it was likely we would have to interact with him, which circumstance forced us instead to interact with each other.

Our relationship was hardly a bloom in spring. Our first few encounters at the chapel were silent, glances of recognition and no more, not even a nod. If my father had cause to wonder what an eight-year-old boy was doing in this house of God, he presumably concluded it was grief, while I wondered if there was not an air of guilt which drove my father to such piety. For my part, I increasingly found my father's attendance at the chapel an annoying distraction, then a curiosity, for I was embarking on that most clichéd journey of the ignorant in an attempt to understand my situation, and attempting to commune in my soul with some form of deity.

My reasoning was the standard line of all of us who kalachakra, those who journey through our own lives. I could find no explanation for my predicament, and having concluded that no one else I had ever encountered was experiencing this journey through their own days again and again, logic demanded that I consider myself either a scientific freak or in some way touched by a power beyond my comprehension. In my third life I had no scientific knowledge, save that shallow stuff acquired from reading glossy magazines printed in the 1970s with predictions of nuclear destruction, and could not imagine how my situation was scientifically possible. Why me? Why would all of nature have conspired to put me in this predicament, and was there not something unique, something special about the journey I was taking which implied a purpose, more than some random collision of sub-atomic events? This premise accepted, I turned towards the most popular supernatural explanation available, and sought answers from God. I read the Bible from cover to cover, but in its talk of resurrection I could find no explanation for my situation, unless I was either a prophet or damned, and thin enough evidence either way to make a decision on that front. I attempted to learn of other religions, but at that time and in that place data on alternative belief systems was hard to collate, especially for a child barely expected to be able to scratch his own name, and so, more out of default convenience than any particular leaning, I found myself turning to the Christian god as having not much else to go on. Thus you could find me in the chapel, still praying for an answer to a nameless question, when,

"I see you come here often."

My father.

I had wondered, could my situation be inherited? But if it were so, would my father not have said as much? Could any man be so shallow, so captured by his pride and the times, as not to speak to his son of a predicament so horrific as this? And then again, if my situation were inherited, why would there be such consistency of behaviour from my father, where surely knowledge would induce change?

"Yes, sir." An instinctive answer, instinctively rendered. I find as a child my default position is polite affirmation of the often unwise and frequently incorrect assumptions of my elders. On the few occasions I've tried rebellion I have either frustratingly been dismissed as opinionated and precocious or, on several occasions, my actions have been an excuse for the lash. What "Yes, sir" gains in neutrality, however, it lacks in social advancement, and so our conversation lagged.

At last, "You pray to God?"

I confess it took a while for the banality of this question to penetrate. Could this man, half of my own genetic material, muster nothing more? And yet to dazzle and confound the situation I replied with another round of, "Yes, sir."

"That's good. You've been raised well."

He sounded satisfied at that, which perhaps in my enthusiasm I interpreted over-liberally as parental pleasure. Having achieved so much with our conversation it seemed as if he would leave, so I went in with, "What do you pray for, sir?"

Coming from an adult, the question would have been blunt and intrusive. From a child, unable to understand the answers that might be given, I suppose it was almost sweet, and I played this part with what I had practised in front of the mirror as my most innocent face. Regrettably, being merely young has never guaranteed me an aura of naïveté.

He considered for a long time, not so much his answer as his confession to a stranger, then smiled and chose the shallower option. "The same as all men. Fair weather, good food and the embrace of my family."

I suspect my incredulity at these sentiments was visible on my face, for his own twitched in an uncomfortable recognition of failure and, to compensate for the same, he proceeded to ruffle my hair, awkwardly, briskly, a gesture curtailed as quickly as it had begun.

It was my first meaningful conversation with my biological father, and it was hardly an omen of good things to come.

# Chapter 22

The Cronus Club is power.

Make no mistake, for that is what it is.

Laziness, apathy and a lack of interest: these are what restrain the exercise of its resources. Fear too, perhaps. Fear of what has been and what will come. It is not entirely true to say that we who are kalachakra can live our life free of consequence.

I killed myself in in my fourth life to escape Phearson and his tape machine, and in my fifth I did indeed seek the counselling that Virginia had suggested. I do not regain consciousness all at once; there is no one flash of memory being restored, but rather it is a gradual recollection that begins at my third birthday and is complete by my fourth. Harriet said I cried a lot in the early years of my fifth life. She said she had never seen such a sad infant. I realise now that, in a way, the process of recalling my previous death was almost a natural working-through of it, a reliving step by step, as my mind integrated it into who I was.

I sought counselling, as I said. Virginia was correct that the medical services would hardly do, and our chaplain, as established, was of very little use. By the time I remembered what I was, and where I had come from, I could see the beginning of Harriet's decline, and read the gaunt recognition in Patrick's face as his wife began to wither before his eyes. Cancer is a process on which the healthy cannot impose. I was a child and could not express myself to these two people who, in my own, slow way, I had come to love. I needed the help of a stranger, needed the means to express myself to someone else.

I wrote to my father.

He may seem an unlikely choice, an unusual confidant. Needless to say I could not tell him all – there would be no reference to my true nature, no telling of the future past or mention of my age. Rather, I penned my letters in a stiff adult's hand, signing myself Private Harry Brookes, late of my father's division. I wrote it as an apology, as a confession, told him that he would not remember me but that I remembered him, hoping for his understanding, his attentive ear. I told him of being captured by the enemy in the First World War, making up the details of my arrest from the books I had read and tales I had heard. I told him of being interrogated, and here I wrote it out in full: the beatings and the pain, the humiliations and the loss, the delirium and the drugs and the moment I tried to make it end. Over several months and many letters, I told him everything, adapting only the names and times to suit my confessional, and transforming my successful suicide attempt into merely suicide attempted.

"Forgive me," I wrote at the bottom. "I did not think I would break."

He didn't reply for a very long time. I had given him an entirely fictional address to send his response to, knowing full well that I would be the boy sent with the mail to the post office. Private Harry Brookes poured his heart out to a distant stranger who made no reply, but I knew that what I needed was not so much the comfort of return, but to speak of what I had been. The telling was all, the reply merely a courtesy.

Yet I longed for it with a childish passion that I could not fully attribute to my hormones and physical biology. I began to grow angry in my father's presence, knowing that he had received the letters of Private Brookes and read them, and marvelling that he did not weep and could maintain such a carapace of stone in the face of my genuine anguish. My fury must have been visible briefly on my face, for my grandmother spoke to Harriet and exclaimed,

"That boy of yours is a vile little wretch! He gives us such terrible looks!"

Harriet chided me, but she, more than any other, I think, could sense the thing beneath the surface which I was trying to express and dared not say out loud. Even Patrick, not averse to the willow wand, seemed to beat me less in that life for my transgressions, and my cousin Clement, usually the bully of the household, hid from me in the house.

Then at last my father replied.

I stole the letter off its silver plate by the door before any in the household could see and ran to the woods to read it. His handwriting, infuriatingly, was a lot like mine. How insufferable, I concluded, to have inherited so many genetic traits from this overindulged man. Then I read, and my anger diminished.

*Dear Private H. Brookes,*

*I have received and read your letters with interest, and cordially thank you for your courage and fortitude in both enduring what you have endured, and expressing the truth of it to your superiors. Please know that I bear you no ill will for anything you may have expressed to the enemy, for no one could have suffered what you suffered and been less the man. I commend you, sir, and I salute you.*

*We have seen things that men cannot name. We have learned, you and I, to speak a language of bloodshed and violence; words do not reach deep enough, music is no more than hollow sound, the smiles of strangers grow false. We must speak, and dare not, cannot, unless it is in mud and the screams of men. We have no kin but each other, for our loves to our mothers and our wives demand that we protect them from what we know. Ours is the fellowship of strangers who know a secret that we cannot express.*

*We are both of us broken, shattered, hollow and alone. Only for
the ones we love do we remain, painted dolls in the playhouse of
this life. In them we must find our meaning. In them we must
hold to hope. I trust you find the one who gives you this
meaning, and remain always,*
    *Your sincere friend,*

    *Major R. E. Hulne*

I burned the letter after reading it, and scattered its ashes
beneath the trees. Private Harry Brookes did not write to my
father again.

# Chapter 23

There is an art to navigating London during the Blitz. Certain guides are obvious: Bethnal Green and Balham Undergrounds are no-goes, as is most of Wapping, Silvertown and the Isle of Dogs. The further west you go, the more you can move around late at night in reasonable confidence of not being hit, but should you pass an area which you feel sure was a council estate when you last checked in the 1970s, that is usually a sign that you should steer clear.

There are also three practical ways in which the Blitz impacts on the general functioning of life in the city. The first is mundane: streets blocked, services suspended, hospitals overwhelmed, fire-fighters exhausted, policemen belligerent and bread difficult to find. Queuing becomes a tedious essential, and if you are a young man not in uniform, sooner or later you will find yourself in the line for your weekly portion of meat, to be eaten very slowly one mouthful at a time, while non-judgemental ladies quietly judge you. Secondly there is the slow erosion – a rather more subtle but perhaps more potent assault on the spirit. It begins perhaps subtly, the half-seen glance down a shattered street where the survivors of a night which killed their kin sit dull and numb on the crooked remnants of their bed. Perhaps it need not even be a human stimulus: perhaps the sight of a child's nightdress hanging off a chimney pot, after it was thrown up only to float straight back down from the blast, is enough to stir something in your soul that has no name. Perhaps the mother who cannot find her daughter, or the evacuees' faces pressed up against the window of a passing train. It is a death of the soul by a thousand cuts, and the falling skies are merely the laughter of the executioner going about his business.

And then, inevitably, there is the moment of shock. It is the day your neighbour died because he went to fix a bicycle in the wrong place, at the wrong time. It is the desk which is no longer filled, or the fire that ate your place of work entirely so now you stand on the street and wonder, what shall I do? There are a lot of lies told about the Blitz spirit: legends are made of singing in the tunnels, of those who kept going for friends, family and Britain. It is far simpler than that. People kept going because that was all that they could really do. Which is no less an achievement, in its way.

It seemed perverse for 1st July 1940 to be such a pleasant day. Without the wind, it would have been too warm; without the sun, the wind would have been too cold, but today these elements seemed to have combined into perfect harmony. The sky was baby-blue, the moon was going to be full that night, and so the men and women passing briskly through the square had a rather downcast look, cursing the heavens under their breath and praying for fog and rain. I sat on the north side of the square above the steps down to the fat, shallow fountains and waited. I had come early – nearly an hour before the specified 2 p.m. – to scout the area for whatever signs of danger I hoped I would be able to recognise. I was a deserter. My call-up had come in 1939 and, aware of my appointment with Virginia, I had fled, to the shame of Patrick and quite possibly my father. Like many of our kin, I had taken care in my fourth life to note one or two useful events, including the clichéd but essential winners of races and sporting events. I didn't make indiscriminate money off this knowledge, gleaned from a sports almanac in 1957, but used it as a basis to achieve that level of outward comfort and stability that was so important if you were to be considered for a comfortable and stable job. I chose an accent that was almost as parodied as Phearson's received pronunciation, letting a little of my natural voice drop into it whenever I wished to impress potential employers with how hard I'd worked at my social status. Indeed, that thing I loosely described as my "natural voice" had become so distorted by travels, time and languages learned that I often found myself verging on a parody of my colleagues, unconsciously acquiring their syntax and tone. To Patrick I talked as a northerner, to my grocer as a cockney and to my colleagues as a man dreaming of working for the BBC.

Virginia, it transpired, made no such allowances.

"Hello, dear boy!" she exclaimed, and at once I recognised her, though it had been twenty-two years since she had slipped me a penknife in a house in the north. She was younger, a woman in her forties, but still dressed for a soirée where the jazz was cool and the men were willing, no concession made in any aspect of her being for the nannying concerns of the present.

I stood at once, an awkward formal gesture, which she immediately dispelled by grabbing me by the shoulders and giving me a kiss on either cheek in recognition of a fashion yet to come. "Harry!" she exclaimed. "My goodness but you are young at the moment, aren't you?"

I was twenty-two, dressed to convince the world that I was a rather youthful twenty-nine and worthy of consideration in all things. The effect was more of a child playing in his father's clothes, but then I have never truly mastered my own body. She had her arm hooked into mine and was leading me towards Buckingham Palace – not yet damaged by the Dornier bomber that would eventually hit Victoria station, but that event was only a few months away. "How was the last one?" she asked brightly, sweeping me off down the Mall like a country cousin come to town for a family holiday. "The femoral artery is such a gusher once it gets going, and far fewer little nerve endings round there. I did try to bring you something chemical but it was all done in such a hurry – terrible fuss!"

"Was death the only option?" I asked weakly.

"Darling!" she exclaimed. "You would only have been hunted down and interrogated more, and frankly we couldn't be handling that. Besides –" a surreptitious nudge that nearly knocked me off my feet "– how would we have known you were really one of us, if you didn't make this meeting?"

I took a slow, steadying breath. This meeting – this already rather strange meeting – had cost me my life and twenty-two years of expectation. "May I ask, are you going to walk away rapidly in the next fifteen minutes? I only enquire because I have several hundred years of questions, and need to know whether I should start prioritising."

She gave me a playful slap on the arm. "Dear boy," she replied, "you have many centuries left in which to ask whatever you like."

# Chapter 24

The Cronus Club.

You and I, we have fought such battles over this.

No one knows who founded it.

Or rather, that is to say, no one knows who has the first idea.

It is usually founded in Babylon around about 3000 BCE. We know this because the founders tend to raise an obelisk in the desert, in a valley with no particular name, on which they write their names and often a message for the future generation. This message is sometimes sincere advice –

BEWARE LONELINESS
SEEK SOLACE
HAVE FAITH

– and material of that sort. Occasionally, if the founders are feeling rather less reverent towards their future readership, they leave a dirty joke. The obelisk itself has become something of an object of fun. One generation of the Cronus Club will often have it moved and hidden in a new place, challenging future descendants to find it. The obelisk remains hidden in this manner for hundreds of years until at last enterprising archaeologists stumble upon it and on its ancient carved stone they too leave their messages, ranging from

IN TIME ALL THINGS ARE REVEALED

through to the rather more mundane

HARRY WOZ 'ERE.

The obelisk itself is never quite the same from one generation to another: it was destroyed in the 1800s by zealous Victorians for being just a little too overtly phallic in its design, another sank to the bottom of the sea while being transported to America. Whatever its purpose, it remains a declaration from the past to all future members of the Cronus Club, that they, the kalachakra of 3000 BCE, were here first and are here to stay.

The rumour goes, however, that the first ever founder of the Cronus Club was not from the deep past at all, but was instead a lady by the name of Sarah Sioban Grey, born some time in the 1740s. A kalachakra, she was one of the first pioneers to actively seek others of her kin, accumulating over many hundreds of years and dozens of deaths a picture of who else within her home town of Boston might be of a similar nature. Kalachakra generally occur at a rate of one in every half million of the population, so her success at finding even a few dozen cannot be underestimated.

And of these few dozen, it quickly occurred to Sarah Sioban Grey that they represented not merely a fellowship in the now, but also a fellowship of the yet to come and what had been. She looked at her colleagues and perceived that where the oldest was nearly ninety years old, this would make him a child at the turn of the century, which she was too young to experience; and where the youngest was merely ten, this made him a grandfather by the time of the American Civil War, and thus a visitor to a future she could never know. To the old man from the past she said, "Here is my knowledge of future events – now go forth and make gold," and indeed, when she was born again in the 1740s, the old man was already knocking at her door saying, "Hello, young Sarah Sioban Grey. I took your advice and made gold, and now you, little girl, need never work again." She then returned the favour to the child who would live to see the Civil War, saying, "Here is gold which I will invest. By the time you are grown up and old, it will be a fortune and you need never work again. All I ask in return for this investment is that you pass the favour on to any others of our kin you may meet in the future, that they too are safe and comfortable in this difficult world." And so the Cronus Club spread, each generation investing for the future. And as it spread forwards in time, so it also spread backwards, the children of now speaking to the grandfathers of yesterday and saying, "The Cronus Club is a fellowship of men – go find for yourself the grandfathers of your youth and as a child say to them, 'This thing is good.'" So each generation set out to find more of its kind, and within just a few cycles of birth and death, the Club had spread not only through space, but also time, propagating itself forwards into the twentieth century and back into the Middle Ages, the death of each member spreading the word of what it was to the very extremes of the times in which they lived.

Of course, it is more than possible that the story of Sarah Sioban Grey is a myth, since it was so long ago that none of the Boston Club members can even remember, and she long since disappeared. It was, however, the story that Virginia told me as she sat me down in a blue armchair beneath the portrait of a long-dead member in what was known as the red room of the London branch of the Cronus Club, and if nothing else, she clearly enjoyed the telling.

As the Cronus Clubs are hardly fixed in time, so they are rarely fixed in space. The London branch was no exception.

"We've been in St James's for a few hundred years," explained Virginia, pouring another glass of finest black-market brandy. "Sometimes we end up in Westminster though, occasionally Soho.

It's the 1820s steering committee! They get so bored being in the same place, they move buildings, and we're just left staggering around trying to work out where the Club has gone."

Where the Club was now was a few streets north of St James's Park, south of Piccadilly, tucked in between bespoke tailors and mansions for the declining rich, a single brass plaque on its door declaring, TIME FLIES. NO TRADESMEN PLEASE.

"It's a joke," she explained when I asked. "That's the 1780s bunch. Everyone's always leaving each other little notes for posterity. I buried a time capsule in 1925 once with a vital message for the Club five hundred years from now."

"What's in the capsule?" I asked.

"A recipe for proper lemon sherbet." She saw my face and spread her arms expansively. "No one said it was easy being on the end of linear temporal events!"

I drank brandy and looked around the room again. Like so many giant properties in the wealthy parts of London, it was a throwback to a time when colours were rich, tastes were prim and mantelpieces had to be made of marble. Portraits of men and women dressed smartly in the garments of their time – "Apparently they'll be worth something one day. Damned if I know why and I've snogged Picasso!" – lined the walls like memorials to the departed in a crematorium. The furniture was plush and rather dusty, the giraffe-built windows were criss-crossed with tape, "To appease the locals, darling. Nothing's going to get hit round here but the wardens kick up such a fuss."

The halls were silent. Crystal chandeliers tinkled gently when planes went overhead, the lights burned low in a few rooms behind the blackout blinds, and no one was to be seen.

"Countryside," explained Virginia brightly. "Most of them pack out by July '39. It's not so much the bombing, you see, as the ghastly sense of oppression. Our members have been through it so many times before that really they can't be buggered, so they ship off to somewhere nicer, brighter, with good ventilation and none of this tedious war business to bother them. A lot go to Canada, especially from the rather more oppressive clubs – Warsaw, Berlin,

Hanover, St Petersburg, all that crowd. One or two stick around for the excitement but I can't be bothered."

Then why was she here?

"Keeping the ship afloat, dear boy! It's my turn, you see, to keep an eye out for our freshest members. That's you, by the way – you are our first new member in six hundred years. But there's also several members being born about now – their mothers take such a sentimental view of their boys departing to conflict that, what can I say, discretions are brought into question. One has to stick around to make sure their childhoods aren't too rough. A lot of the time money solves things, but sometimes –" she took a careful sip from the glass "– one has to arrange things. Evacuation and that sort of business. Parents can be such a bore."

"Is that what you do?" I asked. "You . . . cater for the childhood period?"

"It's one of our primary roles," she replied airily. "Childhood is the most taxing time of our lives, unless of course you're genetic-ally predisposed towards a ghastly death or some sort of inherited disease. We have all the knowledge and experience of a dozen lives, and yet if we tell some boring linear adult that they really should invest in rubber as it's going to be the most marvellous thing, we just get a pat on the head and a cry of 'There there, Harry, go back to your choo choo set' or whatnot. A lot of our members are also born rather poor, so it helps to know that there is a society of mutually understanding individuals who can see that you get a decent pair of socks to wear and ensure that you don't have to waste several tedious years of your life, every life, learning your ABC. It's not just the money," she concluded with a flare of satisfaction, "it's the companionship."

I had a hundred questions, a thousand, all reeling round inside my head, but I couldn't pin any of them down so fell back weakly on, "Are there any rules I should know about?"

"Don't bugger about with temporal events!" she replied firmly. "You did cause us a bit of embarrassment in your last life, Harry – not your fault of course, not at all; we've all been in difficult situ-ations – but Phearson had enough information to change the

100

course of the future, and we really can't have that. It's not that we aren't concerned, it's that these things can never be fully predicted."

"Anything else?"

"Don't harm another kalachakra. We really couldn't care what you do to everyone else as long as it's not particularly obscene and doesn't bring attention to us, but we remember, and it's just not on. Be good!"

"You mentioned contributions . . ."

"Yes, if you do get a chance to make a massive, obscene amount of money, please do put some aside for our childhood benevolent fund. The future generations are so appreciative."

Was that it?

No, not quite.

"Not so much a rule, Harry darling," she explained, "as good advice. Don't tell anyone where or when you're from. Not in so much detail."

"Why?"

"Because they might kill you with it," she replied brightly. "Of course I'm sure they won't – you seem like a charming young man – but there's been a few, and so you see it's not considered good form. Don't ask, don't tell – that's the policy round here."

And she explained.

# Chapter 25

The first cataclysm began in 1642, in Paris.

The man who brought about the cataclysm was an unassuming gentleman by the name of Victor Hoeness. An ouroboran, he went through the usual traumatic first phases of life before the local Cronus Club found him, calmed him down and explained that actually he was neither possessed nor damned, as far as anyone could tell. The son of a gunsmith, he saw the very worst of the Thirty Years War, a conflict which embraced all the usual early-modern socio-economic causes of war, and then turned it into a crusade. In the name of one, men are permitted to kill; in the name of the other, they are commanded to destroy. Needless to say, most Cronus Club members during the conflict like to move to less fraught areas of the world, such as into the rather more stable heartland of the Ottoman empire, where, while the sultans may be mad during this time, at least their mothers are not. Victor Hoeness, however, refused, insisting that he remain in the Holy Roman Empire. He was counselled against interfering and swore that he was merely acting as a passive observer, documenting all that he saw. Indeed, for several lifetimes the notes of Victor Hoeness provided an excellent historical source, with several kalachakra themselves failing to realise that it was the careful documentation of one of their own kind that had produced such sterling primary evidence. Other members of the Cronus Club were concerned: it wasn't that Hoeness was unstable; rather, if anything, he was too calm, too collected. He moved through suffering, destruction and dismay, documenting all he saw, like a mist through the forest. He sought no companionship, took no sides, made no acquaintances, removed himself from personal danger where permissible, and even the few deaths he suffered during the war – for no one could fully predict the wild bitterness of those times – he took with a calm grace and resignation, proclaiming afterwards that he wished he had bribed the executioner to put gunpowder into the flames that burned him, or remarking that being impaled on a spear was a far quicker demise if they could just slice open the liver entirely, instead of merely puncturing the gut. His colleagues found themselves in a rather difficult position, for how can you express to a man that his apparent stability and self-control are, quite possibly, irrational, inhuman and the symptom of some deeper ill, when all your evidence for the disease is that it is not there? Over time, Hoeness's remarkable utility as a primary historical source led him into correspondence with future Cronus Club members. Questions would be posed from the early 1800s or twentieth century, relayed back down through time from the child of the 1850s to the grandfather who would be a child again by 1780, who could then pass it back to the grandparent of the 1710s and so on and so forth until, with as few generations as possible to corrupt the message, one of his own time could put the question to Hoeness directly. He would then inscribe his reply on some well-lasting material and leave it with the Cronus Club to deliver to its future correspondent, and posterity. Many of us who have dabbled in academia have used this technique. Often it is abused for academic advantage as, if we lack a source for a particular time, with some polite enquiry and a little persuasion amplified down the generations, not only may an answer be found, but it can be acquired through genuine documents of the time itself which can withstand the scrutiny of our less imaginative peers. Assuming, of course, you're still interested several lives later, when the message may finally arrive.

For Hoeness, however, his price for delivering such excellent documentary evidence was to begin to ask questions himself. Notes were sent forward through time or, if it was felt that paper might not survive the journey, stones inscribed with his message and left at pre-agreed stations where war, urban expansion and agricultural revolution were judged likely to leave it untouched. So he began to enquire about the future, and again the Chinese whispers sent back their vague replies. He learned of the siege of Vienna, the decline of the Ottoman empire, the War of the Spanish Succession, revolution in France, revolution in America, and even distant whisperings of events further on – pogroms become massacres and a world where freedom was wealth and God was a name used to frighten children.

He accepted these musings with the same cool nothing with which he could see children butchered before their mothers' eyes and lines of men stand not forty yards apart blasting at each other with lead while their commanders cheered them on. People considered it strange – remarkable even – but by now all attempts to understand the mind of Victor Hoeness had deteriorated into the tired apathy that is the curse of so many of our kin.

Then, one day, he went to Paris. He took with him very little but his words, and with the simple power of these inveigled himself into the court of the French king.

"I am Victor Hoeness," he is meant to have said, "and I come to you to tell you about the future."

Which then he proceeded to do.

When people asked him why – why are you telling *us* specifically? – he replied, "Your nation is still the most powerful in Europe despite your civil conflicts. The Holy Roman empire is weak, the Spanish king is a weakling, the Pope is powerless in the face of military might, and I need a strong king. I will give you knowledge of ideas yet to come, of philosophies not yet named. I will give you weapons, strategies, medicines; I will give you knowledge of your enemy and the lands beyond these, for I have journeyed to the Pacific and seen the sun rise across the Indian Ocean. I have dined with Mughals and mandarins, heard the running waters of the Congo, smelled the spices in the bazaar and eaten shark meat pulled from beneath the ice. Let us, you and I, make a new world. Let us make a better world."

And after some understandable scepticism, the French king listened to Victor and the world began to change. Victor had no delusions as to the nature of his project – there would be blood and, he knew, it would be more than probable that this revolution, global in its scale, would consume the men who made it. Charles II died before he could ever reclaim the English crown, while the Thirty Years War was brought to a sudden and abrupt end by the intervention of a combined French Catholic–Huguenot army, fighting with rifled guns and the tactics of Napoleon. Victor knew he could only do so much. His life expectancy even with careful living was unlikely to exceed sixty, and he could not waste more effort and time travelling to Istanbul, Varanasi or Beijing or taking a journey across the sea to the colonies of the New World. His policy was to focus intense effort within a compact area and to attempt to change the world from Europe. He knew that he could not see the end of his revolution, which he had precisely calculated would require at least a hundred and twenty years to achieve some form of stability, so he sought two means to secure his legacy in this wildly altered world. One of these methods was to seek the assistance of Cronus Club members, who, seeing what he was undertaking, divided almost exactly in half to support or reject him. Those who were willing to assist he named his vanguard of the future. Those who refused he had incarcerated in the deepest dungeons he could find. Not killed, he insisted, but incarcerated so that they would live as long as possible in his new world and perhaps, before they died, observe his success.

By the time he finally did die, the map of Europe was entirely changed. France ruled from Lisbon to Krakow, Calais to Budapest. The Ottoman empire sued for peace and gave up its North African colonies in an attempt to win the respect of the French king; the English parliament, with nowhere else to turn, offered its crown to Louis XIV, leading swiftly to rebellion, and bloody suppression by the new monarch. But the most devastating change to the history of the world was its technology. Ideas breed ideas, and Victor, largely unwittingly, had with his minor knowledge of future advancements started a process which would change the face of the planet. In 1693 the first steam train made a test journey from Paris to Versailles; in 1701 an ironclad warship destroyed the Barbary pirates in only two and a half hours of bombardment off Algiers. Armies collapsed and nations sued for peace in the face of this technological onslaught, but the populations themselves, whether for faith, or land, or pride, or mother tongue, resisted until resistance became their identity, and took the weapons of their oppressors and, as men will, made them better. And as war does, technology advanced – bigger, faster, harder – so when Edo was bombed in 1768 its anti-air guns were able to down a third of its attackers, and when at last in 1802 the word went out to the bunkers over the underground radio it was "Fight to the last man and gun!"

Victor Hoeness did not live to see the end of his dream, which came on 18 November 1937 when a group called the Prophets of a New Dawn broke into a missile silo in southern Australia and launched three of its missiles, triggering global retaliation and the nuclear winter which blotted out the sun. By 1953 all life was dead on the surface of the planet, and the entire process began again.

# Chapter 26

Victor Hoeness, when told of these events by his kin, did not believe.

When they insisted that this was the word being whispered down the Cronus Club, he merely demanded better notes so that he could attempt to fix the problems at inception.

But there was, for the Cronus Club, a far bigger problem to fix. Victor Hoeness had, to their mind, committed mass murder. Not exactly of the human race – that was merely one temporal outcome, one life in which all had withered and all had died and that was that. His sin was far greater for, by his deeds, whole generations of kalachakra had simply not been born.

"Not so much a rule, Harry darling," Virginia had explained, "as good advice. Don't tell anyone where or when you're from."

I watched her, that night in London, rolling the brandy glass between her fingers, her gaze fixed on nothing much as the sun faded and the city turned black. "Death," she explained, "can be achieved in one of two ways. I don't mean the rather tedious death that our bodies force us to endure every life; not at all. I mean a death that remains, a death that matters. The first death is the Forgetting. The Forgetting can be chemical, or surgical, or electrical, and is used to achieve a complete wipe of the mind. Not name, nor place of birth, nor the first boy you ever kissed will remain after the Forgetting, and for us what is this if not a true death? A clean slate, a chance to be pure and innocent again. Naturally we kill everyone who's been through a Forgetting as soon as we can perceive that their minds are gone, so that they don't start their next childhood with even the slightest hint of what they are. And when they die and begin again, we can be immediately there in their second life to help and assist them, teach them to grow accustomed to what they are without any of that tedious madness-suicide-rejection business. A lot of us have done at least one Forgetting, although, given the difficulty of the task, it doesn't always take. They tell me —" brandy ran up the side of the glass, then slowly seeped back down "— that I have Forgotten before. Though everyone seems embarrassed to say so."

A moment, a second when the ripples went out of the drink in her hand, perfect stillness as Virginia tried to remember a thing she had chosen to forget.

"There is no loss, if you cannot remember what you have lost," she explained at last. "Personally, I feel a great sense of relief. You wipe away the scars of your former life as well as the memories. You wipe away the guilt. I do not say that I have lived a guilty life, of course; merely that the silence of my peers when I ask about the subject does not bode well for the things I cannot remember."

A *tick tick tick* of the grandfather clock in the hall. Soon sirens would sound, and stop, and the city would listen for the low drone of the bombers, the deep clearing of death's throat as he prepared to sing.

"The second death," she went on, "is the death of not being born. It is really rather controversial among us, for it throws into doubt all the scientific theories currently extant about our very natures. It has been observed that if a kalachakra is aborted before consciousness in one life, then in the next the child will not be born at all. It is the true death, the destruction of both mind and body, and, unlike the Forgetting, there is no coming back from it, no healing of mental pathways. It is simply the end. So you see, dearest Harry, there is nothing so prized by our kind as this – who you truly are, who your parents were, and your place and time of birth. This information can destroy you utterly. And one day you might want to be destroyed, of course. Or to forget. The mind struggles to re-create the joy of a first kiss, but somehow manages to recall the terror of pain, the flush of humiliation and the burden of guilt with a startling clarity."

Franklin Phearson.

I'm a good guy, Harry. I'm a fucking good guy.

My skin was white above the bone where it gripped the brandy glass.

Looking back, I ask myself who precisely knows the circumstances of my birth. Even in terms of those who live purely linear lives, the numbers are very few: my father, my adopted parents, my aunts, my grandmother Constance and perhaps some relatives on my mother's side who suspected but could not precisely name my origins. These were unavoidable weaknesses, established before I was born, but my bastardy afforded me great protection. No official records exist of my birth or origin until I am at least seven or eight, when an overzealous school monitor notes a gap in her records, and by then I am in a position to expunge the record as soon as it is made. The shame of being illegitimate in the 1920s, especially to a family whose values lingered from an earlier age, kept discussion of my parentage limited to a tight circle and, once the key players were dead, there was no reason for my origins to be advertised at all unless I chose to. In childhood I am blessed by being rather stunted until I am a teen, and then experiencing a rapid growth spurt rather late – it confuses any guesses as to the precise date of my birth. In adulthood my father's overbred features seem to grow confused as they mingle with my mother's genes, so I can appear to be convincingly twenty-two or thirty-nine at any given moment, as long as I choose my clothes carefully. My hair turns white almost overnight, but stress can alter my physiology, so again the exact date of my birth is hard to guess in later years; and extensive travel has so corrupted my accent that now I find I have almost none of my own, but rather adapt at once to whatever the local requirements appear to be with an ease that borders on the sycophantic. In short, the disadvantages of my normal life, if we are to call it that, are blessings for my secret being, and even as Virginia recounted the final days of Victor Hoeness, I sat back in my chair and considered all this with a growing sense of security.

"Now Victor," she explained, "really rather buggered things up for the future generations. Whole generations of kalachakra simply were not born, and being not born kalachakra once, they were not born again. The world continued as it always had been, Victor's experiment having been terminally ended by death, but the cries for vengeance came whispering down from those few lucky ones who had survived the future apocalypse, telling of whole Clubs wiped out, thousands of years of history and culture which must now be rebuilt from the ground upwards. Not to mention, of course, the rather premature destruction of the world for everyone else on it, but they really didn't count in the scheme of things."

I didn't question this world view, nor why should I? Victor Hoeness had unleashed four hundred years of war and suffering on the world and then he'd died, and none of it had mattered, for when he was born again, things were as they had always been. I was in the Cronus Club now, the past and the future a few whispers away, the secrets of my very existence, I felt, within my grasp. These words were merely stories.

"Those were cruder times," Virginia explained. "There wasn't any room for niceties."

And it was in this spirit that Victor Hoeness was tracked down in the city of Linz, aged eleven years old, where he was already preparing for another stab at changing the nature of the universe. He was taken from his home and tortured for eleven days. On the twelfth he broke and confessed to his true place of birth, parents, home, point of origin. He was kept captive while painstaking research was made into the veracity of his story and, when it was found to be true, the Cronus Club assembled to decide what to do with him.

"Cruder times, cruder times!" exclaimed Virginia.

What they decided was that merely killing Victor outright was not enough. Death, as has been established, holds little fear – it is but the flesh. The mind is the source of what we are, and it was the mind that they were determined to destroy.

They imprisoned him, not merely away from society but in complete physical immobility, in a crude medieval straitjacket entirely made of metal. They cut out his tongue, cut off his ears, pulled out his eyes, and when he had recovered from all of those, they cut off his hands and his feet as well, just to guarantee that he wasn't going anywhere. Then they force-fed him down a hollow wooden rod rammed into his throat, keeping him alive in his own silent, wordless, blind madness. They managed to do this for nine years before finally he choked to death, and died, they said, smiling. He was twenty years old.

But the vengeance of the Cronus Club extended beyond death.

Born again where he had begun, the baby Victor Hoeness was at birth snatched from his crib and taken again to a place of imprisonment. By the age of four he'd reached consciousness and, examining him, the members of the Cronus Club concluded there was still enough of his mind left alive that he could be judged responsible for his acts. So it began again: eyes, ears, tongue, hands, feet, all with careful medical precision to ensure that he didn't die in the process, but all, of course, without painkillers. This time they managed to keep him alive for seven years; he died aged eleven.

"It's surprisingly difficult to hold a grudge over a few hundred years," explained Virginia. "Hoeness may have died when he was eleven, but his captors went on living for maybe thirty, forty, fifty years afterwards? After a while the note – 'Must torture Victor Hoeness' – becomes so low down on your to-do list, especially with death in the way between you and doing it – that frankly when the duty comes around again it seems like something of a bore."

Nevertheless they persisted, and once again examined Hoeness for signs of his old self. This time, however, the baby Hoeness,

111

though born with perfectly functional hands and ears and eyes, seemed incapable of using any of them, though the apparatuses were entirely there. Even as a baby, before achieving full consciousness, he was declared a broken child and his own parents considered giving him away to the care of the church or, so it was whispered, to the rather rougher care of the unloving street. Times were hard – crude, as Virginia would say.

The Cronus Club once again met to make a decision, and all but one voted to end Hoeness's life for good, terminate his mother's pregnancy before he was born and end the cycle of vengeance. The only one who rejected the vote was an ouroboran by the name of Koch, and he . . .

"We call them mnemonics," explained Virginia. "To put it simply, they remember everything."

I think she must have seen my eyes light up, my face turn towards her at these words. If she understood my reaction, she was kind enough not to say so. "The general case with us is that, after a few hundred years or so, we begin to forget. It's perfectly understandable really; the brain is only so vast and it is the natural process of ageing to lose some of what we had. I personally start suffering from dementia around the age of sixty-seven, and I must tell you, being an infant overcoming those recalled symptoms is a thoroughly demoralising process. Mental illness is a deadly threat with our kind. Please do seek help should you be in that predicament, Harry."

"I wrote letters to my father," I confessed, the words barely audible to my ears.

"Marvellous, marvellous stuff! Positive attitude. Naturally one of the great advantages of having a fallible memory is that one is still capable of being surprised. Another is that one is capable of overcoming the past. You will find that while facts and figures may remain with you, especially if you attempt to recall them, furious emotions that burned inside begin to diminish. Some won't. If you are a prideful person then slights will always linger with you, and frankly there's nothing you can do about that save forget. If you are especially soppy then you may always regret a lost love, even several

112

lives down the line. However, in my experience, time smooths all. One obtains a kind of neutrality after a while, a battering away at the edges as one begins to perceive through endless repetition that this slight was no such thing, or that love was merely a fancy. We have the privilege of seeing the present through the wisdom of the past, and frankly such an honour makes it very hard to take anything too seriously at all."

Koch was an anomaly of our kind, a kalachakra who recalled all, including things most had forgotten.

"Mnemonics," said Virginia, "are usually rather strange."

My heart, tight in my chest.

I had come this far to find my people, and here it was already, spoken in innocence. Mnemonics are rather strange. To a certain class of society, in a certain corner of England, there is no greater failing.

"Koch spoke up, when the Clubs were deciding what to do with Victor Hoeness," she explained. "'This is not the first cataclysm,' he said, 'but the second. You do not remember it, for it was many hundreds of lives ago, and thousands of years. Perhaps if you do remember it, it is merely as a vague darkness in your minds, a distant memory. But I know of it, for I lived through it. A thousand years before now, another of our kin did exactly as Hoeness has done, and it ripped the future apart like a cutlass through soup. How long will we live before we reach one of the two only conclusions left to us? That if anything is to ever change, we must make sacrifices and challenge this rigid system within which we live. Or if nothing is to change at all, then we must watch our own kind constantly, and punish ruthlessly, and live without remorse. You have already decided on Hoeness's fate, but let my words live as a warning to you all.'

"And perhaps the other kalachakra were a little afraid when they heard all this. Or perhaps, as I personally feel is more likely, they regarded it as rather self-important grandstanding from a less than civilised member of their clique. Either way, the decision had been made and the blind, dumb, deaf, crippled child who was Hoeness had a sword driven though his tiny heart in the night.

His executioner then proceeded to live until he died, and at his death was reborn again, some fifteen years before Hoeness's birth. At the age of fourteen years old, this executioner journeyed to Linz, where Hoeness was to be born. He found himself a place as a domestic servant in the house of the Hoeness family itself, and observed both mother and father, noting in full detail the days up to the nine months before Hoeness was to be born. As soon as the mother began to show signs of pregnancy, the executioner carefully fed her yew bark tea. Regrettably the taste was so repugnant that Hoeness's mother barely swallowed a few gulps before spitting the rest out, and so, falling back on something of an ugly back-up plan, Victor Hoeness's executioner drew his blade, pinned his mother to the floor and cut her throat. He remained long enough to ensure that his victim was dead, then cleaned himself up, laid her out for burial, left a few coins for the father, and went on his way.

"And so it was that Victor Hoeness came never to be born."

# Chapter 27

I am mnemonic.

I remember everything.

You need to understand this if you are to understand the choices I was to make.

For a while I doubted, wondered if what I possessed was not perfect recall but a perfect fantasy, the ability to cast my mind to any time, any place, and fill in gaps that suited some picture of myself.

But too much evidence corresponds to what I believe and I now realise that, down that path, there lies only inaction and madness.

Hundreds of years, thousands of lifetimes before I was born, a man called Koch advised that we, the Cronus Club, either seek to change the world, or become brutal arbitrators of our own kind. I ask myself what sights he had seen to make him so sure of his path, and whether he has any forgiveness left for others, or himself.

All of which brings us back to where we began.

I, dying my usual death, slipping away in a warm morphine

haze, which she interrupted with all the charm of a rattlesnake in a feather bed.

She was seven, I was seventy-eight. She perched on the side of my bed, her feet dangling off it, examined the heart monitor plugged into my chest, observed where I'd disconnected the alarm, felt for my pulse, and said, "I nearly missed you, Dr August."

Christa, with her *Berliner Hochdeutsch*, sat on the side of my bed, telling me about the destruction of the planet.

"The world is ending. The message has come down from child to adult, child to adult, passed back down the generations from a thousand years forward in time. The world is ending and we cannot prevent it. So now it's up to you."

# Chapter 28

"Consider," Vincent, my sometime student in Cambridge, would exclaim. "The very notion of time travel is, in itself, paradoxical. I build a time machine – impossible – I travel back in time – impossible – and step out on to the earth in say 1500. I speak to no one, I do nothing, I spend no more than ten seconds in the past before leaving again – impossible – and what have I achieved?"

"Very little at great expense?" I suggested, pouring myself another glass of whisky.

If I had, in my sixth life, any concerns that it was unfitting for a should-be professor to spend most of his time arguing with an undergraduate student rather than sitting in silence at high table with his peers, those concerns had vanished with my further acquaintance with Vincent. His complete lack of interest in my supposed status had cultivated a complete apathy towards it on my part too, and of all my colleagues he seemed the only one with the remotest interest in the unfashionably modern ideas with which I tormented 1940s academia.

"Our impossible time traveller has, in the ten seconds he spent in the past, inhaled eight litres of air, one part oxygen to four parts nitrogen, exhaled eight litres of air in which the carbon dioxide content has been marginally increased. He has stood upon a muddy patch of ground in the middle of nowhere, and the only creature which observed his passage is a startled sparrow which has now taken flight. Beneath the soil a single daisy has been crushed."

"Ah, but in that daisy!" I intoned, for this was a regular rant of Vincent's.

"Ah, but in the sparrow!" he retorted. "The sparrow took flight in alarm, and the falcon which was diving to eat it is now diverted, and the falconer has to run further afield to reclaim his bird, and in running further afield—"

"Sees the master's daughter in flagrante with the butcher's son!" I lamented. "And catching them so unprepared, cries out, 'You rascals!' at which all intercourse ceases and the daughter who should be pregnant is not at all—"

"And does not have her child!"

"And that child does not have a child, being, as it is, not born—"

"And a hundred generations later our brave traveller finds himself no longer in existence because his ancestor was caught with the butcher's son and so, being non-existent, he cannot return in time to prevent his own birth by the startling of a sparrow, and so, therefore, is born, and so he can return and prevent his birth and . . . Are we to posit God?" blurted Vincent suddenly. "Is that the only way out of this trap?"

"God?" I queried.

"We are to suppose," he retorted, dumping his surprisingly spry though hardly nimble frame back down in my second-favourite armchair, which now bore the imprint of his body well into its cushions, "that there are only two solutions to this paradox? That one – the universe, finding itself unable to sustain this great burden on its being, simply ceases to be? Or that two – the universe, finding itself still somewhat confused, fixes itself in a way beyond our ken and which, by its express interest in the events of our time traveller, rather does imply conscious structure and thought more than a mere amalgamation of matter might be expected to provide. Are we to posit God?"

"I thought we'd concluded that this hypothesis was impossible."

"Harry!" snapped Vincent, throwing his hands up into the air. "How long have we sat here?"

"I assume you query not some imposed measurement of time, rather how long since you first walked into my rooms to refute my errors?"

"Whenever," he replied, "we come close to the thorny uncertainties of this life, whenever we bring into question the notion of what if, you retreat from the argument like a cocker spaniel from a bulldog's bone!"

"I see no point arguing on a subject upon which, by all scientific measurements of the time, we cannot gather any data that might give us an answer," I replied.

"We cannot measure gravity, not in any practicable sense," retorted Vincent, his face settling into something of a sulk. "We cannot say how fast it is, or even what it is, yet you believe in it as much as —"

"Through observable effect."

"So you limit our debates based on the tools available?"

"A scientific argument must have some degree of data, some ... some sniff of theoretical basis behind it; otherwise it's not a scientific argument, it's a philosophical debate," I replied, "and therefore hardly my department."

Vincent gripped the arms of his seat, as if only that solid presence would prevent him springing up in rage. I waited for the tantrum to pass, "A thought experiment," he said at last. "You will at least tolerate that?"

I gestured vaguely over the lip of my glass that, just this once, I might be open to the idea.

"A tool," said Vincent at last, "for the observation of everything."

I waited.

There seemed nothing more.

"Well?" I asked at last. "I'm waiting for the development of the argument."

"We accept the existence of gravity not because we can see it,

119

or touch it, or say with any great certainty what it is, but because it has observable consequences which can be predicted through consistent theoretical models, yes?"

"Yesss ... " I concurred, waiting for the snag.

"From observable effects, we deduce non-observable consequences. We observe that an apple falls and say, 'It must be gravity.' We watch the refraction of light through a prism and declare it must be a wave – and from that deduction more deductions follow on behaviour and effect, amplitude and energy. So, by very little effort you can quickly theorise your way to the very bottom of things based on rather crude observable effect, as long as it fits the theory, yes?"

"If you're about to propose a better method than the scientific one ... ?"

He shook his head. "A tool," he repeated firmly, "that can deduce ... everything. If we take a building block of the universe, the atom, say, and announce that it has certain observable effects – gravity, electromagnetism, weak nuclear, strong nuclear forces – and proclaim these to be the four binding forces of the universe, then, if this is so, should it not be theoretically possible to extrapolate from this one tiny object, within which the very basis of everything is contained, the entire functioning of creation?"

"I can't help but feel we're straying back into God's territory," I reminded him.

"What is science for, if not omnipotence?"

"Are you looking for an ethical answer, or an economic one?"

"Harry!" he blurted, jumping back to his feet and pacing the slim area of floor I'd carefully cleared some months ago for just this purpose. "Always you dodge the question! Why are you so afraid of these ideas?"

I sat up a little straighter in my chair, his indignation reaching almost unusual levels. There was something odd in what he was saying, a little warning at the back of my mind which slowed my speech, made me answer with more care than usual. "Define 'everything'," I said finally. "I assume that your ... tool, if you like, your hypothetical, impossible tool, will, by deducing the state of all matter in the universe, be deducing both past and future states as well?"

"It would stand to reason, yes!"

"Allowing you to see everything that is, and everything that was, and everything that will be?"

"If time is considered to be non-absolute, then yes, again, I think that's reasonable."

I raised my hands, placating, thinking it through slowly. Alarm was growing at the back of my mind, seeping into my throat, trying to get past my tongue, which I moved so carefully. "But by the very act of observing the future, you yourself change it. And so we're back with our time traveller who stepped from his machine and saw the past. You, in seeing the future, will model your behaviour differently or, if not that, the future will be entirely tempered by the single moment in which you came to know it, altered by the act of being observed, and we return again to a paradox, to a universe that cannot be sustained, and even if that were not enough, surely we must ask ourselves what will be done with this knowledge? What will men do when they can see like gods, and what ... and ... "

I put my whisky glass down to the side. Vincent was standing still in the middle of the floor, his back half-turned to me, fingers splayed at his side, body stiff and straight.

"And," I murmured gently, "even if we were not worried about men obtaining godhood, I would raise this concern – that the strong nuclear force upon which your hypothesis depends won't be posited for another thirty years."

Silence.

I rose from my chair, frightened now by Vincent's stillness, by the muscles bunching along his back and shoulder, locked tight.

"Quarks," I said.

No reaction.

"The Higgs boson, dark matter, Apollo Eleven!"

Nothing.

"Vincent," I breathed gently, reaching out for his shoulder, "I want to help."

121

He jerked at my touch, and I think we both felt a rush of fight-or-flight adrenaline in our systems. Then he seemed to relax a little, head turning down, and smiled a distant smile at the floor, half-nodding in recognition at a thought unseen. "I wondered," he said at last, "but hoped you weren't." He turned sharply, swiftly, staring me straight in the eye. "Are you one of them?" he demanded. "Are you Cronus Club?"

"You know about the Cronus Club?"

"Yes, I know about it."

"Why didn't you—"

"Are you? For God's sake just answer me, Harry."

"I'm a member," I began to stammer. "Y-yes, of course, but that doesn't—"

He hit me.

I think I was more surprised than genuinely hurt. I'd encountered violence and pain, of course, but in this life I'd had such a comfortable existence I'd almost forgotten the feeling. If I'd been braced, I might have stayed standing, but shock more than anything else knocked me back into a pile of books. I was aware of the taste of blood in my mouth and a tooth wobbling at the touch of my tongue which had not wobbled before. I looked up into Vincent's face and saw coldness mingled with maybe – unless my mind imagined it – maybe a shimmer of regret.

Then he swung his fist once more, and this time surprise didn't have time to get a look-in.

# Chapter 29

"I hate to be the one to ask this," she said. "But if the world is ending, what are we really expected to do about it?"

Twelfth life.

Aged six, I wrote a letter to the London branch of the Cronus Club, requesting enough money to get me to London and a standard Club letter inviting me to join a prestigious school. The money was left in a dead letter drop, at my request, in a village called Hoxley, where some many lives ago I had fled from Phearson by the light of the moon.

I wrote a letter to Patrick and the dying Harriet, wishing them the best and thanking them for their time, and set out. In Hoxley I collected the money from its stash in a tin box beneath a hazel tree, and bought myself a fare to London. The baker smiled at me as he passed by in the street, and I felt Phearson in my belly, heard his footstep in my ear, and held on to the wall, wondering why my body refused to forget a thing which my mind had long since passed on by.

I took a cart to Newcastle, and when the ticket inspector on the train asked me if I was accompanied, I showed him the letter inviting me to attend a school and told him my aunty was waiting at London.

My aunty for the purposes of this life's adventure was Charity Hazelmere.

"There's the boy!" she hollered brightly as the conductor escorted me carefully from the train. "Harry, come along at once!"

There are many ways a child may be lifted from his linear parents. The dead letter drop I have referred to, along with the payment of suitable monies and provision of suitable documents, is a generally accepted and popular one. It provides enough resources for the kalachakra to make his own way to the nearest Cronus Club without necessarily exposing vital information such as where the kalachakra lives and is raised. It does, however, provide a degree of exposure in that it can narrow a search to an area. A generally more established rule is for a dead letter drop to be placed in a region where the recipient knows his parents are likely to take him at some point in the early years of his life, thus securing supplies and discretion in one swoop. The only danger of such an arrangement of course being the unlikely event that the family does not conform to expectations.

If discretion is not a concern – and arguably why should it be for the most affable and innocent of our kin – then direct intervention is also sanctioned, and no one did direct intervention quite like Charity Hazelmere. With her patrician nose, operatic voice and collection of stiff black bodices, which I have never seen her vary in all her lives, she is every adult's nightmare of a fiend headmistress, her merest glance over the half-moon spectacles slung by a chain and balanced on the end of her nose enough to reduce mere mortals to quivering doubts and fear. She has cajoled, bullied, badgered, hounded and occasionally plain kidnapped kalachakra children from their trembling parents, all in the name of a quieter life for her charges and with the express hope that in years to come other kalachakra will have the good sense to do the same for future members of our kin.

For all this, her views are arguably rather parochial.

*

"It's all very well to ask us to get involved," she exclaimed. "But how?"

Twelfth life.

It's rare to see a gathering of the Cronus Club. Members drift in and out all the time, but a full regional assembly – invitees summoned by cards with gold trim, agenda: the end of the world – is a sight to see. At six years old I was the youngest. At eighty-two, Wilbur Mawn was the oldest. As a child Wilbur had met the Duke of Wellington, and when growing up as a young man in London he had swapped cards with men who had fought for, and against, revolution in France. Now he was to be our next messenger, a man shortly due to die, who could, by his death, bring the message back to 1844 – the world is ending and we don't know why. So what are you going to do about it?

"Nothing!" declared Philip Hopper, son of a Devon farmer with a taste for adventure that had led him to die in the Second World War six times, the Korean War twice, and Vietnam once, as a rather decrepit war correspondent no army would employ. "The factors are too many, the information too vague! We either need more information or nothing at all, since we can't begin to determine what's at work here."

"I think," suggested Anya, a White Russian refugee who tended to abandon the White Russian cause for a more comfortable life abroad in 1904 with a sigh of inevitability, "the issue concerns the speeding-up. The end of the world is speeding up – it is happening earlier in every life. That implies that the cause is changing, and what, we must ask, is the cause of change?"

Eyes turned to me. I was both messenger boy and, by dint of being the youngest, the most widely assumed to be in touch with modern scientific reasoning on the subject, if you considered the 1990s to be modern.

"In every life we lead, regardless of every death we pass," I said, "the world around us is unchanged. There is always rebellion in 1917; there is always war in 1939; Kennedy will always be shot and trains will always be late. These are linear events which do not vary, as far as we can observe, from life to life. The only variable

125

factors are us. If the world is changing, we are the ones who change it."

"Against the rules of the Cronus Club!" interrupted Charity furiously, never one to be distracted by the bigger picture.

"The question therefore becomes," I went on, legs dangling from the chair on which I was perched, "not why is the world ending. But who?"

# Chapter 30

Killing an ouroboran is hard, but I would argue that killing a linear mortal can often be harder, for you cannot simply prevent their birth in one life and have that serve as death for all. Each murder must be conducted each life, a matter as routine as brushing teeth or trimming nails. The key is consistency.

It was 1951 and I was living in London.

Her name was Rosemary Dawsett: she was twenty-one years old and liked money. I was lonely and liked her. I won't pretend it was a profound relationship, but it was, in its own way, reasonably honest. I didn't ask for exclusivity, and she didn't attempt to extort, though she could see that I was a reasonably wealthy gentleman. Then one day she missed our meeting, and I went to her lodging and found her, in the bath, wrists slashed. The police called it suicide, dismissing her as one more dead tart, but I looked and I saw. The blade had gone too deep into her right wrist, slashing the tendons; she couldn't have been strong enough to hold it for the next cut on her left, and besides there were no hesitation marks, no signs of doubt, no note, no shuffling around as she tried to get the angle right or worked up her courage. As someone practised in the art of self-destruction, I knew a murder when I saw it.

The police refused to investigate, so I took over. The evidence was sickeningly clear to find, once you looked. Fingerprints, one even in the blood itself, and the madame downstairs had a list of all Rosemary's regulars and thought she had seen one Richard Lisle leaving as she had come home. Getting his address was a matter of a few polite phone calls, getting his fingerprints was a case of approaching him in a pub, buying him several pints and listening to his ramblings, which ranged from a discussion of fine art taken from a textbook to loud and raucously cheered remarks about the bloody Pakis and wogs. His voice was the overly slippery upper-class accent of a middle-class man with aspirations and elocution lessons. In thirty years it would be a parody accent, used by comics to expose the sad cliché of the lonely man who believed that Ascot was sacred and could never quite get a ticket. In a merciful mood I might have felt sorry for this little man, striving to be accepted by a portion of society that didn't just ignore him, it didn't even notice him knocking. Then I took his beer glass home and checked his prints, which matched the print in the blood on the side of the bath, and any sympathy I might have felt was gone.

I sent my evidence – beer glass, analysis of the blood patterns, the fingerprint in the blood – to Scotland Yard, to a detective called Cutter who had a reputation for imagination and prudence. He interviewed Lisle two days later, and that, from what I could tell, was the end of it. Two days after that another prostitute hanged herself, and there were self-defence marks on her wrists and arms, chloral hydrate in her bloodstream. This time, though, warned by the visit from the police, Lisle had been careful and left not a fingerprint behind.

I had not committed murder at the time, although I had killed. By this point I knew of seven men I had killed directly, six of them in the Second World War and one in self-defence. I also calculated that I had contributed to the deaths of many hundreds more, through acts as banal as fixing the wheel on a B-52 or proposing a more reliable timer which could later be used on a bomb. I considered whether I had the courage to commit actual, cold-blooded murder, and concluded with mild regret that I did. I informed myself that I had the decency to be ashamed, but what little comfort that was compared to the certainty that I would commit this act. I would kill Richard Lisle.

I prepared carefully. I bought a boat under an assumed name for cash in hand, a crabby tin thing with a lower deck that stank of the slick white fungus which infested its walls. I bought petrol and food, hydrochloric acid and a hacksaw, careful to spread my purchases over as wide an area as possible. I bought gloves and rubber overalls, examined the tides on the Thames and observed the traffic in the night. I acquired several ccs of benzodiazepine and rented a room opposite the pub where I had first acquired Richard Lisle's fingerprints. I waited until one night – a Tuesday, the smog thick green over the streets – when he came to have a drink, and went in. I joined him, remembering our old acquaintance and asking how he had been. He was gleeful, happy, a gleam of sweat about his face and a loudness in his speech that at once set alarm bells ringing in my mind. What had he done to induce such delight? I examined him, every part, for a sign of something amiss, and smelled the fresh soap in his hair, saw how scrubbed his nails were, how fresh and clean his clothes were despite the settling lateness of the hour, and knew with that irrational part of the mind that rationality always denies that I had come to him a few hours too late. Rage flared up inside me and briefly my plan was forgotten, my efficient, organised scheme. I still smiled, and smiled, and we staggered out together into the coal-hung air at closing time, hanging off each other, best of friends, our skin smeared black by the air we breathed. But as we staggered away up the street, one of those lingering terraced streets of tiny houses that still hid beneath the craters of the East End, he looked up at the sky and laughed, and I punched him and punched him again, and when he fell I straddled him, grabbing him by the throat and screamed, "Where is she? Who was it this time?" and punched him again.

In the rush of adrenaline, in my rage, smothered by the smog and hidden by the dark, all my plans, my careful, reasoned plans were forgotten. I barely felt the shock against my knuckles as I drove my fists into his skull. Nor did I register the flick knife that he drove up through my abdomen and into the bottom of my left lung until, drawing breath for another strike, I realised I had no breath to draw. His face was jelly but I was dead. He pushed me off him and and I fell like soggy pudding into the gutter, the dirty water flecking my face. He crawled over to me, his breath wheezing, blood popping and bubbling out of the end of his shattered nose. Awareness of the knife in his hand gave me an awareness of what he did with it, so I felt the next three strokes as he drove it into my chest. Then I felt nothing at all.

# Chapter 31

Many, many lives later, I sat down opposite Virginia in the lounge of the Cronus Club and said, "His name is Vincent."

"Darling, that's hardly much to go by."

"He's one of us. Ouroboran. I asked him about the Cronus Club, and he attacked me and walked away."

"How immature of him."

"He has ambitions."

Virginia was more than capable of being uninterested when she wanted to be. She wanted to be now. She stared at the ceiling as if it was the most fascinating thing in the world and waited for the rest.

"The message keeps coming down to us from the future generations – the world is ending, the world is ending. Nothing changes about the established course of linear events – nothing – except us."

"You suggest this . . . Vincent . . . may be the 'who' which leads to the 'what'?"

"I . . . no. I don't know. I'm suggesting that one of his character, someone who is one of us but not one of us, is someone seeking an answer . . . mindless of the consequences . . . that's what I suggest."

"And Harry," she murmured, "you appear to have an idea of what you desire to do next."

"We look for anomalies," I explained firmly. "The Cronus Club looks for events which should not be happening in their time periods, changes to the normal course of things. I think I've found one."

"Where?"

"Russia."

She sucked in her teeth thoughtfully. "Have you spoken to the Club? To Moscow, St Petersburg – Leningrad, I suppose we must call it, ghastly though it is?"

"I sent them a message via Helsinki. I'm going to Finland tomorrow morning."

"If you're already pursuing this, why do you tell me?"

I hesitated, then, "Should something unfortunate happen, I'd ask that you pass my suspicions on to others. But ..."

"You're concerned that if one of our kind is altering established events, they may have informants within the Club." She sighed. I wondered how long she'd held on to this thought, and how many of our peers considered it too. Were we, all of us, so used to apathy and deceit that not one had bothered to raise the question of it? Did we all take betrayal so much for granted? Then, what good could be achieved, other than to spread suspicion without a cure? "But," she went on, brightening a little, "you, dear boy, clearly trust me enough to inform me of your concerns. But not Moscow or St Petersburg. Oh, Harry, your time as an intelligence agent has done nothing for your socialite reputation."

"I wasn't aware I had a socialite reputation."

"Quite. Harry." A note of what, I imagined, passed for genuine concern slipped into her voice. "I understand how exciting it must be to be informed that the world is ending, what a marvellous adventure this must present for you. Repetition is dull; stimulation is vital to stave off the decline of faculties and will. But the simple, mathematical truth is that, between us and the events unfolding of the future, there is an almost infinite range of possibilities and permutations, and to think that we can, in any meaningful way, affect this, now, is not merely ludicrous, it's really rather childish. I have no objection to you doing whatever it is you wish to do, Harry – it is, after all, your life, and I know that you won't cause any especial embarrassment for the Club while doing it – but I just don't want to see you get too emotionally involved."

I considered Virginia's words. She was, physically, older than me, but after a few deaths such things rarely counted. It was more than likely that she had been through more lives than me, but again, after the first few centuries, most kalachakra reached a plateau where time hardly mattered and the soul barely changed. Yet Virginia had always been a figure of seniority to me, the woman who had saved me from Phearson, introduced me to the Club; for her these memories would fade, and with the passing of experience perhaps our relationship would change, but for me the recollection was as strong as ever.

I remembered Christa standing by my bedside in Berlin.

In 1924 I had travelled to Liverpool to perform a similar service. The man dying had gone by the name of Joseph Kirkbriar Shotbolt, born 1851, dies, on average, 1917–27. Statistically, Spanish flu was his most common killer, along with three members of his near family, twelve cousins and roughly a quarter of the waterside community where he sometimes retired. "Can't shake the bugger!" I'd heard him exclaim on those few occasions he'd outlived it. "Damn plague just follows me anywhere!"

This time he'd missed Spanish flu by the rather sensible precaution of spending the last years of the war on an island in Micronesia which hadn't yet been marked on the atlas, but whose name in the tongue of its native people translated as Teardrop Blessing. The rather less fortunate outcome of his escaping the flu was the acquisition of of a parasite which caused his feet to swell to quite appalling size, bursting out of his socks in their disfigured redness, and which, more crucially, created a series of cysts on his kidneys and liver which induced the septicaemia from which he was dying when I finally met him.

A kalachakra tends to recognise another when he sees him – not necessarily through any instinct, as my relationship with Vincent was to testify, but through the incongruity of circumstance and a certain bearing. A six-year-old boy visiting the bedside of a man dying in a whitewashed infirmary in Liverpool from a parasitical infection that the doctors were at a loss to cure tends to induce a certain circumstantial recognition that needs no greater introduction.

Once a giant of a man, the onset of death had wrinkled Shotbolt up like a burned chip. Every joint seemed bent a little beyond comfort, the tendons seizing up, and the heavy pain medication he was on had only accelerated the liver failure which was turning his skin a very noticeable and rather pungent yellow. His hair had fallen out, including eyebrows and eyelashes, and as he lay alone, dying his last, the swollen knuckles on his hand stood out bulbously above the bed sheets where he clutched them to him against a deep-seated ache that no doctor could cure.

I had met Shotbolt only a few times before, though he did not remember me, but recognition of what I was was there immediately.

"From the Club, are you?" he grumbled, his voice surprisingly heavy for a man so close to the end. "Tell 'em if it's a cure, I don't bloody want it. Laudanum, thanking you kindly, that'd be what I need."

I flicked through the chart at the end of his bed. The drips fed into his body were mostly saline, a half-hearted attempt at liquid sustenance after his digestive system had packed up. The bottles were glass drums, heavy, a leak in one where the rubber had cracked around the nipple of the jar. "Oh God," he groaned, seeing me read. "You've trained as a doctor, haven't you? Can't stand bloody doctors, especially when they're five years old."

"Six," I corrected. "And don't worry; you'll be dead within a week."

"A week! I can't be sitting around here for a bloody week! You know those bastards won't even give me something good to read? 'Mustn't get excited, Mr Shotbolt,' they say. 'Now, Mr Shotbolt, can you make it to the potty?' The potty! Do you know that's what they actually call it? I've never been so humiliated in all my life."

The way he spoke implied that here was a man for whom once-in-a-lifetime outrages had been a fairly common occurrence in times past, and would probably be again. I chose not to debate the point and, satisfied that for all his medication Shotbolt still had some semblance of coherence, I sat down on the edge of his bed and said, "I've got a message."

"It had better not be a question about Queen bloody Victoria," he growled. "Can't stand all these academics wanting to know about her stocking size."

"It's not a question," I repeated patiently. "More of a warning. It's been passed down from generation to generation, trickled down from the future."

"What've we done this time?" he grunted. "Too much ice and not enough fire?"

"Something like that. Apparently – and I feel a little embarrassed telling you this – but apparently the world is ending. Which is, in and of itself, no great surprise. But the end of the world is getting faster. And that's something of a stumper."

Shotbolt considered this a while, fingers still tight around the edge of his sheets. Then, "At last," he exclaimed. "Something new to talk about!"

Almost exactly thirty years later I boarded a flight from Heathrow Airport to Berlin Templehof, changing passports on my way through customs, heading east in search of something new.

# Chapter 32

There are certain rules to a successful deception, of which my personal favourite is – stick with what you know. That is not to say that truth should ever be incorporated into your lies, but rather that good research is the key to a consistent lie. It was in 1956 by no means impossible for a citizen of the West to enter the East – far easier, in fact, than for a citizen of the East to head to the West – but to declare yourself as such was to invite immediate attention and scrutiny, and this was, I felt, something I could not necessarily afford.

I had, in my twelfth life, after receiving Christa's message, embarked on what I believe would come to be known, in the 1990s, as a portfolio existence. I travelled extensively under the flimsy cover of "executive businessman" and dabbled with whichever intelligence services I felt might be of most use to me in order to keep as broad an eye as possible on global events. In 1929, aged eleven, I bought up stocks as the markets collapsed, and by 1933 I was the sole shareholder in one of the fastest-growing investment brokerages in the northern hemisphere. An actor by the name of Cyril Handly was paid a very reasonable wage to impersonate me, it being unwise for a fifteen-year-old boy to be caught as CEO of a large investment company. He was precisely what a chairman should have been – dignified, well built, with a carefully cultivated accent, refined tastes and a reasonable but not unhealthy belly on him, and his combination of judicious silence and fiery retribution worked well in the office until in 1936 his enjoyment of the role became a little too much to tolerate when he began sacking reliable members of staff during board meetings. I relocated the company to Switzerland, paid Cyril off with a retirement home in Bali, and employed a rather younger actor to impersonate my son, newly risen to become head of the company, buying his complicity with a mixture of reasonable fees and, in a twist that surprised me more than anyone else, regular lessons in economics, finance and accountancy which led to, by 1938, my having complete confidence in his ability to run the company with the barest interference from me.

"Invest in American arms, steel, chemicals and petrol," was the only guidance I gave him in 1938, as the world slid towards war. "Pull out of the Skoda arms factory, and withdraw all foreign personnel from Singapore."

By 1948, Waterbrooke & Smith – two names chosen for no reason other than their entire lack of connection to myself – was one of the most successful companies in the northern hemisphere, with extensive and occasionally illegal contacts in South-East Asia and Africa, and growing interests in Chile, Venezuela and, in a move which I quietly had to question, Cuba. The company was successful, unethical and above all provided me with a continual influx of both ready cash – a mild interest – and global information, without my ever having to show my face.

It was one report, a tiny note in the hundred that arrived at my door every week, which sent me to Russia. The title of the document read, "Limited Exposure to PJC/9000 Portable Radio (Commercial)".

In it an analyst briefly discussed the company's recent investment in a radio transmitter-receiver set which had gone on the market in West Germany some two months before, whose range and quality of signal had been recognised and rewarded in the last week by a contract with the air force to fit out its stations with the new equipment. Technical specs were attached, and flicking through them I saw nothing remarkable until my eye, wandering down the page, glimpsed the operational frequency of the transmitter. It was some two hundred thousand hertz outside the normal range of the equipment of the time, and while this relatively low number, in terms of radio frequencies, might not have set off many alarm bells, the mechanism by which it appeared to achieve this effect was something which should not have been invented, let alone been available on commercial markets, for another thirteen years.

# Chapter 33

Asked to think about East Germany in the 1950s, picturesque is not the word which leaps to mind. World War Two had not been kind; the Soviet tanks as they ploughed towards Berlin had not been kind. The years of uncertainty until the elections of 1948, when certainty became rather too certain indeed, had not been kind, and finally the dawn of the 1950s had brought with it a certain grey resignation. The flat landscape left no place to hide the harsh realities of an economy where intellectualism was bourgeois, labour was freedom, and brotherhood was obligatory. The people had been promised cars, so incredibly unreliable little bangers which leaped like startled hippos over every pothole, slamming the heads of the many people crowded into the tight back seats, were wheeled out with the pomp of cardboard coffins. The people had been promised food, so forests were torn down and wheat sown where no farmer would have dreamed of growing it, while industrial fertilisers stained the flat still waters of the northern lakes a scummy grey-brown.

Yet, for all this, one or two bastions of tradition survived, largely through government omission. The confiscation by the Soviets of much of Germany's industrial equipment after the war had ranged from factory machinery down to the smallest farmyard truck, and in corners of the countryside there existed now a population of hardy widowed women who slogged through the fields, scythes in hand, their heads covered with bright scarves and their backs bent beneath the baskets that carried their crops. Blink, and you might imagine it was some idyllic rural scene. Look again, and you might see the hunger in the women's eyes and the weight upon their shoulders as they stooped to toil.

I was travelling to meet Daniel van Thiel. By buying the company which distributed the anomalous radio, I had acquired information as to its origins, which were, to my surprise, eastern European, the key breakthrough attributed to van Thiel, a former communications engineer in the *Wehrmacht* who, at the tender age of nineteen, had been one of the few to escape the *Kessel* around Stalingrad, put on a flight in honour of his "exceptional skills". His evacuation was one of the few acknowledgments the German high command had been willing to make that the army trapped on the Volga was doomed. Over ten years later, van Thiel had conveniently discovered his communist zeal, receiving further education not only in East Germany, but in Moscow too, returning from five years of study to reveal designs which my company marketed as "revolutionising communication!" and which I personally felt were still in need of fuller development. He was like an ancient architect given sudden knowledge of the wheel, who had used it to create a pyramid, failing to appreciate that it might be handy on a chariot too.

I was travelling as Sebastian Grunwald, a journalist working on an article entitled "Future Heroes of Our Socialist Revolution". Van Thiel lived in one of the few towns which might almost be called picturesque in that the tide of industry which was yet to come had not yet reached its high-water mark and pulled down the grey stone cottages, little winding streets and stone-black chapel with its miraculously preserved deep-stained-glass window showing Christ upon the mountain. He lived with his sister, who had dressed in her finest, faded clothes for the occasion and who brought us home-made biscuits and Austrian coffee as we sat in van Thiel's small sky-blue living room.

"The coffee was a present from Vienna," he explained as I redundantly opened my notebook for the interview. "Life is good for us now. Everyone's going mad for East German products."

Talk to anyone in any sort of public capacity at the time and they would tell you that life was good. Cause and effect were tricky little numbers – the cause need have no direct relation to the effect as long as the effect was prosperity and happiness under the GDR's regime.

I asked my questions, careful to surround what I actually wanted to know with as much fluff as I could.

How long had he been interested in radios?

Really, really, a father who was an amateur engineer . . .

. . . he'd listened to the radio during the bombings, an advance warning when the sirens failed . . .

. . . and how had his success affected him?

Proud, proud to be German, proud to be communist, of course.

Was his sister proud?

Was he looking for a wife?

What would he be doing next for his country?

Did he have any other interests or hobbies?

No, of course not, dedicated to his work, a good worker . . .

. . . and what of his time in Russia? It must have been incredibly informative.

"Incredible. Incredible!" he exclaimed. "So welcoming, so warm – I hadn't expected it at all. 'Comrade, there is no German and Russian; we are all communists!'" He mimicked a Russian accent while explaining this, an affectation which slightly threw me. My German is essentially native, but lack of practice takes its toll even on those of us who are mnemonics, and tuning both ear and voice to a regional accent takes time which leaves little room for comedy.

And the idea for the device? Where had that come from?

A mischievous look passed across Daniel's face. "I worked with some great men," he explained. "We were all united by finding a common cause."

It was so much of a slogan, so much a cliché, that I had to smile, and he smiled right back, recognising the emptiness of his own words and enjoying their effect on me. Then he reached out, took the pencil from my hand, pushed my notebook on to the table and closed it. "The Russians," he said, "have bad breath and can't cook for shit. But their science – their science is why they won the war."

You jest, surely you jest, I intoned. The number of people, the strength of their ideology, the industrial base . . .

"Bullshit! I met people there, men and women doing things . . . The Soviets, they've seen the future, that's why they're going to win, why they were always going to win. What I did . . . drop in the ocean."

And the future? What was this future that the Russians had seen?

That would be telling. He laughed, and in another time and another place he might well have gone on to tap the side of his nose. Suffice to say, tomorrow was going to be here today.

Come on, I whispered, come on! Do a favour for a journalist hack who needs to make his bosses happy. Give me a name, just one name – someone you met in Russia, something that inspired you.

He thought about it a while, then grinned. "OK," he said. "But you didn't get this from me. The guy you need to look out for, the man who's going to change everything . . . his name is Vitali Karpenko. If you ever go to Moscow, if you ever get to meet him, remember – he's going to change the world."

I smiled and laughed, dismissing the idea with a shrug, and picked my notebook back up to ask the rest of the empty questions I had prepared. When I left, van Thiel shook my hand and winked and said I was on to a good thing in my line of work. Germany would always need people who understood the big ideas. Four days later he was found hanging from the quaint wooden rafters of his traditional wooden house by an old bit of hemp rope. A note on the desk stated that he had betrayed his country by selling his ideas and his soul, and he could no longer live with the grief. The verdict was suicide, and the bruising around his ribs and hands dismissed as incidental injuries sustained post-mortem, when the police came to cut him down.

Two days after that, under the name Kostya Prekovsky, I boarded a cargo ship hauling coal to Leningrad, one set of travel documents in my pocket, another stowed in the false bottom of my bag, and an escape passport already deposited in an unused signal box just beyond Finland Station, ready should I need it. I was looking for Vitali Karpenko, the man who could change the future.

# Chapter 34

It is not I, but he, who takes the night train across Europe.

It is perhaps the universal experience of travellers – I have only my own view to judge it by – but there is a moment, in the dead hours of the night, when a man may sit upon a platform in an empty station, waiting for the last train upon a long journey, and regardless of the personal experience of that individual, he ceases to be an "I" and becomes a "he". Perhaps another creature stirs in this dead place: a traveller, back bent, eyes too weary to read a book; a government apparatchik on his way back from an unsuccessful meeting straight to an early-morning reproach; two or three strangers gathered beneath the hissing white lights whose sound is inaudible by day, when the trains race through the station and doors clatter and clunk, and which by night become the base sound of the universe. When the train pulls in, it seems to be a long way away for a very long time, then suddenly here, and longer than you had imagined. The doors bend in the middle as they open, heavy and unwieldy. The toilets stink of urine, the nets above the seating sag from too much baggage for too many shaking miles. Three people board the last train to Leningrad, and no one gets off.

I sit by the window, a false name in my passport, a dozen languages mixing in my mind, not sure which one will make an appearance on the end of my tongue, and look at my reflection in the window of the carriage, and see a stranger. Someone else travels on the sleeper train through Russia, alone with the beating of the bumpers beneath the wheels of the cart. Someone else's face is too white against the blackness outside. Someone else's head bumps against the cold window with each jerk of the engine, each shriek of the brake.

Thoughts, at such times, happen not in words but in stories told about someone else's life. A child approached a man, dying in Berlin, and said the world is ending, and these words meant nothing at all. Death has always come to the man as death always will, and frankly the man couldn't be more or less interested in death than in a curious tropical beetle, save that death brings with it the tedium of youth once again. Bombs have fallen and people have died, and frankly why should a change in the process of these events be of any interest, since the outcome is always the same?

And then again.

Vincent Rankis hit a professor in Cambridge, punched him right in the jaw, and for what? For two words uttered in hope – Cronus Club.

A child threw himself from the third floor of an asylum; a wandering monk asked a Chinese spy how to die, and Vincent Rankis exclaimed at the wonders of the universe, and wanted more.

*What is the point of you?*

A man on a train to Leningrad hears the voice of Franklin Phearson in his mind, and is briefly surprised to see his own features flinch in the window. What is that? Is that pain at an unwelcome recollection? Is that guilt? Regret?

*What is the point of you, Dr August? Do you think all this was just a dream?*

An argument with Vincent in my rooms in Cambridge.

*We also posited a parallel universe which you might be able to save from the trials of war. We even hypothesised a world in which you yourself could experience the joy of said peace, paradox being left aside.*

When I am optimistic, I choose to believe that every life I lead, every choice I make, has consequence. That I am not one Harry August but many, a mind flicking from parallel life to parallel life, and that when I die, the world carries on without me, altered by my deeds, marked by my presence.

Then I look at the deeds I have done and, perhaps more importantly considering my condition, the deeds I have not done, and the thought depresses me, and I reject the hypothesis as unsound.

What is the point of me?

Either to change a world – many, many worlds, each touched by the choices I make in my life, for every deed a consequence, and in every love and every sorrow truth – or nothing at all.

A stranger takes the train to Leningrad.

# Chapter 35

History often forgets about the siege of Leningrad, focusing instead on its southern counterpart, Stalingrad. In that the Nazis' retreat from Stalingrad has widely been seen as a turning point, the focus is understandable, but as a consequence it is easy to overlook the siege that Leningrad, a fine city of wide promenades and ancient jingling trams, endured for eight hundred and seventy-one days of unrelenting war. Once the home of tsars, then the heartland of the revolution, it seemed remarkable to me that any semblance of the royal city had survived the beating it had taken, and indeed, in the suburbs all the way through to the heart of the city, an architecture of pragmatism and speed had taken over, of squares and rectangles and grey tarmac before brown walls. History was of little interest to the Soviets, unless it was the history of their success, and, as if embarrassed by the fine stone houses that still survived around the canals of the inner city, the high walls of the old town were plastered over with posters proclaiming STRIVE FOR VICTORY! and CELEBRATE COMMUNISM AND UNITE IN LABOUR! and other such azures of wisdom. The Winter Palace stood rather awkwardly in the midst of all these ugly good intentions, a monument to a bygone era and testimony to the regime which had been overthrown. To celebrate the Winter Palace would have, in some quaint way, glorified its previous occupiers, but to destroy it would have been an insult to those men and women of 1917 who fought against it and all it stood for, and so it and much of Leningrad remained standing strong, walls too thick to be more than scratched by bullets or cracked by ice.

The Leningrad Cronus Club resided, to my surprise, not in one of the great buildings of the old city, but in a far smaller, more modest tenement tucked in behind a Jewish cemetery, whose stones were long-since overgrown and whose trees dangled heavy over its high grey walls. The Club's gatekeeper and, as it turned out, one of the few remaining members, introduced herself simply as,

"Olga. You must be Harry. You won't do at all – those boots are quite wrong. Don't stand there – come in!"

Olga, fifty-nine years old, grey hair plaited down to her waist, shoulders bent slightly forward to give her chin a jutting, pro-truding quality that her face itself did not merit, may once have been a beautiful young woman at whose lightest step upon tiny feet the heart of many an aristocrat raced; but now, as she grum-bled and grunted at the creaking pipes that ran up the staircase of the tenement block, she was almost a child's caricature of that crea-ture called a crone. Green tiles on the floor and faded cobalt-blue paint on the walls were the tenement's only real concession to vitality, and the doors that looked out on to the winding staircase upwards were kept firmly shut, "To keep the heat in!"

It was March in the city, and though the air was still biting cold, the snow was beginning to melt, whiteness giving way to a per-petual shimmer of grey-black as five months of embedded dirt, soot and grime was revealed from beneath the crystal piles shoved up against the roadside. The worst of the ice had gone from the roofs, but these masses of shovelled snow remained, insulating themselves, monuments to the fading winter that had gone before.

"I've got whisky," she said, waving me to a padded chair by the orange-banded electric fire. "But you should have vodka and be grateful."

"I'll have vodka and be grateful," I said, slipping into the soft padded furniture with relief.

"You speak Russian with an eastern accent – where did you learn?"

"Komosomolsk," I admitted, "a few lives ago."

"You need to speak with a western accent, because you look soft," she chided. "Otherwise people will ask. And your boots – far too new. Here." Something metal flashed across the room and landed in my lap. It was a cheese grater. "Have you never been to Russia before?" she demanded. "You're doing this all wrong!"

"Not on a Russian passport," I admitted. "American, British, Swiss, German—"

"No no no no! All wrong! No good, start again!"

"Forgive me," I blurted as Olga sat down in front of me with an unmarked vodka bottle and two intimidatingly large glasses, and I set to work with the cheese grater on my boots. "But I expected there to be more people at the Club. Where's everyone else?"

"There's a few sleeping upstairs," she grumbled, "and Masha's got a toy boy in again, which I don't approve of. They drop in sometimes when passing through, but that's all they ever do these days – pass through. Not like the old days."

There was a misty gleam in Olga's eyes at the mention of the old days, but it was quickly supplanted by a focus on the vital business of drinking and chastising. "Your hair is disgusting," she exclaimed. "What colour do you call that? Carrot? You'll have to dye it at once."

"I was going to— " I began feebly.

"The papers you used to get in, burn them!"

"I've already thrown them—"

"Not throw, burn! Burn. Can't be bothering with people coming here causing us trouble! With so few members in the Club the bureaucracy is endless, endless!"

"Forgive me asking, but what is the status of the Leningrad Club?" I enquired. "The last time I came here glasnost was in full swing, but now ... "

She snorted derisively. "The Club," she explained, thumping

149

the bottle with each word on to the tabletop, "is in the shit. No one can be bothered to stay – no one! In the good old days there were always one or two who worked their way into senior party ranks, just to make sure anyone born into this place would have a reasonable friend at court, but now? 'It's too unreliable, Madam Olga,' they whine. 'Doesn't matter what we do, or whose side we're on, we keep on being purged and shot, it's just not worth the effort. And if we're not purged in the 1930s, we're purged during the war, and if we're not purged during the war, we're purged by Khrushchev. We're bored with this game.' Weedy little arses! They don't have any sticking power, that's the problem! Or it's 'We want to have the good life, Madam Olga. We want to see the world,' and I exclaim, 'You're Russian. You could spend a hundred lifetimes and never see all of Russia!' but they can't be bothered." Her voice dripped scorn. "They don't want to waste their time and energy on being in their native lands so they all cross the borders and emigrate, but they still expect to be looked after when they're born again, little whiny snots!"

I flinched as another good slam of the bottle on the table threatened to topple both glass and furniture. "I'm the only one who sticks around, the only one who bothers to look out for our up-and-coming members! You know I have to get money sent in from other clubs? Paris, New York, Tokyo. I've got a rule now. If you pick up one of *my* members, then any money they contribute gets sent straight back to me! No one argues," she added with satisfaction, "because they all know I'm right. It's only visitors come to gawp who keep things interesting now."

"And ... what about you?" I hazarded. "What's your story?"

For a second her chin drew back, and there it was, the flash of the woman Olga might have been, beneath the layers of jacket and wool. Gone as quickly as it had come. "White Russian," she proclaimed. "I was shot in 1928," she added, sitting up a little straighter at the recollection, "because they found out that my father was a duke and told me that I had to write a self-criticism proclaiming that I was a bourgeois pig, and work at a farm, and I refused. So they tortured me to make me confess, but even when

I was bleeding out of my insides I stood there and said, 'I am a daughter of this beautiful land, and I will never participate in the ugliness of your regime!' And when they shot me, it was the most magnificent I had ever been." She sighed a little in fond recollection. "Course now," she grumbled, "I can see their point of view. Takes having lived through the revolution to notice just how hungry the peasants are, and how angry the workers get when they run out of bread, but at the time, when they pulled the blindfold over my blood-soaked face, I knew I was right. The course of history! I've heard so much crap about the course of history."

"I take it the Club doesn't have many contacts in the administration." This would be something of a blow. In my time in SIS one of the few lessons I learned was that almost no one had good sources in positions of Soviet power during this period, as much from the endless cycle of purges which Olga described as from any lack of effort in developing suitably placed moles. Even Waterbrooke & Smith had a bare minimum of contacts within Russia, and I had been largely relying on the Cronus Club to come good for me.

Then Olga grinned. "Contacts," she grumbled. "Who needs contacts? This is Russia! You don't ask people to help you. You tell them. In 1961 the commissar who lives two doors down is arrested for keeping a rent boy in a dacha on the river; the boy had lived there for ten years, so lives there now! In 1971 a grave is uncovered in the bottom of the butcher's garden – the wife who 'vanished' in 1949, he had no idea where. In three years' time the commissioner of police is going to be arrested on the testimony of his deputy, who needs a bigger house because his wife is pregnant again from her affair with her sergeant lover . . . Nothing changes. You don't need contacts – what you need is money and dirt."

"And what dirt do you have that could help me?" I asked.

"The head of physics at the academy," she said briskly. "He's interested in the universe, wants to find out where we're all from – that stuff. For five years now he's been secretly swapping letters with a professor of astronomy at MIT via a mutual friend in Istanbul who sends the mail with his cousin when he runs soap in

151

and moonshine out on the black market. There's nothing political, but it's enough."

"You've used this before?"

She shrugged. "Sometimes. Sometimes he goes for it, sometimes he doesn't. He's been shot twice and exiled to the gulags three times, but usually, if you handle him right, he comes good. You get it wrong, that's your own fault."

"Well then," I murmured, "I'd better not get it wrong."

# Chapter 36

Blackmail is surprisingly difficult to pull off. The art lies in convincing the target that whatever harm they do themselves – for, by definition, you are compelling them rather than coaxing them into obedience – is less than the harm which will be caused by the revelation of the secrets in your power. More often than not the blackmailer overplays their hand, and nothing is achieved except grief. A light touch and, more importantly, an understanding of when to back away is vital to achieve success.

I've employed plenty of dirty tricks to achieve my goals; employing them against people I like is harder. Professor Gulakov was a man I liked. I liked him from the moment he answered his door with a polite smile of enquiry, a grizzle-chinned man in a thick brown jumper, to the moment he offered me thin boiled coffee in a china cup no thicker than a fingernail and invited me to sit down in a room laden with scrounged, begged and borrowed books. In another life I might have enjoyed his company, shared thoughts on science and its possibilities, hypothesised and debated with him. But I was here with a very precise purpose, and he was my means to achieve it.

"Professor," I said, "I am looking for a man by the name of Vitali Karpenko. Can you find him for me?"

"I don't know this man," he replied. "Why do you want to see him?"

"A relative of his died recently. I was instructed by his lawyer to find Karpenko. There is a matter of some money."

"Of course, I'd help you if I can . . . "

"I'm told Karpenko is a scientist."

"I don't know all the scientists in Russia!" He laughed, uneasily swirling the coffee around his cup.

"But you could find out."

"Well I . . . I could make some enquiries."

"Discreetly. As I said, there is a question of some money, and his relative did not die within Russia." Gulakov's face twitched – he was beginning to sense where this might lead. "I understand," I went on calmly, "that you have dealings with scientists outside the Soviet Union?"

His hand stopped still, but the coffee kept tumbling around inside his cup, whipping up the granules from the bottom. "No," he said at last. "I don't."

"A professor in MIT, do you not correspond with him?" My smile was fixed, but I couldn't quite meet Gulakov's gaze, my eyes transfixed by the coffee in his cup. "There's no harm in that," I added brightly, "no harm at all. Science should be beyond the boundaries of politics, should it not? I merely suggest that a man of your influence and ability should have no trouble – discreetly – finding this Vitali Karpenko, if you wanted to. The family would be very appreciative."

My work done, I shifted the subject at once and for another half an hour talked about Einstein and Bohr, and the question of the neutron bomb, though in truth Gulakov made little more than empty noises to my speech, and then I left him alone in silence to consider his next move.

\*

154

Gulakov didn't call for three days.

On the fourth the phone rang in the Cronus Club, and he was there and frightened.

"Kostya Prekovsky?" he asked. "It's the professor. I may have something for you."

He was talking slowly – a little too slowly – and there was a clicking on the line like the amplified rattle of an insect's skin.

"Can you meet me in twenty minutes? At mine?"

"I can't get to yours in twenty," I lied. "Can you make it to Avtovo Metro?"

His silence – a little too long. Then, "Half an hour?"

"I'll see you there, Professor."

I was reaching for my coat even before the receiver was down. "Olga!" I sang out, voice echoing round the hard, empty corridors of the Cronus Club. "Do you keep a gun anywhere on the premises?"


I had never fully understood the hypocrisy of the Soviet metro systems, for it seemed that the world above and the world below ground were from different universes, let alone different times. The Leningrad Metro had been open less than a year, extensions already planned, and the stations on its one gleaming line were palaces of crystal decadence. Twisting columns and mosaics which, at their best, were triumphs of modern art and, at their worst, gaudy declarations of vanity and ego, lined the tiled platforms like palace viewing galleries. It was a system where the clock didn't count down to the next train, but up from the last, daring the passenger to believe that, in this perfect world, you would never have to wait more than three minutes for anything.

It was also, in terms of any pursuers who might be out there, something of an unknown factor. The system presented problems to local agents in that, in the few months since it had been open, it seemed unlikely they would have developed a method of operating in it, and crowds have always been a friend to anonymity. So, for that matter, has Russia's need for large warm hats and bulky clothes worn tight against the winter. Short of a society where religion obligated modesty, a Russian winter could do wonders for thwarting facial recognition.

I arrived early, and so did they. They were easy to recognise, men in dark coats who didn't board the train when it came. They were uncomfortable, shifty spots of gloom beneath the brilliant bright walls, aware that when it came to discretion they weren't handling themselves particularly well. One was trying to read a copy of *Pravda*, the other stared at the one-line Metro map with the intensity of a snake trying to work out if it could swallow a goat. On my second pass through the station I also detected the woman, who was doing far better. She'd brought a baby in a pram, a prop the merits of which I was divided on, and her air of dedication towards the infant put the distracted quality of the other two watchers to shame. I caught the train out of Avtovo, rode it a couple of stops, then caught the opposite direction back. I repeated this pattern twice, overshooting Avtovo the first time, looking for the professor. When he turned up, he was the most nervous of them all. Standing awkwardly by a wall, shifting from one foot to the other, he looked as if he wanted to pace but wasn't sure if pacing was appropriate. He held a book under one arm, cover out. It was *The Physical Principles of the Quantum Theory* by W. Heisenberg. Thinking about it retrospectively, I can't help but wonder if the book was an attempt by the professor to warn me that he was being observed. It was certainly a curious choice of reading matter being so prominently displayed, and perhaps he hoped the incongruity, as much as anything else, would alert me to something being amiss. Whatever the case, the fact remained that the professor was under observation but probably had the knowledge I needed. As I rode through Avtovo and beyond, I considered my next move. Attempting to acquire information from him now would be dangerous to say the least; but then, if I failed to make the meeting, there was every possibility that he would be whisked away and my best chance at finding Karpenko gone. It isn't always easy for ouroborans to make bold decisions, spoilt as we are by the luxury of time, but this seemed too good an opportunity to miss, and the consequence of not acting on it too dangerous. I headed back to Avtovo station, and as the train began to pull into the platform, pulled my hat down over my eyes and shouted, "Stop, thief!"

There was no thief to stop, but speed in a crowd can often compensate for this particular problem. I barrelled through the shoulders of the people on the train, elbowing them aside with no regard for age or disposition, until, as the train slowed to a halt and the people turned to stare, I raised my head and shouted, "He's got a gun!" To make my point, I drew my own and fired it once into the wall of the carriage. The doors opened, and the stampede began.

There were certain disadvantages to my technique, not least being that the point of origin of the surge of people was a clear indicator of where I was. However, this was to a degree countered by the chaos that reigned on the platform and by the herd mentality of the people around as they perceived the carriage emptying, heard the cry of "A gun, a gun!" and made their own, potentially unwise, decisions. I like to think I contributed in my own way to the chaos, stumbling into the crowd with my head down and giving an occasional cry of "Oh God, help us" or words to that effect. The finer details of what I said were hardly inspiring, but in that heightened state no one really cared. I was pushed, shoved and stumbled upon, my fellow travellers knocking me aside as thoughtlessly as I had ruined their day, and I went with them, the surge of the crowd sweeping me past the bewildered-looking professor, who pressed himself into the wall for refuge, only to give a surprised whimper as, stumbling through the crowd, I grabbed him by the arm and pulled him after me.

All stations have bottlenecks, and while the crowd wished to run, there wasn't the space to do it, so as we pressed and piled for the exit I pushed my body close to Gulakov, pushed my gun into his belly and hissed, "I know they're here. Tell me where I can find Karpenko."

"I'm sorry," he whimpered. "I'm sorry!"

"Karpenko!"

"Pietrok-112! He's in Pietrok-112!"

I let go of his arm and plunged back into the flow of people. There didn't seem much point saying anything more. The three watchers on the platform were shouting, moving among us, pulling hats from faces, hollering at commuters to stop, to stay calm. I could see the woman had now a gun in her hand, the pram abandoned, and was shouting at everyone to stand still and present their papers. At the top of the stairs to the outside world more voices were being raised, police, some in uniform, some not, pouring down towards the human weight that wished to go up. However good their security services, the transport system hadn't yet got the message. I heard the rattle of wheels on metal and as the first watcher came near me, a long-faced man in a fur-lined coat, I turned, face an open picture of panic, wailed, "He's got a gun! Oh my God!" and nutted him as hard as I could in the nose, grabbing the gun in his hand and twisting his wrist hard towards the ceiling. I heard a shot, felt the bite of the metal moving beneath my fingers, and someone next to me screamed, a woman, clutching her leg, before I twisted the pistol free and kicked the watcher squarely between the legs. He fell inelegantly to the floor, and as the crowd parted around us like a flower I turned towards the approaching train, slipped the gun into my pocket and ran for the opening doors.

I had never been a fugitive in Russia before.

The feeling was exhilarating at first, until the discomfort of the settling night and the damp cold eating through my boots reminded me that exhilaration held nothing over reliable hygiene and warm sheets. My Kostya Prekovsky papers were now an even greater liability to me than no papers at all – no papers would at least cause bureaucratic delay, whereas the Prekovsky name was instant, guaranteed incarceration or death. I threw them into the slow black waters of the canal, bought a new hat and coat, and in a second-hand bookshop beneath the glowing lights of a doctor's surgery flicked through an atlas of the Soviet Union, looking for Pietrok-112. I couldn't see it. I considered going to the Cronus

Club, but the grief that I would bring upon Olga and her ilk seemed uncivilised in light of her hospitality, and I wasn't entirely sure whether it was the professor's enquiries alone which had led to the appearance of security forces at Avtovo. Instead, I found Pietrok-111 and Pietrok-113 in the atlas, two tiny markers on an empty stretch of nowhere in the north of the country, and considering this as likely a place to start as anywhere, waited until the last tram had slipped into silence, and headed to Finland Station to recover my escape papers. I had left two sets of documents in an empty signal box by the railway tracks, where a man, hopefully in a fur hat, had once spent his days switching points, and where now mice hid from the worst of the winter's cold. The first document declared that I was one Mikhail Kamin, party member and industrial adviser, a position high enough to accord me respect without necessarily inviting security checks. The second was a Finnish passport, stamped already with an entry visa, which I attached to the back of my calf with surgical tape and rubber bands. I then spent a chilly night in the signal box, listening to the mice scurrying below, around and, in one particularly adventurous case, over me, and waiting for sunrise and the journey north.

# Chapter 37

I have spoken before of my rather feeble attempt to kill Richard Lisle, some five lives before I took the train from Leningrad towards a situation which, even then, I felt could only end in blood. Lisle had killed Rosemary Dawsett and he had killed me. I suspected, though of course my death had prevented me from pursuing the investigation, that after my demise he had killed many more and never been caught.

He had killed me in my eighth life, and in my ninth I pursued him. Not the hot pursuit of a righteous avenger, nor the sly chase of a spy waiting to be caught. I had just over thirty years in which to consider my attitude towards him, thirty years in which hatred could cool to practical, business-like assassination.

"I understand why, but I'm not sure I can condone."

Akinleye. Born some time in the mid-1920s, at her oldest she had lived to see planes fly into the World Trade Center. "I remember thinking," she would say, "how frustrating it was that I wouldn't live long enough to see what happened next." But she interrogated the kalachakra of the Club, the younger members, those born in the 1980s and 1990s, who shook their heads sadly and said, "You're not missing anything." Akinleye's father was a

Nigerian teacher, her mother a Ghanaian secretary "who ran the hospital she worked at and everyone knew it, but she was a woman in the 1920s so they called her a secretary anyway". Unlike most of our kin, she didn't require rescuing from her childhood. "My parents give me an unconditional love which I have yet to meet from any adult," she explained. We were lovers whenever our paths crossed, except once when she was giving homosexuality a go, "To see if it's me?" and once when she was married. Her husband was Sudanese – tall, thin, he towered over the room without ever dominating it and was linear and mortal and wildly in love.

"I'm thinking of telling him the truth," she confided one day. I told her about Jenny, the woman I'd loved, and how that had ended, and she tutted and said, "Maybe not then."

From what I heard later, their relationship was long, happy and deceitful until the day he died.

"This man you want to kill," she said, "has he murdered?"

"Yes," I replied firmly. "Not in this life, but in the last."

"But within the course of *his* living memory, not yours – has he murdered?"

"No," I admitted. "Not as far as I know."

We had met in 1948 in Cuba. She was just blooming into her twenties and spending this life, whatever number it was, doing what she had done for every life I'd ever known her – travelling, shopping, wining, dining and having emotionally fraught liaisons with unsuitable men. She had a yacht, and the locals stared as this young Nigerian woman with her flawless English and her perfect Spanish drifted down the quay towards a white beast of a thing, a shark padded in leather and plated with chrome, which she pushed towards any tropical storms with a merry cry of "Give me rain!" I had agreed to stay with her on the open seas for a couple of nights, on the understanding that this was not yet the hurricane season and I had things to do.

"What things?" she demanded petulantly.

"I'm joining the British secret service," I replied, ticking the points off on my fingers; "I want to meet Elvis before he dies; and I need to kill a man called Richard Lisle."

"Why are you joining the spies?"

"Curiosity. I wish to see if there are any truths behind the conspiracy theories I keep reading about during my old age."

Not many women can drink rum disapprovingly, but Akinleye could. "I don't understand you, Harry," she said at last. "I don't understand what drives you. You have wealth, time and the world at your feet, but all you do is push, push and keep on pushing at things which really don't bother you. So what if Lisle killed a few people? He dies, doesn't he? He always dies and never remembers. Why is it your business? Is it revenge?"

"No. Not really."

"You can't expect me to believe you'd go to all this trouble for a few linear prostitutes?"

"I think I can," I replied carefully. "I'm afraid I must."

"But prostitutes are murdered all the time! Report Ted Bundy, track down Manson, find the Zodiac – why do you have to waste your time on this one man? Jesus, Harry, is this your idea of making a difference?"

"I can't make a difference, can I?" I sighed. "There's no tampering with major established events. Ted Bundy will kill; the Zodiac will terrorise California. These things have been and, by the creed of the Cronus Club, must be again."

"Then why get involved? For Christ's sake, just sit back and enjoy yourself."

I craned my head back further to see the light of the stars coming out overhead. "In a little over twenty years man will walk on the moon. Hundreds of thousands will die in Vietnam for no apparently sensible reason, dissidents will be shot, men will be tortured, women will weep and children will die. We know all of this and we do ... nothing. I'm not suggesting we change the world. I'm not suggesting we know how. What will the future be if these things do not come to pass? But we must do ... something."

She tutted.

I found the gesture strangely annoying, an absent little sound on a peaceful night. I turned away, craning my head back further to see deeper into the sky, picking out the constellations. In truth, my

162

own words rang hollow in my ears. I spoke fine sentiments about participation in the world around us, and yet what was my participation to be? The murder of a man who had not, yet, in his life committed murder.

"Linears only have one life," she said at last, "and they don't bother to change anything. It's just not convenient. Some do. Some … 'great' men, or angry men, or men that have been beaten so low that all they have left to do is fight back and change the world. But, Harry, if there is one feature most common to 'great' men, it's that they're nearly always alone."

"It's all right," I said. "I'm not a great man."

"No," she replied. "I guess that just makes you a murderer."

Afterwards I walked along the waterfront alone, as the sea rolled against black rocks and white sand, and Akinleye sailed on to the next party, the next drink, the next adventure.

"Only one thing surprises me any more," she explained, "and that's the things people admit when they're pissed."

I'd almost sighed. The things people confessed, the deepest secrets of their souls, had long since ceased to amaze me.

This I knew for certain: Richard Lisle would kill.

Was I going to wait for the event?

I went to London. Rosemary Dawsett had operated in Battersea, and so to Battersea I went, back into the old smoke-filled haunts hemmed in by smoke-drenched streets. My joining the secret service was as much about their training and the intellectual challenge as any real desire to learn their tales. I put their skills to use now, learned to be grey, a non-event at the back of the room. I observed Rosemary picking up her clients with the delicacy of a torpedo in an oil tanker and felt an odd pull in the pit of my stomach, remembering what had been between us before. Money, I knew, had been between us before, but in loneliness it can become easy to romanticise these things. I hunted out Richard Lisle and watched him watching. He was still several years away from his first murder, a young man with, perhaps, an uncomfortable manner about him, but nothing which suggested to the casual eye what he would become.

He was even vaguely pleasant. He slept with the prostitutes and paid them reliably, had a reputation as a decent lad albeit a slightly odd one. His work colleagues were friendly acquaintances without being friends, and on breaking into his flat in Clapham and examining its contents, I found no black pictures of death, instruments of pain, signs of torture or organic remains. The most unpleasant thing about his flat was the lingering after-smell of corned beef and onion. His radio was tuned to the BBC Home Service, and what few magazines and books he had seemed largely themed around the joys of country living. I could easily picture him, a retired man of sixty-something, walking through gentle countryside in sensible boots, a dog bounding along merrily at his side, before calling in at the local pub, where everyone could call him Rich or Dick or Dicky, and the landlord would always be sure to pour him a proper pint. I see this so easily, almost as easily as I could see the knife in his hand cut through the smog before it sliced into my body.

Yet he had not done this yet.

Could even Richard Lisle be saved?

The voice of Vincent, my sometime student, as we sat together in my study in Cambridge, drinking whisky.

"The question you must ask yourself is this: will the good you do the other man by helping him overcome his problem – whatever that may be – gout, let's say – will the help you do to the other man in overcoming his gout *exceed* the harm, exhaustion and general sense of distaste that you incur to yourself in helping him? I know it doesn't sound very noble, Harry, but then neither does damaging yourself for the sakes of others, as you will then require fixing, and others will be damaged in the attempt, and so it goes on and on and on, and frankly everyone ends up a worse mess than they were to begin with." A pause while he considered his own world view, before adding, "Besides, gout? Are you really going to help someone get through gout?"

Two weeks later I followed Richard Lisle to the home of Rosemary Dawsett. He stayed for an hour and emerged somewhat less groomed and rather content. She stood in the door and smiled at him as he departed into the dark, and the next day I bought a gun.

# Chapter 38

I'd never killed in cold blood before.

Sitting in Richard Lisle's apartment on a winter's night in 1948 when the ice was beginning to scratch its teeth across the inside of the window, waiting for him to come home, I knew that I would be perfectly capable of pulling the trigger. My anxiety, therefore, was not so much as to whether I could commit the deed, but as to how confident I was of this fact. It is not so far from such a state of mind to absolute sociopath, I reflected. Would it be appropriate to wail? To sob? To bite my lip, to acquire perhaps a nervous twitch? I hoped that my body, if not my mind, would at least have the good grace to demonstrate some psychosomatic disorder, some unconscious manifestation of guilt at the deed I was about to commit. I spent the long waiting hours sitting in the silence and the dark, reproaching myself for my lack of self-reproach. A self-defeating exercise, but even when the logical absurdity of my own thought processes became apparent to me, I was rather annoyed that even this slim manifestation of conscience was so intellectual. I would have far preferred crying into my pillow at night over this calm analysis of my own moral degeneration.

I broke into Richard Lisle's apartment at 9.12 p.m.

He did not come home until 1.17 a.m.

This wasn't particularly uncharacteristic, but nine o'clock had been the optimum time between neighbours settling down and my entry causing an unnecessary disturbance. I kept the light off to avoid questions and waited, gun in my lap, silently in the chair in the living room, which was also the bedroom and, partitioned by a low work surface only, the kitchen too.

He was tipsy without being drunk when he came in.

The sight of me, black leather gloves and small silenced pistol, brought an instant return of struggling sobriety. Rationality, if not intellect, can still overwhelm alcohol when death is on the line.

I should have shot him right then, but the sight of him standing in the door, keys still dangling from their ring, which was threaded over his index finger, a brown woollen vest pulled over his green woollen jumper and face smeared grey from the smog, froze me as well as him. I had no desire to speak to him – nothing I could possibly say – but as I reached for the trigger he blurted, "I don't have much for you to take, but anything you want is yours."

I hesitated, then raised the gun.

"You don't want to do this." His voice was a bare whisper, his words really rather banal as I was already resolved that this was precisely what I wanted to do, and even if I did not, this was now something that needed to be done. "Please." He dropped to his knees, the tears already flowing down his face. "I never done nothing wrong."

I thought about it.

Then pulled the trigger.

# Chapter 39

I like Russian trains.

Not for comfort, of which there is none, nor speed, of which there is barely any to be spoken about, particularly when you relate it to the size of the country that must be crossed. Not even, particularly, for the view, which is inevitably repetitive, as Mother Nature decrees that her works of wonder can only occur so frequently across such a vast and cultivated space.

I like Russian trains, or at least those I travelled on in the early spring of 1956, so many centuries after I gunned Lisle down in cold blood; I like the trains for the sense of unity that all these hardships create in its passengers. I suspect the experience is relative. Take a long, cold, uncomfortable, tedious journey in a carriage with just one difficult, dangerous or mad individual, and it seems plausible that the entire carriage will be dull and silent, for its own protection as much as anything else. But take that same journey in the company of cheerful companions, and you can find the time passes far more quickly.

My companions as I headed north-east from Leningrad under the cover of my new papers were nothing if not cheerful.

"Where I come from is shit," explained Petyr, a seventeen-year-old boy desperately excited by the prospect of working eleven hours a day in a foundry. "All the people are shit, all the land is shit, and shit doesn't even make the land less shit. But where I'm going – there I'm going to be something, I'm going to do something, and I'm going to meet a girl who wants to be with me and we're going to have babies, and our children, they're not going to have to know the shit that I have."

"Petyr is very keen," explained Viktoria, a quieter nineteen-year-old looking forward to studying agricultural policy. "My parents will be so proud. My mother, she can't even read or write!"

The rattle of a small wooden box announced the advent of Tanya's domino set, and as we huddled away from the mist-stained little windows and deeper into the moist interior of each other and the carriage, counters were laid and hopes dashed with the strategic planning and emotional commitment of Napoleon concocting a long campaign. I have no illusions about my companions – their enthusiasm was naïve, their hopes rash and their ignorance as to the outside world bordered on the intimidating. I could picture Viktoria fifty years from now, lamenting the loss of those Good Old Communist days, much as Olga now lamented the departure of the tsar; and Petyr, when tested, slammed his fist against his thigh and proclaimed, "We didn't win the war because of all those bastards who disagreed with Stalin!" Is there innocence in ignorance? And if there is, do we tolerate others for their innocence's sake? Sitting inside that train as the steam of our breath crawled up the walls and the carriage jumped over every join in the track like a young gazelle, I found I had no satisfactory answer to this question.

After seven hours of dominoes, even my companions were silent, dozing upright against each other's shoulders and necks. I sat squashed between a shoemaker and a soldier returning home and considered my next step. I was looking for Pietrok-112, and it seemed likely that whoever was trying to prevent me from finding it would be able to predict my movements. Given this, entering undetected could well prove a problem, even with new papers, and the sensible course of action would be to retreat and try another day.

Therein lay the concern: which other day would I try, and what if the trail I was following had run dry by the time I returned? How long did I dare leave this matter resting, and was I prepared to let it go? I was a hunted fugitive, a stranger in a strange land, and I had been neither for more than a hundred years. The discomfort of my predicament was apparent in my grumbling stomach and the ache in my perpetually turning neck, but I had papers, a gun and money, and the exhilaration of my situation had sent adrenaline pumping through my veins like never before. I resolved to press on, knowing that the rational justification for this act was flimsy, and choosing not to care.

There were guards waiting at the end of the line. Local boys who'd received a telephone call, average age twenty-three, average rank private. It seemed likely they had a description but no picture. I lifted a near-empty bottle of vodka from the open bag of one of my travelling companions, swilled some round my mouth, rubbed more into my neck and hands like a perfume, rubbed my eyes until they watered, and joined the queue coming off the train. The sun was setting already, an angry small ball of light on the grey horizon, dull enough to stare at. The platform was slathered in thin black mud, snow-crusted in the shade, sodden in the dwindling light.

"Name!"

"Mikhail Kamin," I slurred, huffing heavy breath into their faces. "Is my cousin here yet?"

The guard examined my papers – perfect – and my face – less so. "Remove your hat!"

I removed my hat. It's easy to overplay alcoholic stupor; my personal preference is to merely highlight those characteristics which you might be manifesting anyway, in this case subservience. I twisted the ear flaps of my hat between my fingers, chewed my bottom lip and peered up at the guard from beneath the furrow of my eyebrows, neck curled in and shoulders hunched like a wading bird.

"What is the purpose of your journey?"

"My cousin," I mumbled. "Bastard's dying."

"Who is your cousin?"

"Nikolai. He's got this really big house. You should do something about him because he's always had this really big house and I asked if I could stay some time but he said no."

I treated the guard to another fragrant blast of breath and saw him flinch. He passed back the papers, nose crinkling in disgust. "Get away," he grunted. "Sober up!"

"Thank you, comrade, thank you," I intoned, bowing my way from his presence like a mandarin from a Manchu emperor. I slipped and stumbled my way out into the muddy street, splattering black stains of slime up my trousers as I went.

The town, if we could call it that, went by the name of Ploskye Prydy, and as I walked down its one still street I half expected to find that the fronts of the wooden shacks sinking slowly into the mud were exactly that – fronts with no backing, a Soviet answer to the cowboy movies, from one of which, any second now, a wildly screaming Cossack would come bursting, pursued by an angry peasant maid with a cry of "God damn you! God damn you to hell!" No such adventure struck. It seemed little more than a place where the railway stopped, a transit town built to service the journeys of people heading to other destinations. The roads were defined merely by the place where the mud was most pressed down; the one store had a sign in the porch which declared, NO EGGS, and the old veteran on his crutches in the door, an obligatory feature of all good cowboy movies, droned the same two lines of the same forgotten song like a tape stuck in a loop. Nevertheless, in its own small way Ploskye Prydy stood as the gateway between civilisation and the land beyond, a ploughed expanse of black mud and drooping trees as far as the eye could see. The only structure of any note was a large brick building on the side of the tracks, where the air simmered and the chimneys choked blackness into the sky: a brick maker's kiln, providing material for the newer developments further north with translated names as glamorous as Institute-75 or Commune-32, a place for all the family.

I bribed my way on to the back of the brick maker's truck, heading north, towards Pietrok-111, and spent three black but warm hours sitting between still-cooling bricks, which slid and rattled uncontrollably from side to side as we bounced along the one arrow-straight road to the north. Once the worst of the brick falls had happened, and I was relatively secure in a den of tumbled building blocks, it was almost possible to doze, cocooned in the warmth of the cooling slabs, until with a shudder the truck came to a stop and the back was pulled down with a cheery cry of "Pietrok-111. Hope you enjoyed the ride!"

I climbed out blearily from the back as the brick maker and his assistant began throwing the bricks into a mish-mashed pile on the side of the road, like a newspaper boy hurling his daily delivery at the door of a rude neighbour, chatting away brightly as they did so. I blinked against the dim lights of the town, making out apartment blocks, one general store and, towering over it all, a refinery whose flares of burning gas were the only signs of colour in the dead-black night. The stars overhead were tiny numerous waters, frozen in a cloudless sky. I found Polaris, turning my face further north, and asked of my companions, "How far is it to Pietrok-112?"

They laughed. "Another two hours' drive, but you don't want to go there! It's all soldiers and scientists there, comrade."

I thanked them profusely and headed into what I suppose we should call the vibrant throbbing heart of the town.

It seemed unwise to seek out lodging. There was no reason to believe that the authorities weren't yet pursuing me. The night was too cold to sleep outside, those pools of water which had by day melted in the darkness now turning to treacherous slabs of black ice. I wandered through the unlit streets, feeling my way by the walls, the fires of the refinery and the cold silver of the stars, until at length I stumbled on the town bar. It wasn't advertised as such, and made no invitation to strangers, but it was that universal place that springs up in all towns where there is nothing to do – perhaps once it had been a private home which had simply forgotten to close its door to strangers, and was now transformed into a small warm den with a stove set in the centre of the room, where men could sit in silence, focused on the entirely serious business of drinking themselves blind on moonshine. My presence aroused the odd stare but no comment as I slipped down by the stove and offered the two-toothed woman in charge a few roubles for a glass of alcohol only a few steps above antifreeze and a bowl of rice and beans.

"I'm going to see my cousin," I explained. "He's dying. Do you know anyone who can take me to Pietrok-112?"

"Tomorrow, tomorrow," mumbled the crone, and that, it seemed, was all that there was to say.

# Chapter 40

I had slept, despite myself, and when I was shaken awake, my hand went instantly to my pocket, feeling for the gun, imagining guards, soldiers, retribution. Instead a bright-eyed man with an almost spherical face and a grin that twitched the ends of his tiny ears with its enthusiasm stood over me. "You wanted to go to Pietrok-112, comrade? I'll take you!"

His price was extortionate; his means of transport an ex-*Wehrmacht* staff car. It takes a great deal to surprise me, but I stared at this thing in astonishment. The metal around the doors and fender was rusted to a crinkled orange, the seats a tangled mess of springs and stuffing, re-upholstered with the remnants of old blankets, but the Nazi emblem was still clearly visible on the front and sides, and as I gaped the young man beamed with pride and exclaimed, "My father killed two colonels and a major, and didn't even damage the paintwork while doing it!" He stood by the car, illustrating the momentous deed. "Bham! Bham, bham! Soft-nosed revolver bullets, that's what it took. Three shots, three corpses. My dad was blown up by a tank in Poland, but he left us the car. You want a ride?"

As vehicles went, it wasn't the most discreet I could imagine, but it was operational and heading where I needed to go.

"Thank you," I mumbled. "It'll be something new."

On the journey to Pietrok-112 I sat in silence, huddled against the tearing wind, and considered my next move. I had come this far, as much for curiosity as any coherent plan of what I'd do when I got there. It was clear that the authorities would be on the alert for me, and I had neither the equipment for a discreet entry nor, I suspected, the luck left in me to deceive my way inside. The question was therefore increasingly becoming, was I prepared to die for my answer? Death in some form seemed likely, considering my circumstances, and I'd far rather a quick and easy death than a prolonged bout of questioning in the Lubyanka. It felt like an insufferable waste of time to die so young in this life, with all the tedium it entailed, and I was absolutely determined that I would not die prior to acquiring as much information as I could about Vitali Karpenko and Pietrok-112. A suicide mission then? Was that what this was going to become? I was prepared to go through with it as long as the information acquired appeared to outweigh the boredom death induced. I considered my situation and knew that emotionally I was already committed, even if intellectually the rationale was flimsy. It was an adventure, a dangerous, reckless, unwise adventure, and I had had so few of these in my time.

If Pietrok-111 was a one-horse town, Pietrok-112 was the glue factory where that horse went to die. A chain fence circled a low mess of cabins and rectangular concrete slabs, windowless, nameless, soulless. The road ran straight to a gate, where a sign proclaimed, PIETROK-112 – PASSES MUST BE SHOWN. Two guards in militia uniform were huddled in a small white shed by the gate, listening to the radio. One of them scurried out as we approached, hailing us to stop. He seemed to recognise my driver, giving him a warm pat on the shoulder, but as he approached me, his expression hardened. His fingers tightened on the rifle strap slung across his back, and there was more than just routine caution in his voice as he barked, "Comrade! Your papers!"

Having embarked on a suicide mission, I decided to follow it through with aplomb. I got out of the car, marched straight up to the soldier and replied, "That's comrade Captain, and you are?"

He stood to attention, looking as surprised as I was that this reaction, drilled into him during his training, had become such a physical instinct. The trick with a truly successful intimidation is not to rely on volume or obscenity, but to cultivate that quiet certainty which informs any listener that your people will do the shouting for you, should the moment come. "Where's your commander?" I added. "He is expecting me."

"Yes, comrade Captain," he barked out, "but I need to see your papers, comrade Captain."

"I am Mikhail Kamin, internal security."

"I need to see your pa— "

"No, you don't," I replied softly. "You need to see the papers of farmers delivering grain, of commissars carrying last week's mail, of petty officers who went on the piss last night. You need to see the papers of people who don't have the big picture. What you do not need to see, my son," translating the full meaning of "my son" from cockney gangster into Soviet paranoia is not as simple a linguistic adaptation as you might expect, "are the papers of a man who isn't here. Because I'm not fucking here. Because if I was fucking here, you'd have one hell of a fucking problem, you see?"

The boy was almost shaking with the two conflicting terrors inside him – terror of the known retribution which would strike for disobedience of his superiors, terror of the unknown which would come from disobedience of me. I decided to sway the matter for him.

"I'm glad you're doing your duty, son," I added, resisting the urge to clasp him by the shoulder with a too-hard grip, "but your duty is, if you don't mind me saying so, so far beneath the big picture right now that even thinking about it is giving me a squint. So why don't you walk me to your commander like a good soldier and keep an eye on me, and I won't have to stand around here freezing my fucking balls off in this fucking waste of a fucking place while the shit hits the fan. What do you say, lad?"

Translating the connotations of "lad", as deployed in its most patronising form by red-faced landowners of an uncertain social class, was if anything an even more engaging linguistic challenge than "my son". Sometimes, brute will is the way to deal with a problem, particularly when that problem has been trained from birth to respect the bullies who run the state. The guard knew that there was a security alert – of course he did, his voice as much as any other circumstance had told me as much – and was it therefore such a surprise that someone from the internal security services had turned up at his door to speak to the commander? Certainly no foreign agent would ask as much. Perhaps it wasn't so implausible. Perhaps thinking was above his grade.

"Please come with me, comrade Captain!"

He even saluted as he let me into the compound.

# Chapter 41

I once spent time working in a settlement in Israel which reminded me somewhat of Pietrok-112. I was going through a pastoral phase, having spent a good hundred and twenty years indulging in wine, women and song. Ironically enough, it was Akinleye, the queen of a good time, who inspired me to move to the Promised Land, where I would, so my reasoning went, rediscover man's purer nature through hard work and agrarian toil. She, who had derided my ambition to kill Richard Lisle, was living at the time in Hong Kong. The year was 1971. I was fifty-two years old and wondering whether heroin addiction was such a bad way to go.

"Don't you see how lucky you are?" she asked, lying on a recliner beneath the stars as the needles were prepared by her silent-footed maid. "You can do things to your body that no one else would dare. You can die of happiness and come back to die again!"

"Are they clean?" I asked, observing the needles carefully on their small silver tray.

"Jesus, Harry, what does it matter? Yes, they're clean. I get them straight off this guy Hong, a triad boy."

"How'd you meet a triad boy?"

She shrugged. "They run all the good-time houses in this place. You got money and a sense of fun in this town, you meet people, you know? Here." She slipped off the recliner and, giggling a little at her own good nature, rolled up my sleeve for me. As I get older, the veins on my arm become bluer, or perhaps the skin whiter, and she chuckled to see the blood bulge in the crook of my arm as she pulled the tourniquet tight. The concern in my face must have showed as she picked up the first needle of amber fluid, because she grinned and slapped my skin playfully. "Harry! You're not going to tell me that you've never done this before?"

"By the time I had the cash and the time," I replied firmly, "I'd also had several lifetimes of exposure to the notion that it was a bad thing."

"You mustn't let yourself be influenced by what the linears say," she chided. "We're not like them."

She was good with a needle – I hardly felt it go in.

Euphoria is, I believe, the term they use to describe the sensation, and upon experience I found it to be an entirely useless definition, as it relies on comparatives that are not apt to the situation. A happiness beyond compare, a contentment beyond understanding, a bliss, a travelling, a freeing of the mind from the flesh – these are all, in their ways, an appropriate description of the process, but they mean nothing, for no recollection can re-create them and no substitute mimic them. So, having known what euphoria is, it remains precisely that – a word with longing attached, but no meaning when actually experiencing the thing. My arms and legs were heavy, my mouth was dry, and I did not care, for my mouth was not mine. I knew that I was still and time was moving, and wondered how it had taken me so long to comprehend that this was the nature of time itself, and wished I had a notebook to hand so I could jot down these thoughts – these profound, beautiful thoughts I had never thought before, which would, I felt certain, revolutionise the way mankind worked. I watched Akinleye inject herself, and inject the maid, who lay with her head in Akinleye's lap, a dutiful kitten as the drug did its work,

178

and I wanted to explain to them that I'd had the most extraordinary idea about the nature of reality, seen the most incredible truth, if only I could make others understand it!

Opiates suppress sexual desire, but I knew that Akinleye kissed me. We were not young lovers any more, but then it didn't matter, for our love was a thing which, like euphoria, could not be explained to those who did not experience it. I knew that the maid was dancing, and so Akinleye and I danced too, and then the maid danced down the length of the deck, whirling and spinning, until she reached the prow of the ship. We followed, my legs too heavy to move by themselves, so I dragged myself along the floor with my arms, face down on my belly, craning my neck to see Akinleye put her lips to the maid's neck and whisper the secrets of the universe into her ears. Then the maid laughed some more, stood up on the railing that ran round the edge of the ship, spread her arms wide and let her own weight take her down, face first into the water.

Her corpse washed up two days later on the beach.

The coroner's ruling was suicide.

She was buried in an unmarked grave, no family to mourn her. Akinleye had left the port without telling me her servant's name. Three hours after the coffin was covered, I went to Israel, signing on as a worker in a settlement beneath the turbulent ranges of the Golan Heights. I was not Jewish and had no political affection for the state, but a farmer had offered me the chance to pick oranges for him over the summer, and I had nowhere better to go. For seven months I woke at dawn and worked with a basket on my back, ate flat bread at supper and read no words, watched no TV, heard no radio and spoke to no one beyond the settlement walls. I was housed with thirteen other workers in a wooden shack of low bunk beds, and when I failed to do a satisfactory job accepted the chiding of the farmer like a little boy. The family whispered that I was mentally damaged in some way, unable to understand why this white-haired Englishman would have travelled to the sun-drenched hills of a foreign land to crawl in dust and dirt for his days. Sometimes the boys from the local villages would come and stare, and none of us went outside the settlement alone for fear of being attacked by the families whose land the settlement had taken. In time, none of us left the settlement at all, but hid behind the high white-stone walls from a hostile society only a bullet away from retribution.

I worked until the day the farmer's wife sat down beside me and said,

"I think you need to let it go."

She was a large woman, a black wig on her head, a black apron around her belly.

"This thing you carry inside you," she said at last. "I don't know what it is. I don't know where you got it. But Harry," and her hand slipped round the inside of my thigh as she spoke, "the past is the past. You are alive today. That is all that matters. You must remember, because it is who you are, but as it is who you are, you must never, ever regret. To regret your past is to regret your soul."

Her hand wandered up my leg. I caught it by the wrist before it could finish its journey and laid it carefully down in her lap. She sighed, turning her head slightly away, her shoulders to the side. "It was only a second," she explained. "For a second my hand touched yours, but that second is gone, and cannot be seen, heard or felt ever again. This second is gone too, the moment in which I spoke by your side. It is dead. Let it die."

So saying, she stood up briskly, patted down her apron, the skirt around her buttocks and back, and went back to work.

I left in the night, leaving not a sign behind.

# Chapter 42

Fifteen years earlier, and a few centuries later, and Pietrok-112 reminded me of that farm in Israel. Silence in the night, long, low sheds of bunks for its workers, a fence to cut it off from the rest of the world – a hostile, frightening world of darkness and things that rattled in the night. Where the Golan Heights had stood above us as a monument to the god of another tribe, in Pietrok-112 the mountains were of unmarked concrete, temples to a new, rational deity of atoms and numbers.

I walked at the self-important speed of all managers visiting an insubordinate. There were more guards on duty by the first gate into that concrete canyon, which extended as far down into the earth as it did up. They looked at me with suspicion, but the deference of my escort gave me a certain credibility, and they asked no more.

Corridors of concrete beneath white strip lights; signs gave no more indication of which way to go than B1 or G2. Notices on the wall advised that radiation badges must be worn at all times, but it was no nuclear testing site. A poster showing the triad of scientist, soldier and happy industrial worker leading the way across golden fields, the sun glowing at their backs, reminded all passers-by of the bigger picture. Civilians were plentiful, mixed in among the guards. Lab coats were out, heavy quilted jackets were in, but the place was no industrial warehouse. Heavy shutters isolated the more sensitive areas, or access to them, with giant warnings proclaiming, NO UNAUTHORISED ACCESS.

The commander's office was a small raised room overlooking a delivery platform that led to the outside world. A black and white picture on the desk showed a man holding a very large machine gun, strings of bullets slung across his shoulders like a gangster's fashion prize. The radio was playing greatest communist hits of the 1940s, songs with refrains such as "We march through our brother's blood, raise our children to the sun" or "In the motherland we work for our loved ones and our comrades" and other poetic statements of intent. The commander himself was a man who'd been compressed to thinness – a protruding nose and squashed face sat on a matchstick frame that could only have been achieved through some horrific medical accident. His brown eyes flashed up from a bank of telephones as we entered, and at the sight of me he barked, "What is this?"

Having begun boldly, I decided to continue so, and reaching into my pocket for my papers, making a show of having a hard time finding them, I barked, "Mikhail Kamin, comrade, state security. My office rang."

"Never heard of you."

"Then you should get a better secretary," I barked, "because I've been travelling for eight fucking hours to get here and I'm damned if I'm going to waste another second on some bloody memo. Have you received the latest description?"

The commander's eyes flashed from me to the private. This was a man paid to think, a man who really should not have permitted anyone to talk to him with less than suitable rifle-point deference. I could see his mind heading in a direction I didn't want it to go, so slammed my fist hard on to the tabletop to drag it back and snapped, "For Christ's sake, man, do you think the mole is going to sit around waiting for you to sort the paperwork out? We need to move now before he receives the warning."

Tyranny can do marvellous things for a person's independent will. The commander's eyes flashed to sudden, focused attention. "A mole? I've heard nothing of this. Who are you again?"

I rolled my eyes with a little too much drama, turned to the private and barked, "You – out!"

He obeyed with the shuffle of a man not quite sure where his loyalty lies, mind going one way, legs taking him the other. I waited for the door to close, leaned forward on the table, looked the commander deep in the eye and said, "Get on the phone, and get me Karpenko."

Hesitation resolved itself into action.

"I don't know you," he repeated firmly. "You come in here, making these accusations . . . "

I pulled the gun from my pocket. The Mikhail Kamin papers came too, unprofessionally tangled up in the depths of my coat, but as they tumbled on to the table they only mildly undermined the emphasis of the moment. "Vitali Karpenko," I repeated softly. "Get on the phone and bring him here."

Heroism fought with pragmatism.

To my relief, pragmatism won. I really had no idea what I was going to do if it hadn't.

# Chapter 43

I will never fully understand the notion of a suicide mission. For us it is relatively simple, entailing only the considerable boredom of youth as its primary consequence. Certainly I regretted how likely it seemed that I was going to have to blow a hole in my own skull to escape the situation I had so effectively talked myself into, but by far the more intimidating prospect would have been capture and questioning, and I considered a few years' boredom to be infinitely preferable to that.

But I have seen men for whom death truly is the end walk towards their demise for reasons no greater than that it was what they were told to do. On the beaches of Normandy, where the bodies floated in the water beside the falling ramps of the landing craft, I saw men run into machine-gun fire who would say, "Hell, I never thought it would come to this, but now I'm here, what's a guy to do?" With no going back, and no going forward, they went to their deaths with no better plan immediately to hand, having gambled that their choices would not narrow so far, and having been found to be wrong.

For my part, it seemed likely that I would die in this place for little more than a speculation. For a crystal in a radio which was a few years ahead of its time; for the name of a man who saw the future; for a secret hidden by men with guns.

The commander was so good as to point all of this out to me. "You're going to die here," he explained as we sat in his office, waiting for Karpenko to come. "Make it easier for yourself."

I grinned. "Make it easier for yourself" implied that death was my primary concern, as well as being a phrase I associated with New York policemen rather than Soviet commanders in a hidden base. My levity surprised him, his thin grey eyebrows twitching over his paper face. "You're handling this very calmly," I pointed out, "for a man on the wrong end of a gun."

He shrugged. "I've had my time and lived it well. You, though – you are a young man. You will have things which tie you to this world. Are you married?"

"That's a very pious question," I answered. "Will it have the same emotional implication if I say that I enjoy living in sin?"

"What else do you enjoy? Perhaps you can enjoy them again."

"That's a really nice thought –" I sighed "– and I'm grateful for it, but there comes a point when one realises that gratification of the flesh is only so fulfilling. It's fantastic while it lasts, but comes with so many questions of emotional baggage and doubt that frankly I begin to question whether the grief involved outweighs the satisfaction gained."

To my surprise, he raised his eyebrows. "You clearly aren't having the right sort of gratification."

"A professional ear masseuse in Bangkok once said exactly those words to me."

"You're not Russian," he suggested.

"Is there something wrong with my accent?"

"No Russian would do this."

"That's a terrible indictment of the Soviet spirit."

"You misunderstand. You do not appear to be in a fragile enough state to have chosen this as your particular suicide, and yet neither do you seem to have an agenda which could further the cause of others. I see in you no clear explanation for what you do . . . "

185

"So why assume I'm foreign?"

He shrugged. "Call it instinct." That was a little distressing. Instinct was one of the few factors which I had no great ability to alter or control. "Comrade," he went on, "you seem too intelligent to be doing this for nothing. Is there really no other path open to you?"

"None which engages me so much," I replied. A knock at the door cut short any further soul-searching. I gestured at the commander to be silent behind his desk and, tucking the gun into my coat, slipped on to the one stool besides his desk.

A nod, and the commander called,

"Enter!"

The door opened. The man who came in was already in the middle of a sentence, which had clearly begun for him some several seconds before actually receiving permission to come inside.

" . . . very busy right now and really can't be—"

The sentence stopped.

The man looked from the commander to me, and his face broke into a smile. "Good God," he said, each word dropping like a pebble in a pond. "Fancy seeing you here."

# Chapter 44

Many lives ago, in that busy summer when Vincent Rankis and I first began to truly examine each other's minds, and before that cold night when he learned of the Cronus Club and left me with some light bruises and some heavy doubts for my pains, we went punting down the river Cam.

I have never liked punting, always feeling that, as means of transport went, it was one of the least sensible available and, more to the point, as it appeared to be practised in Cambridge, a skill as much valued in the incompetence as the mastery. A good trip on the river would not be complete for both students and some of my peers unless it involved hitting a bridge, causing a pile-up, running aground on a muddy bank, dropping the pole in fast-flowing waters and, ideally, at least one person falling in. I have similar feelings about gondolas in Venice, where the skill of the pilot is almost entirely cancelled out by the size of the fee and the sense that you are, in your own naïve way, contributing to a cliché that will in later years serve more gondoliers to defraud more tourists of their cash.

"That's your problem, Harry," Vincent had explained. "You've never understood the concept of doing things by halves."

I had grumbled my way to the riverbank, and grumbled my way on to the punt, and grumbled as we bumped our way between students, and grumbled as Vincent opened up his wicker basket, packed for the purpose, to produce flasks of gin with a dash of tonic, and perfectly cut cucumber sandwiches.

"The cucumber sandwiches," he'd explained, "are vital if we are to fulfil our roles."

"What are our roles?" I sulked.

"We are the living proof of the notion that rationality and intel-lectual vigour are slaves to social pressure and pleasant sunlight. For you and I may know, Harry," he exclaimed, sloshing the pole through the water with pointed enthusiasm, "that this is a truly ridiculous pastime for any self-respecting scholar of the universe to indulge in, and yet, for no rational reason that I can possibly devise, this is what *must* be done."

Our companions giggled.

I wasn't at all convinced by Vincent's choice of associates for this trip. I'd only met them at the riverbank, and their presence had further added to my sense of impending doom. She was Leticia, and she was Frances, but which was which I still couldn't quite put my finger on. They were dressed very properly in high-buttoned summer dresses and with their hair immaculately curled by their ears, but alas, from their propriety also came their frivolity, for they knew – of course they knew! – that taking a punt ride with two young bachelors in the summer sun was very much something Mother Would Not Approve Of, and any other thoughts they might have had on the course of our journey were rather sub-sumed by this all-encompassing revelation.

"Leticia's father is something in biochemistry," Vincent whis-pered in my ear, "and Frances has been claimed, apparently, by Hugh, who's a thoroughly repugnant creature but is playing tennis today down on the lawns. When we get there, Harry, I'm afraid it's either your or my ghastly duty to ensure that one of us kisses Frances on the lips, for Hugh to see; better not get the timing wrong, else we'll have to go through the entire procedure again until he notices."

I begged tutor's privilege, announcing it was bad enough to be seen to be on the river with students, let alone kissing one. Vincent sighed profoundly, and when we got to the lawns he did, indeed, as promised, contrive to drop the pole into the river and insist that myself and Leticia paddle against the current to collect it while he engaged in the loud and important business of temporarily seducing Frances. The calamity of our situation drew everyone's attention; the sight of the small, slightly round figure of Vincent entering into a sensual embrace with the spry Frances held it, and his work was done.

To my surprise, as I dried my freezing hands on my trousers and returned the pole to the safety of the punt, I realised I was laughing. Quite when the absurdity of the situation had begun to outweigh my resentment at its circumstances, I couldn't say, but no matter how hard I tried, I found it almost impossible to maintain a foul mood. Even the cucumber sandwiches, thin, tasteless and forlorn, entertained me for all of the above qualities. I had a worry that Leticia, feeling left out, expected me to do something sensual with her too, and my polite refusals to do so led to a rumour within the campus that I was, in fact, gay and enjoyed Vincent for his body, not his mind.

"Damn me, it's nice that someone does," said Vincent when the rumour reached his ears. "It's a lot of hard work, falling back on intellectual brilliance and emotional intelligence to seduce girls these days."

Should I have seen the clues?

Should I have spotted what Vincent was?

He was a novelty. He was unusual, ridiculous, brilliant, sombre and absurd. He was innovation in a stodgy town. When the day was done, and our companions had been returned to the stony embraces of their families, unsullied if not uncorrupted, we sat in my rooms, drinking the last of the gin – a nearly empty bottle being far sadder, in Vincent's mind, than a finished one – and discussed once again the perpetual subject of Vincent's final-year thesis.

"I don't know, Harry. None of it seems really ... important enough."

Not important enough? The turning of the stars in the heavens, the breaking of the atoms of existence, the bending of light in our sky, the rolling of electromagnetic waves through our very bodies . . .

"Yes yes yes." He flapped his hands. "That's all important! But ten thousand words of thesis is . . . well, it's nothing, is it? And then there's this assumption that I should focus on one thing alone, as if it's possible to comprehend the structure of the sun without truly understanding the nature of atomic behaviour!"

Here it was again, the familiar rant.

"We talk about a theory of everything," he spat, "as if it were a thing which will just be discovered overnight. As if a second Einstein will one day sit up in his bed and exclaim, 'Mein Gott! Ich habe es gesehen!' and that's it, the universe comprehended. I find it offensive, genuinely offensive, to think that the solution is going to be found in numbers, or in atoms, or in great galactic forces – as if our petty academia could truly comprehend on a single side of A4 the structure of the universe. X = Y, we seem to say; one day there will be a theory of everything and then we can stop. We'll have won – all things will be known. Codswallop."

"Codswallop?"

"Codswallop and barney," he agreed firmly, "to paraphrase Dr Johnson."

Perhaps, I suggested, the fate of the universe could briefly take second place to the thorny issue of graduating with honours?

He blew loudly between his lips, a liquid sound of contempt. "That," he exclaimed, "is precisely what's wrong with academics."

# Chapter 45

"Good God," he said. "Fancy seeing you here."

He was only a few years older since I'd seen him last, those centuries ago, still a fresh-faced young man barely clipping his early thirties. Somehow he'd managed to find a pair of grey suit trousers and well-kept brown leather shoes, polished up bright to wear. An oversized greenish tunic was more in keeping with his Soviet style, and a thin beard of fragile curls was an attempt to enhance his age, and he was Karpenko, and he was Vincent Rankis. He was followed almost immediately by two armed guards, rifles raised. They at once shouted at me to get down, to put my hands above my head, but he silenced them with a gesture.

"It's all right," said the man known as Karpenko. "Let me handle this."

Vincent Rankis, sometime student, as British as they came, his Russian flawless, his eyes full of recollection. The night he'd attacked me in Cambridge, he'd also vanished from his rooms. I'd used every resource in my power to track him down, but every name had led to an empty nothing, every enquiry ended in a failure. Vincent Rankis, I'd been forced to conclude, had, legally speaking, never existed. But then neither had I.

For a moment I couldn't speak, all the tactics and questions I'd had in mind briefly suspended at the sight of him. He took the opportunity to flash me a brilliant smile, before glancing at the commander and saying, "Comrade, may I have the room?"

The commander looked to me, and through lips turned to sand I mumbled, "Fine by me."

The commander rose carefully, walked to Vincent and paused, turning his head by the young man's side to murmur, quietly but audibly, "He has a gun."

"That's fine," replied Vincent. "I'll handle it."

With a nod, he dismissed the other soldiers and, moving around the commander's desk, settled himself down in the large chair with an easy confidence, folding his fingers together in front of his chin, elbow resting on his crossed-over knee.

"Hello, Harry," he said at last.

"Hello, Vincent."

"You here about our Daniel van Thiel, I assume?"

"He pointed the way."

"Self-important little man," said Vincent. "Had this incredibly annoying habit of telling everyone how brilliant they were, which was of course nothing more than a demand to be informed how brilliant he was himself. I'd hoped he'd help resolve some of the monitoring issues we've been having, but in the end I had to let him go. Little wart was bright enough to remember a few technical specifications, though. Should have killed him months ago. And your journey here – via Professor Gulakov? Did you like him?"

"Yes, very much."

"I'm afraid he's been sent away for re-education."

"I'm sorry to hear that. But then this is a very gun-heavy operation you seem to be running. Had to kill many to preserve it?"

He puffed impatiently. "You know how it is, Harry. Can't risk introducing too much new technology into the course of the linear timeline without being able to control the consequences. Risks drawing attention, rocking the boat – you're Cronus Club, you must know all about that. Speaking of which . . ."

he flicked a fingernail casually against the ridge of its neighbour, making a soft *thwap-thwap* noise " . . . should I be expecting the combined forces of the world's Clubs to descend on me any second now?"

"The Clubs know my suspicions, if that's what you're wondering, and are under orders to pursue the matter if I vanish."

He groaned, throwing his eyes up to heaven in exasperation. "That's incredibly tedious, Harry, actually. What people never realise about the Soviet Union is how much bureaucracy there is at the middling level. It's all very well if you're the general secretary – people know better than to take notes then – but for anyone further down than Politburo there's a huge amount of documentation that has to be accounted for whenever shutting down or moving these projects."

"Doesn't sound very secure," I admitted.

"Politics," he spat. "Everyone is always looking for material to use against everybody else – my point being, Harry, I could really do without the frustration of having to move bases again. Do you think the Club will find you, if you vanish?"

"Maybe," I replied with a shrug. "Is that the situation we're looking at here? Am I going to vanish?"

"I don't know, Harry," he murmured thoughtfully. "What do you think?"

For the first time our gazes locked, and there was no student there, no young man wanting to go punting on the Cam with a girl called Frances to embarrass a rival, but an old, old man in a young man's body, staring out from those still-round eyes. I pulled the gun from my coat, laid it quietly in my lap, finger inside the trigger guard. The movement caused his eyes briefly to flicker, before settling back on me.

"Not for me, I trust?"

"Just in case reporting back becomes difficult."

"Of course – a bullet for your brain. How determined of you. Although . . . " he shifted gently in his seat, shoulders twitching in what might have been a shrug " . . . what do you really have to report?"

I sighed. "I don't suppose it would be too much for you to tell me what's going on here?"

"Not at all, Harry. Indeed, it is my hope that, once you are aware, you may even join us." He stood, gesturing courteously towards the door. "Shall we?"

# Chapter 46

My father.

I think of my father.

Both of them, in fact.

I think of Patrick August sitting silently across from me by the fireside, peeling the whole skin off an apple, one twist of the fruit at a time.

I think of Rory Hulne, an old man with a great swelling in his left leg, who in one not so special life in 1952 sent a letter informing me that he was holidaying on Holy Island; would I join him? I was a professor of mathematics, married to a doctor of English literature, Elizabeth. Lizzy wanted children and berated herself for the fact that we seemed unable to have them. I loved Lizzy as a loyal companion and a kind soul, and stayed with her until her death in 1973 from a series of strokes which left her largely paralysed down the left-hand side, and did not seek her out in future lives.

I am on Holy Island, the letter said. May you join me?

"Who is this Mr Hulne?" asked Lizzy.

"He was the master of the house where I grew up."

"Were you close?"

"No. Not in this life."

"Why in God's name does he want to see you now?"

"I don't know."

"Will you go?"

"Maybe. He will be dying by now."

"Harry," she chided, "that's an awful thing to say."

It was seven hours by train to Alnmouth, the train pausing at Newcastle to let the black-faced driver take his deserved break on the green wooden benches of the red-brick station. When he pulled his cap off, there was a line of soot across his forehead, stopping at the headband, and two owl-circles around his eyes when he lowered his goggles. A child waved at me excitedly from its mother's lap on the opposite platform. I waved back. The infant kept waving for the fifteen minutes we were in the station, and, wearily, I felt obliged to return the gesture. By the time we left, my arm ached, as did my smile, and the feeling that this journey was a terrible mistake grew on me. I flicked through the newspaper on my lap, but had read it some few lives ago and grew irritated by its naïve coverage of events yet unfolding. The crossword in the back frustrated me – I had answered nearly every clue three lives ago, when I attempted this same crossword during a break from the Europe desk at the Foreign Office, and three lives ago I had been stumped by the very same clue which now I could not penetrate: "Hark – a twist in the road, I perceive", eight letters and, I was infuriated to find, as impossible now as it had been those centuries before. Maybe, for one life only, I could be the man who wrote to the newspapers to complain.

The tide was in, Holy Island cut off from the mainland, the causeway visible only as a few sticks protruding above the surface of the water. I paid an old man with a rowing boat full of crab cages and no crabs for a ride across the water. He said nothing the entire length of the journey, and rowed with a rhythm so steady you could have set a pacemaker by it. As he rowed, the fog rose up across the water, smothering land and sea, obscuring the black remains of the castle that crowned the island's hill. By the time we reached the shore, the fog had cut visibility down to a few white cottages peering out from the edge of the hill, through which the mournful call of the thick-fleeced lost sheep wailed. The island was yet to discover its role as a tourist temple, selling almost-home-made jam and practically-hand-made candles, but had a reputation as a place where people went to be alone, to forget and, yes, even to die beneath the old Celtic crosses. It wasn't hard to find my father – the strangers in town were all well noted. I was directed to a room above a small-doored cottage owned by a Mrs Mason, a cheerful, rose-faced woman who could crack a chicken's neck between thumb and forefinger and who didn't believe in this new-fangled NHS business, not when there were gooseberries in the garden and rosehip cordial in the kitchen cupboard.

"You be here for Mr Hulne?" she asked brightly. "I'll bring up some tea."

Up a staircase designed to decapitate anyone higher than seven years old, through a wooden door with a black iron latch on it was a room with a small orange fire burning against the wall and a series of poorly painted images showing still waters bedecked with lilac flowers. There was a small single-person bed and a rocking chair by the fire. In the rocking chair, more blanket than man, was Rory Edmond Hulne, and he was, right on schedule, dying. From the yellow tinge at the end of his flaking nails to the protruding weakly throbbing veins on his chicken-neck, he was a man for whom little more could be provided than palliative care and a little emotional redemption. It took very little to assess which one I was.

I perched on the end of the bed, put my bag down on the floor and, as his eyes flickered open against the gum that weighed his lashes down, I said, "Hello, Mr Hulne."

When had I seen him last? A warm May in 1925 of this life, when I had, as I always did, finally mustered enough self-awareness and recollection to regain my former self and composure, and had written in my firmest hand to the Cronus Club, requesting extraction from the tedium of childhood. Charity Hazelmere, that great matron of the Club, had replied at once, informing Patrick and Harriet that a generous scholar was offering to pay for the education and board of deprived youths, and my name had been put forward for a position. A figure had been named, and I had absolved my foster-parents of all guilt at my departure by exclaiming gleefully how exciting the prospect would be, and how I had longed for a chance to better myself, and would write home often, though they could both of them barely read. They had packed my one bag of tatty clothes and put me in the back of my foster-father's cart to take me to the station, and Rory Hulne had come out of his house to watch me go, and stood in the door, and said nothing. In some lives, as we went through this ritual, he would come to shake my hand and tell me to be a brave young man; not this time, though quite what it was in my behaviour that so altered his, life to life, I can never say.

That had been nearly thirty years ago. On the few occasions I returned north, to spend Christmas silently with Patrick or to attend Harriet's funeral – that constant fixture of my childhood – my father had not been there. Away on business, or taking the waters, or up in town, or other such emptinesses of occupation. Yet now, here he sat, dying before my eyes, alone in a cottage on an island, no signs of wealth or power about him, a frail old man by a fire.

"Who are you?" he murmured, voice grown as thin as his frame. "What do you want?"

"It's Harry, sir," I replied, the deference of youth intruding despite myself. "Harry August."

"Harry? I wrote you a letter."

"That's why I came."

"Didn't think you would."

"Well ... I did."

Hundreds of years of living, and why could this man still reduce me to empty platitudes, make me feel a child again, hiding from the glare of a master?

"Are you well, Harry?" he asked, as the silence grew too thin and high between us. "Are you rich?"

"I do all right," I replied carefully. "I teach mathematics."

"Mathematics? Why?"

"I enjoy it. The subject is . . . engaging, and the antics of the students are always curious."

"You have . . . children?"

"No. I don't."

He grunted, a sound which conveyed to me almost satisfaction. A wrist flicked towards the fire, a command to put another log on. I did, crouching down by the brazier and poking it with the end of a stick before tossing that too into the flames. When I straightened up, he was staring right at me with a face that would one day be my own, and though his body was fading, his mind was still very much alive. He grabbed my arm as I moved back to the bed, holding me in place, staring up urgently into my eyes.

"Do you have money?" he demanded softly. "Are you rich?"

"I told you, Mr Hulne, I teach—"

"I heard you were rich. My sisters . . . the house . . . " A flicker of pain passed over his face, his hand falling from my wrist as if it suddenly lacked the strength to hold on. "Soon there'll be nothing left."

I sat down cautiously on the edge of the bed. "Do you need . . . a loan, Mr Hulne?" I spoke very slowly, to keep my rising anger out of my voice. Had I been summoned after twenty-seven years to serve as a walking bank to a man who wouldn't even acknowledge me his heir?

"The Depression . . . " he grunted. "The war . . . the new government, the land, the times . . . Constance is dead, Victoria dead, Alexandra has to work in a shop – a shop of all things. Clement will inherit the title, but he's drinking it all – all of it, all gone. We sold half the land to pay the debt on the mortgage, not even the mortgage itself! They'll take the house and fill it with union men," he spat the words, "with middle-class bankers and their spawn, with lawyers or accountants. They'll auction it all off, all of it, and there'll be nothing left. All gone. All for nothing."

I had to force my body into stillness, felt the twitch in my knee, wanted to fold my arms, cross my legs, as if the very muscles in my being had to express their rising hostility.

"Is there something you want to say to me, Mr Hulne?"

199

"You always liked Alexandra, didn't you?" he said. "She was nice to you when you were a child, yes?"

"She was kind," I admitted. "In more ways than I suspect I saw."

"Clement is a disgusting little creature," he added bitterly. "Do you know he's had three wives? He wants to sell it all and move to California."

"Mr Hulne," I repeated, harder now, "I don't see what it is you expect me to do about this."

His eyes flickered upwards, and there was liquid brimming on the bottom of the gummy eyelids. As so often is the case with men who refuse to cry, the awareness of his own tears seemed to cause them to rise even faster, shame mixing with grief, and even as they began to dribble down his face he clung to the side of the chair, refusing to acknowledge their presence on his skin. "You can't let it die," he whimpered. "It's your past too, Harry – the house, the lands. You understand, don't you? You want to keep them alive too."

"As the poet says – the times they are a-changing," I replied firmly. "Or perhaps he hasn't said it yet, but time will cure that absence. I am sorry for your situation, Mr Hulne. I regret that Alexandra is in difficulty; she was always kind. But Clement was a bully, even as a child, and the house was a monster of stone-praised vanity and quiet tragedy. Constance was a tyrant, more focused on perceptions than truth; Victoria was a drug addict; Lydia was an innocent who you tormented beyond—"

"How dare you!" His body jerked as if he would rise from the chair and hit me, but he didn't have the strength to do it, so stayed put, shaking all over, the tears fading now against the rising flush in his cheeks. "How dare you? How dare you speak of them like ... like you knew, like you ... ? You were a child, you left us! You left us and never looked back. How dare—"

"Tell me," I cut in. His voice was angrier, but mine was more powerful. "When you raped my mother, did she scream?"

He could have gone either way. The rage was there in him, ready to plough straight through my words, but instead, it seems, they ploughed through him, knocking him back against his seat

200

and pinning him there like a butterfly. I made sure he stayed put, adding, "I met a woman called Prudence Crannich once, who delivered a baby in the women's washroom of Berwick-upon-Tweed station, on New Year's Day. The mother died, but I tracked down her family and listened to her mother – my grandmother – tell the story of Lisa Leadmill, who went down south to find her fortune and who met her death in the arms of strangers. Cold is an enemy in trauma care – it slows down clotting, making it easier for patients to bleed out. Perhaps, if I'd been born in summer, my mother would have lived. Of course no one but you and Lisa will ever know if you truly raped her, but she was a young lonely woman in the house of an angry, potentially violent master who believed that his wife had betrayed him and was himself quite probably psychologically damaged from his time at the front. I imagine you caught her by the arm and kissed her, loud and rough, so that your wife would know you had done it. I imagine she was terrified, not understanding her role as a pawn in your marriage. You tell her that her position is becoming untenable; she begs you not to do it. You say that it'll make things easier for everyone, that if she screams the household will know and she'll be sent out without pay or references, branded a whore – better to be docile, better to be quiet . . . I suppose you could tell yourself that it wasn't rape, if she didn't scream. Did she scream when you pushed her down? Did she scream?"

His knuckles were yellow-white where they gripped the chair, his body still shaking now but not, I felt, with rage.

"There was a time," I went on, calmer now, "when I wanted to know you. I wrote you a letter once, telling you about the horrors I'd seen, the sins I'd committed, the pain I was in. I needed a stranger who cared, someone who was obliged by the bond of blood between us to understand but not judge. I thought perhaps you could still be my father. You replied as one soldier to another, but I realise now I've never really been a son to you. An heir, perhaps, a bastard heir, a sign of shame, a reminder of your failings, a retribution in human form, but never really a son. I don't think you've ever really had it in you to be what a father should."

I picked up my bag, getting to my feet and turning to the door. "I thought for a moment," I continued, "that you might be about to propose that I, as your blood, inherited Hulne House. I wondered if you believed that I might feel a fondness for the place, a desire to preserve it, that Clement lacks. Or if, with my humble origins, I might be so awed by the gift that I would somehow turn it into a monument to you and your name. As it is, I feel I should tell you that, were you to give me the house now and all its lands, and the home where I grew up under Patrick and Harriet's care, I would raze it all to the ground, to the very lowest foundation stone, and transform it into ... a pleasure centre for bankers and their children, or a casino for the quirky, or maybe I'd just leave the land barren, and let the earth reclaim its own."

I turned to leave him.

As I got to the door he called after me, "Harry! You can't ... It's your past, Harry. It's your past."

I walked away and didn't look back.


Two lives later I did come into possession of Hulne House. The catalyst was, aged twenty-one, attending my grandmother Constance's funeral. I had never been to her funeral before, never wanted to. Aunt Alexandra, who all those years ago had saved my life and insisted I was taken in, and who would always, in every life, save me, fell to talking to me by the graveside and we grew, in our way, close. She was the strongest of the family, saw the way the wind was blowing and let it carry her in its path. I never found out what she said to my father, but three months before his death he changed the will, and I inherited the estate. I kept it exactly as it was, not a brick changed, and turned it into a charitable trust for the treatment of mental illness. At my next death it was of course restored to its usual state beneath the watchful eye of Constance, but I liked to think that somewhere, in a world lost to my sight, Hulne House had finally made a difference.

# Chapter 47

Vincent, walking by my side through a Russian military research base.

Mr Hulne, if only you could see me now.

He let me keep the gun as we walked through the belly of his facility. What was it to him? Killing him would gain me nothing, and killing myself at this precipitous time would also gain me nothing but the irritation of going through puberty again. People moved out of his way, their eyes flickering to me in doubt, but no one questioned him. In his shabby jacket and rolled-up socks, this young man was clearly in charge, clearly a source of reverence, and a wave of his hand opened every sealed door, cleared every armed patrol.

"I'm glad it's you," he remarked as we headed deeper down, until the air grew cold and heavy with moisture. "When I realised that a piece of my technology had made it on to the open market before its time, I rather hoped the Cronus Club would be too busy drinking to pay the matter any attention. I was surprised anyone even noticed – but pleased that of all the people to notice, it was you, Harry. Is it Harry at the moment?"

I shrugged. "Harry's as good as anything else. What about you? How did you end up Vitali?"

A dismissive shrug. "I tried working through the American industrial complex for a few lives," he grumbled, "but keeping any sort of technological innovation private in that environment is almost impossible. If it wasn't businessmen or greedy scientists, it was army generals or State Department officials demanding to know how many I could produce, and how fast. Terribly crude nation, America. At least with the Soviets the culture is bred to secrecy."

The further we went, the colder it grew, and the thickness of the trunking and cables in the corridor increased until the walls were almost entirely lost behind pipes and wires fatter than my arm. "How have you been since I saw you last?" he added airily. "Did you get your professorship?"

"What? Yes, eventually. Only after Fred Hoyle threatened to punch me though."

"Dear me, what a violent academic career you had."

"In fairness, you and Hoyle were the only two individuals in that entire life who came close to physical violence."

"I'm glad to think I was keeping good company. Here, you'd better take one of these."

He handed me a thin, clear badge. I examined it – a simple radiation token, crude in that it could only tell you if you'd been exposed, rather than how bad your condition was.

"Vincent, you seem far too sophisticated to be building nukes for the Soviets," I tutted. "What is your arrangement, precisely?"

"Oh, I build nukes," he said, airily pulling back a lock on a metal door the size of a small castle. "But I'm very careful to ensure that clever men don't reach their full potential, and minor errors of manufacturing are introduced into the final process so, when the device goes up, it can do so on a historical schedule. I'm sure even the Cronus Club would notice a shift in the global arms race."

"And no one asks any questions?"

"As I said," he replied brightly, "remarkable system the Soviets have."

The door, during all this, had been sliding back with glacial sluggishness. Now it stood open, and Vincent stepped into a cavern of iron and electricity. All the trunking in the building seemed to converge here, and the air was notably warmer than in the gloomy corridors which had led down to this depth. Fans greater than the propellors on the *Titanic* whirred and hummed, and at the centre of all this stood a monolith of a machine. Where the Americans might have attempted to dress up their creation, Vincent and his team had gone for pure, practical functionality, parts welded together by brute force, the innards hanging exposed, cables labelled with white tape and pen, the only lights flashing those which actually, desperately, urgently needed to flash. It looked like the DIY class of a technological god who had run out of heat shrink tubing even before he'd begun. Men and women in little white badges scurried beneath the hulking shadow of this creature, dragging ladders across the floor to climb up to some unseen access port high above its warping pyramid base.

"What do you think?" asked Vincent brightly.

I felt the weight of the gun in my pocket and replied as calmly as I could, "That rather depends on what I'm looking at."

"Harry," he chided, "you disappoint me."

His disappointment was an invitation for deduction. Reluctantly, I deduced. "All right." I sighed. "You're clearly operating solid-state computing of a kind that won't be invented for a good fifteen years; over there I can see liquid cooling units which again I doubt will come into use for another seventeen years. The radiation badges combined with the lead-lined walls everywhere imply a radiation source, but you're clearly not running reactors as there's not enough water nearby for you to cool the system – unless, that is, your reactor technology is more than fifty years ahead of the time?"

"No reactors," he agreed. "But you're correct as to the radio-active source."

"Criticality is a concern," I went on, "but not a big enough one for you to have men in hazard suits running around. The large amount of networking coming off the machine suggests you're feeding data out as well as energy in; that implies experiments which are being monitored rather than a fully fledged manufacturing process. In conclusion ... you're studying something, probably sub-atomic, using technology decades ahead of its time, in a secret base in the middle of the USSR, and – this is what continues to baffle me – you seem pleased at this precise situation."

Indeed, he was beaming proudly at his machine. "Of course I'm pleased, Harry," he said. "With the insights we glean from this machine, we can change everything."

"Everything?"

"Everything," he repeated, and by the look in his eye I actually thought he might mean it. "Would you like to help?"

"Help?"

"Help," he parroted, "being a deed that is the opposite of hinder?"

"Even were this entire enterprise not in violation of everything the Club stands for –" a rolling raspberry noise was made at this suggestion "– I really don't know what it is I'd be helping with."

He put his arm over my shoulder, hugged me to his side like a long-lost friend. Was this the man who, so many centuries ago, had kissed Frances by the lawns and punched me to the floor for being kalachakra? "Harry," he said firmly, "what would you say to building a quantum mirror?"

# Chapter 48

"A quantum mirror—" he began.

"Phooey," I replied.

"A quantum mirror—"

"Claptrap."

"A quantum mirror!" Vincent was getting annoyed, worked up, the way he so often did during our talks.

Cambridge again.

Memories again.

It seems to me that in the course of my knowing Vincent my mind always turns back to the good times, to the days before complexity, before the end of the world.

"Are you quite ready to listen?" he demanded.

"Pass me another slice of chicken and some mashed potato, and I'll sit in silence and even prepare my best expression of interest for the moment," I replied.

He duly topped up my plate with a healthy portion of chicken and an obscene quantity of mash. "A quantum mirror," he tried again, "being a theoretical device for the extrapolation of matter."

"When you say extrapolation—"

"I thought you were going to be silent? Eat your food."

"I'm eating," I replied, pointedly forking in a mouthful of potato.

"Consider Darwin." I managed not to make a spluttering sound, and my effort itself earned me a glare. "He journeys to islands cut off from the rest of the planet and observes creatures and their patterns of living. These sights have been seen before, these sights will be seen again, but for Darwin, observing the world around him, they are the beginnings of a logical extrapolation. Observe, he says, how creatures adapt to their environments. Marvel at the bird which dives so perfectly off the rock to fish for its prey; see how similar it is to another animal thousands of miles away which could well be of the same species, except that its prey lives in caves and so it develops a long beak. Observe a worm, observe an insect, observe the crawling of a crab along an ocean floor, and from all this –"

"Pass the gravy," I grunted.

The gravy was passed without missing a beat. "– and from all this there comes the most marvellous of theories – a theory of evolution. Extrapolation, Harry. From the smallest thing, great wonders are exposed. Now we as physicists—"

"I'm a physicist; you're still a student, and I don't know why I tolerate your company."

"As physicists," he ploughed on, "we – my recipe for gravy is superior to yours – aren't looking at animals or the behaviour of birds; our material, the matter we observe, is in the atom itself. What if we can take this single, simplest of things, and put it to the same process that Darwin did? From a proton, a neutron and an electron we can deduce the forces which bind them together, which must therefore bind the universe together, bind space together, bind *time* together, and hold up a mirror, as it were, to the nature of existence itself . . . "

"A quantum mirror!" I concluded, waggling my fork melo-dramatically. "Vincent," I added, before his indignation could overwhelm mine, "that's precisely what science *does*."

"It's what it aims to achieve," he corrected, "but the tools we're limited to – three-dimensional objects which we can perceive within the visible spectrum, the human brain itself – are utterly insufficient to the task. What we need is an entirely different tool for the understanding of matter, an entirely different way of comprehending the very building blocks of reality, from which comprehension the whole universe may unfold. What do you think?"

I thought about it.

"I think it's claptrap," I said at last.

"Harry—"

"No, wait, stick with me. Leaving aside the theoretical complications, the economic difficulties, the scientific problems, I think it's claptrap from an entirely philosophical point of view, one which will make you suitably angry because of its unscientific nature. I don't think, Vincent, that the human race has the *capacity* to fully comprehend the whole universe."

"Oh, but please—"

"Wait, wait just a moment! I think what you describe – this entirely impossible device, may I add – which will, through some method I cannot begin to guess at, explode our understanding of the universe and create a theory of everything capable of answering every question starting with how and finishing up with the far more difficult why, this ... miraculous device, is nothing more and nothing less than a do-it-yourself deity. You want to build yourself a machine for omnipotence, Vincent? You want to make yourself God?"

"Not me, God, not me ..."

"To know all that is, all that was, all that could be—"

"The purpose of science! A gun is only a gun, it's men who misuse it ..."

"That's all right then. Bring on omnipotence for the human race!"

"'God' is such a weighted term ..."

"You're right," I snapped, harder than I'd meant. "Call it a quantum mirror and no one will even begin to suspect the scale of your ambition."

"Maybe that's it," he replied with a shrug. "Maybe all God ever was was a quantum mirror."

# Chapter 49

I said, "Can I have some time to think?"

"Of course," he replied airily.

"Do you mind if I keep the gun?" I added.

"Of course not. If you don't mind, would you be comfortable waiting in a cell?" he asked. "There's a lot of sensitive equipment down here which you might get blood on, should you choose to blow your brains out."

"That would be frustrating," I agreed. "Lead the way."

They led me to a couple of cells. I supposed that no good secret research station was complete without them. They were cold, the beds concrete set into the wall. Vincent promised someone would bring blankets, and he was as good as his word. A hot thick soup with dumplings was also provided. The guard pushed everything nervously across the floor to me, his eye still fixed on the gun at my side. I smiled nicely at him and said not a word.

A quantum mirror.

Vincent Rankis – Vitali Karpenko – whatever his name was – was actually attempting to build a quantum mirror.

All of time and space, all that was or could be, laid out before you like the map of creation. A machine which could, from a single atom, extrapolate the wonders of the universe.

Explain how we came to be.

Why we came to be.

Even us, even the kalachakra.

I sat and thought.

Thought about Cambridge and our arguments over roast chicken.

About Akinleye pushing the needle under my skin.

Richard Lisle, shot in the chest before he could commit his crimes.

Lizzy, who I had loved, and Jenny, who I had loved in a completely different way, no less honestly, no more truly. Crawling at Phearson's feet; Virginia at my door – the femoral artery is best, such a gusher – Rory Hulne at my grandmother's funeral, and the look on my father's face as I left him to die. Standing by Harriet's graveside again and again, life after life, a child unable to take the hand of my foster-father, Patrick August, who would wither away inside, even as his body lived on.

What is the point of you?

The world is ending.

Now it's up to you.

Did she scream?

It's your past, Harry. It's your past.

Are you God, Dr August? Are you the only living creature that matters? Do you think, because you remember it, that your pain is bigger and more important? Do you think, because you experience it, that your life is the only life that gets counted?

That's all right then! Bring on omnipotence for the human race!

What is the point of you?

Are you God?


Apparently I thought for nearly a day.

When I'd done, I banged on the cell door. The same nervous guard who'd left the dumplings opened it, eyes flickering to the gun in my hand.

"Hello," I said, passing him the weapon. "Tell Karpenko yes. My answer is yes."

211

# Chapter 50

I once met a kalachakra by the name of Fidel Gussman. It was 1973; I was in Afghanistan to see the great Buddhas before the Taliban came to power and destroyed them. I was travelling as a New Zealand national, one of the easier passports to move about with, and trying to brush up my Pashto in the process. I was fifty-five years old and had spent a good deal of my life hunting down messages left in stone by previous members of the Cronus Club. It was a running game – a joke left from AD 45 for future Club members which, if I could disinter, I would add my name to before burying in a new place, leaving behind a new set of suitably cryptic clues for future generations to solve – a sort of international time capsule for the overly bored. If feeling generous, participants also buried hidden treasures of a non-biodegradable kind. By far the most magnanimous contribution to the hunt had been a hitherto lost work of Leonardo da Vinci buried by a kalachakra from Renaissance Italy in a sealed jug of wine beneath a shrine to Santa Angelica in the highest part of the Alps. The helpful clues left behind had almost entirely been in the form of lewd rhymes, making the eventual discovery of the bequeathed artefact something of a treat. These games, more than anything else, took me round the world, and it was while visiting the Buddhas of Afghanistan that Fidel Gussman came calling.

You could see him approach from a mile off – a great man with a swollen neck riding on the roof of one of a convoy of trucks which kicked up yellow dust higher than their bobbing radio aerials. The people of the village scattered when he came into town, fearing bandits, and indeed bandits are precisely what they looked like. I made no attempt to hide – a fair-skinned New Zealander in the middle of Afghanistan doesn't have many places to go to ground – and stared down this European-faced arrival and his multinational convoy of AK-toting men as a tourist might stare at an obstructive police officer.

"Hey, you!" he called in heavily inflected Urdu, gesturing me over to his truck. If it had been any colour other than the summer soil before, now there was no way to tell. The engine ticked, unable to cool in the blasting heat, and already pans were coming out and being laid on the bonnets, ready to fry the mid-morning breakfast – no need for flames. I approached, quietly counting up the weapons and making an assessment of the type of men who'd so rudely disrupted my sightseeing. Mercenaries and thieves, I decided, the only sign of uniform being a red bandanna that each wore somewhere about their person. The man who'd called to me was clearly their leader, a great smiling face above a stubbly beard.

"You're not from around here – you CIA?" he demanded.

"I'm not CIA," I replied wearily. "Just here to see the Buddhas."

"What Buddhas?"

"The Buddhas of Bamiyan?" I suggested, doing my best not to let my contempt of this bandit's ignorance show. "Carved into the mountainside itself?"

"Hell yeah," mused the man on the truck. "I've seen them. You're right to go now – twenty years from now they won't even be standing!"

I stepped back, surprised, and had another look at this ragged, smelling, dust-covered man. He grinned, touched his hand to his forelock and said, "Well, nice to meet you, even if you aren't CIA."

He hopped down from the truck and began to head away.

I called out, surprised at myself for even doing it, "Tiananmen Square."

He stopped, then swung round on the spot, toe pointing up and ankle digging into the dirt as he did, like a dancer. Still grinning his easy grin, he swaggered back towards me, stopping so close I could feel the stickiness coming off his body. "Hell," he said at last. "You don't look much like a Chinese spy neither."

"You don't look like an Afghan warlord," I pointed out.

"Well, that's because I'm only passing through this place on the way to somewhere else."

"Anywhere in particular?"

"Wherever there's action. We're men of war, see – that's what we do and we do it well – and there's no shame in that because it'll happen without us anyway, but with us –" his grin widened "– maybe it'll happen that little bit faster. But what's a nice old gentleman like you doing talking about Chinese geography, hey?"

"Nothing," I replied with a shrug. "The word just popped into my head. Like Chernobyl – just words."

Fidel's eyebrows flickered, though his grin remained fixed. Then he gave a great chuckle, slapped me so hard on the shoulder that I nearly lost my footing, stepped back a little to admire his handiwork, and finally roared out loud. "Jesus, Joseph and the Holy Mary," he blurted. "Michael fucking Jackson to you too."

We ate together. The family whose house we ate in were told in no uncertain terms that they were going to receive guests, but Fidel's men at least supplied most of their own bread and threw bottle tops at the kids, who seemed excited enough to collect these trinkets. The mother stood in the door, watching us through the blue veil of her burka, daring us to break a single one of her pots.

"I'm born in the 1940s," explained Fidel, tearing off hunks of roast lamb from the bone with an impressive set of well-worn teeth, "which is shit, because I miss a lot of the good stuff. I'm usually OK to go do the Bay of Pigs though, and obviously – hell – obviously I do Vietnam. I spend a lot of time on the conflicts in Africa too but, you know, so much of that is just about scaring the

214

natives and I'm like, where's the craft in that? Give me proper war to fight, damn it; I'm not some psychopath who likes seeing infants cry! Iran and Iraq are starting to get good round this time, though Iran's no fun once the shah's gone, I can tell you that. Kuwait's a good 'un, and I've tried the Balkan shit too, though again that's all so much 'Kill the civilian, kill the civilian, run from the tank!' and I'm like, Jesus guys, I'm a fucking professional, do you have to give me this shit?"

"Are you a soldier most of your lives?" I asked.

He tore off another strip of meat. "Yeah. My dad's a soldier, which is where I guess I got it from – spend a lot of kiddy years growing up on Okinawa and, my God, the people there, they have something, I mean like, something iron inside, you gotta see it. I'm paid up with the Club," he added, an afterthought needing clarification, "but all that sitting around, all that sex and the politics? Jesus, the politics, it's all so-and-so-said-this-three-hundred-years-ago and so-and-so-slept-with-such-and-such-but-then-so-and-so-died-and-got-really-jealous, and I just can't be having that. I mean, I dunno, maybe it's the Club I grew up with – do you find it like that?"

"I don't spend much time with the Club," I admitted, embarrassed. "I get easily distracted."

"Hey, for immortals, Club guys are really inconsistent? You know they killed me with an overdose once? I was like, Jesus guys, I'm only thirty-three and now I've gotta go through potty training again? What the fuck?"

"I tend to self-medicate in my later years," I admitted. "Midsixties, early seventies, I always get the same disease . . . "

"Fucking tell me about it," he groaned. "Small-cell lung cancer, aged sixty-seven, bham! You know, I've tried smoking, I've tried not smoking. I've tried clean living, and every time I get the same fucking disease. I asked a medic once why that should be, and you know what she said? 'Hey, stuff just happens.' I mean, fuck me."

"So," I asked carefully, deciding not to elaborate on my own medical career, "why war?"

He eyed me beadily over the rapidly appearing whiteness of the

215

lamb bone. "You done much fighting? You look like you might have been old enough to do a bit of World War Two, no offence to you."

"I've seen a few wars," I admitted with a shrug, "but I tend to steer clear. Too unpredictable."

"Fuck, man, that's the whole fucking point! You're born knowing everything that's gonna happen in your lifetime, every fucking bit of it, and you're like 'Let's just watch'? Screw that – let's get out there, let's live a little, get surprised! I've been shot –" he bristled with pride "– seventy-four times, but only nineteen of those bullets were fatal. I also been blown up by a hand grenade and stood on a mine, and this one time, back when we were fighting the Vietcong, I got stabbed to death with a sharpened bamboo stick, can you fucking believe it? We were clearing this patch of jungle which didn't even have a fucking name, and the place stank cos the air-force boys, they'd fried the land to the left and the land to the right – funnelling the guerrillas into a killing zone, they called it – and Jesus, we'd done some killing, and I'm feeling on top of the world, I mean like, knowing every second could be my last, it's this buzz, this amazing buzz. And I don't even hear him, I don't even see this guy; he's just there, coming out of the ground, and I get a shot off which takes out his stomach and he's gonna bleed to death, but that doesn't even slow him down – he's on me, bham, bham! Guy can't have been more than sixteen years old and I thought, hell yeah, you're a sight worth seeing."

He threw the chewed bone out of the door for a three-legged dog to hobble over and gnaw on. Wiping his hands on his shirt, he grinned at me and said, "You Cronus Club boys, you're all so scared of doing something different. Problem is, you've gone soft. You've got used to the comfy life, and the great thing about the comfy life is no one who has it is ever gonna risk rocking the boat. You should learn to live a little, rough it out – I'm telling you, there's no greater high."

"Do you think you've ever made a difference to the course of linear events?" I enquired. "Have you, personally, ever affected the outcome of a war?"

"Fuck no!" He chuckled. "We're just fucking soldiers. We kill some guys, they kill our guys, we kill their guys back – none of it fucking means anything, you know? Just numbers on a page, and only when the numbers get big enough do the fat cats who decide this shit sit down and and go, 'Wow, let's make the decisions we were always gonna have to make anyway.' I'm no threat to temporal events, partner – I'm just the fire in the stove. And you know the best bit?" He beamed, climbing to his feet, tossing a fistful of bunched-up notes into the corner of the hut, like a master throwing scraps to a pet. "None of it fucking matters. Not one bullet, not one drop of blood. None of it makes any fucking difference at all."

He made to go, then paused in the doorway, grinning, his face half in the shade of the hut, half in the blinding white light of day. "Hey, Harry, you ever get bored of this archaeology shit, or whatever it is you do, come find me on the thin red line."

"Good luck to you, Fidel," I replied.

He grinned and stepped into the light.

# Chapter 51

"It's yes," I told Vincent. "The answer is yes."

We sat in the commander's office of the Pietrok-112 facility, the commander having tactfully vacated the space, and I waited, knees crossed and hands folded, watching Vincent watch me.

Finally Vincent said, "May I ask why? It seems like a remarkable change of heart from your previous stance of 'Claptrap.'"

I looked up to the ceiling for inspiration and noted a thin line of black bugs marching in an orderly way across the surface, out of the loose end of the light fitting. "I could tell you," I suggested, "it's because of the scientific challenge, the curiosity, the adventure, and because, ultimately, I believe it can't be achieved, so where's the harm? I could say it's a rebellion against the Cronus Club, against their policy of sit still and do nothing, of drink and fuck and get high across the globe, because that's all there is to do and all there ever will be. I could tell you that the past is the past, and nothing has any consequence, and I'm tired of a life where nothing I do has any meaning for anything more than myself, and that over the years I've grown numb inside, hollow and empty, and I drift from situation to situation like a ghost visiting an old graveside in search of an explanation of how he died, and in my search

I have found nothing. Nothing that makes any sense. I could tell you that I share your ambition. That I want to see with the eyes of God. That is what we're talking about here, ultimately, isn't it? This machine, this 'quantum mirror', whatever the hell that even means in practical terms ... it's merely a scientific instrument like any other, but a scientific instrument to answer the why, the what, the how of ... everything. To know everything. Why we are. Where we come from. Kalachakra, ouroboran. For all of humanity's history we've tried to find answers to what we are, and why. Why should the kalachakra be any different? I could give a lot to have that kind of knowledge, and no one else has given me even the slightest glimmering of an answer, of an approach to an answer. You offer a plan, if nothing else."

I shrugged, leaned back deeper into the chair.

"Or, more to the purpose, I could tell you very simply that it's something to do, something which might actually change the way I live. So damn everything else."

Vincent thought about it.

Smiled.

"OK then," he said. "That's good enough for me."


Even now, knowing what I do, I cannot lie.

Ten years I spent working on the quantum mirror.

For kalachakra, ten years is nothing in the grand scheme of things, but then, no one, not even we, live in the grand scheme of things. Three thousand, six hundred and fifty days, give or take the odd break for holidays, and each moment was ...

... revelatory.

For so many years I hadn't properly worked, not truly. In my early lives I'd held down the occasional job – doctor, professor, academic, spy – but they had only been means to an end, a means to knowledge and understanding of the world around me. Now, as I set to work on Vincent's impossible project, like a student graduating at last I unleashed my knowledge, turned it to its ultimate purpose, and for the first time in all my lives understood what it was for your work to become your life.

I was happy, and marvelled that I hadn't long before realised this was what happiness was. The working conditions were far from luxurious – Vincent had to make some concessions to the state within which he worked, after all – but I found I had no problem with this. The bed was warm, the blankets were thick, the food, while hardly tasty, was filling after a long day. Twice a day, every day, Vincent insisted that we went above ground to experience the sun or, more often, the lack of sun and the biting wind off the Arctic, with a cry of, "It's important to stay in touch with nature, Harry!"

He extended this principle even into winter, and I spent many miserable hours huddling in the biting cold as my hair, eyebrows and tears froze solid against my skin while Vincent paraded up and down barking, "Won't it be marvellous when we go back inside?"

Had I not been too cold to reply, I might have said something cutting.

I was accepted by all because Vincent accepted me. No one asked any questions and no one questioned the fear behind their colleagues' silences, but as the time passed it became clear from both my working and social life that Vincent had collected some truly extraordinary minds to assist him in his work.

"Five lives, Harry!" he exclaimed. "Five more lives and I think we'll have it!"

This long-term plan, requiring as it did five deaths to fulfil it, he shared only with me. We were still so far from achieving the breakthroughs Vincent wanted, so far from even having the equipment to begin to study the problems of how and why – every how, every why – that there wasn't any point even mentioning the idea. Instead we worked on components, each one of which was itself revolutionary for the time and whose purpose was, as Vincent put it, "To kick the twentieth century firmly into the twenty-first!"

"I intend to have developed an internal Internet by 1963," he explained, "and have microprocessors really sorted by 1969. With any luck we can take computing out of the silicon age by 1971, and if we're still on schedule I'm aiming for nano-processing by

1978. I tend to die," he added with a slight sniff of regret, "by the year 2002, but with the head start this life gives me, hopefully next time round we'll have microprocessors up and running by the end of World War Two. I'm thinking of setting up in Canada next time – I haven't picked the brains of many Canadians lately."

"This is all very well and good," I remarked during a quieter evening as we sat playing backgammon in his quarters, "but when you say you shall take the discoveries of this life and implement them in your next, it does rather imply that you will be able to recall every detail of every technical specification, every diagram and every equation."

"Of course," he replied airily, "I shall."

I dropped the dice and hoped that my clumsiness looked like a deliberately crude roll. I stammered, "Y-you're a mnemonic?"

"I'm a what?" he demanded.

"Mnemonic – it's how the Club describes people who remember everything."

"Well then, yes, I suppose that's precisely what I am. You seem surprised?"

"We're – you're very rare."

"Yes, I'd imagined so, although I must say, Harry, your recollection of your scientific days seems flawless – you're an absolute bonus to our team."

"Thank you."

"But I take it you too forget?"

"Yes, I forget. In fact, I can't remember whose move it is – yours or mine?"

Why did I lie?

Years of habit?

Or perhaps a recollection of Virginia telling the story of that other famous mnemonic Victor Hoeness, father of the cataclysm, who remembered everything and used it to destroy a world. Perhaps that was it.

The world is ending.

Christa in Berlin.

It didn't matter.

221

It doesn't matter.

Death must always come, and if the reward for our actions was an answer – a huge, beautiful answer to the oldest of questions, *why* we are, where we come from – then it was a price worth paying.

So I told myself, alone in the darkness of a Russian winter.

There was an art to the secrecy that Vincent and I practised during that time. Both of us were aware of theory and technological developments twenty to thirty years ahead of their time. Both of us had flawless memories of the same, though I always chalked my recollections up to a good head for numbers. The skill lay in introducing our ideas in such a way as would permit the highly intelligent individuals Vincent had surrounded himself with to make the consequent breakthroughs as it were for themselves. It became something of a game, a competition between us, to see who could drop that subtle idea which might lead the chemist to a connection, the physicist to revelation. The magnitude of the task in a way offered us benefits, as it was too great for either of us to comprehend, and so we broke it down into smaller parts. We would need an electron microscope – a concept we were both familiar with but neither one of us had studied or used. We would need a particle accelerator, which again we both knew we desired but neither one of us had built. On occasion even the discussion of a concept was enough to provoke unexpected bursts of brilliance from our researchers, who, giddy with the success after success rolling out of the labs, never paused to question just how or why these revelations were occurring.

"By the end of this life," stated Vincent firmly, "I intend to have the technology of 2030 at my disposal, whatever that may be. It's a good communist attitude – one must always have a long-term plan."

"Are you not concerned," I enquired, "about what happens to this technology after your death?"

"There is no 'after my death'," he replied grimly.

I would like to say that this question troubled me more than it did. I recalled our discussions on the very nature of kalachakra. What are we, how do we live? Are we, in fact, little more than consciousnesses flitting between an endless series of parallel universes, which we then alter by our deeds? If so, the implication rather was that our actions *did* carry consequences, albeit ones which we would never perceive, for somewhere there was a universe where Harry August had turned left and not right at his fifty-fifth birthday, and somewhere a universe in which Vincent Rankis had died, leaving behind a post-Soviet Russia with a technological database decades ahead of its time.

The world is ending.
  Christa in Berlin.
  The world is ending.
  It must be one of us.

"The world is ending," I said.

It was 1966, and we were on the verge of testing Vincent's first cold fusion reactor.

Cold fusion technology, in my opinion, could save the planet. A renewable energy source whose primary waste products are hydrogen and water. In the streets of London smoke still blackened the faces of travellers. Grey clouds rose above the coal stacks of my home country, oil clung to ruined beaches where a container ship had sunk, and in twenty years' time thirty men would die from breathing in the smoke that roared out of Chernobyl's shattered fourth reactor, and hundreds of thousands would later be dubbed "liquidators" – soldiers who shovelled radioactive soil into underground mines, builders who poured liquid concrete over a still-burning uranium heart, firemen who threw shovels of sand on to flaming nuclear fuel even as their skins prickled with the insidious caress of radiation. All this was yet to come, and even then cold fusion would be nothing more than a dream; yet here we stood, Vincent and I, ready to change the world.

"The world is ending," I said as the generators built up, but I don't think he could hear me over the sound of the machinery.

Our test was a failure.

Not this life, it turned out, were we going to crack one of the greatest scientific quests of the twentieth century. Even Vincent, it turned out, even I, had our limitations. Knowledge is not a substitute for ingenuity, merely an accelerant.

"The world is ending," I said as we stood together on the viewing gallery, watching our apparatus being pulled away.

"What's that, old thing?" he murmured, distracted by the disappointment and the need to put on a brave face.

"The world is ending. The seas boil, the skies fall, and it's getting faster. The course of linear temporality is changing, and it's us. We did this."

"Harry," he tutted, "don't be so melodramatic."

"This is the message that has been passed down from child to dying old man down the generations. The future is changing and not for the better. We did this."

"The Cronus Club was always stodgy."

"Vincent, what if it's us?"

He looked at me sideways, and I realised he had heard me after all, over the sound of the machinery, over the sound of a machine which would one day beget a machine which would beget a machine which would beget the knowledge of God, the answer to all our questions, the understanding of the universe as a whole.

And he said, "So?"

Four days later, once it was evident from the growing number of results coming in from the fusion experiment that we had failed, but were still, in accordance with the 99.3 per cent probability of the same, alive, I requested a holiday.

"Of course," he said. "I entirely understand."

I was given a lift in an army car to Pietrok-111; from Pietrok-111 a different car took me to Ploskye Prydy, and it occurred to me that I hadn't left Vincent's lab for ten years. Time had not been kind to the landscape: what few trees there had been had been removed, leaving ugly stumps in the earth beyond which great walls of concrete proclaimed that here the people laboured for bread or here they toiled for steel or here there was no sign at all except a warning against any and all trespassers and that anyone coming within sight of the walls after 8 p.m. would be shot. Only one train a day left Ploskye Prydy, and the town was not renowned for its food and board. My driver took me to his mother's house. She fed me plates of steaming beans and preserved fish and told all the secrets of the village, of which she seemed both the greatest source and, I suspected, the prime originator. I slept beneath an icon of St Sebastian, who had died shot through with arrows and who Catholic iconography tended to depict dying in his underpants but who here wore cloth of gold.

The train back to Leningrad was silent, none of the garrulous youngsters I had ridden with on my first journey to the north. A man was transporting several boxes of chickens. Four hours into the journey and the uneven tracks – more so than I remembered – sent one flying, and its prisoner, white-feathered and red-eyed, spent nine glorious minutes in freedom, hurtling up and down the carriage, before a militia man with scaling skin and a suggestion of melanoma about the jaw, reached out with a single gloved hand and caught the bird by the throat. I saw its neck stretch, and the creature seemed as grateful as an animal with a brain the size of a walnut can be to be restored to its master and its cage.

I was not officially met when I finally crawled off the train in Leningrad, the sky already black and rain tapping against the old slanted roof, but two men in wide-collared coats followed me as I left the station in search of a place to spend the night, and stayed outside the boarding house in the shadow of the street as the cobbles danced with rushing water. During the few days I spent in the city I came to know my watchers well, a six-man team in total, who I mentally dubbed Boris One, Boris Two, Skinny, Fat, Breathless and Dave. Dave earned his name by his uncanny physical resemblance to David Ayton, an Irish laboratory engineer who'd once destroyed my coat with a mug of sulphuric acid, only to beg a new one from the store, sew on my name overnight, and even attempt to smear a precise replica of the coffee stains and chemical erosions into the back and sleeves which had made my coat so distinctly mine. Sympathy for the effort involved far outweighed my ire, and now Soviet Dave earned my respect as well by his good-natured attitude to my shadowing. The others, especially Boris One and Boris Two, who mirrored each other in clothes, bearing and technique, attempted to conduct entirely covert surveillance of a most distracting kind. Dave afforded me the respect of being fairly overt in his observation, smiling at me across the street as I passed in acknowledgment of his own discovery and the futile nature of his role. In another time, I felt, I would have enjoyed Soviet Dave's company, and wondered just what stories lurked behind his polite veneer, to have made him a security man.

For a few days I simply played tourist, as much as anyone could in the city at the time. In one of the few cafés to grudgingly merit the name, where the chef's speciality was variations on the theme of cauliflower, I was surprised to encounter a team of sixth-form schoolboys from the United Kingdom watched over by the ubiquitous Soviet minders.

"We're here on a cultural exchange," explained one, prodding his bowl of cauliflower special dubiously. "So far we've been beaten at football, hockey, swimming and track athletics. Tomorrow we're going for a sailing trip, which I think means we're going to be beaten at rowing."

"Are you a sports team?" I enquired, eyeing up the portly bearing of some of the boy's companions.

"No!" he exclaimed. "We're language students. I signed on because I thought they'd let us see the Winter Palace. Although yesterday evening Howard beat one of their boys at chess, which caused quite the stir. He's been asked not to show us up like that again."

I wished them luck, earning a wry smile and a polite wiggle of fork in acknowledgment.

That night a hooker was waiting by the door of my room. She said her name was Sophia and she'd already been paid. She was a secret fan of Bulgakov and Jane Austen, and asked, as I was reputed to be such an educated man, if I wouldn't mind talking German, as she was still struggling to get the accent right. I wondered if this was Soviet Dave's idea, or Vincent's. I saw no obvious signs of physical abuse or disease, and tipped her generously for good company's sake.

"What do you do?" she asked me as the headlights from a passing car defined the arc of a sundial across the ceiling, blooming, travelling and gone.

"I'm a scientist."

"What kind of scientist?"

"Theoretical," I replied.

"What kind of theories?"

"Everything."

She found this briefly funny, then was embarrassed to find something funny which I could not. "When I was young," I explained, "I looked to God to find answers. When God didn't have anything, I looked for answers in people, but all they said was, 'Relax, go with it.'"

"'Go with it'?" She queried my American idiom, pronounced in German, using her native Russian.

"Don't fight against inevitability," I translated loosely. "Life is until it is not, so why get fussed? Don't hurt anyone, try not to give your dinner guests food poisoning, be clean in word and deed – what else is there? Just be a decent person in a decent world."

"Everyone's a decent person," she replied softly, "in their own eyes."

She was warm against me, and my fatigue gave my words a slow certainty, a weight that, during more alert hours, I usually shied from as being too weighty for polite conversation. "People don't have the answer," I concluded softly. "People . . . just want to be left alone and not bothered. But I am bothered. We ask ourselves 'Why me?' and 'What's the point?' and sooner or later people turn round and say 'It's a coincidence' and 'My purpose is the woman I love' or 'My purpose is my children' or 'To see this idea through,' but for me and my kind . . . there is none of that. There must be consequences to our deeds. But I can't see it. And I have to know. Whatever the cost."

227

Sophia was silent a while, thinking it through. Then, "Go with it." She said the unfamiliar words carefully, and, grinning, tried them again. "Go with it. You talk about decent people living decent lives as if that doesn't mean anything, like it's not a big deal. But you listen – this 'decent', it is the only thing that matters. I don't care if you theorise, Mr Scientist, a machine that makes all men kind and all women beautiful if, while making your machine, you don't stop to help the old mother cross the street, you know? I don't care if you cure ageing, or stop starvation or end nuclear wars, if you forget this –" she rapped her knuckles against my forehead "– or this –" pressed her palm against my chest "– because even then if you save everyone else, you'll be dead inside. Men must be decent first and brilliant later, otherwise you're not helping people, just servicing the machine."

"That's not a very communist viewpoint," I breathed softly.

"No, it is the most communist view. Communism needs good people, people whose souls are –" she pushed harder against my chest, then sighed, pulled away entirely "– kind by instinct, not by effort. But that is what we most lack, in this time. For progress, we have eaten our souls up, and nothing matters any more."

She left shortly after midnight. I didn't ask for where or whom. I waited with the light out in my room for the dead hour of the night when the mind shifts into a numb, timeless daze of voiceless thought. It is the hour when all things are lonely, every pedestrian walking flat-footed over blackened stones, every car swishing through deserted streets. It is the utter silence when the engine stops in a flat, ice-drifting sea. I pulled on my coat and slipped out into it through the back door, circumventing Boris One and Breathless as I headed into the night. The secret to being unafraid of the darkness is to challenge the darkness to fear you, to raise your eyes sharp to those few souls who stagger by, daring them to believe that you are not, in fact, more frightening than they are. Easy, in this place, to remember Richard Lisle and the streets of Battersea, dead girls by the door. Leningrad had been built as Russia's European city by a tsar who'd travelled the world

228

and decided to take some of it home with him. Had Brezhnev travelled the world? The question surprised me, as something I did not know the answer to.

A corner. The streets in Leningrad are largely flat and sharp, a smell in the summer of algae on the sluggish canals, a madness in the city from the white nights; in winter euphoria at the first clean snows, then dullness as the freeze truly sets in. I walked by memory, turning a few times more than was strictly required to check on the presence of any would-be followers, until at last I came to the small wooden door of the Cronus Club.

Or, more accurately, the place where the small wooden door of the Cronus Club had been.So shocked was I to discover that the door was no longer there that for a brief moment I almost doubted my own infallible memory. But no, observing the street and my surroundings, this was the place, this was the porch, this the square patch of land where the Club had once stood and where now, built with tasteless 1950s brutality, a concrete plinth squatted instead, showing on its top a curious curve of stone crossed with an iron bar, and whose caption, chiselled into the stone, proclaimed:

IN MEMORY OF THE ULTIMATE SACRIFICE OF THE
GREAT PATRIOTIC WAR, 1941–1945

Nothing more remained.

Members of the Cronus Club leave signals for each other in order to find companionship in adversity. Entries in *Who's Who*, messages left behind the counter of a nearby pub, stones laid in earth for future generations to gather and speculate on, hints as to a place to go inscribed in the black ironwork of the drainpipes hanging from rooftops. We are hidden, but the simple fact of our existence is so patently absurd that we do not need to hide much deeper than in plain sight. Over the next three days I lived a harmless tourist life around the city, walking, looking, eating and spending my evenings reading in my room, at night slipping out past my warders to seek out the clues of the Cronus Club, any sign as to its fate. I found only one: a tombstone in the local cemetery for OLGA PRUBOVNA, BORN 1893, DIED 1953; SHE SHALL RISE AGAIN.

Beneath this tombstone was a much longer inscription in, of all things, Sanskrit. Translated, it read,

> IF THIS MESSAGE HAS BEEN AFFIXED TO MY TOMBSTONE, IT IS BECAUSE MY DEATH WAS VIOLENT AND UNEXPECTED. BE MINDFUL THE SAME DOES NOT HAPPEN TO YOU.

# Chapter 52

A dilemma.

To stay or to go?

What was I to make of the destruction of the Leningrad Cronus Club?

No degree of naïve optimism could dissuade me of the likely notion that Vincent was, somehow, behind this event.

No degree of self-deception could convince me that, in some way, I too was to blame – by my silence, by my vanishing to join the very cause I had set out to defeat.

And what now that I had learned of this truth – this old truth, years old, which had happened behind my back? Did it change anything? Did it change the essential wonder of our research, the breathtaking scope of Vincent's vision? Was it not true that the project we were embarking on, the question we pursued, was bigger than any mere blip in the present, any tiny alterations to the future? It was absurd – patently absurd – to let such things influence my decisions, and yet, even as I firmly rationalised this fact, I knew quite plainly that my decisions were affected, and I would not be the same when I returned.

Return I did.

Fleeing Russia would have been problematic, and I had every confidence that, as it had been all those years ago, the simplest escape would be death. Why alert anyone to my contemplating this by attempting a crude physical escape? Escape from what? To what purpose? There were questions I needed answered, and if they were to end in my demise, it would be a death of my choosing, once I had as full a picture as I could find. Planning and questions, they were my food for the journey back to Pietrok-112.

"Harry!" He was waiting for me as I stepped through the goods door, blushing with enthusiasm. "Good holiday, well rested, yes? Excellent! I really need your brains on this one. It's going to be beautiful when we solve it, simply beautiful!"

Vincent Rankis, did he ever sleep? "God for a pocket calculator," he added, sweeping me down the halls. "Do you think it would be a waste of time developing a pocket calculator? I suspect that the time saved in having one to hand would vastly exceed the time wasted in bringing the technologies up to necessary scratch, but one never can tell with these productivity calculations, can one? How many decades do we have until they invent the management consultant? How many decades after that, I wonder, until they abolish it?"

"Vincent—"

"No, no time to take off your coat. I absolutely insist, we're at a critical moment."

"Afterwards," I interjected firmly, "we need to talk."

Strange how the approach of "afterwards" can weigh on a mind. I knew every number in front of me and every outcome of the equation on the board yet could barely concentrate or say a word. The others joked that my holiday had made me soft, that my mind was addled with pretty girls and too much drink. I nodded and smiled, and after a while, seeing just how distracted I was, they stopped joking and just got on with their work without me.

Afterwards should have been dinner, but Vincent, bursting with energy, was far too preoccupied.

Then it was the evening and he was wondering if we should try working through the night.

By the time I'd convinced him this was a poor idea, we'd already begun, and it wasn't until two in the morning that I grabbed him by the sleeve, dragged him away from the blackboard and exclaimed, "Vincent!"

It was a rare breach of protocol to use his English name in front of others. His eyes flashed quickly round the room to see if anyone had noticed, but if they had, they ignored it. "Yes," he murmured distantly, attention flowing back to me in little parts. "We were going to talk, weren't we? Come into my office."

Vincent's office was his bedroom, and his bedroom was a cell like any other, small, windowless, humming with the sound of pipes and vents passing overhead. A small round table, a little too low to comfortably get your knees under, and two wooden chairs were the only furniture besides the wall-set single bed. He gestured me to a chair and, as I sat, pulled out a bottle of malt whisky and two shot glasses from beneath the bed, and laid them on the table.

"I had it imported through Finland," he said, "for special occasions. Your health." He toasted me, and I chinked glasses back, barely letting the drink wet my lips before setting it back down on the tabletop.

"I apologise for my insistence in there," I began at once, for it's always easier with Vincent just to get on with things. "But, as I said, we need to talk."

"Harry," he sounded almost concerned as he settled down opposite me, "are you all right? I don't think I've ever seen you so urgent."

I pushed the glass a little further into the centre of the table and attempted to arrange my thoughts in some sort of order. My desire to speak to Vincent had somewhat undermined the focused list of matters I needed to discuss; now I struggled to reassemble the cold plan of my train ride beneath the furnace of the moment.

Finally, "You destroyed the Leningrad Cronus Club."

He hesitated, looked briefly surprised, then turned his face away. It was an oddly animal movement, eyes focusing down into the depths of his whisky as he considered the accusation. "Yes," he said at last. "I did. I'm sorry, Harry. I'm somewhat playing catch-up – the reports from your watchers indicated you went nowhere near the property." A sudden flash of a smile. "I suppose I should expect that they would be reluctant to admit to their own incompetence in keeping you away, however. Did you like Sophia, by the by?"

"She seemed perfectly pleasant."

"I know it's a terrible thing to say, but sometimes, I feel, a man just needs to unwind. Yes, I destroyed the Leningrad Cronus Club. Was there anything else you wished to say?"

"Are you going to inform me that it was for my sake? To prevent my colleagues tracking me down, to hide the betrayal?"

"Of course it was, and don't you feel that 'betrayal' is rather a pejorative term? The Cronus Club are interested only in the endlessly repetitive present; you and I are working for much, much more. You believe that as much as I, yes?" He topped up my whisky glass as he talked, even though I'd hardly drunk a drop, and sipped his. If his hope was that I would follow his example, he was disappointed. "Surely this doesn't trouble you? It was merely to cloud the trail. And if you insist on using 'betrayal', I must remind you, purely in the interest of academic precision, that I was never of the Cronus Club. You are. The betrayal that you refer to was entirely yours, your choice, made freely and in full conscience. If you had any doubt about what we are doing here, and how wrong the Club is in its policy, you could have blown your brains out ten years ago. You could have blown them out today."

"Join or die?"

"Harry." He tutted. "Don't use the words of linear mortals in arguments with me. The idea that their philosophy, their morals, can be applied to either of us isn't merely absurd, it's intellectually weak. I do not say we must live without standards, merely that the adoption of mortals' rules is almost as feeble a choice as living with no rules at all."

234

"The laws of mortal men, the ethics, the morality of living, have been formed over thousands of years."

"The laws we live by, Harry, have been forged over hundreds, and are not enforced by fear."

"What happens here when you're done?" I asked softly. "What happens to the men and women of this place, to our ... colleagues?"

His fingers rippled round the edge of his glass, just once. Then, "I can see that you know what the answer must be, and that it distresses you. I'm sorry, Harry, I didn't realise you were becoming so reflective."

"Do you not say it out loud," I asked, "because you're ashamed or simply too much of a delicate flower?"

Another ripple, just once, like a pianist warming his fingers for a concerto. "People die, Harry," he breathed. "It is the fundamental rule of this universe. The very nature of life is that it must end."

"Except for us."

"Except for us," he agreed. "All this –" a gesture with the end of his little finger around the room, a flicker of his eyes "– when we are dead, will no longer be. Will not have been. Loved ones we have watched die will be born again and we will remember that they were loved, but they will not know us, and none of this will matter. Not the men who lived or the men who died. Only the ideas and memories they made."

(Are you God, Dr August? Are you the only living creature that matters?)

(There is a black pit in the bottom of my soul that has no limit to its falling.)

"I think we need to stop," I said.

Now he set down his glass on the table and leaned back, one leg folded over the other, hands tucked into his lap, a troubled schoolteacher trying not to let his anxiety show to the distressed pupil. "All right," he said at last. "Why?"

"I'm scared that we're going to eat our own souls."

"I didn't ask for a poetical answer."

"This ... machine," I said carefully, "these ideas we're exploring, memories we're making, if you want. This theory of everything, answer to all our questions, the solution to the problem of the kalachakra ... it is a beautiful idea. It is the greatest thing I have ever heard, and you, Vincent, are the only man I've met with both the vision and the will to pursue it. It is majestic, and so are you, and I am honoured to have worked on it."

"But," he prompted, the tendons standing up around his windpipe, the soft hollow of his wrist.

"But in the name of progress we have eaten our souls up, and nothing else matters to us any more."

Silence.

I watched the thin lines of his tendons grow whiter against his skin.

Then, in a single motion, he downed the rest of his glass, laid it with a chink on the tabletop.

Silence.

"The world is ending," I breathed at last. "This message has been passed down from child to dying old man, whispered down the generations. The idea is too big to comprehend – much like the ideas you seek to answer. But there are people behind it, lives that are being destroyed, broken and lost. And we did that. The world is ending."

Silence.

And then, as abruptly as he'd drained his glass, he stood, paced once across the room, spun on the spot, hands behind his back like the schoolteacher he should have been, and proclaimed, "I question your use of 'the'." I raised my eyebrows at this, inviting the inevitable explanation. "We are not destroying *the* world, Harry," he chided wearily, "only *a* world. We are not scientific monsters, we are not madmen out of control. It is undeniable that we will affect the course of temporal events – we have no choice but to affect the course of temporal events – but it is only one world which may be changed. We live and we die, and all things return to how they were, and nothing we did before matters."

"I disagree. We are changing people's lives. It may not matter to us; it may be . . . irrelevant, in the grand scheme of things. But in the grand scheme of things there are billions of people in this century alone who believe it to be very relevant indeed, and though we may have more time than they do, they still have the greater mass. Our actions . . . matter. We have a responsibility to consider the small as well as the big, merely because that is what the whole world around us, a world of conscious, living beings, must exist upon. We are not gods, Vincent, and our knowledge does not grant us the authority to play the same. That's not . . . not the point of us."

He puffed in exasperation, throwing up his hands and then, as if the rest of his body had to join in, prowled round the small room. I stayed still, watching him move. "No," he said at last. "I concur, we are not gods. But this, Harry, this is what will *make* gods, give us the vision of the creator; this research could unlock infinity. You say that we are causing harm. I do not see it. A message passed down through the Cronus Club? It means nothing, and you and I are both aware that no permutation of mathematics nor analysis of history could possibly suggest that our devices have led to this end, the factors are too great and varied. Do you assume that humanity must destroy itself with knowledge, is that your implication? For a man who advocates the value of short-term life, I find that a highly pessimistic view."

"There are theoretical implications for the quantum mirror in your ideas. What if—"

"What if, what if, what if!" he snapped, spinning on the spot to change the direction of his pacing. "What if we are causing harm in the future? What if our actions are changing lives? What if, what if, what if! I thought you were the level-headed one, for whom 'what if' was a theoretical anathema." His scowl deepened into his face, and suddenly he turned, slamming the palm of his hand against the wall. There he stayed for a moment, waiting for the shock of the noise to fade to deepest silence. Without looking at me he said, "I need you on this, Harry. You're more than just an asset, more than just a friend. You're brilliant. Your knowledge, your ideas, your support . . . I could unlock the secrets of

237

existence, of *our* existence, in just a few more lives. I need you to stay with me."

"Working on this," I admitted, "has been the single most exciting time of my lives. And it may be so again. But here, now, until we fully understand the consequences, I think we should stop." He didn't answer so, rashly, I pushed on. "If we talk to the Cronus Club ..." a grunt of contempt, fury at the idea " ... we can send questions further forward in time, to members whose understanding of the technology may be more advanced. We can see what effect, if any, our research has on time, on people—"

"The Cronus Club are stagnant!" he snarled. "They will never change, never consider developing because it threatens their comfort! They would suppress us in a shot, Harry, maybe even try to wipe us out. People like you and me, we are a threat to them, because we cannot be content with wine and sun and endless, pointless, questionless repetition!"

"Then we don't tell the Club," I replied. "We leave a message in stone, requesting information, ask that the answer is whispered back through time. We can stay anonymous, and once we know—"

"Thousands of years!" he spat. "Hundreds of generations! Are you prepared to wait?"

"I know you've been working on this longer than I—"

"Dozens of lives, centuries of my life, from the first stirring of consciousness in my father's arms to the day I die, this, Harry, *this* is my purpose." Now he turned and fixed me with a stare from which I refused to flinch. "You won't stop me, will you, Harry?"

A plea and a threat?

Perhaps.

Something tightened inside.

"I will always be your friend, Vincent," I replied. "Nothing less."

Did that part of my soul which curled up in knowledge of the lie curl up inside him too? Did we both recognise our own deceptions in that deep part of our beings that had no need for rational thought?

If he did, he moved straight through the second, waving it by like a casual acquaintance seen on the other side of a busy street. He slipped back into his chair, picked up the empty whisky glass, scowled to see it drained, laid it down again. "Can I ask you to take some time to think?" he said at last. "A week, maybe? If at the end of it you still feel the same ... "

"Of course."

" ... we'll work something out. I would be heartbroken if you went, Harry, truly I would, but I understand if ... conscience ... stands between us."

"Let's see how it is in a week," I replied with a shrug. "After all this, it would be hypocritical to rush into things."

Half an hour later I was back in my room, and not ten seconds after the door snapped shut was reaching for my travel bag and warmest clothes, and wondering about the best way to escape.

# Chapter 53

Did I ever tell you about the time I was kidnapped by Argentinian bandits? I was a businessman, which was to say I was taking the profits from a company while other people did the legwork and feeding most of my resources into the Cronus Club, as befitted the basic tenets of the institution. I was living in Argentina and, rather naïvely, had assumed that I was keeping my head down and causing very little trouble.

I was kidnapped while driving to market. They were rather unprofessional about it, taking my car out with a sideswipe that overturned it and could well have killed me then and there. As it was, I dislocated my shoulder and cracked a couple of ribs, and considered myself lucky to have done no worse.

As I crawled from the wreckage of my car, two men in ski masks came barrelling out of the pickup which had swiped me on the potholed road, grabbed me by an arm each and, screaming, "Shut up, shut up!" in heavily accented English, dragged me into the rear of their vehicle. The whole escapade can't have taken more than twenty-five seconds.

I was too groggy and confused to do anything other than obey, and lay face down with my hands above my head for the duration of the journey, where under more prepared or kinder circumstances I might well have made a better strategic assessment of my kidnappers. I was aware by the increasingly poor roads and rapidly rising humidity that we were heading into forest and felt no particular surprise when we finally came to a stop in a small round clearing of no discernible merit and I was pushed to a mud floor shimmering with larvae. They bound my hands with rope and covered my head with a cloth that stank heavily of roasted coffee, and dragged me through the forest. As will happen when you have a bewildered, injured, blindfolded prisoner on rough paths, I only made it a few miles before I tripped and sprained my ankle. A row ensued as to what to do with me next, and eventually a rough stretcher was cobbled together from crooked branches that stuck into my spine as they pulled me to their camp. There, to my great disappointment, the ski masks came off, and I was crudely shackled with a rusted chain to a post set in the ground. A newspaper carrying the day's date was laid at my feet, a photo taken and, eavesdropping on to the gabble of my hosts, I discovered that a ransom for some $300,000 was to be demanded.

My company could have paid the fee ten times over, but, listening to my captors, who still hadn't realised that I spoke a word of Spanish, I concluded that it was unlikely I would live to enjoy the cost-benefit analysis. As they clearly considered me a weak foreign businessman, I played the part, groaning as my shoulder and ankle began to swell against my clothes. It took very little play-acting, for they'd shackled my sprained ankle to the post and very quickly the flesh was pressing against the metal in hot, throbbing agony. Eventually, realising that a dead hostage was a useless hostage, they unshackled me and gave me a crutch to walk on, and a boy, barely fifteen years old, took me down to the nearby stream to wash my face and neck. He had a Kalashnikov, the universal weapon of all budget warriors, but he could barely hold it and I doubted if he knew how to fire the thing properly. I collapsed into the stream and, when he came to check on me, hit him round the side of the head with my crutch, beat him into submission and drowned him beneath the thin, shallow water, sitting on his spine and pressing my elbow into the back of his skull with all the weight and strength I had.

Examining my surroundings and my damaged leg, it seemed unlikely that escape would happen, and I resolved that, since I would almost certainly die in this place, I may as well die by the means of my choosing. So I limped back to the camp, preparing to go out in a blaze of glory. Somewhat embarrassingly, the first guard I came upon was having a piss by some trees and, while my sense of professionalism suggested merely snapping his neck and being done with it, I was, I concluded, not exactly SAS competent. Instead, I shot him in the buttocks, and as he screamed and the others came running, I got down on my belly and shot out the kneecaps of the first man to come into view.

To my surprise, no one else came.

Then a voice called out in broken English, "We do not want fight you!"

I replied in Spanish. "You don't appear to have a choice."

A pause while this information settled in. Then, "We'll leave the map and water – clean water! And food. We'll leave you the map, water, food. We'll wait twenty-four hours. That will give you time to get to the truck. We'll not follow! You take the map!"

I called back, "That's very kind of you, but really, if you don't mind, I think I'd rather just slog it out here and now, thank you very much."

"No, no, no need!" he called back, and really, I was beginning to doubt the commitment of these bandits to their task. "We'll wait twenty-four hours and go. Won't bother you again. Good luck!"

I heard the sound of movement between the leaves, of metal things being overturned, footsteps heading away.

I must have lain there for an hour, an hour and a half, waiting for the end. The forest stirred. Ants crawled into my shirt and considered eating me, but I clearly wasn't their choice of meal, and they crawled on. A snake slithered through the undergrowth nearby but was more afraid of me than I was of it. Dusk began to settle, and there was silence in the camp. Even the man whose kneecaps I had removed was silent. Perhaps I'd hit the femoral artery. Perhaps the pain had become too great to bear. At last, boredom more than anything else and a recollection that death was not my primary concern here pushed me to my feet, and, rifle in one hand and crutch in the other, I limped into the camp.

It was indeed deserted.

A map, water canteen and tin of cooked beans had been carefully laid out on the central table, along with a handwritten note.

The note said, in English,

"*Many, many apologies.*"

That was all.

I put the canteen over my shoulder, the map in my pocket and began the slow limp back to civilisation.

Whoever the bandit was, he had told the truth. I was never to see him again.

# Chapter 54

Regrettably, my escape from the Argentinian forests was not, I suspected, going to be in quite the same league as leaving Pietrok-112. Certainly, the actual leaving of the facility should present no problem, for there was no reason for the guards to suspect my purpose and there is nothing as reassuring as a friendly face, a polite wave and a man heading about his – presumably vital – business. It would be once outside, in the big beyond, that movement would become difficult. Acquiring an easy means of suicide would be vital, I decided, should it seem that capture was likely. The decision which remained was this – did I risk an overland route, striking out through the vast emptiness of northern Russia, using size and space to deceive my inevitable pursuers, or did I follow transport lines and try to lose myself in the Russian transit networks, creeping my way through cities and towns towards the western borders? I was more comfortable with the latter option, but rejected it. There were too few transport networks out of Pietrok-112, too many bottlenecks which could be sealed with a simple phone call, and even were I to somehow make it to a populated area and lose myself in the crowd, I doubted if national borders or state treaties would hold back the search. I knew too much, and was both too valuable and too much of a risk to the secrecy of Vincent's project.

Overground it would be, surviving to the best of my ability in the tundra. I had experience of living off the land, of both reading the simplest path and hiding my own trail. However, these were not the fertile lands of northern England where I had been raised, but a thousand-mile hostile nothingness. Suicide was still a firm option on the table, but death by starvation was unacceptable.

Did I have time to plan?

Time to prepare a stash, gather together the necessary tools?

I doubted it. There had been a look in Vincent's eye. He knew, as I knew too, that I was no longer his man. I did not doubt that the man who had torched the Leningrad Cronus Club would soon strike against any threat to his security. I had to get out before he could take action against me, and time would be short.

I threw together only what I'd need to survive. Money was irrelevant, as was a change of clothes beyond a pair of socks to keep dry. Paper for kindling, matches for fire, electric torch and spare batteries, a penknife for cutting wood, a metal cup from beside my bed, the plastic sheeting from my rubbish bin, needle and thread. I packed fast but carefully, slung my bag over my back and headed to the lab to pick up a small lump of black magnet and a length of copper wire, waving cheerfully at the lab assistant as I did so, for I was often to be seen grabbing random bits. I broke the lock into the canteen stores and grabbed as many tins of salty food as I could find, burying them in my bag, but was interrupted by a sound in the dining room outside, forcing me to scurry for cover. The noise went by and I marched upwards, heading back through the cold corridors of Pietrok-112 towards the armoury. I would need a weapon, light and reasonably adaptable. No Kalashnikov this time; a revolver would do. The armoury was guarded, but the sergeant on the door knew me and smiled as I came up to him, right up to the moment where my arm went across his throat and a tin of sardines crashed down against the side of his skull, plunging him into darkness. I fumbled for the keys on his belt, and found none. Cursing, I turned to the armoury door. Unconsciousness in humans is usually of two sorts – brief or terminal – and I doubted if my sardine-led assault on the sergeant was going to buy more than a few minutes. Was there time to pick the lock? I tried, using the copper wire from the lab and my penknife, cursing at the crudity of my implements, biting my lip every time a tumbler slid into place. A click, a turn, the darkness of the armoury beyond. I stepped inside, turned on the light and . . .

"Hello, Harry."

Vincent stood right there, calm as anything, leaning against a box of grenades. For a moment I was frozen in his stare, a thief caught red-handed: no denial, no chance to beg or run. I said, "In the time it takes me to load and fire one of these guns . . ."

"No," he agreed. "You won't make it."

He didn't move, didn't try to stop me. I sighed. At the end of the day, having nothing better to do, I had to try. I grabbed the nearest pistol, had the safety off and the empty magazine out in a click, reached down for the live ammunition on the shelf below, grabbed a fresh magazine, pushed it into the butt, felt it lock, raised it to fire – not at Vincent, but at me – when several thousand volts administered from behind sent my body first into paralysis, then convulsions, then nothing at all.

# Chapter 55

A padded suit in a padded chair in a padded cell.

How had I worked in this place for so long and not found this room?

Bright light and an IV drip. The drip fed into a vein in my hand. My hand was strapped to the chair at the wrist. I wondered if anything would be achieved by trying to wrench the drip out of my skin. In the long run, probably not. There were straps along the length of my arm, stopping at the bend in my elbow. More straps across my legs, around my ankles, across my chest and even, to my annoyance, my forehead. It was designed to make death by anything other than an act of God impossible. I reflected that it was probably also the best my posture had been for a very long time and was thus innately uncomfortable.

Vincent sat in front of me and said nothing.

A phrase written on his face.

Not angry – just sad.

I wondered if, in another life, Vincent had been a primary school teacher. He would have excelled at the task.

Finally I said, "Assuming I refuse to eat or drink, how long do you think you can keep me alive with nutrients and force alone?"

He almost flinched, pained by the vulgarity of the task in hand. "In a few years' time the IRA hunger strikers will live for over sixty days before death. I'm hoping, however, that we can find some better way of sustaining you than by putting a tube down your throat."

My turn to flinch. Sixty days is a long time to be a prisoner with no thought of escape but a prolonged, painful death. Did I have the will to refuse food when dying of starvation? I didn't know. I had never put it to the test. Could my mind reject life even when my body screamed for it. It depended, I concluded, on what that life was for, and worth.

Silence.

I couldn't remember there ever being silence between us before this day, or at least a silence which was not one of shared excitement and contemplation. There seemed no need for communication, no need to spell out all the obvious things which polite society required were said. Indeed, it seemed to me that in that silence we said it all anyway, and almost at the exact instant I had run out of things I wished to say to Vincent in the imaginary conversation in my mind and begun back again on a loop of it, he raised his head and declared,

"I need to know your point of origin."

The question stunned me, though it shouldn't have.

"Why?" I asked, mouth suddenly dry.

"Not to kill you," he blurted hastily, "Dear God, I would never do that, Harry, never, I swear. But I need you to know that I know it. I need you to realise that you could be aborted in the womb, not-born. I need you to know that, so that you will keep my secrets. I know you will never again be my friend, but the rest . . . is more important."

I considered the implications, not for my own life – the threat against that was suddenly very clear – but for Vincent. He was younger than me, born later in the century, and therefore the idea that he could somehow be a threat to me, prevent me even being born, was impossible, unless he had assistance. Someone of an older generation, someone who would be alive in 1919, ready to

248

poison my mother before I could be created. An ally in the Cronus Club? A collaborator in his dream, as I could no longer be?

He watched me, no doubt following the direction of my thoughts, then added, "I would rather not take the information by force, Harry. But if I must, I must."

A snap back to the present, focus on reality. "You'll torture me?" I asked. No point dancing around the words, and I was mildly pleased to see him flinch at the idea. Less pleased to see how readily he accepted it.

"Yes, if I must. Please don't make me."

"I'm not making you, Vincent; the decision is entirely yours. I'd like just to clear myself of any moral responsibility for that particular act before you do it."

"You know everyone breaks, Harry. Everyone."

A memory. Franklin Phearson, sobbing at his feet. Everyone breaks, and that was the truth of it. I would break as well. I would give up my point of origin.

Or I would lie and die.

"What will it be?" I asked airily and was surprised by the giddy lightness of my words. Recollections of Phearson tumbled beneath my thoughts like a quiet sea pulling back for the tsunami, and I rolled along with the waters, no longer in charge. "Are you thinking chemical? I should warn you, they tried antipsychotics on me before and it produces some unlikely effects. Psychological? No, probably not psychological. If I have only sixty or so days before my body is too weak to survive, and while I hate to overestimate my own mental fortitude, time is your enemy. Electrical would be best, but runs a risk to the heart – you do know about my heart, don't you? Extreme cold, perhaps. Or extreme heat? Or a mixture of both. Sleep deprivation as standard but then again—"

"Stop it, Harry."

"I'm just going through the process for you."

He managed to meet my eyes, and I found it easy to meet his. I'd never seen him beg before.

(I'm a fucking good guy, Harry! I'm a fucking defender of democracy!)

"Just tell me, Harry. Tell me when you're born and this won't have to get any worse."

(Christ, I'm not that guy, I'm just not, but you gotta understand, this is bigger than you or me.)

"I hope you don't mind if I again query your use of the phrase 'have to'." I didn't know who spoke but it sounded like me, albeit a little drunk. "You are under no compulsion to do any of this to me. It's an entirely voluntary action on your part."

"Everybody breaks, Harry."

"I know. But you can't afford to see how long it takes me, can you? So come on, Vincent," I relished his English name, rolled it round my tongue. "You'd better get started."

He hesitated, just a moment, then the begging was gone.

His eyes tightened.

(Make a difference, damn it! Make a difference!)

Franklin Phearson's voice in my ear. Once upon a time he'd made the pain go away and stroked my hair, and I'd loved him for it like a child loves a long-lost mother, and I'd been broken and he'd been right. In his own inestimable, pointless way, he'd been right, and I'd died and that world, to me, might never have been if memory didn't make it so.

With a half-shake of his head, Vincent stood to go.

"Not going to do it yourself?" I called after him. "Whatever happened to moral responsibility?"

"Think about it for a day," he replied. "Just a day."

And he left.

# Chapter 56

One day.

One day to avoid a fate far, far worse than death.

One day in a padded suit strapped to a padded chair in a padded room.

Look for the flaws in the system, any flaw, no matter what.

Chair bolted to the floor, IV drip feeding me the nutrients I would naturally refuse to take. Padded door, guards outside. They were the weakest link. Vincent, in refusing to participate in what would happen next, had left the process open and exposed to manipulation. I had no doubt that he'd ordered the guards not to speak to me, but sometimes even an under-rewarded soldier of the USSR has to take the initiative.

I tugged and writhed against the needle in my hand until at last I managed to pull it free, lacerating the skin across the top of my hand in a great jagged red stripe. I didn't call out, didn't say anything, but let the blood run in great crimson stains over the white padded floor, infusing the cloth with glorious technicolour. The strap across my skull made it impossible for my head to hang, but I closed my eyes and waited with what I hoped was my greatest faraway look. It took the guards shamefully long to check on me and see the blood still dribbling down the chair. They burst in at once, and then an embarrassing conversation took place as to what they should do, and whether to get help.

"Is he unconscious?" asked one. "How much blood has he lost?"

The elder and, I hoped, the senior, inspected my hand. "It's a surface wound," he exclaimed. "He's pulled out the needle."

I opened my eyes and was satisfied to see the man jump back in alarm. "Gentlemen," I said, "I imagine you're under orders not to communicate with me, so let me be blunt and to the purpose. I know you all, I know your names, your ranks, your histories and your homes. I know that you, Private, still live with your mother and you, Sergeant, have a wife in Moscow who you haven't seen for three and a half years, and a daughter whose photo you proudly carry in your pocket and show to all in the canteen every dinner break without fail. 'She is my diamond,' you explain. 'She is my wealth.' I have a question for you – just one question, and it's this – do they know nothing? Absolutely nothing about what you do? It's very important you think about this, very important you consider every aspect of every conversation you've ever had with them, for if they know anything, anything at all which could compromise this facility, then of course, gentlemen, they will be next. Your wife, your mother, your daughter – they cannot know a thing. Not even a whisper. That's all I wished to say, and now if you wouldn't mind applying a plaster to my hand, I'll get on with the business of awaiting my torture and inevitable execution, thank you."

They left in a hurry and didn't bring me a plaster.

It may have been twenty hours later, it may have been two, and Vincent was back. The sergeant from before stood in the doorway as he talked, watching me nervously over his employer's shoulder.

"Have you considered?" Vincent asked urgently. "Have you decided?"

"Of course I have," I replied lightly. "You're going to torture

252

me, and I'm going to tell you an endless series of whatever it is I think you want to hear, to make you stop."

"Harry," urgency, desperate and low in his voice, "it doesn't have to be this way. Tell me your point of origin and no harm will come to you, I swear."

"Have you considered the point of no return? That moment when the damage you've done to my body is so great that I no longer care, nor consider it worth my while, to say anything at all? You must be hoping that you won't reach that moment before you break my mind."

He leaned back, face hardening at my words. "This is your doing, Harry. This is something you're doing to yourself."

So saying, he left me. The sergeant stayed in the door, and for a moment our eyes locked.

"Nothing at all?" I asked as the door swung shut.

They began only a few minutes later. To my surprise, they opened with chemicals and a twist on the usual theme of the same, a partial paralytic, locking my diaphragm in place so I choked and suffocated, the air turning to lead in my lungs, blood and head. Some movement was still possible, the dose cleverly judged, so for an hour, maybe more, maybe less, I sat gasping and gaping for air, the sweat running down my face and spine, vision on the edge of darkness but not quite going over. Vincent had hired a professional. A small man with a neat moustache, he had his tools laid out – always for my scrutiny – on a tray before him, and like an athlete in training gave some time for rest between each new application of pain. At the end of every rest he asked the question "What is your point of origin?" and waited patiently for me to reply, shaking his head sadly when I refused to do so. Next up was physical nausea, causing cries not so much of pain but of an animal trapped in its own carcass, of heat upon heat upon heat, of a twisting, a shrinking, a narrowing of the senses until all I could perceive was my own hideously sane delirium.

And there was the sergeant in the door, watching, always watching, and when the torturer took a break to get himself a glass of water, the sergeant came in and took my pulse, looked into the pupils of my eyes and whispered,

"She knows I took the train to Ploskye Prydy, the end of the line. Is that too much?"

I just smiled at him and let him answer the question for himself.

Somewhere between the sickness and the suffocation Vincent came in and held my hand. "I'm sorry, Harry," he said. "I'm sorry."

I tried to spit at him, but my mouth was dry, and he left again.

They brought in the car battery long before, I think, they intended to use it. It was merely another object of interest, a thing to be placed on display. Sleep deprivation and extreme heat, a variation on the method I had expected, were the first order of the day. Someone with a highly creative appreciation of the use of surround sound and an ear for the unholy had created a soundtrack which oscillated between techno beats, tortured screams and graphic descriptions of violent and violating acts, carried on with Foley effects and in several different languages. If there was any danger that the noise and horror of all this was making me numb, a little too close to sleep, the guards came in and shook me awake, throwing ice water in my face, horror against the heat.

"You're a good man," I told the sergeant when he woke me again. "You know what's right."

"Drink, Harry, drink." Vincent's voice, a whisper in the sudden quiet. I knew he put a damp cloth to my lips and I drank greedily, until my mind crawled back to awareness and I spat the liquid out, spilling it down my chin and front, a thin concoction two parts saliva to one part water. The torturer's moustache was especially fine the day he pulled my toenails out. I imagined him sleeping at night with a net across his face to give it such excellent buoyancy.

"You're a good man," I told the sergeant as he folded up the plastic sheet from beneath my feet, containing its cocktail of torn nail and black blood. "How long until it's you?"

He looked over his shoulder to make sure the torturer was outside, taking one of his many rest breaks to stretch his fingers out after his work, then leaned in close. "I can get you poison," he whispered. He looked. "That's all I can do."

"That's enough," I replied. "That's all anyone can do."

The poison was rat poison, but rats and humans share more than a few passing genetic traits. It was enough. The torturer, ironically, didn't realise what my symptoms entailed until my kidneys were well into failure; even I could perceive the spreading yellowness in my skin was no reaction to having the little bones in my feet crushed one at a time in a vice. I howled with laughter when the torturer realised, shaking in my chair, stained tears rolling down my cheeks at the revelation.

"You idiot!" I shrieked. "You incompetent! You total arse!"

They unstrapped me from the chair and the torturer stuck two fingers down my throat to induce vomiting far, far too late. That was how Vincent found me, on the floor, shaking with laughter in my own blood-flecked puke. The old sergeant stood stiff and steady in the door. Vincent turned from me to the torturer, to the sergeant, and in that instant knew precisely what had happened and how. Anger flickered across his face, and he turned back to me. I laughed the harder to see the look in his eye, but to my surprise Vincent didn't lash out at the sergeant, didn't condemn the torturer, but gestured to two orderlies and barked, "Get him to the infirmary."

They got me to the infirmary.

They even gave me painkillers.

The doctor stared at the floor as she delivered her diagnosis, and my laughter, rather diminished by the loss of hormonal stimulation from my system, was only a smile for Vincent when he came to my bedside. "That was very quick," he said at last. "I didn't expect you to contrive a means of death for at least five days."

"It's been less than five days?"

"Two and a half."

"Good God." Then, "The sergeant's a good man. He didn't like what you're doing. If you shoot him, can you apologise to him first? On my behalf, that is."

Vincent scowled, flicking through my medical chart in the vain hope of finding some indication that I wasn't, in fact, already a long way past saving. I had finished puking, finished shaking and burning. The doctors had got to me in time to prevent cardiac failure, but my kidneys were lost, and my liver would follow soon, and that was enough. I didn't even need to look at a chart to know it was so.

"He'll be moved to another unit," replied Vincent calmly. "I am not in the business of unnecessary death." I nearly laughed again, but breathing was on the way out, so I only managed a grunt. "It's obvious now that I won't get what I want, so of course we'll aim to make your death as comfortable as possible. Is there anything I can bring you?"

"Wouldn't say no to more morphine."

"Alas, I believe you're already at your maximum allowance."

"What's the harm now?" His lips twitched, eyes dancing away. My heart jumped a beat. What more? What more could possibly be done to me in the little time I had left? "Vincent," I murmured, voice slipping low with warning, questioning, "what are you going to do?"

"I am sorry, Harry."

"So you keep saying, and I'm sure every toenail I left behind is grateful for your pity. What are you planning?"

He didn't meet my eye as he said, "I need you to forget."

I was so briefly stunned, I didn't know what to say. He half-shook his head, and for a moment I wondered if he was going to apologise again. The temptation to try and punch him if he did flickered briefly at the back of my mind, not that I could have possibly landed a blow. Instead, he just walked away and refused to look back even when I started screaming again.

They kept me tranquillised for most of my demise, which was a relief. It kept both the pain, and the thoughts of what was next, subdued. I know I dreamed but, for almost the first time, did not remember my dreams, only that they were fast and hot, reality intruding into the stories of my mind as a prickling on my skin that became the claws of insects, a burning in my stomach that became the carrying of my own guts in a shopping bag, the bleeding in my feet which was simply explained by my wandering mind as the slow swallowing of my body whole by a great snake whose body rippled like a harmonic wave with each new gulp of my flesh. By the time its fangs reached my midriff, my feet were already well into the snake's belly, dissolving a bone at a time in the slow pulsing acid.

They cut things fine. I was on pure oxygen and my stats still falling by the time they were ready for me. They wheeled in a new device, patched together from who-knew-what dregs of a mad scientist's mind. It needed its own power supply – a mere two hundred and thirty volts were not enough for this baby. There was some bickering about whether the trolley I lay on should be earthed or not, before one doctor with a great bark of "You're such children!" pointed out that the metal handcuffs which strapped me to its sides would do a perfectly decent task of channelling any current and that everyone was to treat this procedure as being equivalent to a cardio-pulmonary resuscitation, and be it on their own head if they got stung.

I believe I kicked and screamed and begged and fought, but in truth I was probably too tired and too dosed to make more than grunting noises punctuated by the occasional child-like shriek of indignation. They had to use masking tape to attach the electrodes to my skull; getting me to keep the final electrode in my mouth proved more of a challenge until the same doctor who had demonstrated such a sensible attitude to voltage reached the equally sensible decision to administer a paralytic. Sedation, it was judged, would probably not help what they were aiming to achieve, but I was grateful when one of the orderlies leaned over and taped my frozen bone-dry eyes shut. All I was left with was sound. It took them three false starts to get it right, the first charge misfiring as a fuse blew; the second failing to trigger because one of the leads had become detached in the attempt to change the fuse. When they finally got round to the business of sending a few thousand volts through my brain in an attempt to wipe every aspect of who and what I was from my still-thinking mind, it had a slight air of comedic afterthought.

I heard the doctor say, "Can we please get it right this time? Is everyone standing clear? All right, and—"

And that was that.

# Chapter 57

I've only once attended a Forgetting.

It was 1989, in a private room of St Nicolas' Hospital, Chicago. I was seventy years old and doing all right for myself, I felt. I had only received the diagnosis of multiple myeloma a few months ago, which was surprisingly late in my life cycle, and my enthusiasm in my mid-sixties for how little I appeared to be dying a slow and inconvenient death had led to me taking better care of my body than I usually did. I was even a member of a tennis club, something I'd never been in all my lives gone before, and I taught mathematics at a school in the mountains of Morocco for three months of every year, perhaps in an attempt to enjoy the company of the children that I could never call my own.

My visit to this eminently polite room in this eminently polite hospital on the edge of a more polite Chicago suburb, where the American flag flew proud and fresh flowers were put at the end of every patient's bed, every day, without fail, was not on my own account. I had been summoned, and the woman who had summoned me was dying.

Akinleye.

I hadn't seen her since that night in Hong Kong when her maid danced out across the water and she had fled before the sun rose.

They had me put on a sterile robe, and wash my hands in alcohol before going into her room, but the measure was rather half-hearted. The damage had already been done. How a woman with so few white blood cells left in her body was still alive bewildered me, and stepping through the door into the room where she would soon be deceased, I could see how obviously, how clearly, death approached.

Her hair had fallen out, leaving a pocked skull of crude bones protruding up like mismatched tectonic plates. I hadn't ever seen her without any hair before, but now I realised how egg-shaped her skull truly was. To say her eyes had sunk into her sockets would be a lie, rather it was that every ounce of flesh, every line of softness in her features had been eroded away, leaving no more than a skull thinly coated in muscle and protruding remnants of nose, ear, lip, eye dangling off it like baubles off a withered Christmas tree. She was physically younger than I, but in that place, at that time, I was the sprightly infant, she the ancient one, dying alone.

"Harry," she wheezed, and it didn't take a doctor's training to notice the crackle in her voice, the holes in her breath. "Took your time." I pulled up the empty chair by her bed, sat down carefully, bones creaking a little despite my exercises. "You look good," she added. "Old age suits you."

I grunted in reply, the only sound I felt was really apt. "How are you, Akinleye? They wouldn't tell me much outside."

"Oh," she sighed, "they don't know what to say. It's a race as to what will kill me off first. My immune system, you know. And before you tell me that AIDS is a lifestyle disease, I think you should know that you're an idiot."

"I wasn't going to say—"

"The others look at me, you know, as if I was evil. As if having this —" she may have wanted to gesture, but the movement was little more than a twitch at the end of her fingertips "— is somehow a result of being morally bankrupt. Instead of the fucking cheap condom splitting."

"You're putting words into my mouth."

"Am I? Maybe I am. You're all right, Harry, always have been. Stodgy old fart but all right."

"How long have you got?" I asked.

"My money's on the pneumonia getting me – couple of days, maybe? A week if I'm unlucky."

"I'll stay. I'm booked into a hotel down the road . . . "

"Fuck's sake, Harry, I don't want your pity. It's just dying!"

"Then why did you call me?"

She spoke fast and flatly, words that she had already prepared. "I want to forget."

"Forget? Forget what?"

"All of it. Everything."

"I don't—"

"Harry, don't be obtuse. You do it sometimes to put people at ease, but I find it patronising and annoying. You know exactly what I mean. You try so hard to blend in, I find it frankly intrusive. Why do you do that?"

"Did you ask me here to tell me that?"

"No," she replied, shuffling her weight a little in the bed. "Although now you're here, I may as well inform you that this ridiculous notion you have that if people find you pleasant, you'll have a pleasant time in return is stupid and naïve. For fuck's sake, Harry, what did the world do to you to make you so . . . blank?"

"I can go . . . "

"Stay. I need you."

"Why me?"

"Because you're so obliging," she replied with a sigh. "Because you're so blank. I need that now. I need to forget."

I leaned forward in my seat, fingertips steepling together. "Would you like someone to talk you out of it?" I said at last.

"Absolutely not."

"Nevertheless, I feel a certain obligation to try."

"For God's sake, as if you could say anything to me I haven't already said to myself."

I put my head on one side, flicked at the seam of my hospital robe, ran my nails down either side of the line, tightening it to a ridge along my sleeve. Then, "I told my wife."

"Which one?"

"My first wife. The first woman I married. Jenny. She was linear and I was not, and I told her, and she left me. And a man came, and he wanted to know the future, and he wasn't very polite when I said no, and I wanted to die, the true death, the blackness that stops the dark. That's why, in answer to your question. Why I . . . go along with things. Because nothing else I've done seems to work."

She hesitated, sucking in her lower lip, rolling it beneath her teeth. Then, "Silly man. As if anyone else has got the right idea."

The Forgetting. It merits, I believe, a definite article in front of the name, for it is a kind of death. I told Akinleye all the things which she already knew in an attempt to dissuade her. A death of the mind, for us, exceeds a death of the body. There would be pain. There would be fear. And even if she did not feel the loss of knowledge, of mind, of soul which the Forgetting brings, even if she did not regret its absence, having no recollection of what was gone, we who knew her, who were her friends, would be bitterly sorrowful to see her go, though her body lived on. I did not add the last part of my argument, that to forget was to run away. To abscond from the responsibility of the things she'd done and who she'd been. I did not think the notion would hold much sway.

To which she said, "Harry, you're a nice man trying to do your best here, but you and I both know I have seen and done such things as I would not live with any more. I have shut down my heart, cut off what you so charmingly call my soul, because I find that I cannot live with either of them. Do this for me, Harry, and maybe I can have them back again."

I didn't push the argument any further. My heart wasn't in it.

The following morning I went to the Chicago Cronus Club to collect what I needed, and I left a letter to be distributed to the other Clubs informing them that Akinleye would no longer remember who and what we were, and in her new, innocent state, we should watch over her, and only interfere once she had need of our help.

The technology of 1987 was only a little beyond that which Vincent used to wipe my mind. He had the advantage of some foreknowledge; the Cronus Club had the advantage of plenty. We may not tamper much in temporal events, but when it comes to matters of our own survival, the Clubs of the future share their knowledge with the Clubs of the past. I have even heard rumours of a steam-powered device deployed in the 1870s to aid with the Forgetting of its maker, though I have no proof to corroborate this claim, nor probably ever shall have.

Our device was a mixture of chemical and electrical, nodes targeting some very specific portions of the brain. Unlike Vincent's, our device did not require the mind to be conscious for the moment, and as I administered the final sedative into Akinleye's bloodstream, it felt like a kind of murder.

"Thank you, Harry," she said. "In a few lives, when I've settled down a bit, come visit me, OK?"

I promised that I would, but she had already closed her eyes.

The process only took a few seconds after that. I stayed with her when it was done, monitoring her vitals, sitting by the bedside. She'd been right – the pneumonia was going to win the battle of diseases trying to kill her off. Under other circumstances, I would have simply let her die, but the Forgetting had one other, vital step, essential to seeing if it was complete. It happened three nights after the initial shock had been delivered, at two thirty in the morning. I woke to the sound of a voice crying out. It took me a while to recognise the language – Ewe, a dialect I hadn't heard spoken for centuries. My knowledge of Ewe was middling at best, but I had enough to reach out and take Akinleye's hand and whisper, "Peace. You're safe."

If she understood my words, she showed no sign but recoiled at the sight of me and called out again in Ewe for her parents, for her family, for someone to help her. She didn't understand what was happening, looked down at her body and shuddered with pain. Mother, father, God were all begged for assistance.

"I am Harry," I said. "Do you know me?"

"I do not know you!" she wheezed. "Help me! What is happening?"

"You're in hospital. You're ill." I wished my knowledge of the language was better than it was, for the only way I could think of to phrase it was "dying".

"Who am I?"

"You'll find out."

"I'm scared!"

"I know," I murmured. "That's how you know it worked."

I put her back to sleep before she could ask anything more. As a child, born again, she might perhaps remember this encounter, and consider it a dream, but there was no need to give her anything more material than was absolutely necessary. When the nurses came in the next morning to change Akinleye's sheets, she was dead and I was gone.

# Chapter 58

A hospital bed.

Awakening.

A figure by my side.

Vincent, folded up beneath the curves of his arm, sleeping, his head resting against the mattress where I lay.

I woke from my own Forgetting, from my own encounter with mental death, and I was . . .

. . . still myself.

Still me.

Still Harry August and I remembered . . .

. . . everything.

I lay still a while, not daring to move in case I woke Vincent with my stirring, and my mind raced. I was still a prisoner in Pietrok-112. I was still a threat to Vincent. I was still dying, my body consumed by the poison I had ingested, but my mind – my mind was my own. Like I had with Akinleye, Vincent would want to test this hypothesis when I woke, would look for any sign that there was still a Harry left in my mind. I would not give it.

Some part of me must have twitched because Vincent jerked awake at my side. Seeing my eyes open, at once he leaned forward and examined me, as a doctor might examine a patient, looking for responses behind my eyes. I considered speaking, considered reverting back to my native tongue, to my native voice, as Akinleye had, but it seemed an over-complication. Instead I opened my mouth and made an empty baying animal sound of distress, which hardly took any mimickry to achieve, so ravaged was my body by poison and pain.

"Harry?" Vincent was holding my hand, as I had held Akinleye's, and his face was a picture of concern. "Harry, can you hear me?" He spoke Russian, and I just wailed the louder. Seeing this, he switched to English. "Are you all right? Are you OK?"

He was playing the concerned friend. The cheek of it almost roused me to reply, but there was so little time left, so little life, best not to squander it now. Besides, in the time I had been unconscious more tissue had died inside my body, and now all I could do was lean over the side of the bed and heave up a stomach full of acid and blood. I like to think some of it got on Vincent's shoes before he managed to jump back. My head was pounding, and someone had lined the inside of my eyes with Velcro, which crackled around the inside of my skull whenever I tried to look. My left eye kept going off in its own direction, creating a bewildering picture of a room with a gap down the middle as my brain tried and failed to join up the confusing sense data coming into its core. Poor old Vincent – the timing couldn't have been worse for him – not enough time to see if I was faking before I would inevitably die. He chose a bolder test. Leaping back from my bed he waved at two guards, barking in Russian, "Take him!"

They took me, one arm each, and dragged me out of my bed. They hauled me down the corridor – I was in no fit state to be anything other than hauled – and dropped me on my knees in a shower room where a lifetime ago I'd had an encounter with a very friendly lab assistant called Anna. Vincent stood in the door and barked in English, "Kill him!"

What was I meant to do? There was a risk that, by demonstrating comprehension of the order, I would show that my grasp of language had survived intact. Then again, if I took my own impending death too calmly, that might suggest that I had a residual awareness, an understanding that death was a relief in this scenario. Thankfully, the wretched state of my own body did most of the work for me as, finding itself dragged down a hall and deposited so unceremoniously, it duly went into convulsions which, I suspected, were the penultimate step in departure anyway, and I didn't even notice when the bullet went into my brain.

# Chapter 59

My thirteenth life began ...

... exactly as it always had.

Berwick-upon-Tweed, the ladies' washroom. After all the drama I'd been half wondering if I'd wake up the son of a king. If there was any form of divine justice in this universe, it was clearly taking its time in getting round to the affairs of the kalachakra.

The usual process. Passed over to Patrick and Harriet, raised as their own. I began to reclaim memory by the age of three and was, I am informed, a remarkably quiet child of very little note. Aged four I was on the verge of full faculties, and by my sixth birthday I was ready to go out into the world and declare to all members of the Cronus Club the simple truth of Vincent's plans and the things he would do to achieve them.

I wrote to London, to Charity Hazelmere and the Cronus Club, telling them everything. Vincent Rankis, the quantum mirror, Russia – everything. I felt that there was no time to bother with the whole rigmarole of removing me kindly from my family, so informed Charity that I would be stealing the necessary money and writing myself a suitably adult-sounding letter, and making my own way to Newcastle to explain everything to her in person. All she needed to do was wait for my telegram and meet me at the station. This haste and urgency, I later realised, probably saved my life.

I received no reply, nor expected one. Charity was always reliable in matters of infant kalachakra. I stole some shillings from Rory Hulne's desk, wrote myself a very fluent and eloquent letter informing any readers that the bearer of this note was heading to school in London and should be assisted by any willing adults in his path, and, armed with my best – and indeed, only – pair of boots and a sack of stolen fruit, I set off for Newcastle. Getting transport from the local village was impossible – far too easy to confirm with my parents whether they had given me permission for my adventure – but by walking through the night I reached, of all places, Hoxley, where once I had fled from Franklin Phearson and his interest in the future, hundreds of years ago. By presenting my letter and earnestly informing the postmistress that I was an orphan bound for London, I was given not only a ride on the back of her rattling truck, along with two yews and a lazy Labrador, but also some hot bread and lard to see me through.

At Newcastle I went straight to the telegram office. Getting my telegram sent was difficult, mostly because the desk was too high for me to reach, but a kindly lawyer waiting in the queue lifted me up to perch on the counter's edge as I explained firmly in my piping voice what my mission was, presented my letter and announced I was to wait for my aunt. After some hesitation, my message was sent, and the stationmaster asked me if I had a place to stay for the night. When I said no, he tutted and said it wasn't right for a boy so young to travel alone, and he was thinking of calling the police, but his wife commanded him to leave me alone and, at her behest, I was given a blanket and a pot of soup and told I could stay as long as I wanted in the office behind the ticket counter, and she'd keep an eye out for my aunty. I thanked her, not least because having to deal with adults' endless interest in a lone six-year-old boy travelling to London would have been tedious.

I waited.

269

The longest Charity had ever taken between receiving my telegram and reaching Newcastle was eleven hours, and on that occasion heavy snow had disrupted her journey. After eight hours the stationmaster's wife asked me if I had anywhere else to go, or if I knew anyone, and the stationmaster tutted again and said he was definitely going to call the police, because it wasn't right at all, not at all this sort of funny business. I asked to go to the toilet and crawled out the back window while they stood outside.

I stood guard the next day on the hill overlooking the railway bridge within easy running distance of the station. With every train that crawled in from the south, I slunk down to the platform's edge to look for Charity.

Charity did not come.

I admit I was at a loss. In all my time with the Cronus Club Charity had been a trusty staple of my youth, or if she had not, someone else had come in her stead. And now ... I was completely bewildered. A reliable support had been pulled out from beneath me, a crutch on which I hobbled through the hardest part of my life. Should I write again?

Caution instantly advised against it. There were too many questions unanswered, too many dangers still lurking. Vincent had wanted to know my point of origin, but as I was his elder the implication was clear – he must have a colleague, someone older than either him or me, who was capable of killing kala-chakra in the womb. The realisation that this must be so suddenly made the preservation of my greatest and only secret essential – under no circumstances must Vincent or his potential, unseen associates learn where I came from. My mind raced. Had I revealed too much in my letters to Charity? My intent hadn't been to disguise my origins; it was merely the case that she and I were so practised in the art of lifting me out of my childhood I hadn't felt any great need to expound further on the theme. What about past lives? I had given addresses – never my true address, merely locations near enough to the hall for me to monitor the mail – for previous letters to extract me from my childhood. Could they reveal my location? Certainly they would

270

narrow the search down uncomfortably. It wouldn't take a great deal of research to find boys of an appropriate age and quality in such an isolated area.

Then again, was I in any formal records? My illegitimacy, for so much of my life a curse, was suddenly a great blessing, for it occurred to me that there could well be no formal indication of my existence. My biological father would not acknowledge me, and my foster-father despised paperwork nearly as much as he raged whenever candles burned down needlessly, which was to say, disproportionately. Would anyone have even made any effort to prove I existed?

I had memories of my first life, when such things had mattered to me – memories of trying to draw my pension, of having to pay National Insurance for the very first time, bureaucracies confused by my existence. Even the name I gave myself was not true. I was no more Harry August than I was Harry Hulne; by the strict letter of the law I was the son of Lisa Leadmill, died 1919, who gave me no name more than a few syllables whispered on a bathroom floor.

But the simple fact was, I was not dead.

I had not been terminated before I was born.

If Vincent was making efforts to find me in this life, if he was sending out an ally – maybe several – who were older than himself, then clearly they had not succeeded in determining my true point of origin, and I did not think I had given enough information to Charity for them to do so.

And what of Charity?

What of her fate? Why did she not come?

This last matter, more than any other, prompted me to my course of action. I sneaked back into Newcastle station and boarded the first train to London.

I didn't buy a ticket.

No one prosecutes a six-year-old for fare-jumping.


Back to London.

London in 1925 was a city on the verge of change. In Stoke Newington the day I arrived the mayor installed a new horse

271

trough for passing beasts to drink at, and within a few hours of its ceremonial opening it was struck by a car that lost control on the corner. Everyone knew that change was coming, but as no one quite knew what shape that change would be, society seemed to wobble, balancing on a precipice, the old clinging on with one hand as the new pushed and shoved with the other. Costermongers fought with grocers, Labour with Liberal, while the Tories stayed aloof, reluctantly resigned to the reforms that were inevitable but tactfully hoping their rivals would push through the most controversial measures. Universal suffrage was the banner of the moment, as women who'd fought for political equality now turned their attention to social equality – the right to smoke, drink and party like any man about town. It was everything that my grandmother Constance would not have approved of, but then she had never really approved of anything since the 1870s.

It was easy for a boy to pass through these streets. Packs of infant thieves still abounded in the alleys and outside the brothels around King's Cross, and Holborn, for all its aspirant imperial grandeur, was as yet all façade and no belly. I moved with confidence, eyed up by the coppers but not stopped, heading deeper into the city, in search of the Cronus Club. The coal-soaked air turned white stone black; even the newer buildings were already scrawled with initials and messages scraped into the dirt. But there was the passage where the Cronus Club had been, where I had first met Virginia that warm summer's day at the height of the Blitz, and we had talked of time and protocol, and lounged between the dust sheets. There the door, and there no sign. Not a brass plaque. Nothing at all.

I knocked anyway.

A maid in a stiff white apron and hat that was three parts frill to one part headpiece answered.

"Yeah?" she demanded. "What you want?"

I lied instinctively. "Do you buy oranges?" I asked.

"What? No! Push off!"

"Please, ma'am," I blurted. "Finest Cronus oranges."

"Piss off, you little tyke," she retorted and, for good measure, gave me a half-hearted prod with her foot as she slammed the door shut in my face.

I stood, stunned, in the street, staring at nothing.

The Cronus Club was gone. I looked frantically for signs, for clues, messages left in iron, in stone, hints in any form as to where it could be – nothing. Turning wildly in the street I looked up for a notch in a gutter, for any smear of a suggestion, and saw a curtain twitch overhead.

My heart froze.

But of course.

Stupid stupid stupid.

Of course, even if you'd destroyed it, you'd leave watchers on the Cronus Club to see who came out of the woodwork.

Well, I'd come out of the woodwork all right, with the intelligence of the idiot child I appeared to be.

I didn't try to fight, didn't try to see who was looking at me from behind the grubby brown curtain overhead. I simply put my head down and ran.

# Chapter 60

I had no choice.

I slunk back to Berwick.

Back to Hulne House, back to Patrick and Harriet, to Rory and Constance. Back to where I'd come from, back where it all began.

I arrived, four days after I'd left, grimy, tired, bedraggled. A thief child who'd run away and found nowhere to run to. Harriet wept when she saw me, held me close and rocked me in her arms, sobbed until my clothes were damp with it. Patrick took me out the back and gave me the worst hiding of my life. Then, he dragged me up to the house and made me apologise, still bleeding, to Mr Hulne and all the family, who told me I was very lucky that I wasn't being thrown out entirely, to starve like the little brat I was, and that from now on I would have to work every day and every night until I'd made it up to them, nasty, ungrateful child that I was.

I took my beating and humiliation in silence. I had no choice. The luxury, the lifeline of my last few lives had been pulled out from beneath my feet. I was six years old. I was seven hundred and fifty. I was being hunted.

The Hulnes refused to pay for me to go to school, and Patrick, humiliated by my escapade, didn't argue the point. Harriet began dying early in this life, and I wondered if, in my way, I had contributed. I stayed by her bed to the end, feeding her poppy juice thieved from my aunt Victoria and holding her hand in silence. Perhaps my vigil gave me some credit in Patrick's eyes, for her funeral was the first time he looked me in the face since I had run away, and after that the beatings grew less.

In the wake of Harriet's death, and refusing to see her unacknowledged nephew grow up entirely wild, my aunt Alexandra secretly took to teaching me letters. Naturally, I knew all she had to say, but I was so grateful for the company, for the conversation, the books and the encouragement she gave me that I indulged her, a tiny compensation for her great gift. Five months in, Constance found out, and the argument between the two was audible even from the fish pond outside. Alexandra had more guts than I'd given her credit for, as her visits, in the aftermath of the argument, became even more regular. She was impressed by how fast I learned and, having no children of her own, failed to appreciate fully how abnormal my development was. As she became more a part of my life, Patrick grew less, until, by the age of twelve, barely a word passed between us, and no more seemed required.

I was biding my time and had very little choice but to do so until such time as I could pass for an adult. By my fifteenth birthday I considered that I could perhaps get away with the deceit, and, as manner is half the battle, I certainly had the bearing and intellectual capacity to pull it off. I went to Alexandra, asked to borrow some small amount of money, wrote her a letter thanking her for her kindnesses, and another to Patrick expressing the same, and left the very next day without looking back.

My task was that of a historian. I needed to learn the fate of the Cronus Club without exposing my own survival. It seemed likely that, whatever had happened to the Club, those in the know would be hiding. It also seemed likely that, no matter how determined Vincent's reach, he could probably not influence kalachakra more than a few generations older than his own. There would have been a London Cronus Club before, maybe not in the 1900s, but possibly in the 1800s and surely in the 1700s, or even if Vincent had somehow managed to stamp out all trace of it so far in the past, there would be other branches, in other cities, which he had not affected. I had to find them.

I began my research in the University of London library. Security was almost non-existent, and it was easy enough to pass as a student, swaggering my way into the reading room to pull out tomes on the social history of London. I also began, very cautiously, sending out feelers to other cities. Telegrams to academics in Paris and Berlin, never kalachakra themselves but those who might have an interest in society, enquiring after the Cronus Club on their turfs. Paris came back with nothing, and so did Berlin. In desperation, I sent messages further afield. New York, Boston, Moscow, Rome, Madrid – all silent. The Beijing Cronus Club was, I knew, in too much turmoil at this time anyway to necessarily answer enquiries, as it spent a large part of the 1920s–40s as a shadow Club, referring its members to more prosperous and reliable institutions. Finally I received a hit from a collector of trivia in Vienna, who reported that in 1903 a organisation called the Cronus Club had held a party for the city's ambassadors and their wives, but in all the troubles of the First World War it had closed its doors and never reopened them.

In London I scoured the history books and finally found a reference in the *London Gazette* to the Club. In the year 1909 the directors of the Cronus Club were closing its doors owing to "a lack of suitable member interest". That was almost all I could find.

1909.

The date gave me a clue and to a degree some relief. The Cronus Club had existed until the end of the nineteenth century, which suggested that whatever allies Vincent might have, they could not extend too far back in time. A child born in 1895 would by 1901 have recovered enough mental faculties to hunt down kalachakra at their point of origin and terminate their births. By 1909 the trend would have been noticed, the threat to the Club clear, and suddenly the organisation which was meant to protect its members would be a trap, a lure, and a danger to all who sought its aid.

Then again, even if the London branch was being so targeted, I couldn't believe the scale of these events, global in their proportion. No one, not even Vincent, could possibly have discovered the points of origins of so many ouroborans and wiped them out, not on such a massive scale. Even as that thought passed through my brain, another promptly occurred – that Vincent did not necessarily need to know the points of origins of Club members to kill them; he merely needed to make them forget. That would do the job well enough, and whole generations of the Cronus Club would tumble. Finding mature Cronus Club members would be easy enough, and I had no idea what kind of action Vincent had taken against them in my last life, since I had died too young to observe. He could have had forty years, maybe more, in which to hunt down every kalachakra on the planet and wipe their thoughts or, as he had intended to do with me, determine their point of origin. Either would be devastating and yes, potentially damaging on a global scale.

If this was so, then I needed to find a survivor, someone to confirm my suspicions.

I headed to Vienna.

# Chapter 61

The Vienna Cronus Club stood – or rather, had stood – over-looking the Danube on the edge of town, where the waters flood out fat and rolling, their tossing surfaces hinting at the great currents dragging beneath. The city was, by the time I arrived, little more than a pleasure palace for the gently declining aristocracy of what had once been the Austro-Hungarian empire, who would, in very few years, be ruled by Hitler and his proxies, then Stalin and his. But for now they danced and made music, and tried not to consider these things yet to come.

I had come to Vienna for the very simple reason that it was the only Club I had heard of, in all my enquiries, where it seemed an older generation had willingly dissolved the society. In London all trace of the Cronus Club had been wiped away, and I had received no answers as to my enquiries in other cities, but here, in Vienna, there was some hope that, in dissolving the Club, the directors had left a clue in the stones. Something that Vincent may have missed.

I dressed myself as a student of Austrian history and spoke German with a slight Magyar accent, which entertained my hosts no end. I paid my way through a mixture of deception, theft and, that oldest trick for the oldest kalachakra, remarkably accurate predictions as to what would win at the races. And as I worked, scouring the grounds of the former Club, tearing through the local civic records, I asked myself why had the Forgetting not worked on me?

I could think of only one simple answer – I was a mnemonic like Vincent. But then ... did Vincent know as much? The destruction wrought on my kind was a clear indication of how much Vincent knew and how far he was prepared to go with his ambitions, but in my case how much did he truly know? He had a rough idea of my age and possibly my geographical origins, but he couldn't be sure that my name was my own, nor could he know with any certainty that I remembered a thing. This latter could be a great advantage to me as long as I remained undiscovered. Being caught digging up dirt on the Cronus Club would be highly incriminating and reveal that the Forgetting had failed entirely. While my identity remained hidden, however, I could be the unknown thorn in Vincent's side.

With this in mind, I lived an endlessly changing series of lives. I stayed in no place for more than a few days, changed my clothes, my language, my voice, on a regular basis. I dyed my hair so often that it quickly became a brittle mousy mess, and grew such an apt forger of documents I was offered a commission in Frankfurt to do a job lot for a criminal mob. I left no traces of myself: no pictures, words, letters, names, documents; I kept my notes entirely in my mind, won only as much money as I absolutely needed from gambling and maintained no close friends. I never wrote to Hulne House, nor told, I think, a single honest truth about myself in all the time that I searched. I was going to be Vincent Rankis's nemesis, and he was not going to see me coming.

Three months it took me, which felt like two months too long to search. The Cronus Club directors had been careful, burying all traces, but one, a Theodore Himmel, had left a note in his will stipulating that an iron box be buried at the foot of his grave. The note was tiny, a quirky proviso in the documents of a man dead for over thirty years, but it was enough. I sneaked into the cemetery in the dead of night and by the glow of a torch dug down to the coffin of Theodore Himmel, scraping away until I struck metal.

There was the iron box, black and dented, buried as had been promised in his final will and testament. It had been welded shut, and it took me three hours with a hacksaw to cut my way inside.

In the box was a stone, written on in three languages – German, English and French. The writing was tiny, crammed into every curve of the rock, and the message read

*I, Theodore Himmel, who am of the kin known as ouroboran, the snake that swallows its own tail, leave this message for future descendants of my kind who may seek knowledge of my fate. As a child I was saved from the weariness of my life by the Cronus Club, who came to take me from poverty into riches, companionship and comfort. As an old man, I sought to do the same for the younger generations of my kind, a service I have performed for many lives before this one. Yet in this life it was not to be.*

*Up to the year of Our Lord 1894 the children of our kind had all been born as they should be. Yet from that fated year onwards more and more of our kin have been born with no memory of what they are, and there are some indeed who are not born at all. It would appear that in their previous life they were captured by a force unknown, and their minds, their souls, the repositories of a great knowledge and character accumulated over hundreds of years, destroyed. It is a sin against learning, a sin against men, a sin against all our kind, and I have seen my friends, my colleagues, my family, reduced to infants again. For them there is no Cronus Club, and I can only pity the journeys they must undertake in their next lives, as they go through the pain of rediscovery once again.*

*If you read this, know that I am dead, and that the Cronus Club in this life has been damaged beyond repair. Do not seek it, for it is a trap; do not enquire after others of your kin nor trust them. For so many to have forgotten so much, for*

280

*some to have been destroyed absolutely before their birth, can only be treason.*

*I ask you to bury this stone again, for any others who may come to find it, and pray that the Cronus Club will rise again, as our future lives roll by.*

I read it only once, by the light of my torch, and then, as requested, returned it to the bottom of the grave.

# Chapter 62

I had to find Vincent Rankis.

Infuriatingly, I knew that doing so would not prove easy and, perhaps yet more infuriatingly, that to do so actively in this life would arguably expose me to far greater danger than if I were to do it in the next. If I were caught in this life, it would be proof sufficient that the Forgetting had not worked, and I had little doubt that next time Vincent would not be so sloppy as to let me take rat poison before he had finally extracted my point of origin. Likewise, if I were to pop up on the social radar as too prominent or powerful a figure, it could well lead to questions being asked by linears, as well as kalachakra, as to my origins, and that information was now the most precious I possessed.

With all this in mind, and for the first time in my lives, I became a professional criminal.

My intention, I hasten to add, was not to accumulate wealth as much as contacts. I needed to find those ouroborans who were still alive, still remembering – those who had survived Vincent's purge – but I clearly could not use the Cronus Club to do so. Likewise, I could not use legal means and risk my enquiries being traced back to me, so I established for myself layers of security to prevent both police and anyone else who might be looking from stumbling on my true identity. I began as a money launderer, with the advantage that I both knew my way around major banking institutions and had foreknowledge of where would be wise and unwise to invest. The Second World War disrupted crime to a degree, in that it took a lot of the big business away from my clients and reduced whole economies to black market enterprises over which I had very little control, but the years which followed were ripe for exploitation. I was a little disappointed at how easily the techniques came to me, and how ruthless I quickly became. Clients who violated my advice, or who flaunted their riches in a way liable to bring attention to me, I dropped at once. Those who sought my identity too closely, I cut off. Those who listened and obeyed my strict precepts of business I rewarded with heavy returns on investment. Ironically, a lot of the time the front companies I passed the money through were so successful that they began making profits greater than the illicit activities which had funded them, at which point I was usually forced to close them down or disconnect them from the crime, to prevent too much scrutiny from the tax authorities of the countries where they were based. I never conducted my business face to face but sent plausible proxies, as I had done so many years ago when working for Waterbrooke & Smith. I even hired Cyril Handly, my in-pocket actor from a previous life, to conduct a few exchanges for me. He stuck to the script well this time, largely because I kept him away from the drink, until one day in 1949 when, in Marseilles, a gang of dealers suffering from revolutionary pretensions stormed the meeting he was attending, gunned down all who resisted and hanged the survivors from a crane, a warning to their rivals that they were moving on to this turf. The attacked crime syndicate retaliated with blood and fire, which got them nowhere. I lifted every centime of every franc from their bank accounts, grassed up every accountant and every front man who'd ever worked for them, exposed their shell companies to the force of the law and, when it seemed that this was only going to rouse them to greater stupidity, I poisoned their leader's dog.

A note left around the dog's neck proclaimed, "*I can reach you in any place, at any time. Tomorrow it will be your daughter, and the day after, your wife.*"

He left the city the next day but posted a tactlessly high bounty on my head before he did, which he could not afford to pay. No assassin ever claimed it. No assassin ever knew where to look.

By 1953 I had informants and contacts across the surface of the globe. I also had a wife – Mei – who I had met in Thailand during one of my flying visits and who wanted a visa to the USA. I gave her this visa and set her up in comfortable middle-class gentility in the suburbs of New Jersey, where she learned English, attended society gatherings, meddled in charities and kept a very polite young lover called Tony, who she loved deeply but would, out of good manners to me, always shoo out of the house before my return. For my few expenditures I received regular meals of an extraordinarily high quality, companionship when required and a philanthropic reputation. Indeed, I had a problem with what to do with the excess money I was receiving, and relied heavily on anonymous donations to charity to remove the compromising wealth from my possession. Mei excelled in this task, visiting the offices of every potential recipient and examining, in the finest detail, records of their words, deeds and actions before permitting the dump. Sometimes the glut of income was so embarrassingly large and Mei's scrutiny so thoroughly fine that I had to go behind her back and give an anonymous donation to a charity she didn't approve of, simply to save time. We were never in love, nor ever needed to be. We had what we desired and that was all, and to the day she died she was loyal to both Tony and me, believed my name was Jacob and I was from Pennsylvania. Or if she doubted, she never questioned.

All of this was fine and well, but its ultimate purpose was still hidden even from my wife. As my criminal contacts grew, so my ability to tap into sources of knowledge expanded, and by the 1950s I had policemen, politicians, civil servants, governors and generals either under my thumb or within my grasp. Considering that the information I wanted from them was so minimal, so simple, they must have been grateful that I was the one doing the pushing. My enquiries came through in the form of data on this or that building, or this or that name, ferreting out in my own side-winding way the fates of the Cronus Clubs across the world and of their members, who had lived, or died, or Forgotten. Sometimes I struck lucky: in 1954 I stumbled quite by chance on Phillip Hopper, the son of the Devon farmer, who in this life had inherited his father's business and was now, to my mild delight, producing clotted cream in vast quantities from his herd of fat, overbred cows. The fact he was working on his father's land did not bode well for his memory, as I had never, in all my years, seen Phillip do a stroke of work, but in a spirit of adventure I packed Mei on to a flight to England, bought her a straw hat, took her to see the Tower of London and finally jumped on a train with her to the south-west, where we spent a very pleasant holiday walking the cliffs, looking for fossils and growing really rather tubby on fruit scones. Only on the penultimate day, as if by chance, did Mei and I wander past Phillip Hopper's farm, climbing over the fence and down to the cottage door to see if we could buy some of his famous clotted cream.

Phillip himself answered the door, and there was no doubt, none at all, even in that first second, that he had lost his memory. It wasn't simply his circumstances, his accented farmer's voice or the look of blank ignorance when he saw me, and the flicker of contempt when he heard my fake American accent; it was a deeper absence. A loss of time, experience, knowledge – a loss of all the things that had made this man who he had been. Phillip Hopper, like so many ouroborans, had at some point in his last life been captured by forces unknown and the very essence of who he was wiped from his memory.

He sold us the clotted cream, and I am ashamed to say we had eaten all of it by the time our train got back into London the following morning.

# Chapter 63

There would be, I concluded, chaos in my next life.

Lying next to Mei in our polite suburban home, paid for by drug smugglers and fraudsters, I would stare at the shadows of leaves swaying across the ceiling and consider questions hundreds of years apart.

Those kalachakra whose memories had been wiped would wake with the same confusion and madness that I myself had experienced in my early lives. Usually, after a Forgetting, Cronus Club members would appear in the second life to shield the terrified child from the worst traumas of that experience and to guide them through that most difficult of times. But to do so now, with Vincent clearly aware of the identities of so many kalachakra, risked an exposure for those of us – however many there were – still with our memories intact. And yet what if we did not? Future generations of the Cronus Club, for hundreds of years, were relying on the twentieth-century members to protect them, to assist them. What would they do without the groundwork we laid?

They would find their way, I concluded, as they had no choice in the matter. The more pressing question lay in the here and now – what would *I* do, one of the privileged few who still recalled the nature of my own being, when in the next life the asylums of this world began to fill with men and women whose minds had been ripped apart by Vincent?

I needed to find a Cronus Club which had not been touched by Vincent Rankis's purge, even one would be enough, whose members still knew who they were.

By 1958 it was apparent that the only Club I was likely to find which would fit this description was in Beijing.

It was not a good year to visit Beijing. The Hundred Flowers Campaign had been briskly and effectively terminated when the communist government of China realised that granting cultural freedom was not the same as winning cultural praise; now the Great Leap Forward was commencing, in which the people of the nation would be fired up to advance China, sacrificing tools and metal, time and energy, lives and strength for the good of the nation. Anywhere between eighteen and thirty million people would die of the starvation which ensued. Getting in as a Westerner was almost impossible, but I had enough criminal contacts in Russia to acquire a cover as a Soviet academic sent to Beijing to share knowledge of industrial techniques and expand my knowledge of Mandarin.

Speaking Mandarin with a Russian accent is extremely difficult. Of all the languages I have learned, Mandarin took me the longest, and having to replicate the suitable tones while simultaneously presenting myself as a rather bumbling Soviet scholar was an exercise that caused me considerable distress. In the end I chose to emphasise my Russian accent over any great accuracy in language, producing endless sly smiles from my hosts and the nickname of Professor Sing-Song, which fairly quickly became the name by which all knew me anyway.

Even though I was, technically, an ally from a friendly nation, my movements in Beijing were heavily restricted. It was a city going through tumultuous change but, with the state of the country being what it was, that change was hideously piecemeal.

Whole districts of old Qing housing had been knocked down in a go, though no resources existed to replace the lost abodes. Great skyscrapers had been begun but then could not be completed, so a roof was slotted on some four floors up as if to say "This was our plan all along." Posters were everywhere, and the propaganda was some of the most colourful and, to my sensibilities at least, the most naïve I had ever seen. Ranging from the traditional staples of communist rule – images of happy families striving together against a red sky in a well-tended field – through to more unusual campaigns, such as suggestions that keeping potted plants would encourage clean living, or exhortations to mind your personal hygiene for the good of the nation, they reminded me of a sort of school art project plastered across the city. Nevertheless, the fervour behind much of the propaganda could not be denied, at least among our louder hosts, who spouted the rhetoric of the time with the passion of priests and who would, in a few years yet to come, probably believe the Cultural Revolution to be the greatest time of their lives. It was a reminder of the old truth that for tyranny to flourish all it required was the complicity of good men. In China at that time how many millions of good men, I wondered, were silently watching while this louder, snappier minority of believers marched and sang their way towards famine and destruction?

By day I taught classes of hard-faced earnest young technocrats everything I could remember about Russian industrial dogma of the time. I even drew up entirely fictitious graphs and charts, discussed non-existent steelworks and ways of motivating the workers, and took questions at the end of every session such as,

"Professor Sing-Song, sir, is it not encouraging ideological weakness to offer rewards to supervisors for increasing factory output? Should not the supervisor always remain equal to all his workers?"

To which the answer was, "The supervisor is a servant of his workers, for they are the producers and he is not. However, there must be a clear leadership figure in every organisation, otherwise we have no means of gathering information on its success or failure, nor can we rely on universal policies being implemented at the lowest level. In the matter of rewarding the supervisor for success, we find that if you do not, the motivation of the supervisor and the workers declines, and they may not struggle as hard in the following year."

"But sir! Would not a campaign of indoctrination in correct thinking be the appropriate response to this?"

I smiled and nodded and spoke utter, empty, vapid lies.

I had, very specifically, requested that my time in Beijing be limited to three months. I did not think I could sustain my deception any longer than that and wished to have an effective extraction route available should my cover ever be blown. I had also established links with the triads in Hong Kong, and, at my request and to their great trepidation, they had sent a team of five men north, ready to assist me at any given moment. Neither the men nor the triad appreciated that it would be I myself in Beijing using their resources, but rather assumed, as always, that I was operating through a proxy. The first time I met them, I was alarmed to see how poorly their clothes blended with their surroundings, for they still carried hints of Hong Kong bling about them – new shoes and clean trousers, soft skin, and, to my horror, one even smelled of expensive aftershave. I berated them in a mixture of Russian and Mandarin, and was slightly comforted to discover that their Mandarin was excellent, albeit with strong Hunan accents. As I worked, they went in search of the Cronus Club, spreading out through the criminal underworld of Beijing one cautious whisper at a time, for the government was nothing if not savage to criminals it caught.

The Beijing Cronus Club.

I had been reluctant to try it even at the beginning of my mission, for in the twentieth century it had a rather dubious reputation among the Clubs of the world. For so much of its existence Beijing is a stable, pleasant, reliable Club – something of a tourist destination, indeed, for if you can make the journey to its door it offers a degree of stability and luxury unrivalled by most other Clubs until well into the 1890s. However, from 1910 the Club increasingly shuts down, becoming much as the Leningrad Club was in 1950 – a shadow Club, a place to support its youth but little more. By the 1960s the Beijing Club is a bare whisper on the air, and several times, despite the best precautions of its members, it has fallen victim to the Cultural Revolution. In Soviet Russia, that kind of attack on luxury and intellectualism may be bribed or blackmailed into submission, but during the madness of those months not even the kalachakra can accurately predict the outcome of events.

The Club has also suffered other problems in the twentieth century, a large number of which are ideological. Its members have always been very proud of China, of their nation, and for several lives most will fight on this or that side during the prolonged civil war. However, eventually the more pragmatic members will come to realise that nothing they do will alter the course of events, and several leave, bitter and disappointed at the fate that awaits their country. Those who stay, and there are many indeed, are often caught up in a battle between national pride, an awareness of the bigger picture which many of their linear contemporaries lack, and the same ideological fervour which has so often destroyed the Club itself. When all you can see day in and day out are banners proclaiming the glory of communism, and your whole intellectual world is defined by this great rallying cry, against which you have no tool or defence, then, like a prisoner in a jail cell, those walls become your life. So it can be with the Beijing Cronus Club, and its members – fiery, passionate, angry, bitter, incensed, committed, rejected – carry a dubious reputation in the twentieth century. I am told that in the twenty-first the Club's nature changes again, and it becomes more of a place for luxury and security, as it had been before, but I have never known those days.

Finding the Beijing Club at the best of times is tricky.

These were quite possibly the worst of all times to even consider looking, but to look I had no choice.

It took two months, and I was already beginning to struggle under the pressure of colleagues at the university whispering that Professor Sing-Song was not doctrinally correct. The doctrine I spouted was, in fact, absolutely correct for the times we lived in, but I had underestimated how quickly the times changed and, vitally, how much more important the interpretations of rivals were than the truth of what you said. I calculated I only had a few weeks until I was deported, and deportation would be the soft option.

When the message came through, it wasn't a moment too late. It took the form of a small folded slip of paper under my door, written in Russian. It read, "*Have met a friend. Drop by for tea, 6 p.m. beneath the lantern?*"

"Beneath the lantern" was established code for a small teahouse, one of the very few teahouses still left in Beijing, which had been kept open largely for the benefit of the party elite and visiting scholars such as myself, to enjoy the service of attentive young women who could be extra-attentive for only a little more incentive. The madam of the teahouse wore a plain white robe at all times, but her hair was done up in a great crown of metal sticks and jewels, and I had never seen the smile falter, even for a second, on her wide round face. To show the teahouse's commitment to the Great Leap Forward, all the low metal chairs on which guests had previously been sat had been contributed to industry, and now guests sat on red pillows on the floor. The move had been met with great praise from the party secretaries who drank there, and eventually a gift of twenty lacquered wooden seats from one secretary in particular, who found his knees could no longer handle sitting cross-legged.

I met my informant, one of the triad boys, on the corner of the tight alley where the teahouse resided. It was raining, the hard northern rain that blows in from Manchuria and makes the tiles of the curving roofs clatter with every heavy drop. He began to walk as I approached, and I fell in some fifty yards behind him, checking the streets as we moved through them for informers, eavesdroppers, surveillance. After ten minutes of this he slowed his pace for me to catch up, and we walked while talking beneath his umbrella, as the streets of the city bounced and sparkled with rushing water.

"I've found a soldier who'll take you to the Cronus Club," he whispered. "He says it must be only you."

"Do you believe him?"

"I checked him out. He's not with the PLA, even though he wears the uniform. He says to tell you that this is his seventh life. He said you would know what that means."

I nodded. "Where do I meet him?"

"Tonight, Beihei, 2 a.m."

"If I don't contact you in twelve hours," I replied, "you're to pull out of the city."

He nodded briskly. "Good luck," he hissed and, with a single shake of my hand, slipped back into the darkness.

Beihei Park. In spring you can barely move for the throngs of people come to enjoy the fresh flowers and leaves on the trees. In summer the surface of the lake thickens with water lilies, and in winter the white stupa is disguised behind the frost in the trees.

At 2 a.m. in 1958 it is a good place to get into trouble.

I waited by the westernmost entrance to the park and monitored the progress of the rain as it seeped through my socks. I regretted that I had not seen Beihei in happier times and resolved that, should I live to the early 1990s, I would come back here as a tourist and do the things that tourists do, perhaps choosing an affably harmless passport to travel on, such as Norwegian or Danish. Surely even the most vehement of ideologues couldn't find anything wrong with Norway?

A car came up the empty street towards me, and of course the car was for me. There were few enough cars on the streets of Beijing, and I felt no great surprise when it came to a stop directly in front of me, the door was pushed open, and a voice called out in clear, crisp Russian, "Please get in."

I got in.

The interior of the car stank of cheap cigarettes. There was a

292

driver in front, and another man in the passenger seat, a military cap pulled down across his forehead. I turned to the third man, who'd pushed open the rear door for me to get in. He was small, silver-haired, dressed in a neat grey tunic and trousers. He had a gun in one hand, and a sack, also smelling of cigarette smoke, in the other. "Please forgive this," he said as he pulled the sack over my head.

An uncomfortable journey.

The roads weren't much to speak of, and the car's suspension had been welded in by a stonemason resentful of his change in career. Whenever we neared a crowded area, I was politely asked to put my head down beneath the front seats, an action which required considerable shuffling of knees as the front seats were a bare breath away to begin with. I sensed the move into country-side by the swelling of the engine as we reached open roads, and was politely informed I could sit up and relax but, please, not to remove the bag from my head.

As we travelled, the radio played recordings of traditional music and selected highlights from Mao's greatest speeches. My com-panions, if I can call them that, were silent. I didn't know how long the drive took, but by the time we came to a stop I could hear the first trillings of the dawn chorus. There were leaves rustling against each other in the damp morning breeze and thick mud underfoot as I was guided, still blindly, out of the car. A step up to a wooden porch, the *swish* of a door sliding sideways, and just on the inside of the porch the same polite voice of the man with the gun asking if I minded them removing my shoes. I did not. I was patted down briskly, professionally, and led through to another room by the arm. The room smelled ever so slightly of smoked fish, and as I was guided awkwardly into a low wooden chair, a source of warmth off to my right, another odour – green tea – was added to the medley.

The bag was removed, at last, from my head, and looking around I found myself in a square rush-floored room of eminently trad-itional design. There were no ornaments save for a low wooden table and two chairs, one of which I sat in, but a great window looked out in front of me on to a small green pond, over whose surface the morning insects were beginning to flick with the approach of dawn. A woman came in, a pot of tea balanced expertly on a tray, and carefully laying out two china cups, she poured me some of the brew. The other cup was filled and set opposite me, though there was as yet no one to drink it. I smiled, thanked her and drank my cup down whole.

Waiting.

I waited, I estimate, fifteen minutes, alone with the pot of green tea and a cooling cup.

Then the sliding door at my back moved again, and another woman entered. She was young, barely more than fifteen years old, wearing flat sandals of woven reed, blue trousers, a quilted jacket and a single lilac flower in her hair. She folded herself neatly into the chair opposite me with the merest smile of acknowledgment, took her cup of green tea, rolled it beneath her nose once, to take in the by-now cold odour, then sipped it carefully.

She eyed me, I eyed her a while. At last she said, "I am Yoong, and I have been sent here to determine whether or not to kill you." I raised my eyebrows and waited for the rest. She laid her cup carefully back down on the tray, fingers straightening as she adjusted the little vessel to place it in perfect alignment with the pot and my own empty cup. Then, folding her hands in her lap, she went on, "The Cronus Club has been attacked. Members have been kidnapped, their memories erased. Two have been terminated before they are born, and we are still mourning their departing. We have always lived discreetly, but now we feel that we are under threat. How do we know that you are not a threat to us?"

"How do I know that you are not a threat to me?" I replied. "I too have been attacked. I too was nearly destroyed. Whoever is behind this must have had access to and knowledge of the Club. This is an attack hundreds of years in the making, maybe thousands. My concerns are as valid as yours."

"Be that as it may, you sought us. We did not look for you."

"I came looking for the only Cronus Club which I know of as still being remotely intact. I came to pool resources, to determine if you had any information more than I currently possess which could help me track down the one behind all this."

She was silent.

Irritation flared up in some pit of my soul. I had been patient – thirty-nine years of patience, no less – and was taking a considerable risk by even showing myself to these people. "I understand," I went on, trying to keep the rising frustration out of my voice, "that you are suspicious of me, but the simple truth is, if I were your enemy, I would not be placing myself so absolutely in your power. I have gone to great lengths to hide my identity, it is true, but this is only to hide my point of origin and physical location from whoever is attempting to destroy us. I can give you some intelligence as to who our mutual enemy might be; I hope you believe it is in your interests to share any information you may have as well."

She was silent a good long while, but by now my irritation was nearly on par with my self-control, and I felt that to say anything more would probably be to lose any restraint I had left. Abruptly she stood up, gave a little half bow and said, "If you would wait here, I will consider this matter further."

"My cover is a Russian academic," I replied. "If I am to be detained indefinitely, I hope you will supply means of extraction, should the need arise."

"Of course," she replied. "We would not wish to inconvenience you unnecessarily."

So saying, she left as abruptly as she had arrived.

A few seconds later the smiling man with the gun came back into the room. "Did you enjoy the tea?" he asked, pulling the sack back over my head and guiding me to my feet. "It's all in the simmering, you know!"

They deposited me back where they'd found me, outside Beihei Park. I had half an hour to get to a class, and ran wildly through the streets, making it two minutes late to the classroom. My students, far from reproaching me for my tardiness, chuckled, and I gave a breathless lecture on agrarian collectivisation and the benefits of chemical fertilisers before dismissing them three minutes early and running even faster than I'd run from the park for the nearest toilet. No one ever considers the question of bladder when dealing with matters of subterfuge.

For four days I waited.

They were four infuriating days during which I knew perfectly well that my alibi was being checked and every aspect of my cover story examined by the Beijing Cronus Club. I was confident that they would find nothing. I had put enough safeguards between Professor Sing-Song and myself to necessitate a lifetime of investigation. On the fifth day, as I was walking out of the university and heading for my hall, a voice said from the shadow of a door, "Professor?"

I turned.

The teenage girl I had met in the house by the pond stood there, wearing khaki and carrying a satchel over one shoulder. She looked even more a child than before, dressed in her baggy-panted uniform. "May I speak with you, Professor?" she enquired. I nodded, gesturing towards the street.

"Let me get my bicycle," I said.

We walked together sedately back through the city streets, my foreign skin and undeniably quirky nose attracting all the usual stares, only enhanced by the presence of the girl by my side. "I have to congratulate you," she murmured as we walked, "on the thoroughness of your preparations. Every document and contact indicates that you are who you claim to be, a great achievement considering that you are not."

I shrugged, eyes scanning the street, looking for anyone who took too great an interest in our discussion. "I've had a while to get this sort of thing right."

"Perhaps it was your skill with subterfuge which saved you from being targeted?" she mused. "Perhaps that was how you escaped the Forgetting?"

"I was dead by Watergate," I replied. "I suspect that played a bigger part."

"Indeed. There was no indication of anything amiss until 1965. That was the year Club members began to disappear. At first we thought they were simply being assassinated, their bodies buried in unmarked graves – such things have occurred before, when linear authorities take too much interest in us – and will occur again, I think. But our own deaths and returns to life showed a far more sinister trend. Those who were kidnapped and killed had their memories destroyed first, which is a form of death that the Club cannot tolerate or accept. Here in Beijing we have lost eleven members to the Forgetting, two to pre-birth death."

"From what I've gathered from the other Clubs," I replied softly, "that seems a fairly average pattern."

"There are more patterns," she added with a stiff nod. "No one killed pre-birth was prior to 1896. This implies that their murderer is too young to act before that time. Assuming consciousness and faculties are obtained between four and five years old—"

"That puts our murderer's birth at approximately 1890, yes," I murmured.

Another strict nod of agreement as we rounded a corner. Students bustled against us, scurrying by to classes. Several groups marched together, carrying giant banners proclaiming STUDENTS UNITE FOR THE GREAT LEAP FORWARD! and other such tokens of impending calamity.

"The pre-birth killings appear to be targeted against older members of the Club," she went on. "It would appear the intention is to remove the most active members of our kind who might be in a position to interfere at the start of the twentieth century. Naturally their removal has an impact on the future generations of the century, who are more grievously affected by their loss than if, for example, you or I were removed."

"Don't be so hard on yourself," I joked, and she did not even flicker a smile.

"In 1931 there is a brief acceleration in the pre-birth murder rate. Where, before, the worldwide average for Club losses was six

297

a year, concentrated mainly in Europe and America, in 1931 there is a spike to ten losses a year, including three in Africa and two in Asia."

"The murderer reaching maturity," I suggested. "Growing more active?" Yet even as the words passed my lips, I discarded them for the more obvious, more simple possibility. "Another kalachakra, one born later, is joining the killings." I sighed. And of course I knew who.

"This seems most likely," she confirmed. "The year in which the killings spike suggests a birthday around 1925."

Yes, I could well believe Vincent was born in that year. "What about the Forgettings?" I asked. "Is there any pattern there?"

"They began in 1953, starting with the Leningrad Cronus Club. At first we assumed the Club had suffered some great political damage through the actions of the linears, but in 1966 both Moscow and Kiev were hit, with 80 per cent of the members of those Clubs kidnapped, their memories erased, and the bodies destroyed."

"Eighty per cent?" I couldn't keep the astonishment out of my voice. "That high?"

"Clearly the perpetrator has been monitoring the Club's activities for a long time, taking note of its members. By 1967 most Clubs in Europe had been hit, as well as five in America, seven in Asia and three in Africa. Those members who had evaded attack were sent underground and all Club houses ordered closed until 2070, by which date it was assumed our attacker would be deceased. Messages were left in stone for future generations warning them of the danger. So far we've received no whisper reply."

As the girl talked, my mind raced. I had known the situation was bad, known that Vincent had spread himself far and wide, but this? This was on a scale I hadn't even considered possible.

"By 1973 the attacks on our kind were slowing, thanks to the methods employed for our own protection, but those survivors who were not exemplary in their security still risked exposure and the Forgetting. In 1975 a final bulletin was issued from the Beijing

Cronus Club, urging all surviving members to take their own lives at once, to evade any pursuers in this life. Regrettably –" a twitch in the corner of her mouth that might have been sorrow "– we did not predict that after the mass Forgettings inflicted upon us our enemy would then seek to destroy so many pre-birth. We believed our attacker to be a linear agency, perhaps a government apprised of our existence. We did not realise that the perpetrator could be one of our own. The loss has been extraordinary. We tried to find out who was attacking us, who was bringing us down, but this . . . crime . . . was planned, organised and executed with a stark brutality that left us reeling. We had grown complacent, I believe. We had grown lazy. We will not be caught so off guard again."

For a while we walked in silence. I was still too stunned to speak. How much had I missed, courtesy of my early death? And to what extent, I wondered, had Vincent's all-out attack on the Cronus Clubs been a consequence of my actions, of my refusing to cooperate and threatening to expose him once and for all? Clearly the attack had been planned for a long while, but was I not partially responsible for bringing it to a head?

"The pre-birth murders," I said at last. "If they've been going on since 1896 of this life, that gives you over fifty years to investigate them. Do you have any leads?"

"It's been difficult," she conceded, "our resources limited. Those who died – we did not know their points of origin and can only conclude that they have been murdered by the simple fact that they have not been born. However, we have made some progress and narrowed our list of suspects down. In its way –" a wry smile now, as humourless as a tomb "– the loss of life among our people makes it easier to predict who might be our villain. By focusing on a specific time, a specific place, there are only so many candidates for this deed."

"Do you have names?" I asked.

"We do, but before I tell you all, I must ask you, Professor, what it is you intend to offer me."

For a moment I nearly told her all.

Vincent Rankis, the quantum mirror, all our research together.

But no. Too much danger, for where could knowledge of this have come if not from me?

"How about a vast organised criminal network that spans the globe," I said, "capable of finding anyone, anywhere, and buying anything, at any price. Will that do?"

She considered.

It would do.

She gave me a name.

# Chapter 64

I met Akinleye several times after her Forgetting. Once, in the life that immediately followed, I went to the school where she was studying, shook her hand and asked her how she was doing. She was a bright teenage girl, full of prospects. She was going to move to the city, she said, and become a secretary. It was the greatest ambition a young girl could have, a towering pinnacle of hope, and I wished her luck with it.

In the life after that I visited her again, this time when she was a child of seven. She'd come to the attention of the Accra Cronus Club – who in any case were keeping an eye out in that general area – as a child her parents called mad. They'd tried everything, from the shrieks of witch doctors to the chanting of imams, and still, they cried, Akinleye, their beautiful daughter, was mad. Already, the Accra Club proclaimed, Akinleye was a suicide threat.

I went to visit her before that could happen and found she had been given over to the care of a doctor who kept his patients shackled to their beds. Epileptics, schizophrenics, mothers who'd seen their children die, men with limbs hacked off, driven mad by infection and sadness, children in the last throes of cerebral malaria, their bodies twitching, were all kept together in the same ward, to be treated with one spoonful of syrup and one spoonful of lemon juice every half-hour. My fury at the doctor was so great that, on leaving the place, I requested the Accra Club to have it torn down.

"It's like this all over the country, Harry," they complained. "It's just the times!"

I wouldn't take no for an answer, and so, reluctantly, and to get rid of me, they had the building knocked down and a neat, square hospital put up in its place, where one fully trained psychiatrist cared for thirty patients, whose numbers swelled to nearly four hundred in the first three months.

Akinleye, undersized and underfed, stared at me wildly when I came to visit.

"Help me," she sobbed. "God help me, I am possessed by a demon!"

A seven-year-old girl, rocking in despair, possessed by a demon.

"You're not, Akinleye," I replied. "You are whole; you are yourself."

I took her with me back to Accra that very night, to the Cronus Club, whose members greeted her as the old friend she was and gave her the greatest meal of her lives so far, and showed her luxury, and told her she was sane and well, and welcome among them.

Many years later I met Akinleye in a clinic in Sierra Leone. She was tall and beautiful, trained as a doctor and wearing a bright purple headscarf in her hair. She recognised me from our meeting in Accra and asked me to join her on the terrace for lemonade and memories.

"They tell me that I chose to forget my life before," she explained as we sat and watched the sun set over the shrieking forest. "They tell me that I had grown tired of who I was. It is odd knowing all these people have known me for hundreds of years, yet they are still strangers. But I tell myself it is not me they have known – it is the last me, the old me, the me that I have forgotten. Did you know that me, Harry?"

"Yes," I replied. "I did."

"Were we ... close?"

I thought about it. "No," I replied at last. "Not really."

"But . . . from your perspective, knowing me as you did, do you think I – she – made the right decision? Was she right to choose to forget?"

I looked over at her, young and bright and full of hope, and recalled the old Akinleye dying alone, laughing as a maid danced out into the waters off the bay of Hong Kong. "Yes," I said at last. "I think you were."

# Chapter 65

My thirteenth life.

In Beijing I was given a name. A name whose owner was of the right age, right geographical base, right access to information, to have killed so many kalachakra before they could be born. There was no motive given, no understanding of what could have driven this name to do such acts, but looking at it hard and long, I began to fear that it might be right.

I sneaked out of China at the end of the week and was back in New Jersey three days later with my wife, her lover, thick carpets and solid brick walls.

I took my time. I investigated as only a criminal mastermind can investigate – slyly, cruelly, savagely and with a great deal of ruthless corruption. Dates and places, times and rumours, snatches of gossip and stamps pressed into a passport and yes, being the good historian I was, I could see the data begin to coalesce, detect the pattern of movements and say that perhaps this name was indeed responsible for bringing death.

It took a great deal of effort, time and money, but at last, having pressed every resource I had almost to breaking point, I found what I was looking for. I went to South Africa in February 1960 to confront a murderer.

We went to the farmstead as the dusk settled on the land.

A sign by the gate proclaimed that this was MERRYDEW FARM, a place of tough brown soil and tougher orange trees. Summer was at its scorching height, and the truck bounced and rattled over a dust track turned to stone as we clattered towards the glowing lights of the farm. It was the only spot of illumination in this otherwise empty place, tiny windows of tungsten yellow beneath a vast star-spanned sky. In another place, another time, it might have been beautiful, but I was here with seven paid mercenaries and an engineer, rattling beneath an infinite universe towards an encounter with some very finite possibilities. My mercenaries wore balaclavas; so did I. As we arrived at the farm a dog started barking, bouncing round the yard furiously on a length of chain. The door opened, and a man with a shotgun obscured the light, calling dire warnings in Afrikaans. My men bundled out of the truck, weapons raised, and shouted back, telling him he was surrounded. By the time he realised that this was the case, three more men had lobbed gas into the house from the back, blinding its occupants – a black maid and a white wife. Seeing these two subdued, the farmer lowered his gun, begged for mercy, and as his hands were tied together and he was dragged upstairs, swore that he would get us, some day.

The farmer we locked in the upstairs bathroom, the maid handcuffed to the sink beside him, the windows of the house thrown wide open to let the last of the gas clear.

The farmer's wife we kept downstairs. She was old, seventy at least, but I had seen her older in my time. The heat and dryness of this place had hardened her to rock, and she had none of the usual pudginess I associated with her old age. The mercenaries kept her sitting on a tatty sofa in the parlour of the farm, hands cuffed together behind her back, blindfold over her eyes, as I prowled the house, looking for anything amiss. Family photos – the happy farmer and his wife, here on their first tractor, there on a holiday by the sea. Memorabilia of times past and places seen, gifts hand-sewn by a neighbour proclaiming, "*Friendship and love*". Bills suggesting that the orange trade was not necessarily booming at this time. Postcards from a distant cousin, politely informing them that she was well and wishing them the best. Painkillers under the kitchen sink, recently purchased and being rapidly consumed. The farmer – or his wife – was dying, and I could guess who. I looked at the label. They were prescribed to Mrs G. Lill, Merrydew Farm. I wondered what the G stood for, as in another life I'd only ever known her by one name – Virginia. Virginia who'd saved me from Franklin Phearson, Virginia who'd introduced me to the Cronus Club, and now Virginia who'd betrayed us all, murdering us in our mothers' wombs. If I'd given Vincent one drop of information more than I had, she'd have killed me before I was born too.

I went back to the parlour, where my technician was already halfway through setting up the equipment we'd dragged all this way. My mercenaries were under orders not to speak, but at my entry Virginia looked up anyway, head straining round as if through her blindfold, in the direction of the creaky floorboard beneath my boot.

"You don't want money?" she said at last, in Afrikaans.

I squatted in front of her and replied, very softly, "No."

Her eyebrows twitched beneath the blindfold, trying to place my voice. Then her shoulders sagged forward a little, her head bowed. "You must be retribution," she said at last. "I wondered how long you'd take."

"Long enough," I replied, and rattling the little tub of painkillers for her to hear, added, "We nearly missed you this time."

"It's my nerves," she replied. "Quite literally. They're shutting down from the periphery in. I'll suffocate to death or my heart will stop just after I become paralysed from the neck down."

"I'm sorry to hear it."

"I assume you want my birthday?" she added quickly. "It won't be hard to find now you know it's me. If you wouldn't mind not torturing me for it; my heart really will give out very fast."

306

I smiled despite myself, and said, "It's all right. I don't want your birthday."

"I can't give you any information," she added firmly. "I'm very sorry, dear, but I really can't. Not that I know very much worth knowing."

"You must know *why* you did it, why you killed so many of us."

A hesitation. Then, "We're making something bigger. We're making something better. We're making . . . a kind of god, I suppose. Yes, I think that's what we are doing, in fact. A kind of deity."

The quantum mirror. Just enough technology, Harry, just enough lives, and we'll build a machine that can solve the mysteries of the universe. Look at all things, with the eyes of God. How easily the idea seduced.

My technician was ready. He looked at me for approval, and I nodded, stepping back. Virginia flinched as the first electrode was placed against her skull. "W-what are you doing?" she stammered, unable to fully bite back on her fear.

I didn't answer. As the next electrode was settled above her right eye she blurted, "Tell me. I've paid my dues, I've done my bit – always. I always helped the young, got the children away, served the Cronus Club. You can't . . . Tell me."

She was beginning to cry, the tears driving little pink rivers through the thick make-up on her skin. "You can't . . . You can't make me . . . forget everything. I'm . . . I'm not ready. I'm . . . I want to see the . . . see the . . . You can't do this."

I nodded at a couple of my men, who held her steady as the last few nodes were attached. She gasped as a needle was pushed under her skin, a chemical cocktail to soften up the receptors. "If I'm to for-forget," she gasped, "you can tell me your name! Show me your face!"

I didn't.

"Please! Hear me out! He can help you! We're doing this for everyone, for all the kalachakra! We're going to make it better!"

I nodded at the technician. The fat machine, all electric parts and stolen technologies, which we had lumbered down the tracks of South Africa, whirred into life, building up the charge that would be blasted into Virginia's brain. She was shaking now with the tears, and as the charge built she opened her mouth to say something more. The machine triggered, and Virginia collapsed forward – a shell, the mind burned away.

In the years to come the Cronus Club was to debate extensively what to do with Virginia, but in the end they made no radical decisions. The Virginia who had murdered so many of our kind had been destroyed, her mind wiped blank. I had made the decision for them, and that was all there was to say.

# Chapter 66

I spent the rest of my thirteenth life quietly hunting Vincent, and failing.

It is my suspicion that, in the aftermath of his attack on the Cronus Club, he was very deliberately keeping his head down, avoiding the attention of his now roused, if weakened, enemies. Nevertheless, I continued my search, as I have no doubt he searched for me, and occasionally followed the odd lead to unlikely places, always a little too late, a little too far behind. If my security measures were paranoid, I suspect Vincent Rankis in that life was operating on a whole other level. I can only speculate as to whether he was as lonely as I.

I lived far longer than I usually do, pushing both my body and the limits of medical science. No one seemed surprised that a money launderer wanted access to advanced technical equipment, nor did my doctors, after suitable bribes were administered, question why I might so firmly dictate the course of my treatment when the inevitable diseases struck. I had been surprised at how easy it is to corrupt men. Even good men, it seemed, could be swayed once you had them used to the notion that it was acceptable to give them a gift of a bottle of wine, then a gift of a new toy for their kid, then a gift of a day out for the family, then a weekend away, then membership of a golf club, then a new car ... by which point the great mass of gifts already accepted made the rejection of this latest present hard even for the best of men and their status as morally compromised assets complete in both the eyes of criminals and the view of the law. Mei was patiently loyal to the last. Her lover ran away in 1976 and she never sought another, spending her time instead writing furious letters to disreputable companies and campaigning vigorously for the Democrats. We saw in the year 2000 in New York, neither of us strong enough to travel further afield at our time of life, and Mei wept like a true native as George W. Bush won the election.

"It's all gone to hell!" she exclaimed. "There's no talking to people any more!"

We sat in silence watching the twin towers fall in 2001, over and over again, a loop on every screen across the country. Mei said, "I'm thinking of buying a flag to put out in our garden," and was dead three months later. I had never seen the twenty-first century before. I wasn't particularly impressed by the medicine, even less so by the politics, and in 2003, having decided at the ripe old age of eighty-five that another round of chemotherapy wouldn't do any good and that the painkillers I was now physiologically and psychologically dependent on were weakening my mind to the point of no return, I bequeathed half of my fortune to Mei's favourite charity and half to any kalachakra who could find it, and took an overdose one cool October night.

I think there is a study of the effects of narcotic addiction over multiple lifespans. I died in my thirteenth life utterly dependent on medications of a wide and occasionally interacting kind, and to this day I cannot help but wonder whether their effects on both my body and mind do not linger. I know it is absurd to suggest that any event in 2003 can have implications for those of 1919, but one day, with the subject's permission, I think I would enjoy studying the physiology of an infant kalachakra, who died of drug dependency

310

in their last life, to observe whether there are any marked effects on the child.

Whether there were on me in my fourteenth life I cannot tell, as, following the usual course, I did not begin to recover full faculties for the normal passage of years. I made no attempt to contact the Club during this childhood, limiting myself instead to the essential tricks of a youthful ouroboran: theft, manipulation, exploiting sports results and gambling outfits to acquire any money I might need. In truth, I was also still determined to keep my head down, and made no attempts to run away or find Vincent but worked as Patrick August's apprentice in the grounds of the house, as I had done so many lives ago, before the Cronus Club entered my existence. In 1937 I applied for a scholarship at Cambridge to study history, considering that, with so many ouroborans forced to forget and the Cronus Club in such a poor state of affairs, a knowledge of the past and, more importantly, of the means to study it, might allow me to detect patterns in events which I could usefully connect to Vincent in years to come. When I was offered the place, the Hulnes were gobsmacked, not least because Clement, my pasty cousin, had actually been turned down – a thing almost unimaginable for one of his wealth and background at the time. My grandmother Constance, for almost the first time in that life, summoned me to her study.

I had noticed something of a pattern in the Hulnes' relationships with me. For most of my lives my biological father, Rory, ignored me as one might ignore a somewhat embarrassing disease, a thing that is part of yourself but best not discussed with others. My aunt Alexandra showed cautious interest, hidden behind a mask of respectability; Victoria ignored everyone who wasn't of use to her, and I was no different; and my grandmother Constance actively shunned me and yet was also the regular bearer of bad news. If my actions were somehow disreputable – and at that time it took very little for a bastard son's deeds to be considered disreputable – it was Constance more than Rory who did what she doubtless considered to be necessary but dirty work.

So it was then, and as I was summoned into her study, a

311

scholarship boy of eighteen years old, she was already set for recriminations, her back turned to the door through which I entered, a pair of hanging silver earrings bouncing beside the harsh line of her chin. She glanced at me in the mirror by which she adorned herself, before her eyes darted back to the examination of her ears and, without turning, she said, "Ah, Harry. Yes, I did want to see you, didn't I?"

It had been remarkably easy to move beyond the fact that, in my infant years, Constance had wanted to throw me back whence I came. To me, after all, these revelations were hundreds of years old, yet I had to recall that to her the impulse was only as old as my current physical body.

She faffed with her earring a little longer, then turned sharply as if all interest was lost in this task, to stare at me hard down a pointed nose. Whatever unkind genetic pixie had gifted me with my face, it hadn't spawned on her side of the family.

"I hear you are for Cambridge," she said at last. "Not quite as fashionable as Oxford, but I suppose for someone like you it must be a great thing."

"I'm very glad, ma'am."

"Glad? Is that what you are? Yes, I suppose you must be. They tell me that the college was so impressed that they are overlooking your background, is that correct? Your father can't be having letters asking for financial assistance once you're gone, that won't do at all."

"The college have been very generous," I replied, "and I have some other means."

Her eyebrows arched in disdain at this notion. "Do you? Do you indeed?"

I bit back on my reply. "Yes, biological Grandmother. I know precisely who wins the Grand National every year from 1921 to 2004, as well as having an encyclopaedic knowledge of famous boxing matches, football championships and even the occasional dog race for the same time period, in case I am starved of choice." Somehow it didn't seem like an appropriate revelation for the moment.

312

"Of course it's very inconvenient of you to leave at this time," she blurted against my more considered silence. "Your father is hardly as young as he was, and the grounds . . . Well, I needn't tell you how much he's valued his work for this family. I had rather expected you to do the same."

It was a conversation I'd had with Constance every time I'd left the nest for any employment other than national service. At first I thought it was sheer resentment at my potential success, but as the conversations rolled by I had begun to wonder if it were not a deeper anxiety – a desire, even now, to keep control of the boy who symbolised her son's greatest mistake. I remembered Holy Island, my father dying in a room above a cottage, and felt a brief flush of unexpected shame at the things I had said to him.

" . . . it's actually rather ungrateful, I think, for a boy like you to just abandon his home like this."

The words brought me back to my grandmother's study. I imagine there had been some preamble to this statement, but live as a servant long enough and you acquire an understanding of when sound is meaningless. "Ungrateful, ma'am?" I queried.

"You've been a part of this household your whole life," she replied, "practically a part of the estate! And now to just pick up and go, it's really not what we were expecting from you, Harry, I must admit. We all thought rather better of you."

"Better . . . than getting a scholarship to Cambridge?" I suggested.

"Yes, and the backhanded way in which you did that! No seeking permission, no extra studies, no tuition at all, from what I can see. It's not how these things are done!"

I stared at Constance and wondered if, in her way, she wasn't quite, quite mad. Not a neurological madness, not a disease of the mind, but rather a cultural madness, an infection of expectations which corrupted her perception of what should be and what actually was. Under any other circumstances I would have been praised as a genius, an unmitigated hero and quite possibly a model for social reform in stodgy times; but to Constance all these things made me a rebel. I wondered what she would make

313

of the twenty-first century, if she would have wept when the twin towers fell. Was it a world she would have been able to comprehend?

"Are you asking me to stay?" I queried.

"You're a young man," she retorted. "If you want to abandon your father and go off to a place where, I personally feel, you'll be quite unsuited to the life, then of course that's entirely your decision!"

What would this conversation have been like, I wondered, if I was only eighteen years old? Now, in my eight hundred and forty-ninth year, it was almost funny.

I informed her I would consider my position most carefully.

She sniffed some empty words in reply and dismissed me with a wave.

I made it to the end of the corridor before I burst out laughing.

# Chapter 67

Being an undergraduate again brought back memories.

Memories of Vincent, mostly.

Of better times.

When World War Two broke out and I was called up, I managed to get myself assigned to military intelligence. By 1943 I was working on Allied deception plans, agonising about whether cardboard tanks needed to be fully three-dimensional scale models, or if a well painted cut-out, adjusted for the position of the sun, could do the job of confusing a reconnaissance pilot. By 1944 I was so involved with my work that my heart would genuinely skip a beat whenever I heard rumours of a scout plane which had made it over the Kent coast *before* we could fully deploy our models, or which had come a little too low over one of our fake camps. Vincent was briefly forgotten about until in April 1944 a group of visiting Americans, come to inspect one of our phoney landing strips, asked me entirely casually if I had any models of the new jet fighters ready to deploy.

The question caught me so by surprise that it was one of the few moments when I actually doubted my own memory. A jet fighter this early? I knew the jet engine was under development, and tests were being conducted on the technology, but for actual deployment in battle? If such a thing had been even considered, it was in no record of the war I'd read, nor in no life during the war that I had lived, and I had dabbled in some senior positions with access to sensitive information in my time. I made some vague remarks and quickly took our visitors on to explain to them how our radio operators were working round the clock to generate as much radio traffic as possible in Kent between the large numbers of fictional units we'd stationed there, and how we'd be grateful if the US Army could issue us with a wider range of suitable call signs. The meeting done, the visitors adjourned, and I was left to ponder the great mystery of the throwaway question. In the guise of an eager official seeking to do a good job, I sounded out a few contacts in the American air force, looking for information on this new jet engine so that I might better deceive our enemy into thinking we had it, or didn't have it, or whatever it was government policy dictated was the lie of the moment. A few replies drifted back from the ether. Yeah, it was a project some of the boffins were working on, wasn't it? Sorry, Harry, not really my thing. Had I talked to any of the chaps down in Portsmouth? Maybe they'd have something more. Getting nowhere, I nearly let the matter drop altogether, until in December 1945, visiting a friend in hospital in Folkestone, he shook me warmly by the hand, exclaimed how pleased he was to see me and asked me if I'd heard about his new kidney. He even showed me the scar from the operation, which impressed me greatly not least as the first organ transplant operation wasn't due to happen for another five years.

# Chapter 68

The world was changing, and the source of the change was America.

In another time such flagrant and obvious corruptions of the normal passage of things would have brought the Cronus Club tumbling down on their creator's head like the walls of Babylon atop a heretical priest. But the Clubs were not only weakened, but in this life – the second since the massed Forgettings inflicted on its members – hundreds of members were coming into an awareness of who and what they were as though for the very first time. Previously the Clubs had had to process one new member each every century or so, but in this new world the survivors were swamped.

"We could do with your help, Harry," Akinleye said.

Remarkable Akinleye, who had chosen to forget and who, through luck more than anything else, had managed to escape Vincent's clutches when he came after us all, was taking charge. Aged sixteen years old, she was juggling duties in London, Paris, Naples and Algiers, marshalling survivors and caring for the newcomers only just beginning to learn what they were. "I've got kalachakra kids committing suicide; I've got kids in mental institutions, adults getting God, adults not understanding why they shouldn't kill Hitler, and, Harry, I've only been doing this for four lives that I can remember myself. You're one of the lucky few who hasn't lost control. Help me."

Akinleye, the only kalachakra who knew the truth, knew that Vincent hadn't wiped my memory. I didn't dare tell anyone else.

"I think the one who did this is still out there," I replied. "If I can't find him, he'll only come after the Clubs again."

"There's time for revenge later, isn't there?"

"Maybe. But maybe not. Time has always been our problem in the Cronus Clubs. Always had so much; never learned to appreciate it."

I left her to struggle on, and flew to America in 1947, an expert in strategic deception, a scholar of Mediterranean corsairs in the 1720s, a press pass in my wallet for a minor British newspaper looking to expand its focus, and my eyes firmly set on Vincent Rankis, wherever he might be.

Wherever he was, he was certainly busy. Colour TVs were already on sale, and scientists were wondering how long it would be before man walked on the moon. Clearly sooner, their enthusiasm seemed to imply, than I was used to. It was a country in boom, the fervour of those who'd lived through the war combining with an overwhelming sense that this time America hadn't simply won, it was *the* victor, unstoppable, undefeatable, a country that had fought on two fronts and on both fronts had proved itself superior. The nuclear age was upon us and it seemed only a matter of time before everyone wore tight-fitting suits and flew to work with a rocket pack. The Soviet menace was a gathering storm on the horizon, but damn it, Good Americans would triumph over the tiny minority of Bad Americans who were swayed by this doctrine of evil, as Good Americans had triumphed so powerfully before. I had lived a long time in America, in lives gone by, but hadn't before crossed the waters so soon after the Second World War. The civil rights movement, Vietnam, Watergate – these were all to come, and now I was somewhat overwhelmed by the warmth of my welcome, the hearty greetings and genuine praise I received even for such trivial achievements as walking into a drug store and buying a toothbrush ("An excellent choice of toothbrush, sir!"), and the many admonitions to buy household goods which should not – quite simply *should not* – have been. Watching the colour TV in my hotel room, I wondered if Senator McCarthy would do so well in this new world, now the vivid flushes of his skin could be seen in such glorious technicolour. Black and white, I concluded, lent a certain dignity to proceedings that the proceedings themselves probably lacked.

As luck would have it, I was not the only one who had noticed America's remarkable technological breakthroughs. Even linear journalists were printing headlines like AMERICA DOES IT AGAIN! praising some out-of-the-blue discovery. Magazines hailed the years 1945–50 as the "Epoch of Invention", distressing both the ouroboran and pedant inside me, while Eisenhower went on TV to warn, not only against the burgeoning military-industrial complex, but the loss of American Values which this new era of steel, copper and wireless technology might bring. By 1953 street lighting was going halogen, Valium was the anti-depressant of choice and we were all being invited to trade in our clunky, unfashionable glasses for soft contact lenses guaranteed to bring the sparkle back into the corner of your eye. I watched, amazed by the cartoonish quality of it all, as the society of 1953 processed the technology of 1960 with both a ravenous hunger and a slight hesitation as if the generations who were set to rebel weren't quite sure yet what it was they were meant to rebel against.

The most infuriating part of all this was tracing the source of the outbreak. Inventions weren't springing out of one company or one place, but from dozens of companies and campuses across the country, all of which then engaged in bitter patent rows with each other while the technology spread virus-like from mind to mind, unstoppable, uncontainable, out of control. I spent nearly two years trying to pin down where these remarkable ideas were springing from, growing ever more infuriated by the stonewalling and empty shrugs I received for my enquiries even as teams of scientists set to work taking the basic principles behind mundane devices and extrapolating them into something entirely new, entirely their own work, and far, far too advanced for the time of their invention. Perhaps more alarming, for every new device the Americans came up with, the Soviets would send more agents to steal it, and push their own people harder to find the answers for themselves, and so the technology race accelerated.

It took a doctor of chemistry at MIT, one Adam Schofield, to finally give me the answer I needed. We'd met at a talk on "Innovation, Experimentation and the New Age". We had a drink afterwards in a hotel bar and talked about bad cars, good books, disappointing sportsmen and the upcoming presidential race, before finally getting on to the subject of the day's latest developments in biomass energy.

"You know what, Harry?" he explained, leaning in close over the embarrassingly empty bottle of port we'd been sharing. "I feel like such a liar when I take credit for that."

Indeed, but why, Dr Schofield?

"I understand it; I can explain it; we can do fucking amazing things with it – amazing things, Harry, I mean, paradigm-shift-amazing – but the actual idea? I tell people it 'came to me in my sleep'. Can you believe that crap? What a load of bull."

Oh, but no, Dr Schofield, surely not, Dr Schofield, but then where did your ideas come from?

"Some letter in the post! Five sides of fucking science like you would not believe, like you've never fucking seen. Took me four days before I got it, and I was sat looking at it, and, Harry, this letter, this guy, whoever sent it – it was the mother lode."

Did he know who he was?

No, he did not, but . . .

"Do you still have this letter?"

"Sure! Kept in a drawer. I've always been open about this to anyone who asked, because I sure as hell don't wanna get sued if this guy ever comes after me or something, but the faculty, they wanted it done real quiet."

So here it was, here was the big moment . . .

"Can I see it?"

He had, as promised, kept it in a drawer, in an envelope marked "*Dr A. Schofield*". His office was an attempt at wood-panelled antiquity that the building could not sustain. The light on the desk was low, covered with a green shade. I sat and read through the five pieces of double-sided thick yellowish paper on which were scrawled a series of diagrams, numbers and equations which would be in first-year chemistry classes across universities everywhere – in 1991. We kalachakra can change a lot about ourselves, but oddly enough we rarely consider changing our handwriting, and Vincent's headlong scrawl was recognisable anywhere.

I examined the paper, looked for a watermark, found none. Examined the ink, the envelope, for anything – anything at all – which might suggest a point of origin. Nothing. I was many, many years too late. I tried to work out how old Vincent would be now – mid-twenties, at a pinch. Able to blend into any campus in any college in the US. Then again, if this was his method of accelerating technological development, by stimulating the minds of those at its present-day forefront, perhaps he'd struck again elsewhere?

Harvard, Berkeley, Caltech. It took persuasion and on more than one occasion copious amounts of rather pricey alcohol, but there they were, letters on yellow paper several years old. In one or two faculties the professors who received the documents had ignored them, treated them as pranks. Now, as they watched their rivals forge ahead in the field, they kicked themselves and drank a little deeper of their academic sorrows.

But Vincent's method was still only a means to an end. He wished to accelerate modern technology to reach a point where he could recommence his work, find his answers and build his quantum mirror, presumably using technology from some time in the early twenty-first century. I knew now how he was going to achieve this, but I was far too late to the chase to be able to prevent the dissemination of technology which he had begun. Now

321

I needed to discover where the next step was happening, for there Vincent would be. And all the while, as I searched, the technology moved on with frightening speed. In 1959 the first personal computer – rather optimistically dubbed the Future Machine by an inventor so dazzled with his own brilliance he couldn't think of anything better – was on sale. It was the size of a small wardrobe and had a life of approximately four months before the internal parts melted under the strain, but it was nevertheless a sign of things to come. If I'd been less preoccupied with finding Vincent, I might have appreciated the role technology was playing in politics a little further. I'd never noticed Israel invade Syria and Jordan before, although I was hardly surprised when furious local resistance drove even the technologically superior IDF back to more defensible borders. The declaration of holy war in the Middle East toppled the Iranian shah several years earlier than average, but secular strongmen seemed to be the power of the moment, leaping into the vacuum left behind with a new generation of military equipment that put the 1980s to shame. Armies tend to exploit science faster than civilians, if only because their need tends to be more urgent.

By 1964 the Soviets were winding up the Warsaw Pact, and the US declared another great triumph for capitalism, consumerism and commerce, and still technology surged and surged ahead. I'd got myself a position as science editor on a magazine based in Washington DC, in which capacity I also quietly reported to the FBI on the developing crimes of the age, including telephone fraud and the world's first ever computer hack, dated 1965. Had my editor ever learned of my duplicity, I would probably have been sacked on principle, and re-hired for the quality of my scoops and the quirky range of my contacts.

All this I watched with an apparently disinterested awareness, even as the Cronus Club seethed and raged about me. The future was being destroyed before our very eyes, the effects of the twentieth century rippling forward through time. Billions of lives were going to be changed, and possibly billions of kalachakra no longer born or their worlds torn beyond all recognition. We, the children of the twentieth century, were doing this, as blithe and oblivious as a whale to the writhing of plankton in the sea.

"Harry, we have to do something!"

Akinleye.

"Too late."

"How did this happen?"

"Some letters were sent with some bright ideas in them. That's all."

"There has to be something . . . "

"Too late, Akinleye. Much, much too late."

Find Vincent.

That was all there was.

Forget consequences, forget time.

Find Vincent.

I scoured every technology company, every university, interrogated every contact, investigated every rumour and leak. I trawled through shipping manifests in search of the components which I knew would be on anyone's shopping list for a quantum mirror, investigated every scientist and scholar who might be of service to Vincent, who had the appropriate knowledge, and all the time quietly wrote articles on the changing world and the prowess of American technological development.

I was careful too. I operated behind a great range of guises, very rarely revealing my true identity when investigating a story. If I wrote an article on agricultural fertilisers in Arizona, then I would be Harry August – but if a man phoned a nuclear scientist in the night to ask about the latest developments in electron microscopes, he did so under any name, and with any voice, that was not mine. By Vincent's reckoning, I should have forgotten all my past lives save the one immediately after my Forgetting, and this existence should only be my second on the earth. If I were to stumble on Vincent through my research, it had to appear by chance, not intent. My perceived ignorance and weakness were my greatest weapons, to be cherished for a final blow.

And then, without warning, there he was.

I was attending a talk on nuclear technology in the age of the

323

extra-atmospheric long-range missile, which my editor hoped I'd write up under the tag line "Missiles in Space". I found the idea rather unprofessional, as it implied a multiple exclamation mark at the end of the title and possibly an opening paragraph beginning, "There are some ideas too terrible . . ." before swelling to an oratorical climax. A card delivered to my hotel door invited me to discuss these issues further with the sponsor of this event, a Mrs Evelina Cynthia-Wright, who had added in a personal note at the end of the invite how terribly pleased she was to see the media taking an interest in these dire affairs.

With a sense of disappointment already well settled in my bones, I drove out to her house, a great white-walled mansion some three miles from the Louisiana river. The evening was damp, hot and chittering. The vegetation around the sprawling, overgrown estate hung down like it too could no longer bear the heat, while an air-conditioning system straight off the manufacturing line was blasting out steamy clouds from a device the size of a small truck, wedged up against one side of the otherwise venerable property like a technological leech on a historical monument. By the cars lined up around an entirely algae-covered pond, it was clear I was not the only guest, and a maid answered the door even before I could knock, inviting me to take an iced julep, a business card and hand-made peppermint for my pains. The sound of polite conversation and less polite, child-made music drifted out of what I could only call the ballroom, a great high-ceilinged place with wide windows that opened on to the rear garden, an even more excessively drooping jungle than at the front of the house. The music was being produced by a would-be torturer aged seven and a half and her violin of pain. Proud family and polite friends were sat in a small circle before the child, admiring her stamina. As if to prove that this at least was inexhaustible, she began in on another medley. Over eight hundred years of reasonable living had rather dented my adoration for the works of the young. Surely I could not be the only creature on this earth who favoured prolonged incubation as a safer method of development than puberty?

Mrs Evelina Cynthia-Wright was exactly what a grand dame of the Louisiana river should have been – extremely courteous, utterly welcoming and hard as the rusted nails which bound her great property together. Her research was clearly as up to date as her rather ineffective air-conditioning unit, for as I stood scanning the room, considering whether I had made enough of a necessary token appearance and wondering, not for the first time, if journalism was an appropriate response to the encroaching end of the world, she bore down on me like a melting glacier and cried out, "I say, Mr August!" I managed to suppress my flinch and crank up my smile, producing a half-bow to the hand offered to me by the wrist. Even fingers, it seemed, drooped in this weather. "Mr August, it's so good of you to come. I've been such an avid follower of your work . . . "

"Thank you for the invitation, Mrs Wright . . . "

"Oh my, you're British! Isn't that charming? Darling!" A man three parts moustache to one part facial features responded to "Darling!" with the dutiful twitch of one who has chosen not to fight the inevitable. "Mr August is British, would you ever have guessed?"

"No, ma'am."

"I've read so many of your articles, but then I imagine writing in the American way must just come naturally to you."

Had it? Was I permitted to say so? Was this a gathering where all modesty was false, all boasting insufferable? Where, I wondered, did speedy social victory and hasty escape lie?

"You absolutely have to meet Simon. Simon is such a dear and has been dying to meet you. Oh Simon!"

I fixed my smile in the locked position and, upon reflection, that was probably what saved the situation.

The man called Simon turned. He too was sporting a moustache that rolled out from his top lip like a crashing brown wave, and a smaller goatee, which ever so slightly mis-directed the user's eye to his left collarbone. He held an icy glass in one hand and a rolled-up copy of the magazine I worked for in the other, as if about to swat a fly with it, and there were plenty of candidates for the honour. Seeing me, he opened his mouth in an expansive "O" of surprise, for this was a gathering where nothing short of expansive would do, tucked the magazine under his arm, wiped his hand off on his shirt, perhaps to remove the detritus of perished flying adversaries, and exclaimed, "Mr August! I've been waiting so long to meet you!"

His name was Simon.

His name was Vincent Rankis.

# Chapter 69

I was not without my allies.

Charity Hazelmere was not dead.

It had taken me a while to find her, and not until the middle of my fourteenth life did I stumble on her, almost by chance, in the Library of Congress while trawling through a report on developments in modern science. I looked up from a particularly boring passage which had nothing to do with my perpetual investigation into Vincent and his activities, and there was Charity, old – inside, as well as out, leaning on a walking stick for the first time I'd ever known – staring at me from across the other side of the table, not sure if I was enemy or friend.

I looked from her to the rest of the library and, seeing no direct threat, closed my book, returned it carefully to its tray, pointed at the SILENCE PLEASE sign, smiled and walked towards the door. I didn't know if she'd follow or not. I don't think she knew either. But follow she did.

"Hello, Harry."

"Hello, Charity."

A little grimace. Her ancient body was in pain, and I recognised the signs of more than just old age about her. The hair on her head was thinning, but there was a slouch to the left side of her mouth and a weight to her left leg which spoke of more than simple generic decay. "So you remember," she muttered. "Not many do, these days."

"I remember," I replied gently. "What are you doing here?"

"Same as you, I think. I don't usually like to live this long, but even I can see that something's gone wrong with time. All this . . . *change* . . . " The word dripped like acid from her lips. "All this . . . *development*. Can't be having that at all." Then, sharper, "I see you've become a journalist now. Read some of your articles. What the bloody hell do you think you're doing, drawing attention to yourself like that? Don't you know there's a war on, them against us?"

"Them" had to be Vincent, "us" the Cronus Club. I felt a momentary flicker of shame that I was still included in the "us". After all, I had spent more than a decade working with Vincent, and my collaboration and subsequent defection were arguably the trigger for the attacks on the Cronus Club. Whether anyone knew this, I doubted, and nor was I in a hurry to tell.

"If the enemy knows your name, they can pursue you! A low profile, Harry, is vital – unless, that is, you're deliberately inviting trouble?"

To her surprise, and perhaps mine, I smiled. "Yes," I replied softly. "In point of fact, that's exactly what I'm doing. It will make things easier in the long run."

Her eyes narrowed in suspicion. "What are you playing at, Harry August?"

I told her.

Everyone needs an ally.

Particularly one born before 1900.

# Chapter 70

Two things I learned during my career in espionage. The first is that a dull listener is, nine times out of ten, a vastly more effective spy than a charming conversationalist. The second is that the best way to approach a contact blind is not for you to directly engage with them, but to convince them that they want to engage with you.

"Mr August, such a pleasure."

Vincent Rankis stood before me, smiling, offering me his hand, and all those years of preparation, all that planning, all the thought I had dedicated to what I would do if this moment ever came, and for a moment, just a moment, it was all I could do not to plunge the rim of my julep glass into the pulsing softness of his pink throat.

Vincent Rankis, smiling at me like a stranger, inviting my friendship.

He knew everything he had done to me, remembered it with the perfect detail of a mnemonic.

What he did not know – *could not know* – was that I remembered it all as well.

"A pleasure, Mr . . . ?"

"Ransome," he replied brightly, clasping my hand in his and shaking it warmly. His fingers were cold from where he'd held his drink, passing it from hand to hand, and damp with still-clinging condensation from the outside of the glass. "I've read so much of your work, followed your career, you might say."

"That's very considerate of you, Mr ... Ransome?" I nearly stumbled on the enquiry, important to make it clear I didn't know him, but push any lie too far and it begins to totter. "Are you in the trade?"

The trade, to any large profession on the planet, is always whatever craft the speaker happens to practise.

"Good God, no!" He chuckled. "I'm something of a layabout really, terrible thing, but I do admire you journalist chaps, striding about places, putting wrongs to right and that."

Vincent Rankis and his bare, sweaty throat.

"I hardly do that, Mr Ransome. Just earn those dimes, as they say."

"Not at all. Your commentary is engaging – some might even say incisive."

Vincent Rankis sat by my bedside as the rat poison flooded through my veins.

Walking away as the torturer began to pull the nails out of my toes.

Riding a boat down the river Cam.

Hopping with excitement at another experiment. We can push the boundaries, Harry. We can find the answers, all things, everywhere. We can see with the eyes of God.

Not turning back at the sound of my screams.

Take him, he said, and they took me, a bullet to the brain, and here I am, and I will never forget.

He was looking.

God but he was looking, above that brilliant smile and behind those empty, charming lies, he was studying every feature of my face, looking for the lie in my eye, looking for recognition, revulsion, rebellion, some hint that I was still who I had been, that I knew what he had done. I smiled and turned back to our host,

330

heart beating too fast, no longer confident I could stop my body from revealing what my mind would not.

"You clearly have excellent taste in both friends and reading material, ma'am," I explained, "but I trust my invitation here wasn't merely to discuss the incisiveness of my text?"

Mrs Evelina Cynthia-Wright, God bless her, God praise her, had an agenda to push, and in that moment of crisis, that moment when I might have turned and lost my control altogether, she exclaimed, "Mr August, you've got such a journalist's mind! As a matter of fact, there are a few people I'd like you to meet . . . "

And she put an arm around my shoulder and I could have kissed that arm, could have wept into its clean white sleeve, as she led me away from Vincent Rankis and back into the crowd. And as Vincent had not looked back, neither did I.

# Chapter 71

I had him.

    I had him.

    I had him.

    And best of all, I had him without having to expose myself.

    He had sought out me.

    He had come to *me*.

    And I had him.

    I had him.

    At last.

Utterly cool, as the Americans would say.

    Time to play it utterly cool.

    I listened to Mrs Cynthia-Wright's friends discuss in earnest, occasionally frantic tones the threats of nuclear war, the dangers of ideological stand-off, the invasion of technology into conflict, and knew that Vincent was only a few paces from my back, and I didn't look once. Not too cold, not arctic and distant: on my way out of the house I smiled at him and complimented him once more on his excellent literary taste, expressing the hope that he was a regular subscriber to the magazine. He was. What a good man, what a fine bastion of learning in this ever-changing time.

Not too hot either.

I did not shake his hand on the way out, and as I walked back down the drive beneath the now star-studded sky, I did not turn my head to see if he stood in the door.

I had him.

I made it back to my hotel, a second-floor room that stank of the damp mould creeping into every corner of this soggy town, and locked the door, sat down on my bed and shook for nearly fifteen minutes. I couldn't stop, and for a while, as I watched my hands tremble across my lap, wondered what kind of twisted conscious reaction of my mind this was, what manifestation of the many emotions I knew I should feel to see this man who I had hunted for over a century, this man who had come so close to destroying me. But if it was so, still I could not control it, and as I went mechanically through the motions of going to bed, my hands shook, and I smeared toothpaste down my chin.

Had I thought it would work, I would have called the Club at once. I would have summoned up mercenaries, I would have taken up arms myself, and we would have administered the Forgetting to Vincent, right then and there. No question, no trial, no fruitless interrogation for his point of origin, which information, I felt sure, he would not easily give. He was a mnemonic, and if my experiences were anything to judge by, such action could only result in failure, and every chance we had of stopping Vincent could be lost for good.

Having found him, this was a time now to walk away.

He knew where to find me, if that was his inclination.


Three months.

Worse than any torture.

I went about my job, and this time I was scrupulous, I was rigorous, I played the part of a journalist to the full and took no action that could be even considered as remotely researching Vincent. Further, I stepped up other activities that might be considered symptomatic of a ouroboran only two lives on from a Forgetting. I attended churches of various denominations; made and then broke various appointments with counsellors, maintained firm isolation from my peers, and in every way, shape and form lived the life of Harry August, innocent kalachakra slogging through a confusing world. I even took private classes in Spanish, which language I spoke fluently, masking my easy progress by paying my downstairs neighbour's child to do my homework, and that badly, and embarking on a brief and fairly enjoyable affair with my teacher, before guilt at her betrayal of a very absent Mexican boyfriend caused her to break off both relationship and lessons.

Whether I needed to have gone to the lengths I did to maintain this illusion, I do not know. If Vincent was investigating my present conditions closely, he hid it brilliantly. For certain he was investigating my past, looking no doubt for my point of origin. But my allies were in place, Charity and Akinleye, and every document left in the system proclaimed that I, Harry August, had come into the understanding of the British as an orphan abandoned in Leeds, and there remained until my adoption by a local couple by the name of Mr and Mrs August. I knew Vincent would investigate these facts and indeed find a Mr and Mrs August of Leeds who had adopted a boy of roughly suitable age, whose life I had always quietly marked as being a useful alibi for mine and who died in a car crash in 1938, in time for me to claim his paperwork as my own. His accidental death was, in many ways, a great fortune to me as, if it had not occurred, I may well have been forced to kill him in order to safely maintain my disguise.

Whatever the course of Vincent's investigations into these carefully woven lies, he did not approach me for another three months, and I did not seek him out. Then, when he finally did reappear, he did so at two in the morning, on a land line to my apartment in Washington DC.

I answered, groggy and bewildered, which was precisely how he intended me to be.

"Mr August?"

His voice, instantly recognisable. Full wakefulness immediately; the blood raced so fast in my ears I wondered he couldn't hear it as I pressed the phone against my body.

"Who is this?" I demanded, crawling across my bed for the light switch.

"It's Simon Ransome," he replied. "We met at Mrs Cynthia-Wright's soirée?"

Was that what it had been? Perhaps. "Ransome . . . I'm sorry, I don't quite—"

"Forgive me, you probably don't recall. I'm an avid reader of your works . . . "

"Of course!" Was my jubilation at recognition a little too much, a little too forced? This was America, a land of big expressions, and the phone was not the medium for subtlety. "I'm sorry, Mr Ransome, of course I remember – it's a touch early in the morning, is all . . . "

"Good God!" Was his regret a little too forced, a little too over the top? Perhaps, I mused, when this was done we could swap notes on the qualities of each other's deceptions? I could think of no one whose opinion I would value more in this regard. "I'm so sorry. What time is it there?"

"Two in the morning."

"Good *God!*" again, and really I was beginning to feel I should be taking points off Vincent's otherwise flawless performance. I made a mental note to myself that empty banal sounds were far more apposite than grand exclamations of sentiment when it came to such matters. Then again, if his operating assumption was that I was a traumatised innocent stuck in my second life, perhaps he considered it only apt to treat me like an idiot? "Harry, I'm so sorry," and again there it was, the slip of a familiar first name where no such terms should have yet existed. "I was going to invite you to join me for drinks next week, as I believe I'll be in your neighbourhood. How thoughtless of me to forget the time! I'll call back later – a thousand apologies!"

He hung up before I could begin to let him off the hook.

*

335

We met for drinks.

The bar was a haunt for lobbyists and journalists, and beneath the low-wattage bulbs and against the sound of slow jazz, a brief truce was declared and the soldiers were allowed to cross the lines to join strangers at their tables, discussing football, baseball and the latest twists and turns in the ongoing battles of the civil rights movement.

Vincent arrived ten minutes late, dressed in an outrageous white suit and braces. He was, he explained, a layabout with very little do with his life, but the world I inhabited fascinated him, and he hoped I didn't mind his picking my brains. Not at all, I replied, and he insisted on buying the drinks.

I had eaten vast amounts of cheese in preparation for this moment, and drunk copious quantities of water. There is an art to getting drunk in the line of duty, and I was determined that he would catch me neither shirking in my efforts nor off guard as a consequence. The only downside was the regular need to nip to the toilet, but as prices went, I've paid worse.

As we talked, it became evident that Vincent's notion of rich layabout was not necessarily the same as that held by his peers. "Father left me a lot," he explained with a dismissive shrug, "including a degree I never use, a house I never live in and a factory I never visit, but really I can't be bothered with all that."

Sure you can't, Vincent. Sure you can't.

"Your father must have been a rich man."

"So–so, so–so."

The immortal words of the extremely wealthy, whose natural financial saturation point is so high they have been buoyed above the realms of ordinary mortals, and can perceive vast riches beyond the dreams of lesser fishes. Thus, "So–so, so–so", a promise of wealth yet undiscovered.

The question of Vincent's father dangled between us and, as the bait seemed so juicy and tender, I ignored it.

"So what's a guy like you," I wondered, "doing talking to a hack like me?"

"Didn't I say? I'm an admirer of your work."

"Is that it? I mean, you're not ... what, looking to start your own newspaper, or get a job in the trade or any of that?"

"Good God no! I wouldn't know where to begin. Tell you what though ..."

Here it came, the conspiratorial shuffle across the couch, the bowed head, furtive glances at his neighbours: "You wouldn't have some insider dirt, would you?"

What kind of dirt, dear Liza, dear Liza?

"My accountant chappy wants me to buy into a company doing something terribly technical with harmonic resonance, whatever that is. I usually just let him handle these sorts of things, but the investment is really quite high and I wasn't sure if it was going to go anywhere. What do you think?"

I think, Vincent, that when you decided to deploy the notion of an "accountant chappy", you pushed your hand a little too far.

I think it would be easy to kill you now.

I think that, despite everything, I am smiling.

Smiling at your act. At your charm. At your easy manner and little dirty jokes. Smiling because for ten years we smiled and worked together, and for only a few days did you attempt to destroy my life. Smiling because that's the habit that has been set into my features in your presence, though I loathe you beyond all comprehension. Smiling because, despite the lies, despite knowing all I do about you, I like you, Vincent Rankis. I still like you.

"What's the name of the company?" I asked. "Maybe I can check them out?"

"Would you? I don't want you to think that was what this is about – I know that people use others all the time – but honestly, Harry – may I call you Harry – I have been such an admirer of your work I just wanted to meet you, this other business is really on the side ..."

"It's no problem, Mr Ransome – Simon? Simon, it's no problem at all."

"I really don't want to inconvenience you."

337

"No inconvenience. Just doing my job."

"At least let me pay you for your time! Expenses? Expenses at the very least?"

I remembered how easy it was to bribe a good man. Was this Harry August, the Harry I was playing, a good man? I decided he was, he had to be, and like all good men in the presence of Vincent Rankis, he would have to take a fall.

"You buy the dinner," I replied, "and we'll call it even."

In the end I also let him pay for travel too.

The company was everything I should have expected it to be. In the ordinary way of things, it should have been working on developing the next generation of TVs, refining the oscillations in the cathode-ray tube, studying interference and induction through electromagnetic effect. But it, like so many other institutions across the US, had received five pieces of yellow paper on which were laid out in careful detail specs, diagrams and figures relating to technologies some twenty years ahead of their time, and now the company was ...

"Doing really exciting work, Mr August, really exciting, into single-particle beam resonance."

And what did that mean? For my article, of course, for the readers to understand.

"Well, Mr August, if we take, say, a beam of light – a high-intensity beam of light, such as a laser ... "

Of course, lasers in the 1960s, that well-known household tool.

" ... and we fire it at an electron ... "

Naturally, but naturally we spend the 1960s firing lasers at sole electrons – where had I been for the last eight hundred and eighty years?

" ... we can see a transfer of energy occurring and – are you familiar with the notion of wave particle duality?"

Let's imagine that I am.

"F ... antastic! So you must know that what we consider light is now understood to be both a particle – photons – *and* a wave, and it is through harmonic resonance between these waves, which

338

are also particles, that we can begin to see ... Are you sure you understand this, Mr August? You look deeply concerned."

Do I? Bad lunch. Let's call it a bad lunch.

"I am so sorry, Mr August. I hadn't realised! Would you like to sit down?"

Afterwards, I wrote my report for Vincent. I could see the application at once, and more importantly why Vincent would be looking to use the company in question, as its research could be more than useful for his dream device, the quantum mirror, which would look at a single particle and from that derive the answers to everything. Simple, Harry, so simple – if you have the courage to do it.

He was still building it, I knew, somewhere deep in the heart of America – that was the purpose of this whole exercise. I, however, could show no knowledge of the same so wrote up my analysis based largely on the personalities of the people I'd met and whether they seemed to have a viable financial plan, rather than on the science.

We met over dinner – he paid – and he hummed and ah'd and gasped like an expert as he flicked through my pages, finally throwing the whole thing on to the table with a clap of his hands and exclaiming, "This is perfect, Harry, just perfect! Waiter – more sake!"

It was 1969 and sushi was the new fashion in America. The polar ice caps were melting, the skies were turning orange-yellow with the smear of industry, the Soviet bloc was collapsing and there were rumours of a pill for black people fighting for civil rights in the US which would turn their skin baby-white. This, proclaimed Nixon, was the true path to equality. The only reason the world hadn't been nuked, I concluded, was that no one could really see the point of trying.

"Tell me about yourself, Harry. You're British, right?" Here we are, the point-of-origin question, slipped in so subtly, so gently between courses that I almost didn't notice it appear. "You got much family?"

"No," I replied, honestly enough. "My parents are both dead, a few years back now. I never had any brothers or sisters."

"I'm sorry to hear that. They must have been very proud of you, though?"

"I think so. I hope so. They were good people, but with me working over here, and them living over there ... You know how it is."

"Can't say I do, Harry, but I guess I can understand. You from London?"

A good, American question. If in doubt, assume the Brit is a Londoner. "No, further north. Leeds."

"Can't say I know it."

God, but he lied beautifully; it was a masterclass. If I hadn't been concentrating so hard on my own deceit, I would have stood up and applauded. I shrugged, the half-shrug of the restrained Englishman in no great hurry to talk about difficult things, and he recognised the signal and had the good sense to move swiftly on.

I worked several more jobs for Vincent, on the side.

Trips to odd companies, interviews with potential "investors". The pattern was clear to see, and with each new venture I allowed myself to sink just a little deeper into his pocket. In many ways the techniques he used to corrupt me were the mirrors of techniques I had used in my previous life to corrupt others: a dinner became a weekend away, a weekend away became a regular meeting at his local health club. We dressed in not-quite-matching white shorts and T-shirts and played squash like the rapidly middle-ageing men society expected us to be, and had coffee with other members of the club after, and talked about news, and politics, and whether cold fusion would be the way forward. The day a group of Lebanese radicals finally unleashed a chemical bomb on Beirut, I sat with Vincent in the recreation room of the health club and watched journalists in gas masks hiding behind their armoured trucks as the living and the dying crawled out of the smoke-stained killing ground of the city, and I knew we had done this, we had unleashed this technology on the world, and felt the cold hand of inevitability on my back. In 1975 I bought my first mobile phone, and by 1977 was writing articles on telephone scams, computer hacking, fraudulent emails and the corruption of the modern media. The world was moving forward too fast. My time with Vincent offered an idyllic retreat from it all, as he invited me to attend parties at his grand mansion in the heart of Maine, away from the chaos and the rapidly rising body count. He never mentioned his research, his work, and I never enquired.

His father, the mysterious source of his wealth, turned out to be a real individual who had died in 1942, a hero in the Pacific war. His grave was conveniently unmarked and untraceable, but I had little doubt, as I trawled quietly through Vincent's records, that even if there was a body to examine, it would show about as much genetic connection to Vincent as my DNA did to the mysterious Mr and Mrs August of Leeds. It would take more – much more – to spin Vincent's point of origin out of him.

In 1978, the year the Berlin Wall fell and the first attempt at the Channel Tunnel caused a cave-in beneath the sea which killed twelve men and briefly stalled European attempts at economic recovery following the bursting of the dot.com bubble, I was invited, as I had now grown accustomed to being, to another party at Vincent's mansion. The invitation, trimmed with gold, was clearly to a large social affair, but large social affairs served my purposes, for the repetition and volume of the lies Vincent was forced to tell at such gatherings only made it easier to detect the anomalies in his reporting. Nothing was said as to the occasion, but a handwritten note at the bottom of my card told me to "*Hang on to your pyjamas!*"

He enjoyed toying with me, and, in my way, I enjoyed being toyed with. The years had led him to relax a little in my presence, perhaps to believe that I was as harmless as I claimed – Harry August, limited memory, dubious reputation – and hell, but he knew how to hold a party.

I arrived in the evening down the familiar gravel drive to the familiar old grand red-brick mansion which he called his "April–May, August–October" home, finding these the

341

seasons when Maine was at its most pleasing. Where he spent November–March and June–July was anyone's guess, but I couldn't help but wonder if he wore a radiation badge while there. If a Geiger-Müller counter could have done anything more than confirm my suspicions, I would have packed one beneath my dinner jacket, but as it was I needed nothing more than my own awareness of the same to let me conclude that Vincent was still working on the quantum mirror. I wondered how far ahead he'd come.

Five lives, Harry. Five more lives and I think we'll have it!

Those words had been spoken to me two lives since. Was he still on schedule?

"Harry!" He greeted me at the door, embracing me with a Frenchman's charm and a Yankee's enthusiasm. "You're in the pink room – you are staying, aren't you?"

"Your invite said to hang on to my pyjamas, which I could only assume was an invitation for the weekend."

"Marvellous! Come inside, the other guests are already beginning to arrive. I apologise if I have to talk to them, you know how it is – contacts contacts contacts."


The pink room in question was a small room in a tower projecting from one side of the building designed by an architect who'd decided that medieval was modern. It had its own tiny toilet and shower, and a picture on one wall showing a much younger Vincent proudly holding aloft the largest hunting rifle I'd ever seen, one foot on the carcass of a tiger. It had taken me a solid twenty minutes of analysis to determine that the image was in fact a fake, like so many images of Vincent sprawled around the house.

The chatter was indeed rising from downstairs, and as the sun settled below the horizon, the lawn beneath my room was striped with bright beams of tungsten light spilling out of the windows of every room of the house. A band struck up country tunes of a kind designed to rouse the soul, without necessarily inducing embarrassing deviations towards a "Yee-hah!" in a dignified environment. I donned my suit and headed downstairs.

There were some familiar faces in the crowd, men and women I'd been gradually introduced to over the years of my acquaintance with Vincent – Simon Ransome to all and sundry assembled. There were cordial handshakes and enquiries about mutual contacts, friends, family and, as increasingly began to happen at this time of life, health.

"God, I've taken to measuring my blood pressure at home – I go to the doctor and it just soars through the roof!"

"I've been told to watch my sugar."

"I've been warned to watch the fat!"

"Cholesterol, cholesterol, how I dream of a little more cholesterol in my life."

A few more years, I reflected, and my body would begin its usual course of shutting down from the bone marrow out. A few more years, and if I wasn't any closer to learning the secrets of Vincent Rankis, would this life count as a waste?

A sudden tinkling of silver on glass and a burst of polite applause, and there was Vincent, standing by the now-silent band, drink raised and face smiling proudly upon all assembled.

"Ladies and gentlemen –" the beginning of a speech, God how I hated speeches "– thank you all for coming here today. I'm sure you're wondering why . . ."

In my time I've attended eighty-seven weddings, seventy-nine funerals, twenty-nine bar mitzvahs, eleven bat mitzvahs, twenty-three confirmations, thirty-two baptisms, eight divorce tribunals as a witness for one side or another, thirteen divorce tribunals as a mutual friend to cry on, seven hundred and eighty-four birthday parties of which one hundred and eleven had involved a stripper, twelve of them involving, in fact, the same stripper, one hundred and three anniversary parties and seven remarriages after relationship difficulties, and of these I could think of maybe only fourteen speeches that were even remotely, even passably . . .

" . . . and so, ladies and gentlemen, I give you, the bride to be."

I applauded because everyone else did, on automatic, and looked up to behold the linear mortal who Vincent had decided to occupy himself with this time. Would she be a Frances, chosen to make an unseen Hugh jealous while playing tennis on the lawn? Or Leticia, perhaps, pretty but vacant; perhaps a Mei, adding that air of respectability as he went about his nefarious deeds, or a Lizzy, a companion in dark hours, a figure who was nine parts being there to only one part chemistry. She stepped to the front of the room, a woman with a hint of grey streaking the edge of her hair, dressed in a mermaid dress the colour of clotted cream, and she was

Jenny.

My Jenny.

Memory, moving too fast to process.

My Jenny, who I had loved and married, a surgeon in Glasgow at a time when women simply didn't do that, especially not there. I had loved her and told her everything, and it had been too much. My Jenny, who I never once blamed for the fate that befell me, for Franklin Phearson and my death on the floor of his house, femoral artery slashed and a smile on my face. My Jenny, to whom in another life I had whispered, "Run away with me," and she'd smiled and looked tempted, though she could probably not explain why.

My Jenny, and I had told Vincent about her. Back in Pietrok-112, a memory, a night playing cards, a little drunk on vodka, and he'd said . . .

"Damn it, Harry, I may not agree with the Cronus Club, but I do believe it's only healthy for a man to indulge himself sometimes."

Memory, fast.

I'd been looking at Anna, the laboratory technician whose calibrations were fine unto the sixth sig fig, who smiled at me from over the top of her glasses and didn't realise that this was a cliché which just made it all the more delightful. Vincent slapping my shoulder, muttering, "Christ, Harry, whoever said genius had to be tortured? Go for it, I say."

I'd hemmed and hummed, worried about the politics of it, about the things people would say, and we'd played cards that night and drunk vodka as Vincent derided my concerns as being barely worthy of a seventeen-year-old boy, let alone a man well into his twelfth, long life.

"You must have had some girls in your time, hey, Harry?"

"I've always been a little too preoccupied for true love – I'm sure you know how it is."

"Nonsense," he retorted, throwing his fist onto the table hard enough to make our cards bounce across the surface. "Even though I believe with the absolute conviction of my soul that this project, that the quantum mirror, is the greatest quest man can possibly undertake, to see the universe with the eyes of the creator, to answer the greatest questions posed by man; yet I also believe that single-minded dedication to just one thing, without rest, respite or distraction, is only conducive to migraines, not productivity. I have no doubt that the bureaucrats of this place had some statistic on it – a 15 per cent increase, say, in productivity if, every eight hours, a worker is allowed another half-hour for rest. Does the 15 per cent increase outweigh the loss of time spent away from the workplace? Absolutely."

"You suggest . . . therapeutic sex?"

"I suggest therapeutic companionship. I suggest, as you yourself have so often pointed out, that even the greatest minds cannot spend every second analysing the mysteries of the universe, but must, indeed *must* also spend some time of every day wondering why the toilet is so cold, the shampoo so poor and canteen cabbage so lumpy. I do not expect my scientists to be monks, Harry, least of all you!"

"Do you have someone?" I asked. "I haven't noticed . . . "

He dismissed the enquiry with a flick of the wrist. "I didn't say that untoward, unpleasant relationships improve productivity – quite the opposite, in fact. I will not waste my time on pursuing some futile sexual object just because I feel like a little chemical stimulation! However, when I meet someone who I regard as . . . "

"The half-hour rest in your eight-hour day?"

"Quite so. You will be made aware of it."

"Have you been married?" I asked. There was no great intent

to my question, merely curiosity as I threw down my cards, a polite discussion of friendly history.

"Once or twice," he admitted, "when there seemed to be a suitable candidate available. Once, in my very first life, there was a woman who I thought . . . But retrospect is a marvellous thing, and upon my death I discovered I could live perfectly well without her. Occasionally I acquire someone for companionship. Old age can be tedious without a little loyalty. What about yourself?"

"Something similar," I admitted. "Like you, I find that being alone . . . Its drawbacks outweigh its benefits, particularly in later life. It seems that, even when aware of the futility of the lie, the hollowness of the relationship, if hollow is what it indeed is, the urge to be together, with someone . . . is ingrained deeper than I had possibly imagined."

And, without knowing why, I had told him about Jenny.

Jenny.

Naïve to say love of my life.

Love of a life, perhaps.

Foolish to suppose affection could last so long.

A delusion, formed from so many years of lying, of deceit, of being apart from all things because there is no choice. Apart from the Cronus Club for fear of being exposed, apart from Vincent for fear he would deduce my truths, apart from those who lived and those who died and remembered nothing of the same, apart from my family, adopted and true, apart from a world whose passage I could already describe, apart from . . .

Everything.

This racing of my heart.

This stopping of my breath.

This flushing in my cheek.

It is not love.

It is delusion.

Jenny.

Holding Vincent's hand.

With her other she reaches out and slips the glass from between

346

his fingers, placing it on the black surface of the grand piano. This done, her fingers return again to the back of his neck, run through the thin hairs above his collar. She is almost the same height as him, but stands a little on tiptoe anyway, her weight pushing him back. She kisses him, and he kisses back, deep and long and passionate, and the room applauds and as they part his eyes flicker to me.

A second.

Just a second.

What did he see?

I applaud too.

Only later – much, much later – do I permit myself to crawl into the furthest reaches of the garden, sink on to my hands and knees in the damp soil, and weep.

# Chapter 72

Vincent.

My enemy.

My friend.

Of us two I am the better liar.

But you – you have always been a better judge of men.

Was it the final test? The ultimate proof? Could I look into the eyes of my wife as she kissed another man, and shake her hand, and smile, and say how happy I was for you both, receive her kiss on my cheek and hear her voice and know that she was yours, my enemy, my friend, without revealing all? Could I smile as she was led down the aisle, sing my way through the hymns in the church, take the photos as she cut the cake? For Harry, Harry is a journalist, Harry must be good at taking photos, no? Could I watch you whisper words into her ears, and see her laugh, and smell you on her skin, and not rise up in fury, because you took her, not for love, not for passion or companionship or even that therapeutic half-hour in the eight-hour shift. You took her because she was mine. Could I smile at this?

It would appear that I could.

I know now that there is something dead inside me though I cannot remember exactly when it died.

# Chapter 73

We near the end, you and I.

It occurs to me that in all this I have not told you much of my adopted father, Patrick August, or, more specifically, of how he dies. Harriet, kindly Harriet, dies between my sixth and eighth birthdays; Rory Hulne, as you know, dies poor, although not always in the same place. Patrick, silent Patrick, who sat across the fire from me in his grief at his wife's departure, dies in the 1960s, dissatisfied with his lot. He has never remarried in all the lives I've known him, and often the slow decline of the Hulnes nets him in their web, and he finds himself poor, pension-less, alone. I send him money, and each time I do I receive a stiff letter in reply, almost the same word for word in every life.

*Dear Harry,*

*I have received your money. I hope you do not inconvenience yourself by sending it. I need little for I have what I require, and the efforts of the old must turn towards the future of the young. I walk a lot and keep myself in good health. I trust you do the same. My best wishes to you,*
    *Yours,*
    *Patrick*

349

Always, when I send him money he refuses to spend it for at least six months, but hoards it in a box under his bed. I suspect he keeps it to return to me some day, but poverty takes its toll and he is at last forced to spend it for his own survival. I tried once sending him enough for a new house, but he returned my cheque with a letter politely informing me that such wealth was best spent on the young, and he had enough to keep himself in health. I am careful not to visit him for at least two months after any donation, for fear he will mis-interpret my appearance as a demand for gratitude. Even to this day, after all these years, I am still not sure of the best way to make my father's old age a happy one.

My father.

Throughout all this I have referred to Rory Hulne as "my father", which in a strictly genetic sense he is. He has been present through my life, a constant in the shadows, inescapable, unavoidable; and having no better term to describe him than "my father" so he has been described. I could perhaps call him a soldier, a master, a lordling, a man consumed by jealousy, a creature of regret, a rapist, but as each statement would require some sort of conditional, I settle instead for what he is – my father.

And yet he is not half the father that I believe Patrick to have been. I do not deny Patrick's flaws, for he was a cold man, distant in my youth, harsh after Harriet's departure. He used the rod more than a kind man would, and left me to my own devices more than a loving man might, but not once, not in any life which I have lived, did he deploy the ultimate cruelty, and tell me the truth of myself. Not once did he claim to be anything but my father, even as my features evolved into the looks of the man who denied any link with me. A truer man, a man of his word, I have never met.

I went back to that place in my fourteenth life. I had just witnessed Jenny marry Vincent, and of course – but of course – I stayed around and played the part of the excellent friend, smiling and dissembling, laughing at their jokes, smiling at their fondness, indulging their affection, and only when six, seven months had gone by and my credit was assured did I sadly report that I must return briefly to England. Vincent offered to pay for my flight –

by now I was deep in his pocket and very much his man – but I politely refused, saying that this was a private affair. When I left London airport, two men shadowed me to the train. Losing a tail without making it apparent that you're losing a tail can be a tricky business. I used a combination of errand-running, a guaranteed way to force any surveillance into an error, and well-planned spontaneous attendance at private, invitation-only functions to whittle down both the tenacity and morale of my shadowers. By the time I boarded a train for Berwick-upon-Tweed I was confident that I had lost them, without ever once having to break into a run.

Patrick was dead; so was Rory Hulne, and Constance and Alexandra, and all the faces of my youth. Hulne House had been bought by a man who had made his fortune importing heroin from the Golden Crescent and who fancied himself a country gentleman, keeping a dozen dogs and transforming the rear of the house into a giant white-tiled swimming pool for his wife and guests. Most of the grand old trees had been felled, and instead thick-leafed hedges, trimmed into grotesque figures of humans and animals, adorned the old paths and gardens. To prevent calamity, I knocked on the door of the house and asked if I could look around the grounds. I had worked here, I explained, as a serving boy, back in the day, and the drug dealer, delighted by the notion of tales of past glories and country living, gave me a personal tour, explaining all the things he'd done with the place, and how much better it was now that every room had a TV. I paid my way by telling stories of ancient indiscretions and broken promises, sly gossiping in the 1920s and the parties of the 1930s as the shadow of war drew over us, and after, when I had earned my keep, I slunk down to the old cottage where Patrick had lived, and found it overwhelmed with ivy. There was still some furniture inside, an old table, a mattress-less bed, but all things of value had been stripped away by thieves or nature. I sat between the brambles as the sun went down and imagined the conversation I would have with my silent father one day. He would sit one side of the fire, I the other, and, as was the way of it, neither of us would speak for a good long while until at last, I may say,

"I know you are not my father."

I tried the words out loud, just to see how they felt.

"I know you are not my father, but you have been more a father to me than ever my biological father was. You took me when you did not need to, and kept me when you did not want to, and never once broke down and spoke the truth. You could have destroyed me, the child of your master, and you must have been tempted so many times, in ways which you cannot yourself remember, to end it all, to throw me back from where I came. But you never did. And for that, more than the food on my plate or the warmth of your fire, you have been my father."

I think those are the words I would have said, if I had ever found the courage to break Patrick's silence and say them. If there was any point in them being spoken out loud.

Perhaps in another life.

# Chapter 74

In 1983, as the first International Space Station fell burning to earth with the loss of all on board, a glorious attempt at brilliant new science gone tragically wrong as the nations of the earth scrambled to prove themselves better than their neighbours, tens of thousands died in the Maldives and Bangladesh in the worst summer floods of their history. As the seas heated around the polar ice caps, it was apparent even to the most conservative observers that the great technological surge, as Vincent's tampering was increasingly known, was causing more harm to humanity than good. A journalist standing in a field in Wisconsin where five dancing tornadoes spun beneath a lightning-edged sky declared to camera, "Mankind has learned to carve with the tools of nature, but can't yet see the sculpture it will create," and as the first water wars erupted in the Middle East and central Asia, I began finally to see how Christa's prophecy, delivered hundreds of years ago in a hospital room in Berlin, could come true.

The world is ending, as it always must. But the end of the world is getting faster.

Vincent was at the heart of it, but for all that I had passed his ultimate test, stood before him and proved that I could not possibly have my memory, or else surely I would have gone mad, still he was not exposing me to the secrets of his research, the work that was killing the world. Perhaps, I reflected with a degree of irony, the presumed memory loss I was suffering led him to assume I could be of no use to him in its undertaking. Which, in fairness and by this logic, I could not.

He kept me close, however, having drawn me in with wealth and fine living. In time I left my job as a journalist and worked for him instead an all-purpose dogsbody. Investigator, adviser, occasional social secretary, I was what anyone else would have dubbed an overgrown personal assistant; he called me "my Secretary of State".

I flew out to meet people he was considering investing in, lobbied senators, buttered up scientists whose work he was interested in and even, on a few occasions, got him out of paying parking tickets incurred when he decided to stop on double red lines in the middle of city-centre streets. He appeared to respect both my work and my judgement, backing off from projects which I considered unwise and embracing those I regarded as interesting or useful. I must admit, I was occasionally even engaged by the work. By 1983, technologies which I hadn't even seen in 2003 were starting to hit the markets, and I spent every spare minute I could digesting and analysing them, as I felt sure Vincent was, both of us striving to acquire a leading edge for our future lives. Jenny was a constant at all social gatherings. I hid my feelings, but I think she must have sensed something, for one day, when Vincent was in the kitchen finding another bottle of wine, she turned to me across the dining table and said, "Harry, I have to ask this. Do you like me?"

The question went to the base of my spine and sat there like a parasite, gnawing on the white nerves beneath the bone. "W-why do you ask?" I stammered.

"Please – just answer the question. Quickly, please."

"Yes," I blurted. "I like you. I ... I have always liked you, Jenny."

"All right then," she said calmly. "That's all right, then."

And that, it seemed, was all there was to say.

In 1985 I began to experience pain, heaviness in my legs, and after a few weeks of ignoring it, decided to trot off to the doctor for my usual diagnosis of multiple myeloma. The doctor earned my respect for the skill with which she gave the information to me, unfolding it in several careful diagnostic stages, first with abnormalities which *might be*, then with masses which *appeared to be*, and finally, having primed the patient for receipt of the dire news through rounds one and two, with the calm statement that it was, and I should be prepared for a difficult fight. I was so touched by the manner in which she handled this last, crucial phase that at the end of it I stood up and shook her by the hand, complimenting her on her grace and skill. She flushed and mumbled me out of the door with far less verbal poise than that with which she'd informed me I was dying.

Vincent, when he received the news, was outraged. "We must do something! What do you need, Harry? How can I help? I'll make a call to Johns Hopkins at once – I'm sure I've bought them a ward or something recently . . ."

"No, thank you."

"Nonsense, I insist."

He insisted.

Wearily, I went through the motions.

As I lay in a white hospital gown designed to institutionalise any free-spirited individual as quickly as possible, listening to electro-magnets power up around my body, I considered my next step. Certainly I had made progress in this life – I had observed the way Vincent worked, studied his contacts, his methods, his people, and, most important of all, I had convinced him that I was utterly harmless. From a man he'd had killed only a few lives ago, I was now his trusted assistant, confidant and friend.

I was not, however, yet privy to the vital information that I truly required to bring Vincent down and stop the quantum mirror being manufactured, and I either had to endure many long years

355

of questionable medical procedures while trying to find out, or I would die and an opportunity would be missed.

This being so, I resolved to gamble, the most dangerous gamble of my lives.

"I'm not taking the chemo."

1986. We were on the balcony of one of Vincent's many New York apartments, Central Park to the south, the lights of Manhattan beyond, a sky flecked with grey-brown clouds. The air at street level in New York was getting difficult to breathe, as it had become in most big cities. Too many bright ideas had happened too fast – too many cars, too many air conditioners, too many freezers, too many mobile phones, too many TVs, too many microwaves – and not enough time to consider the consequences. Now New York belched brown sludge into the skies and green slime into the waters around the island, and so it was with the rest of the earth.

The world is ending.

We cannot stop it.

"I'm not taking the chemo," I repeated a little louder, as Vincent stirred lemon peel at the bottom of a glass.

"Don't be ridiculous Harry," he blurted. "Of course you've got to do the chemo, of course!"

"I'm sorry, but I'm not."

He sat down on the recliner next to mine, setting the two glasses – one for him, one for me – on the low metal table between us. He looked up at the sky and, taking his time, said, "Why?"

"Chemotherapy is a prison sentence. It is six months of house arrest, of nausea without being able to vomit, of a heady heat without being able to find a deep enough cold, of pain with no remedy, of isolation and discomfort, and at the end of it I will still be here, and I will still be dying."

"You can't know that!"

"I can," I replied firmly. "I do. I will."

"But Harry—"

"I know it," I repeated. "I give you my word – I know it."

Silence a while. He was waiting perhaps. I took a deep breath and got it out of the way. I had told so few people my secret – no one since the attack on the Cronus Club – the fear and nervousness I experienced were genuine and probably only helped.

"What would you say if I told you that this is not the first time I have had this disease?"

"I'd say what the hell do you mean, old thing?"

"I've been through this once before," I replied. "I had chemotherapy, radiotherapy, drugs – everything – but developed metastases in my brain."

"Jesus, Harry! What happened to you?"

"It's simple," I replied. "I died."

Silence.

The traffic grumbled below; the clouds scudded above. I sat and could almost hear Vincent's brain considering where to go. I let him do his own thinking. It would be informative to see where he came down.

"Harry," he said at last, "do you know of a thing called the Cronus Club?"

"No. Listen. What I'm trying to tell you—"

"You're telling me that you have lived this life before," he said, voice deep and weary. "You were born an orphan and you lived and you died, and when you were born again, you were still you, precisely where you started. That is what you are saying, isn't it?"

My turn to be silent.

My turn to think.

I let it stretch and stretch and stretch between us. Then, "How? Tell me how. Please?"

He sighed again and stretched, his legs creaking as he moved. He wasn't so young now, was Vincent Rankis – this was the oldest I'd ever seen him. "Come with me, Harry," he said. "There's something I need to show you."

He stood up and headed into the apartment. I followed, our drinks left abandoned on the table. He padded through into his

357

bedroom, opened the wardrobe and reached through a collection of coats and shirts. For a moment I thought he was getting a gun, for I had naturally searched this place while he was out and found two guns – one kept in a drawer by the bed, one at the back of the linen cupboard. He didn't. Instead, a square metal box was pulled out, a padlock on the front. The box was new – at least new since the last time I'd searched the place – and at my expression of curiosity he smiled reassurance and took it through to the dining room. He had a long glass table, surrounded by eight uncomfortable glass chairs, and he gestured me to sit in one while he unlocked the box and pulled out its contents.

My stomach curled up in my belly, breath caught on the edge of my lips. At the sound, his eyes flickered to me, curious, and I had to disguise my indiscretion with, "You haven't said how you know."

He half-shook his head and put the contents of the box on the table.

It was a crown of wire and electrodes. Leads trailed down from the back, and connectors criss-crossed its surface like hairs on Medusa's head. The technology was advanced – more advanced than I had ever seen – but the purpose was easy enough to deduce. It was a cortical trigger, a mental bomb – a very advanced device for the Forgetting.

"What is it?" I asked.

He carefully laid it down in front of me so I could look. "Do you trust me?" he asked.

"Yes, absolutely."

A Forgetting – would he really do this? Would he dare?

"Harry," he explained softly, "you asked me how I know about your ... predicament. How I know about your past life, why I believe you when you say that you have died once before."

"Tell me."

"What if ... what if," he murmured, "you and I have met before? What if I knew, even when I first met you, that this was not your first life, that you are ... special? What if I told you that we have been friends, not for ten, twenty or thirty years, but for centuries. What if I told you that I have been trying to protect you for a very, very long time. Would you believe me?"

"I . . . don't know. I wouldn't know what to say."

"You trust me?" he repeated urgently.

"I . . . yes. Yes, I do, but listen, all this . . . "

"I need you to put this on." His hand pressed gently against the crown of wires. "There is so much more to you, Harry, than you know, so much more. You think this is . . . your second? Maybe your second life? But it's not. You've lived for hundreds of years. You have . . . so much experience, so much to offer. This will help you remember."

What a look of doe-eyed sincerity, what an expression of passionate concern.

I looked from Vincent to the crown and back again.

Clearly it was not to help me remember.

Clearly he intended that I should forget.

All that time, all those years – and worse, a more troubling question. In 1966, using the technologies of the time, Vincent had forced me to go through the Forgetting, and I had remembered. But this – this technology was at least fifty years ahead of that and I had no idea, no idea at all, whether my consciousness could survive this process intact.

"You trust me, Harry?"

"This is a lot to take in."

"If you need time to think . . . "

"What you're saying . . . "

"I can explain everything, but this way you can remember it for yourself."

Pride.

How dare he think I'm so stupid?

Rage.

How dare he do this to me again?

Terror.

Will I survive?

Can I remember?

Do I want to remember?

The world is ending.

Now it's up to you.

Vengeance.

I am Harry August, born New Year's Day 1919.

I am sixty-eight years old.

I am eight hundred and ninety-nine.

I have directly killed seventy-nine men, of whom fifty-three died in war of one kind or another, and indirectly murdered through my actions at least four hundred and seventy-one people who I know of. I have witnessed four suicides, one hundred and twelve arrests, three executions, one Forgetting. I have seen the Berlin Wall rise and fall, rise and fall, seen the twin towers collapse in flames and dust, talked with men who scrambled in the mud of the Somme, listened to tales of the Crimean War, heard whispers of the future, seen the tanks roll into Tiananmen Square, walked the course of the Long March, tasted madness in Nuremberg, watched Kennedy die and seen the flash of nuclear fire bursting apart across the ocean.

None of which now matters to me half as much as this.

"I trust you," I said. "Show me how this thing works."

# Chapter 75

He set it up in the kitchen. It seemed a very mundane place to erase a man's mind. I sat on an uncomfortable metal chair as he pottered around me like a man trying to find a clean vacuum bag. I flinched as the first electrode was placed against the side of my skull, and he asked immediately, "Are you OK?"

"Fine," I muttered. "Fine."

"Would you like something to drink?"

"No. I'm fine."

"OK."

He eased the hair up from the back of my neck and pushed two more nodes into my skin just beneath the cerebellum. Clearly this was more advanced than the crude methods of Pietrok-112. The metal was cold as he pressed it into my temples, above my eyes, stopping every time I winced to check, are you all right, Harry, are you sure you want to do this?

"I'm sure," I replied. "It's fine."

I couldn't stop myself, couldn't slow my own breathing; it grew faster and faster as the moment of truth approached. He pulled some duct tape out of a drawer and said, "I think it would be safer if we taped your hands down – are you OK with that?"

Sure, why not.

"You look very nervous."

I don't like medical things.

"It'll be fine. This will be fine. You'll be able to remember everything, very soon."

Wasn't that nice.

He taped my hands to the arms of the chair with thick layers of duct tape. I almost wished he'd spit in my eye, declare his loathing of me, at least then I would have an excuse to scream, to rage. He didn't. He checked the positioning of the wires across my skull, across my face, then bent down so his head was entirely level with mine. "It's for the best, Harry," he explained. "I know that won't matter to you, but really, this is how it has to be."

I couldn't answer. Knew I should, and couldn't, couldn't find words between the breath, between the effort of breathing. He stepped round behind me to adjust the leads and I squeezed my eyes tight shut, shaking all over, my toes shaking in their socks, knees turned to jelly, oh God, oh God, oh—

Darkness.

# Chapter 76

You cannot miss a thing you do not remember.

Perhaps Vincent was right. Perhaps he was being kind.

Vincent's new device, his new toy for the Forgetting, had several disadvantages. I believe he hadn't had a chance to test it properly for, at its application, it killed me stone dead.

My name is Harry August, born New Year's Day 1919, Berwick-upon-Tweed station, and I remembered . . .

. . . everything.

Charity came to me when I was six years old, discreetly this time, quietly, slipping into my life sideways through the Hulnes, ready to debrief me, question me about my time with Vincent – no glamour, no shouting, no wealth, no Cronus Club. It took her six months to convince the Hulnes to let her "adopt" me, and as soon as I was out of the house I was whisked away to Leeds, where a new Mr and Mrs August were waiting to raise me in exchange for a heavy donation of cash and a sense of good deeds and charitable works. The paperwork was in place, the groundwork accomplished – Vincent knew where to find me now, if he wanted to look.

Charity said, "You know, Harry, you really don't have to do this. There are other ways."

Of course there are other ways. Let's find Vincent again; let's strap him down and hack off his feet, his hands, cut out his eyes, slice open his nose, carve our signatures in his skin; let's make him swallow hot tar; let's break every bone in his feet one at a time until ...

... until he dies, having told us nothing. Nothing at all. Vincent Rankis is not Victor Hoeness. He knows perfectly well what he is doing, and he will die defending it. So much for torture.

"What if we make him forget?"

Akinleye, a child, stood by the seashore, face furrowed with hundreds of years of concern – how quickly the centuries had caught up with her, how heavy they weighed. Was it a consequence of being reborn so close to the attack on the Cronus Club? Had she been forced by these events to take responsibility? Or maybe we were simply the sum of our memories, and this new Akinleye was the sum of hers.

"I'm a mnemonic." I had never spoken these words out loud. "I remember ... everything. Simply ... everything. Twice Vincent has tried the Forgetting on me, and twice he has failed. He is also a mnemonic. It will not work on him. Or worse – far worse. Like me he will feign having forgotten, and destroy us."

The Cronus Club in my fifteenth life was not the Club of my first eight hundred or so years. Its members were coming back, those who had survived Virginia's purges. Those who had been forced to forget were now on their third lives, and the messages were slowly trickling back through the generations – the Club of the twentieth century is back, and we have dire warnings for all. Messages were received in carved stone from the 1800s, enquiring after us, asking what had happened to the Club to cause the twentieth century suddenly to go so quiet. The messages from the future were darker, passed down from child to pensioner, whispered back from the twenty-first century.

In our last lives, the voices said, the world was not the world we knew. Technology had changed – *time* had changed – and many of us simply were not born. We haven't heard from the twenty-second century at all. We have no idea what happened to them. Please leave your answers in stone.

So the effect of our calamity rippled forward, spreading its wave through time. I dared not give an answer to the future Clubs, not even a time capsule sealed for five hundred years' time. The risk of it being discovered by Vincent in this time, of him learning how close we were to pursuing and punishing him, was too great. I would not risk the safety of everything I had sought simply out of compassion for a century I had not seen.

My contact with the Club was therefore strictly limited. In the early years it was with Akinleye alone – she alone did I trust with the secret of what I was doing. In later years, Charity too was admitted to the fold. Charity's role was crucial, for she generated the paperwork relating to my fictional life that I needed, documents which confirmed the story I had told Vincent in my previous life: of being an orphan, of Mr and Mrs August in Leeds, everything which might be needed to prove to Vincent that I was who I claimed to be. Now, my memory wiped again, I had to live the life of an ordinary linear boy, become my cover story, and so I went to school every day in Leeds and did my best not to embarrass anyone or myself, performing with the aim of achieving an average B+ grade until the age of seventeen, when I was resolved to give myself some chance of going to university and studying something I hadn't studied before. Law, perhaps. I could see myself becoming lost very easily in the dry but thick volumes of wisdom that subject contained.

As it turned out, obtaining B+ came more naturally than I had expected. Questions designed for a fourteen-year-old brain baffled me in my old age. Asked to write an essay on the Spanish Armada, I presented six thousand words charting its causes, course and consequences. I had tried very hard to stop myself, losing nearly three thousand words from the overall bulk before submission, but the more I looked at the question the more I could not conceive what the teacher desired. A blow-by-blow account of events? It seemed the most obvious, and so I tried to give it but found myself utterly unable to avoid writing *why* Philip II chose to link up with the Duke of Parma or *why* the English fleet sent fireships into the Armada off Calais. The eventual grade for my essay was a grudging A– and a note in the margin requesting that I stick to the matter at hand. I chose from that point on to disregard my teacher entirely, and occupied my brain in his class by inventing first a shorthand derived from Sanskrit, then a longhand derived from Korean designed to ensure the minimum motion of the pen between each letter and the most logical calligraphical unity between letters of certain types. When I was finally caught doing this, I was dismissed as the world's most idle doodler, given three lashes on the hand with a ruler and made to sit at the back of the class.

Two boys, a would-be alpha of the pack, supported by an omega too slow to realise that the top dog needed his minion's adoration to assure himself of his superiority, attempted playground bullying after that incident. My name not rhyming with anything particularly obscene that their young minds could come up with, they settled instead for a little pushing, a little shoving, a little shouting, and when finally, bored with their discourse, I turned round, looked them in the eye and politely informed them that I would rip the ears off the next one who laid a finger on me, the omega burst out crying, and I once again received three smacks of the ruler to my left hand and also detention. To spite my teacher, my next week's project was learning how to write ambidextrously, creating no end of confusion as to which of my hands was the one that could be most conveniently smashed about with a stick while leaving me best able to do my homework. My teacher finally realised that I was in fact able to write with either hand just as I was beginning to step up the quality of schoolwork in expectation of the slog through to university, when . . .

"Are you Harry?"

A child's voice, young, interested, unbroken. I was sixteen; the boy looked about nine. He was wearing a grey cap, grey jacket, white shirt, navy-blue striped tie and white socks, which he'd pulled up almost to his pink kneecaps. He held a satchel over one shoulder, and a bag of hard sweets, stuck together on the paper, in his other hand. Vincent Rankis's face still had a lot of growing out to do, and it was immediately apparent that the years between ten and eighteen were not necessarily going to be kind in this regard. The already-thin hair sticking down from beneath his cap foretold its scarcity in later life, but his eyes glistened with the old, familiar intelligence.

I stared at this child, hundreds – maybe thousands – of years old, and remembered that I was just sixteen, an orphaned teenager from Leeds trying to be cool.

"Yeah," I replied in my best local accent. "What's it to you?"

"My dad sent me to find you," he replied firmly. "You dropped this."

He handed me, very carefully, a blue paper notebook. It was cheap and a little tatty, and bore inside some unfortunate child's French homework, pages of the stuff declaring *je m'appelle, je suis, je voudrais* running down neat rulered margins. I flicked through, then looked up to say, "This isn't . . . "

But the boy was gone.

# Chapter 77

I didn't see Vincent again until 1941.

I did indeed study law, going to Edinburgh University to shiver away over great fat books whose pages crunched with the generations of microscopic paper-munching insects who had lived, bred and died between the judgments. Knowing I would be called up, I pre-empted the moment by enlisting in a Highland regiment, and spent three months being trained in the art of charging at dummies, shooting from behind the safety of a hill and shouting "Kill!" until my ears rang with it. I had a distant recollection that my unit would be largely useless until late into the conflict. We would spend a lot of time training, if memory served, in the art of winter warfare, in expectation of an assault on Norway which wouldn't come, and finally be dispatched to Normandy several weeks after the beaches had been secured. The worst we'd have it would be in the Ardennes, and I fully intended to keep my head down when that moment came. This would be the seventh time I had fought in the Second World War.

I saw Vincent Rankis as if by chance, though there was no such thing, during one of our quieter times, waiting for orders in our barracks in Leith. Our days were spent studying maps of places we wouldn't attack, practising manoeuvres we wouldn't perform and waiting for orders we didn't want to receive. Then a sharp "Attention!" and we all snapped up for the arrival of the major and his minions. I was a grudging second lieutenant – grudging in that I didn't especially relish my commission, and grudging in that it had been grudgingly given in light of my merits and capabilities, as compared to the usual requisites for the post. I had only held my commission for three weeks when my captain complained that I just didn't talk properly, and rather than at once slip into the more RP accent that I knew was required, I turned up my northern gruff to the point where my reports frequently needed translating for the unfortunate man, much to the amusement of his highly Glaswegian sergeant.

It was the Glaswegian sergeant who had called us to attention that day, but the major who spoke. He was a decent man who didn't deserve the death by howitzer that awaited him, but his decency was never of a kindly sort, merely the fixed determin-ation that those who died on his watch did not die because of his inaction.

"All right, gentlemen," he grumbled as if the weight of his facial hair prohibited anything but the bare parting of his lips. "We're just having a look round. Lieutenant August, meet Lieutenant Rankis."

I nearly laughed out loud when I saw Vincent dressed up in an officer's uniform, complete with shiny buttons, cleaned hat, smart boots and a salute so sharp you could have roasted a rabbit on it. He was a boy – a sixteen-year-old boy – yet somehow a hint of beard around his chin and an extra pair of socks shoved down the calves of his trousers and across the back of his shirt had been enough to deceive the army into awarding him a commission. I was never more grateful for the poker face years of being a junior officer on the receiving end of ridiculous orders teaches a man, and earned for my pains a flash of brilliant smile from Vincent's teeth and eyes.

"Lieutenant Rankis won't be with us long," went on the major, "so I want you all to impress him, please. If you need anything, Harry there is your man. Lieutenant!"

Another round of salutes. When dealing with senior ranks you had to get used to having a trigger elbow, as well as a trigger finger. I glanced over Vincent's shoulder and saw the sergeant trying not to laugh. Had he too noticed the fresh face on our infant officer, and the slight bulge around his thighs where he'd padded his uniform to more butch and manly dimensions? I focused on my poker face and salute, and when the major was gone shook Vincent's hand.

"Call me Harry," I said.

# Chapter 78

There is a ritual I undertake in nearly every life. It is the assassination of Richard Lisle.

Every life since the first murder I have either dispatched him directly or sent others to do it for me, before he can begin his murdering of the women of Battersea, and every life Rosemary Dawsett and the rest of the girls live a little while longer, not even knowing that their would-be killer is dead. Except for one life, when I didn't send a killer and couldn't make the appointment myself, and Rosemary Dawsett died, her body sliced up in the bathtub. I am now so used to killing Richard Lisle it has acquired a rather ritualistic quality. I no longer bother with any fancy preparations, no words or hesitation. I merely go to his flat one day, settle down in a seat away from the window, wait for him to walk through the door and put two through his brain. I have never felt that anything more is required.

I wonder now if Vincent's attitude towards me was not entirely dissimilar to my regard for Lisle. Posing no threat, there was no need for him to return to me, but yet return he did, like a fond owner checking up on his favourite pet. As I kept Lisle perpetually in my sights, so he seemed to want to keep me close across the lives. Perhaps he considered my personality of such iron stuff that it might one day return to be a danger to him; perhaps he feared I could regain my memory; perhaps I was a victory prize, a trophy, proof of his success. Perhaps he simply wanted a friend whose very nature he could mould, life to life, to his needs. And how co-operative I had been, how helpful and malleable, from the very first to the very last. Perhaps it was all of these things, in ever-changing measure.

Whatever his motives, keep me close Vincent did. By 1943 he was a captain, and I was surprised to receive a transfer to his very specialist unit of what my major termed "boffins, bookworms and other oily chaps". On arriving, I was less surprised to discover that Vincent Rankis had established himself as the go-to man for scientific know-how and expertise.

"Why me?" I asked as he sat me down in his office. "Why did you request I join your unit? I'm a lawyer; I don't know anything about this science stuff."

"Lieutenant," he replied, for I was still a humble subaltern, "you do yourself a disservice. When I met you in Scotland, you seemed one of the most capable men I've ever met, and if this army needs anything, it needs capable men."

Indeed, I was of some use to the unit, for all its great scientific minds were clearly far too great to be bothered with such trivial details as whether there were enough blankets in the barracks, supplies for the canteen and petrol coupons to get them to their meetings and back.

"See, Harry!" exclaimed Vincent in our once-monthly administrative round-up of business. "I told you you'd fit right in here!"

And so, while my old unit fought and died in the forests of France, I played secretary once again to Vincent Rankis and his rapidly growing private empire of brilliant minds. It was clear – politely yet obviously clear – that Vincent was already very rich, though the source of his wealth was not known among the men. However, as my role as administrative assistant grew, so did my access to information, including, eventually, the details of the account into which Vincent's pay was regularly deposited. Armed with this, and an immaculate forgery of Vincent's signature, it was a simple enough matter to head down to the bank and request a complete history of Vincent's transactions – for the tax men, you know how it is. I was lucky. In my last life my exhaustive research into Vincent's finances had revealed only a tangled web of offshore accounts and intricate security procedures which had sent even the finest forensic accountants wheeling off around the world as they traced this piece of income to a sauna in Bangkok, or that to an Indian restaurant in Paris, or thought perhaps they'd found something in a line of credit which ended in the grocery department of Harrods.

This time, with Vincent barely nineteen years old (but doing a passable impression of twenty-five), he hadn't had either the time or the opportunity to spread his finances far and wide, and a few bank details were enough for me to trace his finances back to the 1920s themselves. I had to fight to keep both my excitement and my activities secret. Living in such close proximity to Vincent, I knew I dared not keep any physical record of my activity in the base so spent my time on leave in a small bed and breakfast in Hastings, poring over every line by light turned down low against the blackout curtain, before burning every document I'd found and washing the ashes away. The pattern of his behaviour was in many ways predictable. Whenever he fell short, he gambled, and like all good kalachakra knew the victors of certain key races and bet heavily enough to ensure a good return but widely enough to raise no questions in any one particular location as to how this boy could do so well. However, one detail did catch my eye: during the earliest years in which I could trace his movements, they seemed focused around the south-west of London, and leaving aside the supplementary income provided by the races, he appeared to receive a regular income of sixteen pounds a month up to the start of the war. While there were plenty of innocent explanations for this, I could not help but suspect, could not but begin to believe, that what I was seeing was an allowance from a relative. Perhaps a very close relative indeed.

It wasn't much, but it was a place to start looking, quietly – so quietly.

When VE Day came, I, in my capacity as the only one in Vincent's unit capable of organising a piss-up in a brewery, did exactly that, perhaps as a petty reminder to my peers that, for all they were brilliant, bright, intelligent and quite possibly the future of scientific development, they were nevertheless incapable of running their own day-to-day lives without having someone to organise it for them. Two weeks later Vincent stuck his head round the door of my office. "Harry," he exclaimed, "I'm off out to meet a bird. Could you pop these in the post?"

A great fistful of envelopes was given to me. I glanced at the addresses briefly: MIT, Harvard, Oxford, Cambridge, the Sorbonne. "No problem, sir."

"For God's sake, Harry, surely we can stop using 'sir' now?"

When he was gone, I steamed open one of the letters. Inside, written on thick yellow paper with no watermark, was a very detailed, very well drawn diagram illustrating the uses, functionality and specifications of a microwave magnetron.

I thought long and hard that night about what to do with these documents. They were dangerous, deadly and postal distribution was precisely the same method as Vincent had deployed in his last life for kick-starting technological growth across the globe, only this time – *this* time he wasn't limiting himself to ideas from twenty or thirty years in the future; within those envelopes were ideas that wouldn't be expounded for at least sixty years.

In the end, I went to Charity for advice.

We met in Sheringham, a small town on the north Norfolk coast, where the fish was always fresh and you half imagined the catch had been blasted in across the shingle by the sheer force of the waves which pounded its shore – a salt-sprayed thundering that chafed the lips, dried the eyes and crystallised every hair within a few minutes of exposure to its roar. She was getting old, my ally, and would soon be looking at death. I was on the verge of being discharged from the army, still stuck in my uniform for a few more

374

days, holding tightly on to my hat between my gloved fists as the wind howled in from a thick grey sky.

"Well?" she demanded, as we strode first one way, then the other, along the few yards of beach that weren't foaming white. "What do you have for me now?"

"Letters," I replied. "He's sending out letters again, to all the universities and engineering institutions of the world. Not just America this time – Europe, Russia, China – anywhere with resources and good minds. There's diagrams for Scud missiles, illustrations of wave-particle duality, analysis of heat-resistant orbital shields, analysis of weight-to-thrust ratios for orbital escape . . ."

She waved me to silence with one white-gloved hand. "I think I see the problem, Harry."

"He's told me to post them."

"Are you going to?"

"I don't know. That's why I wanted to see you."

"I'm flattered that you value my opinion so highly." She was waiting for me to talk it through, work it out for myself, so I did.

"If I post these, history will change again. Faster than ever before. I can't predict it, don't know what will happen, but these letters will revolutionise science, cut out forty to fifty years of tech-nological development. The Clubs of the future—"

"The Cronus Club is already in turmoil, Harry. Last time Vincent did this, history itself was changed. Do not delude your-self into thinking it will be turned back by a few lifetimes."

"If I don't post them, my cover with Vincent will be blown. He'll realise that I can remember everything, and we'll be no closer to his point of origin."

"I still say we should just slice his ears off. It worked in the old days."

"He won't talk."

"You seem so sure of that, Harry."

"I didn't, did I?"

She pursed her lips, turned her head away from another great blast of spray across the shore. "I cannot make this choice for you.

375

If you don't post the letters, then we'll have no choice but to pick Vincent up at once and attempt to interrogate the truth out of him. If you do post the letters, then, for this life at least, the world will once again dissolve into chaos. Order will crumble, the natural course of things will decline, and mankind will not be the same again. But . . ."

"But I will still have my position with Vincent, and still have a chance at tricking him into trusting me with his secrets."

"Quite. I do not know this man. I have never met him, nor can I risk meeting him in case he knows who and what I am. I have no doubt that he's already perfecting the technology for the Forgetting, just in case he should encounter more members of the Cronus Club. The choice is yours, Harry. Only you can judge the best way to end this."

"You've been a great help," I grumbled.

She shrugged. "This is your crusade, Harry, not mine. Do what you think fit. The Cronus Club . . . we can no longer judge. We have had our chance."

The following morning I posted the letters and caught the first train out of town before I had a chance to change my mind.

# Chapter 79

After the war Vincent once again established himself as an all-purpose "investor". He didn't have any particular company to front for this, but trotted around the globe as an extremely wealthy enthusiast, picking up bits here and there of whatever it was that seemed to interest him. And I was his personal private secretary.

"I want to keep you close, Harry," he explained. "You're just so good for me."

As his secretary, I had access to information far beyond anything I'd possessed in my last life. Documents he didn't even know existed were continually fed to me from banks, universities, CEOs, charities looking for investment, governments and brokers, and Vincent, in an omission which I can only class as a fatal mistake, didn't even bother to check on them. He was used to me: I was his pet, utterly reliable, utterly dependent, utterly harmless. I was subservient, grateful that he was paying me so much to do so little, excited by the people I met, and, if asked my job title, would reply proudly that I was not a secretary at all, but rather a corporate executive working for Mr Rankis, a fix-it man travelling across the globe with him, living the high life, following in his voluminous coat tails. He treated me very well, both as an employee and as a

377

friend, once again buying my affection through the usual pattern of free dinners – holidays – golf – and gods how I loathed golf – and the regular trips he paid for us to take to his favourite club in the Caribbean. These were all part of my corruption, and so I went along with it to show willing. I like to tell myself I could have been a good golfer, if only I'd given a damn, but perhaps the simple truth is that there are some skills which experience cannot buy.

We shared stories of the war, friends, acquaintances, drinks; slept in the same compartment on overnight trains; sat side by side on the planes across the Atlantic; swapped seats as we drove from meeting to meeting up and down first the east, then the west coast of America. We stood together above Niagara Falls, one of the few sights on this planet which, no matter how perfectly I recall it, never fails to take my breath away, and when working together on business trips, our hotel rooms were adjoining, a connecting door between so we could share a midnight drink when inspiration struck. Many people assumed we were lovers, and I considered what I would do if Vincent proposed the same. Having been through so much, the prospect of sleeping with him was nothing to me at all, and I would have done it without a second thought. The question that remained over the matter was whether I could justify it based on the persona I was currently wearing of Harry August, nice boy from Leeds, raised in an age when homosexuality wasn't merely illegal, it was entirely taboo. If the matter came up, I resolved to have a good, public, old-fashioned crisis of religious faith about it, and if the question still remained, I would succumb only after a great deal of guilt and quite possibly an unhappy love affair. There was no point making things too easy for him. Thankfully, the issue never arose, though everyone, including myself, seemed to be waiting for the moment. Vincent's attitude to love, it appeared, was, as he himself had stated, strictly therapeutic. Destructive passion was foolish; irrational desire was a waste of time, and his mind was always on higher things.

The first whiff of the higher things his mind was on came in 1948 when, as was so often the way, Vincent walked into the small room that served as my London office, slumped down into the chair on the other side of the desk, stuck his feet on the tabletop between my heavy in-tray and my impressive collection of coloured inks, and said, "I'm going to inspect something the boffins are working on tomorrow – want to come?"

I laid down the document I'd been working on and steepled my fingers carefully. Usually, business trips with Vincent ended in a severe hangover, a large cheque and an overwhelming sense of déjà vu, but this time the vagueness and lightness with which he described his intentions intrigued me. "Where is this project?"

"Switzerland."

"You're going to Switzerland tomorrow?"

"This afternoon, actually," he replied. "I'm sure I sent you a memo."

"You haven't sent me a memo for two years," I pointed out mildly. "You just do things and wait for me to catch up."

"And hasn't it worked brilliantly?" he demanded. "Isn't it marvellous?"

"What's in Switzerland?"

"Oh, something they're working on with heavy water and particles and that stuff. You know I don't bother with these kinds of things."

Absolutely I knew he didn't bother with these kinds of things – he'd gone to great lengths to make it clear how little he bothered with these kinds of things, but now I was utterly fascinated for, as the person who planned nearly every aspect of Vincent's life from morning to night, Switzerland presented a tantalising glimpse of that Holy Grail – a secret that had been kept from me. I'd spotted holes in Vincent's schedules, many weeks set aside as "holiday" or "family business" or "wedding" – and how many weddings there'd been – but as I was never required to make travel arrangements for these events I had never known the full details. Now, I wondered, was it Switzerland, with its heavy water and particles and that stuff? Was this the black hole into which so much of Vincent's money had been quietly diverted when he thought I wasn't looking?

"I don't think I want to go to Switzerland this afternoon."

I was so good at lying I barely even had to hear the words I spoke out loud. So good at deceiving and being deceived, I knew already what Vincent's reply would be.

"Come on, Harry. I know you're not doing anything."

"I may have plans with a beautiful young lady interested in my tales of high finance and dirty bars."

"Philosophically speaking, you may. You may have all sorts of options, you may have herpes, but the fact of the matter is, Harry, in simple empirical terms, you don't, so stop pissing around and get your hat."

I stopped pissing around and got my hat and hoped he saw how irritated I was at having to do any of these things.

Switzerland. I find Switzerland most appealing between the ages of fifty-two and seventy-one. Much younger than that, and the clean air, healthy living, reserved manners and somewhat bland cooking puts me off. Any older and all of the above become a depressing contrast to my decaying body and imminent demise. However, between the ages of fifty-two and seventy-one, especially if I'm feeling hearty for my age, Switzerland is indeed a very pleasant place to retire to, complete with bracing breezes, clear pools and occasionally stunning scenery to walk beneath or between and very, very rarely, over.

Vincent had a car waiting for us at the airport.

"You hired this yourself?"

"Harry, I'm not *entirely* dependent on you to look after things, you know."

"I know," I replied. "Philosophically speaking, that is."

He scowled and smiled all at once, and got into the driving seat.

We drove up, and round, and then up a little further, and then round a little further, and then, to my incredible irritation, down a lot and up again. Navigation on the tight hairpin roads that wind through mountains has always frustrated me. Eventually we began climbing higher than we'd climbed before, until the trees turned to sharp-needled pines, and frost began to glimmer in the sweep of the headlights. I looked down sheer drops into valleys sprinkled with lights, and then up at a sky bursting with stars, and blurted, "Bloody hell, where are we going? I'm not dressed for skiing."

"You'll see! Good grief, if I'd known you'd complain this much, I'd have left you back at the airport."

It was nearly one in the morning when we reached our destination, a chalet with a slanting wooden roof and lights already on behind the wide glass windows. There wasn't snow on the ground, but it crackled with frost as I got out of the car, and my breath puffed in the air. A woman waved from the top balcony of the chalet as Vincent slammed the car door shut, then vanished inside to greet us. Vincent scurried with a familiar step down the narrow cobbled path to a side door, which was unlocked, and gestured me in.

The air inside was wonderfully warm, tinted with woodsmoke from an open fire. The woman appeared at the top of some stairs, apparently bursting with joy.

"Mr Rankis! It's so good to see you again!"

She hugged him, he hugged her, and I briefly wondered if there was something more to their relationship than just affection. Then, "You must be Harry, such a pleasure, such a pleasure." Her accent was German Swiss, her age perhaps thirty. She hurried us into the living room, where indeed a fat fire roared in the grate, and sat us down to a meal of cold meats, hot potato and warm wine. I was too tired and hungry to interrogate my hosts, and when Vincent finally declared with a slap on his knees, "Right! Busy day tomorrow!" I only put in a token grumble and went straight to bed.

I woke the following morning with a start.

He was standing, fully dressed for the cold, at the end of my bed, just staring at me.

I didn't know how long he'd been there, watching me. He had a pair of gloves dangling down from his sleeves, sewn on with a long piece of string, like a mother might sew her child's gloves together, but there was no sign of dampness on his trousers or boots, no indication he'd been outside. For a long while he just looked at me, until, shuffling upright, I stammered, "Vincent? W-what is it?"

For a second I thought he was going to say something else.

Then, with a half-shake of his head and a little shuffle to the door, he replied, not looking at me, "Time to get up, Harry. Busy, busy day."

I got up and didn't bother with a shower.

The world outside was blue-grey with a gentle frost. The air bit hard, promising snow. The woman waved from the balcony as we climbed back into Vincent's little car, and then we drove up again, through thinning pine trees and jutting rock, the heater in the car on at full blast, neither of us saying a word.

We didn't go far. It can't have been more than ten minutes out before Vincent made a sharp right and turned into what I first assumed was the entrance to a mine. A short tunnel led to a concrete car park, surrounded by sheer rock walls on all sides, some parts of which had been covered with chain fencing against crumbling. A single small sign declared in French, German and English, PRIVATE PROPERTY, NO RAMBLERS PLEASE. A single security guard, dressed in a fur-lined blue coat, the bulge of his pistol well hidden beneath its shapeless bulk, greeted us with a polite nod of recognition as we parked among the very few cars and very few spaces. A grey door in a grey cliff wall was opened as we approached, a security camera many, many decades ahead of its time peering down at us as we passed.

I had questions but didn't feel that I could ask them. We descended a corridor of stone cut from the walls of the mountain itself, lined with sluggish burning lanterns. Our breath steamed on the air, but as we went further down, rather than grow colder, a warm moisture began to tingle against my skin. I heard voices, rising from below, echoing against the hard, round walls, and as we descended one way, three men, pushing an empty sled, came up the other way. They were talking loudly, but as Vincent approached they fell silent, and remained so until we were deeper into the mountain out of earshot. By now I could hear the gentle hiss of air vents, the rattling of pipes, and the heat was taking on an unnatural mechanical quality, a little too high and damp to have been designed for simple human comfort. The number of people was increasing, men and women of all ages, who all seemed to recognise Vincent and then look away. There were quiet traces of security too, more men in thick coats, guns under their arms and batons on their hips.

"What is this place?" I asked at last, when the sound of voices was enough to muffle the breakage of quiet that my words entailed.

"Do you understand quantum physics?" he asked briskly as we rounded a corner and paused by a blast door for it to be opened.

"Don't be ridiculous; you know I don't."

He gave a patient sigh and ducked beneath the rising door into an even warmer cave. "Well then, I shall keep it simple. Let us say that you observe a waterfall and ask yourself how it came into being. The water flowed downwards and eroded the rock, you conclude. On the higher side of the waterfall, the rock was hard and did not crumble, but on the downward slope, the rock was soft and collapsed beneath the river rushing over it. Having made this deductive leap, you further conclude that water must always flow downhill, and it must erode, and that friction changes energy, and energy changes matter and so on and so forth, are you with me?"

"I think so."

Did he miss me then? Did he miss the Harry August he had argued with in Cambridge and who had cried "claptrap" to his daft ideas? I think, perhaps, he did.

Your fault, Vincent, for killing me.

Twice.

"Well then, let us take it another step. Let us say that you take an atom in the universe, and you observe it closely. This atom, you say, is made of protons, neutrons and electrons, and from this you begin to deduce that a proton must have a positive charge and an electron a negative, and these two attract, and you say that a neutron binds itself to a proton and a force must be exerted to prevent the attractive pull between all these from causing the atom to collapse in on itself, and from that you can deduce ... " He paused, searching for a word.

"Yes?"

"Everything," said so softly, eyes fixed on some other place. "You can deduce ... everything. From a single atom, a single point in time and space, one can examine the fundamental stuff of the universe and conclude, by sheer mathematical process, everything that was, everything that is, everything that must be. Everything."

Another door opened: a room even hotter than the others, fans working desperately to keep it cool, and there it was, nearly seven storeys high, scaffolding running up to its topmost level, men and women – hundreds of them – swarming over its every detail. The air tasted of electricity, smelled of electricity, the noise was almost deafening. He handed me a radioactivity badge, more advanced than anything I'd worn in Pietrok-112, nearly twenty years from now, nearly two hundred years ago, and over the roar shouted, "This is the quantum mirror!"

I looked, and it was beautiful.

The quantum mirror.

Look into it too deep, and God is looking right back at you.

And it was nearly finished.

# Chapter 80

My third life.

I have told you that I wandered for a while as a priest, monk, scholar, theologian – call it what you will – idiot in search of answers, whatever. I have told you of my meeting with Shen, the Chinese spy who respectfully hoped I wasn't there to overthrow communism. I have told you of being beaten in Israel and scorned in Egypt, of finding faith and losing it as easily as a comfortable pair of slippers.

I have not told you of Madam Patna.

She was an Indian mystic, one of the first to realise that the most profitable way to be enlightened was to spread her enlightenment to concerned Westerners who hadn't had enough cultural opportunities to nurture their cynicism. I was one of those Westerners for a time and sat at her feet chanting empty nothings with the rest of them, for a while genuinely convinced – as I was genuinely convinced of most things in that life – that this chubby, cheery woman did indeed offer me a path to enlightenment. After a few months of working for free – which I considered a necessary part of becoming closer to nature and thus myself – in her extensive plantations, I was granted a rare interview with her, and, almost shaking with excitement, sat cross-legged on the floor before the great lady and waited to be wowed.

She was silent a long time, deep in meditation, and we devotees had learned long ago not to question these deep and presumably profound pauses. At last she raised her head and, looking straight through me, declared, "You are a divine being."

As statements went, this was nothing very new for our *mandir*.

"You are a creature of light. Your soul is song, your thoughts are beauty. There is nothing within you which is not perfection. You are yourself. You are the universe."

Chanted by a crowd in a large room, all this could be rather impressive. Now, with this one woman breathily intoning it, I was struck by just how contradictory so much of it appeared to be.

"What about God?" I asked.

This question seemed a little impertinent to Madam Patna, but rather than disappoint an avid follower with a casual dismissal, she smiled her trademark cheerful smile and proclaimed, "There is no such thing as God. There is only creation. You are part of creation, and it is within you."

"Then why can I not influence creation?"

"You do. Everything about you, every aspect of your being, every breath . . ."

"I mean . . . why can I not influence my own path through it."

"But you do!" she repeated firmly. "This life is only a passing flicker of the flame, a shadow. You will cast it off and soar to a new plane, a new level of understanding, where you will realise that what you perceive now as reality is no more than a prison of the senses. You will look, and it will be as if you see with the eye of the maker. You are within creation. Creation is within you. You are an aspect of the first breath that made the universe, your body is made of the dust of bodies that have gone before, and when you die, your body and your deeds give life. You, yourself, are God."

*

386

In later months I grew rather tired of such empty aphorisms, and when a dissatisfied disciple whispered in my ear that our austere, ascetic leader in fact lived a life of wealthy luxury some three miles down the road, I threw down my straw hat and hand scythe, and left to find a better philosophy. Yet, all these lives later, I still wondered exactly what it would mean to see the universe with the eyes of God.

# Chapter 81

"Harry, this is the single most important thing that anyone will ever do."

Vincent in my ear.

So many voices in my ear, so many years to hear them.

"This will change mankind, redefine the universe. The quantum mirror will unlock the secrets of matter, of past and future. We will understand at last those concepts which we only pretended to comprehend – life, death, consciousness, time. Harry, the quantum mirror is ..."

"What can I do?" I asked, and was surprised to hear my own voice. "How can I help?"

Vincent smiled. His hand rested on my shoulder, and for a second I thought I saw the glimmer of tears run along his lower eyelids. I had never seen Vincent cry and thought for a moment that this was joy.

"Stay with me," he said. "Stay here, by my side."

The quantum mirror.

To look with the eyes of the maker.

Vincent Rankis. Fancy seeing you here! We shall hold up a mirror, as it were, to nature itself . . .

Codswallop!

It is either your or my ghastly duty to ensure that one of us kisses Frances on the lips.

Total balderdash!

I'm a fucking good guy!

It's your past, Harry, it's your past.

Rory Hulne, dying alone.

Patrick August, you were always my father.

Silence as Harriet's coffin slips beneath the earth. Silence by the fireside in a cottage overgrown with weeds. There's a drug dealer living in the house where once Constance Hulne ruled with an iron fist, where Lydia went mad and Alexandra saved a baby boy's life, where a serving girl called Lisa Leadmill was pushed back on a kitchen table and did not scream. And from that moment a child would be born who would travel again, and again, and again, the same life, the same journey again and again and . . .

Richard Lisle, dead at my hands, life after life. Please, I never done nothing.

Rosemary Dawsett, cut up in a bathtub.

Jenny, you should be on the news, you should.

Will you run away with me?

Do you like me?

I have always liked you, Jenny. Always.

The bride to be!

Do you approve, Harry? Isn't she beautiful?

Akinleye. Did you know that me, Harry? Was she right to forget?

I personally favour the thigh! A bath helps, but one must make do, mustn't one? Tra la, Dr August, so long and all that!

Virginia, striding beneath the summer sky in London. Killing kalachakra in the womb. Shaking as we made her forget.

You ever get bored of whatever it is you do, come find me on the thin red line!

*Many, many apologies.*

I'm so sorry, Harry. It's for the best. This is how it has to be.

The quantum mirror.

To see with the eyes of God.

The world is ending.

We cannot stop it.

Now it's up to you.

The quantum mirror.

Stay here. By my side.

Vincent, I sabotaged the quantum mirror.

It was easy to do.

I didn't even have to be there. You had concluded that I was no scientist, that I could not help you as I had in Russia, for here was a man who didn't even understand the thinnest Newtonian principle, let alone the technology – nearly a hundred years ahead of what it should have been – that you were unleashing in that mountain in Switzerland. I was your admin man, as I had been now for so many lives, your go-to man for trivial events. For nine months I stayed in those caves in Switzerland, watching the quantum mirror grow, listening to the roaring of the machines with every test, and knew you were close, you were so close now. Reports landed on my desk and you ignored them, believing I could not understand, but Vincent, I was the only other person there who *could*, every dot and every dash, every decimal point and finest permutation of the graph. It was I who, when I should have ordered thorium 234, changed a digit in the paperwork and ordered thorium 231. It was I who cut costs on the boron rods, slicing away a few vital millimetres from the specs; I who shifted the decimal point one sig fig over on the wave calculations. The document was seven pages long, and I moved the point on the very first page so that by the time the calculations had been worked through, the final answer was nine orders of magnitude out.

You will wonder why I did this.

A desire to preserve the universe? It sounds incredibly grand to say it – perhaps I should get myself a T-shirt and a cape to make clear the same? Who are you, god that you would become, to destroy the world in your search for knowledge?

Habit?

I had dedicated so many years to bringing you down, it seemed a waste not to do it.

Jealousy?

Perhaps a little.

Vengeance?

You had been such excellent company, it was sometimes hard to remember this. Centuries are a long time to hold a grudge, but then . . .

Remember.

Remember like a mnemonic, and here we are again, swallowing poison in Pietrok-112 and being grateful for it, feeling the electrodes press into my head, tasting electricity on my tongue, not once, but twice, and the second time you held my hand and said it was for the best, of course, but for the best. Jenny. Do you like me, Harry? Do you like me? Weeping in the cold, your private secretary, your personal dog, your pet, your whatever-it-was-you-wanted-me-to-be. I close my eyes and I remember and yes.

It is vengeance.

And perhaps a very small realisation that something inside me has died and that this is the only way I can think of to get it back. A notion of "doing the right thing" – as if that meant anything to me any more.

I sabotaged the quantum mirror, knowing full well that all these things – a decimal point, an isotope, a boron rod – would be enough. I would set your research back by fifty years, and you wouldn't even look twice at me, never suspect that I had done it.

The test was set for a summer day, not that seasons had much relevance in the hot dampness of the caves. The excitement was palpable in the air. Vincent came into my office, face flushed from his regular jog round the facility, a substitute, I felt, for the freezing jaunts in the open air he'd subjected to me in Pietrok-112. "Are you coming?" he demanded.

I laid down my pen carefully, folded my hands, looked him in the eye and said, "Vincent, I'm very happy that you're very happy, but as I'm sure you know, I've got fifty tins of out-of-date tuna in the canteen, and the passionate, dare I say fiery, letter of complaint I'm in the middle of writing is, without wanting to overblow the matter, a work of epic prose the likes of which the tuna industry has never seen, and you are rather serving as the person from Porlock."

He blew air loudly between his lips like an irritated orca. "Harry, without wanting to demean your works in any way, when I tell you that the test today could be the beginning of a revolution in the very nature of what it is to be human, I'm sure you'll understand that the chastising of the tuna industry can take second place. Now get your stuff together and come with me!"

"Vincent—"

"Come on!"

He hauled me by the elbow. I grumbled, grabbing my radio-activity badge as he hauled me into the corridor. All the way down into the depths of the mountain I protested about unhealthy tuna, rotting salad and the cost of maintaining the electricity supply in this place, and he exclaimed, "Harry! Future of the species, insight into the universe; ignore the salad!"

Down by the quantum mirror there were nearly thirty scientists bundled into the observation gallery, looking down to the great beast itself. It had grown, a great dangling, misshapen rocket of bits added and bits taken away, of rolling cables and flashing interior surfaces, of heat and steam and pressure and a thousand monitoring devices tapped into computers fifty years ahead of their time. I was the only non-scientist in the room, but as the floor around the quantum mirror itself was cleared, Vincent dragged me to the front, exclaiming, "These idiots wouldn't be able to number-crunch if you didn't feed them and help them wipe their bloody bottoms. Come on! You deserve to see this."

I supposed I did, considering that it was my subtle adjustment of the paperwork which would almost certainly lead to the catastrophic failure of the approaching test.

392

A warning siren was sounded three times, telling all personnel to vacate the immediate area of the machine itself. Then the most straight-faced scientist they could find began a countdown, as generators roared into life and a dozen faces stared at rolling banks of increasingly excited data. Vincent was almost hopping up and down beside me, his hand briefly squeezing mine before a sense of masculine decorum snatched his arm away again and he chewed instead on his fingertips. I watched, arms folded, an unimpressed expression firmly on my face as the power in the device swelled to its maximum, and inside its depths hideously fine and fiendishly clever pieces of equipment stolen from a hundred years from now turned, turned, turned, aligned, opened up, drew energy in and spat energy out and . . .

"Sir?"

The voice was a question, raised by a technician at a computer screen. The question was emotional, not objective. Objectively the questioner could read perfectly well the data on their screen, but emotionally they felt the need for support. Vincent sensed it at once, turning on the spot to stare at the unfortunate enquirer even as someone else stood up sharply and barked, "Shut it down!"

They didn't need to say anything more than that, didn't want to say anything more than that, and immediately a hand was slammed down on the emergency cut-out button and the chamber with the quantum mirror in it went dark. So did the observation gallery, a sudden stifling blackness lit only by the grey glow of the screens and the soft blues of the emergency lights set into the floor. I looked round and saw Vincent, skin ghostly, the veins on the side of his neck throbbing far too fast to be healthy, eyes wide and lips slightly apart, staring first at the men and women in the room and then slowly, inexorably, back at the quantum mirror.

The quantum mirror, like the rest of the cavern, should have been in darkness, but we could all see the orange glow rising from its core, a cheerful reddish pinkness spreading down its thinner metal joins, eclipsed only by the black smoke starting to belch from its interior. I could hear a hissing of tiny metal parts under pressure, rising to a screaming, rising to a shriek, and, glancing

393

down at my radioactivity badge, I was probably the only person in the room to see the thin film start to turn black.

"Stop it," whispered Vincent, his voice the only thing in the room apart from the growing grumble of the machine. "Stop it," he whispered again to no one in particular, as if there was anything anyone could do. "Stop it."

The light rising from the machine, a light of burning, a light of parts starting to melt, was rapidly becoming stronger than the glow of the emergency blues. I looked around at a room of frozen rabbits, of collective terror, and with the level-headed attitude of a man who spends his day calculating how much toilet paper a facility might need, I barked, "Radiation! Everybody out!"

"Radiation" was a good enough word, and people scrambled for the door. There was no screaming – screaming would have required an energy which now had to be entirely focused on getting as far away as possible from the rising flood of gamma waves spilling into the observation gallery in deathly silence. I looked at Vincent, and saw that the badge on his shirt was also turning black, oil-black, deathly black, so I grabbed him by the sleeve and hissed, "We have to go!"

He didn't move.

His eyes were fixed on the quantum mirror, reflecting the spreading heat now bursting out of its surface. I could hear the metal singing and knew what was coming next. "Vincent!" I roared. "We have to get out of here!"

He still didn't move, so I swung one arm across his throat and dragged him backwards, like a swimmer saving a drowning man, towards the door. We two were the last in the room, the light in the chamber beyond now too bright to look at, the heat rising, suffocating, pushing its way through the glass. I looked up and saw the paint begin to blister on the metalwork around the room, heard the computers fry, giving up any attempt at staying intact in the face of the rising everything blasting through the room and our bodies like a gale through a cobweb. I heard the glass of the viewing gallery crack and knew with an absolute certainty that the explosion which was about to take place would kill us both, that we were already dead. I shoved Vincent out of the door of the gallery; he landed on his hands and knees, groggy, half-turning to look back at me. The light was unbearable now, blinding, more than just the visible spectrum eating through to my retinas. I fumbled for the emergency handle on the door, felt the metal burn through the skin on my hand with an ironing-board hiss, pulled it down and, as the door began to descend, dived beneath it.

"Run!" I screamed at Vincent, and he, bewildered and staggering, a mere shadow in the tortured static of my vision, ran. I crawled down beneath the bulkhead door as it slammed into place, scrambling out into the darkness of the corridor beyond, got three paces away, and felt the world behind me explode.

Visions of a rescue.

There was metal in my skin, embedded deep.

Stone on my belly.

Dirt in my mouth.

The rescuers wore lead-lined suits, and before they removed me from the smoking wreckage of the corridor, they hosed me down for nearly half an hour. The water ran red for a very long time, before it ran clear.

Darkness.

An anaesthetist asked me if I knew of any allergies.

I tried to reply and found that my jaw was swollen lead.

I don't know what use the question was, or if they asked me any more.

Vincent by my bedside, head bowed.

A nurse changing tubes.

I knew, by the quality of the air, that I was no longer in a cave.

I saw daylight, and it was beautiful.

Vincent sat in a chair at the end of my bed, an IV drip connected to his arm, though he appeared unbloodied, sleeping. Had he left my side? I didn't think so.

I wake, and I feel nauseous.

"Water."

Vincent, there, immediately.

"Harry?" His lips are cracked, his skin is pale. "Harry, can you hear me?"

"Vincent?"

"Do you know where you are?"

As he talks, he checks my vitals, carefully, effectively. He, like most ouroborans, has had some medical training. My vitals are not good, but this Harry August mustn't know that.

"Hospital?" I suggest.

"That's right – that's good. Do you know what day it is?"

"No."

"You've been asleep for two days. You were in an accident. Do you remember that?"

"The . . . quantum mirror," I breathed. "What happened?"

"You saved my life," he replied softly. "You got me out of the room, told me to run, closed the door. You saved a lot of lives."

"Oh. Good." I tried to lift my head, and felt pain run up my back. "What happened to me?"

"You were caught in the blast. If I'd been any closer I would have been . . . but it was mostly you. You're still in one piece, which is a miracle, but there are some . . . some things the doctor will need to discuss with you."

"Radiation," I wheezed.

"There was . . . there was a lot of radiation. I don't know how it . . . But that doesn't matter now."

Doesn't it? That's new.

"You OK?" I asked, knowing the answer.

"I'm fine."

"You look a little pale."

"I . . . I got a lot of radiation too, but you were . . . You saved my life, Harry." He kept coming back to this, incredulity in his voice. "Thank you doesn't begin to cover it."

"How about a pay rise?"

A little laugh. "Don't get cocky."

"I'm going to die?" I asked. When he didn't immediately answer, I gave a small nod. "Right. How long?"

"Harry . . . "

"How long?"

"Radiation sickness ... it's not pretty."

"Never seen myself bald," I admitted. "Did you ... ? Are you ... ?"

"I'm still waiting on test results."

No, you're not, Vincent. "I hope it's ... I hope you're OK."

"You saved me," he repeated. "That's all that matters."

Radiation sickness.

It's not pretty.

You will be experiencing the worst of it, as you read this. Your hair will be long gone, and the nausea will largely have passed to be replaced by the continual pain of your joints swelling up and internal organs shutting down, flooding your body with toxins. Your skin will be peppered with ugly lesions, which your body is incapable of healing, and as the condition progresses you will start drowning in your own bodily fluids as your lungs break down. I know, because this is precisely what my body is doing, even as I write this for you, Vincent, my last living will and testament. You have, at most, a few days to live. I have a few hours.

"Stay with me," I said.

Vincent stayed.

After a while the nurses brought another bed in for him. I didn't comment on the drips they plugged into his veins as he lay down beside me until, seeing my stare, he smiled and said, "Just a precaution."

"You're a liar, Vincent Rankis."

"I'm sorry you think so, Harry August."

In a way, the nausea was worse than the pain. Pain can be drowned, but nausea eats through even the most delicious opiates and cutting chemicals. I lay in my bed and tried not to cry out until at last, at three in the morning, I rolled on to my side and puked up into the bucket on the floor, and shook and sobbed and clutched my belly and gasped for air.

Vincent slipped out of his bed at once, coming over, entirely ignoring the bucket of puke at his feet, and with hands on my shoulders held me and said, "What can I do?"

I stayed curled up in a bundle, knees tucked to my chest. It seemed the least uncomfortable position I could assume. Vomit ran down my chin in thick, sticky bands. Vincent got a tissue and a cup of water and wiped it off my face. "What can I do?" he repeated urgently.

"Stay with me," I replied.

"Of course. Always."

The next day the nausea began for him. He hid it well, sneaking out of the room to puke up in the toilet, but I hardly needed nine hundred years of experience to see. In the night the pain began to take him too, and this time I staggered out of the bed to hold him, as he puked and retched into a bucket on the floor.

"I'm fine," he gasped between shudders. "I'll be fine."

"See?" I murmured. "Told you you're a liar."

"Harry," his voice was acid-eaten, ragged between breaths, "there's something I wanted to say to you."

"Was it 'Sorry for being a damn liar'?"

"Yes." I didn't know if he sobbed or laughed the word. "I'm sorry. I'm so sorry."

"It's OK." I sighed. "I know why you did it."

The lesions, as they broke on my skin, didn't hurt so much as itch. They were a slow splitting, a gentle peeling away of flesh. Vincent was still going through nausea, but as my body began to break down, the pain grew intense again, and I screamed out for comfort and morphine. They dosed us both, perhaps considering it rude to only fill up one patient, least of all the one who wasn't paying for this extensive medical care. That evening a box arrived for Vincent. He crawled out of bed and unlocked the padlock on the front, pulling from the inside of the box a crown of wires and electrodes. With shaking hands, he held it out towards me.

"What is it?" I asked.

"It . . . it will make you f-forget," he stammered, laying it down on the end of my bed as if it was a little too heavy for his tastes. "It will . . . it will take away everything. Everything you are, everything you ... It will take away this memory. Do you understand?"

"What about me?" I asked. "Will it take away me?"

"Yes."

"Bloody stupid then, isn't it?"

"I ... I'm so sorry. If you knew ... if you knew some of the things ... "

"Vincent, I'm not in a confessional mood. Whatever it is, I forgive you, and let's leave it at that."

He left it at that, but the box with its crown of wires stayed in the room. He would have to use it on me, I concluded, before I died, and before he grew too weak to operate it.

In the night we were both in pain.

"It's OK," I told him. "It's OK. We were trying to make something better."

He was shaking, at the limits of his pain meds, and still in pain.

Tell me a story, I said, to distract in this hour of need. Here, I'll begin. An Englishman, an Irishman and a Scot walk into a bar ...

For God's sake, Harry, he said, don't make me laugh.

Then I'll tell you a story – a true story – and you tell me one in reply.

Fair enough, he answered, and so I did.

I told him of growing up in Leeds, of the bullies at the school, of B+ grades and the tedium of studying law.

He told me of his wealthy father, a good man, a kind man, entirely under his son's thumb.

I spoke of trips on to the moor, of flowers in spring and the heather by the side of the railway lines which caught fire in summer and burned down to a black crisp as far as the eye could see.

He spoke of a garden with rhododendron bushes in it, and the whooping of the whistles from the trains on the other side of the hill.

Was this southern England?

Yes, just outside London.

I told him about my adopted parents, and how they were more

to me than my biological father, wherever he was, whoever h
was. How I wished I had the courage to say, You are everything
and he is nothing, and it was not the food on my plate, nor th
roof over my head, but that you never let me down which make
you my father, my mother.

He said, "Harry?"

His voice was choking with pain.

"Yes?"

"I . . . I want to tell you something."

"All right."

"My name . . . my name is Vincent Benton. The gardener
name is Rankis. I hid my true name because . . . I am twenty-fiv
years old. I am seven hundred and ninety-four. My father i
Howard Benton, my mother is Ursula. I never knew my mother
She dies when I am just a child. I am born at home, on 3 Octobe
1925. Apparently the nanny fainted when I popped out. I've neve
told anyone this in my entire life. No one."

"I am who I am," I replied. "That's all."

"No," he answered, levering himself out of bed. "You're not."

So saying, he unlocked the box with its crown of wires an
eased it on to my head.

"What are you doing?" I asked.

"I cannot accept this life," he replied. "I cannot accept it.
cannot. I just wanted someone to understand."

"Vincent . . ."

I tried to struggle but had no strength and little inclination. H
patted my hands away, pressed the electrodes into my skull. "I'm
sorry, Harry." He was weeping. "If you knew what I have done t
you, if you could only understand . . . I'll find you, do you under
stand? I'll find you and keep you safe, no matter what happens.
The whirr of a machine charging, the fizzle of electricity.

"Vincent, wait, I'm not—"

Too late.

# Chapter 82

I was alone when I woke after the Forgetting and, as had been the case before and would be the case, I believe, no matter what was done to my mind, I was still myself.

Still in hospital.

Still dying.

My bed had been moved, or perhaps Vincent's had been moved. The crown of wires had been tidied away, and I floated now in a warm painkiller glow, my flesh bandaged up against its own gradual shedding.

I lay there a while, contemplating nothing at all. Still at last. A thoughtless, wordless silence. After a while I stood up. My legs gave way immediately. My feet were bandaged, as were my hands, and there was no strength in the swollen redness of my knees. I crawled to the door and managed to make my way out into the corridor. A nurse found me, crying out in shock to see me in such a state, and got a porter with a wheelchair, who helped me sit up.

"I'm discharging myself," I said firmly.

"Mr August, your condition—"

"I'm dying," I replied. "I only have a couple of days left to live. I am discharging myself and there's nothing you can do to prevent me. I will sign any document you like to rid of you liability in this regard, but you'd better get it fast because in the next five minutes I am gone."

"Mr August . . . "

"Four minutes fifty seconds!"

"You can't . . . "

"I can. And you will not stop me. Where's the nearest phone?"

They tried to stop me – not with force, but with words, wheedling, dire warnings as to the consequences. I resisted them all, and from the phone at the doctors' station called Akinleye. This done, I wheeled myself out of the hospital, still in my hospital gown, and into the warm summer's air of the street. The sun was setting, brilliant orange-red over the mountains, and the air smelled of cut grass. People lurched back from me in horror, at my skin, at my falling hair, at my bloody robe where the lesions were beginning to leak, at my expression of wonder and delight as I headed downhill, letting the brakes go flying off as I sped towards the horizon.

Akinleye met me on the edge of town, in a small red Volkswagen. I'd had her in the area of Vincent's facility for months, waiting for my call, and now as I rolled my way towards her she got out of the driver's seat and said, "You look awful."

"Dying!" I replied brightly, crawling into the passenger seat. "I need every painkiller you have."

"I have a lot."

"Good. Take me to a hotel."

She took me to a hotel.

Gave me every painkiller she had.

"Pen, paper."

"Harry, your hands . . . "

"Pen, paper!"

Pen and paper were provided.

I tried writing and got nowhere. My hands were, as Akinleye pointed out, not in a very useful state.

"All right, typewriter."

"Harry!"

"Akinleye," I said firmly, "in less than a week I will be dead, and it's a chemical cocktail miracle that I have any conscious faculties as it is. Get me a typewriter."

She got me a typewriter and pumped me full of every chemical our combined medical knowledge could think of, to keep me both lucid and sane.

"Thank you," I said. "Now if you'd be so kind as to leave me enough morphine to fell an elephant and to wait outside, that would be appreciated."

"Harry ..."

"Thank you," I repeated. "I'll visit in the next life."

When she was gone, I sat down before the machine and considered carefully my words.

In time, as the sun finally vanished beneath the horizon, I wrote:

*I am writing this for you.*
*My enemy.*
*My friend.*
*You know, already, you must know.*
*You have lost.*


Vincent.

This is my will and testament. My confession, if you will. My victory, my apology. These are the last words I will write in this life, for already I can feel the end coming to this body, as the end always comes. Soon I will lay all this aside, take the syringe Akinleye has left behind, and stop the pain from carrying on any more. I have told you all this, the passage of my life, as much to force myself to action as for your enlightenment. I know that in this I put myself entirely in your power, reveal every aspect of my being, of the many beings I have pretended to be in the course of this, and of whatever being it is I have become. To protect myself after this confession, I now have no choice but to destroy you

403

utterly and the knowledge you have possessed of me. I force myse
to action.

By now, you will have discovered I am missing from the ho
pital.

Fear will have gripped your belly, a fear that the Forgetting d
not work, that I am fled.

And perhaps a deeper fear, for you are into the art of deducin
all things. Perhaps you have deduced from my absence that mo
than just a fear of dying has caused my departure. Perhaps you ha
realised from my sanity after you attached your little machine th
the last machine you attached did not work, nor the machin
before that. Perhaps you see unfolding before you, as neutro
spreading in a chain reaction, the whole course of these even
every lie, every deceit, every cruelty, every betrayal, unravellin
like an atom before the eye of God. Perhaps you know alrea
what it is I have to say to you, though I do not yet think you c
believe it.

You will send men to find me, and with little difficulty they w
indeed stumble on my corpse. Akinleye will be gone, her wo
done for this day. As well as the empty needle, they will find the
words and bring them to you, I trust, in the hospital. Your eye w
scan this page and with my very first words you will know – yo
will *know* as you already must know, as you can no longer deny
the pit of your belly, that you have lost.

You have lost.

And in another life, a life yet to come, a seven-year-old boy w
walk down a lane beyond south London with a cardboard box
his hand. He will stop before a house whose gardens smell of rh
dodendrons and hear the whistle of a passing train. A father an
a mother will be in that place. His name is Howard, hers is Ursu
Their gardener, who keeps the flowers so fragrant, goes by t
name of Rankis.

This seven-year-old child will approach these strangers an
with the innocence of youth, offer them something from his car
board box. An apple, maybe, or an orange. A caramel sweet,
piece of sticky toffee pudding – the detail is not important, f

who would refuse a gift from such an innocent child? The father, the mother, maybe even the gardener too, for caution is not for such events, each will take something from the boy, and thank him, and eat it as he turns and walks away up the lane.

I promise the poison will be quick.

And Vincent Rankis will never be born.

And all will be as it should.

Time will continue.

The Clubs will spread their fingers across the aeons, and nothing will change.

We will not be gods, you or I.

We will not look into that mirror.

Instead, for those few days you have left, you are mortal at last.

# TO
# MY PAST
# SELF

you could go back and give yourself one iece of advice from a life already lived, what would it be?

## LEAVE YOUR MESSAGE AT

## #HARRYAUGUST

## WWW.HARRYAUGUST.NET

*To my past self: plan ahead and say yes more. #HarryAugust*

*To my past self: May 2009. This too shall pass, this situation will change. #HarryAugust*

*o my past self: set your alarm when drunk on a bus. Waking up in Crouch End rather than King's Cross is a bad idea. #HarryAugust*

*ly past self: school should teach you nothing about life beyond how bad a template it is for the world. #HarryAugust*

# extras

www.orbitbooks.net

**Look out for the thrilling new
Claire North novel – coming soon:**

**No one knows what triggers the first switch . . .**

Just before your life ebbs away, your skin touches another
human being. In that instant, your mind transfers into theirs,
and their body becomes your own.

Now you can move from body to body, never knowing
who you are, or who you could be next. You can remain for a
minute, an hour, a lifetime, and the host won't remember that
you were there.

They call me Kepler. I could be you. You could be me.

**And now I am being hunted. Get ready to run.**

**Read on for an extract . . .**

# TOUCH

## by Claire North

In a few minutes police would shut down the line to Sanayii. In a few minutes someone would see the blood on my clothes, observe the fading red footprint I left with every step.

It wasn't too late to run.

I watched the man in the baseball cap.

He too was running, though in a very different manner. His purpose was to blend with the crowd, and indeed, hat pulled down and shoulders curled forward, he might have been any other stranger on the train, not a murderer at all.

I moved through the carriage, placing each toe carefully in the spaces between other people's feet, a swaying game of twister played in the busy silence of strangers trying not to meet each other's eyes.

At Osmanbey the train, rather than growing emptier, pressed in tighter with a flood of people, before pulling away. The killer stared out the window at the blackness of the tunnel, one hand grasping the bar above, one resting in his jacket, finger perhaps still pressed to the trigger of his gun. His nose had been broken, then restored, a long time ago. He was tall without being a giant, hanging his neck and slouching his shoulders to minimise the effect. He was slim without being skinny, solid without being massy, tense as a tiger, languid as a cat. A boy with a tennis racket under one arm knocked against him, and the killer's head snapped up, fingers curling tight inside his jacket. The boy looked away.

I eased my way around a doctor on her way home, hospital badge bouncing on her chest, photo staring with grim-eyed pessimism from its plastic heart, ready to lower your expectations. The man in the baseball cap was a bare three feet away, the back of his neck flat, his hair trimmed to a dead stop above his topmost vertebrae.

The train began to decelerate, and as it did, he lifted his head again, eyes flicking around the carriage. So doing, his gaze fell on me.

A moment. First stony nothing, the stare of strangers on a train, devoid of character or soul. Then the polite smile, for I was a nice old man, my story written in my skin, and in smiling he hoped I would go away, a contact made, an instant passed. Finally his eyes traced their way to my hands, which were already rising towards his face, and his smile fell as he saw the blood of Josephine Cebula drying in great brown stripes across my fingertips, and as he opened his mouth and began to draw the gun from his shoulder holster I reached out and wrapped my fingers around the side of his neck and

switched.

A second of confusion as the bearded man with blood on his hands, standing before me, lost his balance, staggered, bounced off the boy with the tennis racket, caught his grip on the wall of the train, looked up, saw me, and as the train pulled into Sisli Mecidiyekoy, and with remarkable courage considering the circumstances, straightened up, pointed a finger into my face and called out, "Murderer! Murderer!"

I smiled politely, slipped the gun already in my hand back into its holster, and as the doors opened behind me, spun out into the throng of the station.

if you enjoyed

# THE FIRST FIFTEEN LIVES
# OF HARRY AUGUST

look out for

# THE OVERSIGHT

by

## Charlie Fletcher

# CHAPTER 1

## The House on Wellclose Square

If only she wouldn't struggle so, the damned girl.

If only she wouldn't scream then he wouldn't have had to bind her mouth.

If only she would be quiet and calm and biddable, he would never have had to put her in a sack.

And if only he had not had to put her in a sack, she could have walked and he would not have had to put her over his shoulder and carry her to the Jew.

Bill Ketch was not a brute. Life may have knocked out a few teeth and broken his nose more than once, but it had not yet turned him into an animal: he was man enough to feel bad about what he was doing, and he did not like the way that the girl moaned so loud and wriggled on his shoulder, drawing attention to herself.

Hitting her didn't stop anything. She may have screamed a lot, but she had flint in her eye, something hard and unbreakable, and it was that tough core that had unnerved him and decided him on selling her to the Jew.

That's what the voice in his head told him, the quiet, sly

voice that nevertheless was conveniently able to drown out whatever his conscience might try to say.

The street was empty and the fog from the Thames damped the gas lamps into blurs of dull light as he walked past the Seaman's Hostel and turned into Wellclose Square. The flare of a match caught his eye as a big man with a red beard lit a pipe amongst a group standing around a cart stacked with candle-boxes outside the Danish Church. Thankfully they didn't seem to notice him as he slunk speedily along the opposite side of the road, heading for the dark house at the bottom of the square beyond the looming bulk of the sugar refinery, outside which another horse and carriage stood unattended.

He was pleased the square was so quiet at this time of night. The last thing he wanted to do was to have to explain why he was carrying such strange cargo, or where he was heading.

The shaggy travelling man in The Three Cripples had given him directions, and so he ducked in the front gates, avoiding the main door as he edged round the corner and down a flight of slippery stone steps leading to a side-entrance. The dark slit between two houses was lit by a lonely gas globe which fought hard to be seen in murk that was much thicker at this lower end of the square, closer to the Thames.

There were two doors. The outer one, made of iron bars like a prison gate, was open, and held back against the brick wall. The dark oak inner door was closed and studded with a grid of raised nailheads that made it look as if it had been hammered shut for good measure. There was a handle marked "Pull" next to it. He did so, but heard no answering jangle of a bell from inside. He tugged again. Once more silence greeted him. He was about to yank it a third time when there was the sound of metal sliding against metal and a narrow judas hole opened in the door. Two unblinking eyes looked at him from behind a metal grille, but other than them he could see nothing apart from a dim glow from within.

The owner of the eyes said nothing. The only sound was a moaning from the sack on Ketch's shoulder.

The eyes moved from Ketch's face to the sack, and back. There was a sound of someone sniffing, as if the doorman was smelling him.

Ketch cleared his throat.

"This the Jew's house?"

The eyes continued to say nothing, summing him up in a most uncomfortable way.

"Well," swallowed Ketch. "I've got a girl for him. A screaming girl, like what as I been told he favours."

The accompanying smile was intended to ingratiate, but in reality only exposed the stumpy ruins of his teeth.

The eyes added this to the very precise total they were evidently calculating, and then abruptly stepped back and slammed the slit shut. The girl flinched at the noise and Ketch cuffed her, not too hard and not with any real intent to hurt, just on a reflex.

He stared at the blank door. Even though it was now eyeless, it still felt like it was looking back at him. Judging. He was confused. Had he been rejected? Was he being sent away? Had he walked all the way here carrying the girl – who was not getting any lighter – all for nothing? He felt a familiar anger build in his gut, as if all the cheap gin and sour beer it held were beginning to boil, sending heat flushing across his face. His fist bunched and he stepped forward to pound on the studded wood.

He swung angrily, but at the very moment he did so it opened and he staggered inward, following the arc of his blow across the threshold, nearly dumping the girl on the floor in front of him.

"Why—?!" he blurted.

And then stopped short.

He had stumbled into a space the size and shape of a sentry box, with no obvious way forward. He was about to step uneasily back out into the fog, when the wall to his right swung open.

He took a pace into a larger room lined in wooden tongue-and-groove panelling with a table and chairs and a dim oil lamp. The ceiling was also wood, as was the floor. Despite this it didn't smell of wood, or the oil in the lamp. It smelled of wet clay. All in all, and maybe because of the loamy smell, it had a distinctly coffin-like atmosphere. He shivered.

"Go on in," said a calm voice behind him.

"Nah," he swallowed. "Nah, you know what? I think I've made a mistake—"

The hot churn in his guts had gone ice-cold, and he felt the goosebumps rise on his skin: he was suddenly convinced that this was a room he must not enter, because if he did, he might never leave.

He turned fast, banging the girl on the doorpost, her yip of pain lost in the crash as the door slammed shut, barring his escape route with the sound of heavy bolts slamming home.

He pushed against the wood, and then kicked at it. It didn't move. He stood there breathing heavily, then slid the girl from his shoulder and laid her on the floor, holding her in place with a firm hand.

"Stay still or you shall have a kick, my girl," he hissed.

He turned and froze.

There was a man sitting against the back wall of the room,

a big man, almost a giant, in the type of caped greatcoat that a coachman might wear. It had an unnaturally high collar, and above it he wore a travel-stained tricorn hat of a style that had not been seen much on London's streets for a generation, not since the early 1800s. The hat jutted over the collar and cast a shadow so deep that Ketch could see nothing of the face beneath. He stared at the man. The man didn't move an inch.

"Hoi," said Ketch, by way of introduction.

The giant remained motionless. Indeed as Ketch stepped towards him he realised that the head was angled slightly away, as if the man wasn't looking at him at all.

"Hoi!" repeated Ketch.

The figure stayed still. Ketch licked his lips and ventured forward another step. Peering under the hat he saw the man was brown-skinned.

"Oi, blackie, I'm a-talking to you," said Ketch, hiding the fact that the giant's stillness and apparent obliviousness to his presence was unnerving him by putting on his best bar-room swagger.

The man might as well be a statue for the amount he moved. In fact—

Ketch reached forward and tipped back the hat, slowly at first.

It wasn't a man at all. It was a mannequin made from clay. He ran his thumb down the side of the face and looked at the brown smear it left on it. Damp clay, unfired and not yet quite set. It was a well made, almost handsome face with high cheek-bones and an impressively hooked nose, but the eyes beneath the prominent forehead were empty holes.

"Well, I'll be damned . . ." he whispered, stepping back.

"Yes," said a woman's voice behind him, cold and quiet as a cutthroat razor slicing through silk. "Oh yes. I rather expect you will."

# CHAPTER 2

## A Woman in Black and the Man in Midnight

She stood at the other end of the room, a shadow made flesh in a long tight-bodiced dress buttoned to the neck and wrists. Her arms were folded and black leather gloves covered her hands. The dress had a dull sheen like oiled silk, and she was so straight-backed and slender – and yet also so finely muscled – that she looked in some ways like a rather dangerous umbrella leaning against the wood panelling.

The only relief from the blackness was her face, two gold rings she wore on top of the gloves and her white hair, startlingly out of kilter with her otherwise youthful appearance, which she wore pulled back in a tight pigtail that curled over her shoulder like an albino snake.

She hadn't been there when Ketch entered the room, and she couldn't have entered by the door which had been on the edge of his vision throughout, but that wasn't what most disturbed him: what really unsettled him was her eyes, or rather the fact he couldn't see them, hidden as they were behind the two small circular lenses of smoked glass that made up her spectacles.

"Who—?" began Ketch.

She held up a finger. Somehow that was enough to stop him talking.

"What do you want?"

Ketch gulped, tasting his own fear like rising bile at the back of his throat.

"I want to speak to the Jew."

"Why?"

He saw she carried a ring of keys at her belt like a jailer. Despite the fact she looked too young for the job he decided that she must be the Jew's housekeeper. He used this thought as a stick to steady himself on: he'd just been unnerved by her sudden appearance, that was all. There must be a hidden door behind her. Easy enough to hide its edges in the tongue and groove. He wasn't going to be bullied by a housekeeper. Not when he had business with her master.

"I got something for him."

"What?"

"A screaming girl."

She looked at the long sack lying on the floor.

"You have a *girl* in this sack?"

Somehow the way she asked this carried a lot of threat.

"I want to speak to the Jew," repeated Ketch.

The woman turned her head to one side and rapped on the wooden wall behind her. She spoke into a small circular brass grille.

"Mr Sharp? A moment of your time, please."

The dark lenses turned to look at him again. The silence was unbearable. He had to fill it.

"Man in The Three Cripples said as how the Jew would pay for screaming girls."

The gold ring caught the lamplight as the black gloves flexed open and then clenched tight again, as if she were containing something.

"So you've come to sell a girl?"

"At the right price."

Her smile was tight and showed no teeth. Her voice remained icily polite.

"There are those who would say *any* price is the wrong one. The good Mr Wilberforce's bill abolished slavery nearly forty years ago, did it not?"

Ketch had set out on a simple errand: he had something to sell and had heard of a likely buyer. True, he'd felt a little like a Resurrection Man skulking through the fog with a girl on his shoulder, but she was no corpse and he was no bodysnatcher. And now this woman was asking questions that were confusing that simple thing. When life was straightforward, Bill Ketch sailed through it on smooth waters. When it became complicated he became confused and when he became confused, anger blew in like a storm, and when he became angry, fists and boots flew until the world was stomped flat and simple again.

"I don't know nothing about a Wilberforce. I want to speak to the Jew," he grunted.

"And why do you think the Jew wants a girl? By which I mean: what do you think the Jew wants to do with her?" she asked, the words as taut and measured as her smile.

"What he does is none of my business."

He shrugged and hid his own bunched fists deep in the pockets of his coat.

Her words cracked sharply across the table like a whiplash.

"But what you think you are doing by selling this girl is mine. Answer the question!"

This abrupt change of tone stung him and made him bang the table and lurch towards her, face like a thundercloud.

"No man tells Bill Ketch what to do, and sure as hell's hinges no damn woman does neither! I want to see the bloody Jew and by God—"

The wall next to her seemed to blur open and shut and a man burst through, slicing across the room so fast that he outpaced Ketch's eyes, leaving a smear of midnight blue and flashing steel as he came straight over the table in a swirl of coat-tails that ended in a sudden and dangerous pricking sensation against his Adam's apple.

The eyes that had added him up through the judas hole now stared into him across a gap bridged by eighteen inches of razor-sharp steel. The long blade was held at exactly the right pressure to stop him doing anything life-threatening, like moving. Indeed, just swallowing would seem to be an act of suicide.

"By any god, you shall not take one step further forward, Mr ..."

The eyes swept over his face, searching, reading it.

"Mr Ketch is it? Mr William Ketch ..."

He leaned in and Ketch, frozen, watched his nostrils flare as he appeared to smell him. The midnight blue that the man was dressed in seemed to absorb even more light than the woman's black dress. He wore a knee-length riding coat cut tight to his body, beneath which was a double-breasted leather waistcoat of exactly the same hue, as were the shirt and tightly knotted silk stock he wore around his neck. The only break in the colour of his clothing was the brown of his soft leather riding boots.

His hair was also of the darkest brown, as were his thick and well-shaped eyebrows, and his eyes, when Ketch met them, were startlingly ... unexpected.

Looking into them Ketch felt, for a moment, giddy and excited. The eyes were not just one brown, not even some of the browns: they were *all* the browns. It was as if he was looking into a swirl of autumn leaves tumbling happily in the golden sunlight of a blazing Indian summer.

One look into the tawny glamour in those eyes and Ketch forgot the blade at his throat.

One look into those eyes and the anger was gone and all was simple again.

One look into those eyes and Bill Ketch was confusingly and irrevocably in something as close to love as to make no difference.

The man must have seen this because the blade did something fast and complicated and disappeared beneath the skirts of his coat as he reached forward, gripped Ketch by both shoulders and pulled him close, sniffing him again and then raising an eyebrow in surprise, before pushing him back and smiling at him like an old friend.

"He is everything he appears to be, and no more," he said over his shoulder.

The woman stepped forward.

"You are sure?"

"I thought I smelled something on the air as he knocked, but it didn't come in with him. I may have been mistaken. The river is full of stink at high tide."

"So you are sure?" she repeated.

"As sure as I am that you will never tire of asking me that particular question," said the man.

"'Measure twice, cut once' is a habit that has served me well enough since I was old enough to think," she said flatly, "and it has kept this house safe for much longer than that."

"Are you the Jew?" said Ketch. His voice squeaked a little as he spoke, so happy was he feeling, bathed in the warmth of the handsome young man's open smile.

"I do not have that honour," he replied.

The woman appeared at the man's shoulder.

"Well?" she said.

The chill returned to Ketch's heart as she spoke.

"He is as harmless as he appears to be, I assure you," repeated the man.

She took off her glasses and folded them in one hand. Her eyes were grey-green and cold as a midwinter wave. Her words, when they came, were no warmer.

"I am Sara Falk. I am the Jew."

As Ketch tried to realign the realities of his world, she put a hand on the man's shoulder and pointed him at the long bundle on the floor.

"Now, Mr Sharp: there is a young woman in that sack. If you would be so kind."

The man flickered to the bundle on the floor, again seeming to move between time instead of through it. The blade reappeared in his hand, flashed up and down the sacking, and then he was helping the girl to her feet and simultaneously sniffing at her head.

"Mr Sharp?" said Sara Falk.

"As I said, I smelled something out there," he said. "I thought it was him. It isn't, nor is it her."

"Well, good," she said, the twitch of a smile ghosting round the corner of her mouth. "Maybe it was your imagination."

"It pleases you to make sport of me, my dear Miss Falk, but I venture to point out that since we are charged with anticipating the inconceivable, my 'imagination' is just as effective a defensive tool as your double-checking," he replied, looking at the girl closely. "And since our numbers are so perilously dwindled these days, you will excuse me if I do duty as both belt and braces in these matters."

The young woman was slender and trembling, in a grubby pinafore dress with no shoes and long reddish hair that hung down wavy and unwashed, obscuring a clear look at her face. At first glance, however, it was clear she was not a child, and he judged her age between sixteen and twenty years old. She flinched when he reached to push the hair back to get a better look at her and make a more accurate assessment, and he stopped and spoke quietly.

"No, no, my dear, just look at me. Look at me and you'll see you have nothing to fear."

After a moment her head came up and eyes big as saucers peered a question into his. As soon as they did the trembling calmed and she allowed him to push the hair back and reveal what had been done to her mouth to stop the screaming.

He exhaled through his teeth in an angry hiss and then gently turned her towards Sara Falk. She stared at the rectangle of black hessian that was pasted across the girl's face from below her nose down to her chin.

"What is this?" said Mr Sharp, voice tight, still keeping the girl steady with his eyes.

"It's just a pitch-plaster, some sacking and tar and pitch, like a sticky poultice, such as they use up the Bedlam Hospital to quiet the lunatics . . ." explained Ketch, his voice quavering lest Mr Sharp's gaze when it turned to add him up again was full of something other than the golden warmth he was already missing. "Why, the girlie don't mind a—"

"Look at her hands," said Sara Falk.

The girl's hands were tightly wrapped in strips of grubby material, like small cloth-bound boxing gloves.

"Nah, that she does herself, she done that and not me," said Ketch hurriedly. "I takes 'em off cos she's no bloody use with hands wrapped into stumps like that, but she wraps whatever she can find round 'em the moment you turn your back. Why even if there's nothing in the rooms she'll rip up her own clothes to do it. It's all she does: touches things and then screams at what ain't there and tangles rags round her hands like a winding cloth so she doesn't have to touch anything at all . . ."

Sara Falk exchanged a look with Mr Sharp.

"Touches things? Then screams?" he said. "Old stones, walls . . . those kind of things?"

Ketch nodded enthusiastically. "Walls and houses and things in the street. Sets 'er off something 'orrible it does—"

"Enough," said Mr Sharp, his eyes on Sara Falk who was stroking the scared girl's hair. Their eyes met once more.

"So she's a Glint then," he said quietly.

She nodded, for a moment unable to speak.

"She's not right in the head is what she is," said Ketch. "And—"

"Is she your daughter?" said Sara Falk, clearing something from her throat.

"No. Not blood kin. She's . . . my ward, as it were. But I can't afford to feed her no more, so it's you or the poorhouse, and the poorhouse don't pay, see . . . ?"

The spark of commerce had reignited in his eyes.

"Don't worry about that blessed plaster, lady. Why, a hot flannel held on for a couple of minutes loosens it off, and you can peel it away without too much palaver."

The man and the woman stared at him.

"The redness fades after a couple of days," he insisted. "We tried a gag, see, but she loosens them or gnaws through. She's spirited—"

"What is her name?" said Sara Falk.

"Lucy. Lucy Harker. She's just—"

"Mr Sharp," she said, cutting him off by turning away to kneel by the girl.

"What do you want to do with him?" said the man in midnight.

"What I *want* to do to a man who'd sell a young woman without a care as to what the buyer might want to do with or to her is undoubtedly illegal," said Sara Falk almost under her breath.

"It would be justice though," he replied equally softly.

"Yes," she said. "But we, as I have said many times, are an office of the Law and the Lore, not of Justice, Mr Sharp. And Law and Lore say to make the punishment fit the crime. Do what must be done."

Lucy Harker looked at her, still mute behind the gag.

Mr Sharp left them and turned his smile on Ketch, who relaxed and grinned expectantly back at him.

"Well," said Mr Sharp. "It seems we must pay you, Mr Ketch."

The thought of money coming was enticing and jangly enough to drown out the question that had been trying to get Ketch's attention for some time now, namely how this good-looking young man knew his name. He watched greedily as he reached into his coat and pulled out a small leather bag.

"Now," said Mr Sharp. "Gold, I think. Hold out your hands."

Ketch did so as if sleepwalking, and though at first his eyes tricked him into the thought that Mr Sharp was counting tarnished copper pennies into his hand, after a moment he realised they were indeed the shiniest gold pieces he had ever seen, and he relaxed enough to stop looking at them and instead to study more of Mr Sharp. His dark hair was cropped short on the back and sides, but was long on top, curling into a cowlick that tumbled over his forehead in an agreeably untidy way. A single deep blue stone dangled from one ear in a gold setting, winking in the lamplight as he finished his tally.

"... twenty-eight, twenty-nine, thirty. That's enough, I think, and if not it is at least ... traditional."

And with that the purse disappeared and the friendly arm went round Ketch's shoulder, and before he could quite catch up with himself the two of them were out in the fog, walking out of Wellclose Square into the tangle of dark streets beyond.

Ketch's heart was soaring and he felt happier than he had ever been in his life, though whether it was because of the unexpectedly large number of gold – gold! – coins in his pockets, or because of his newfound friend, he could not tell.

# CHAPTER 3

## A Charitable Deed

If the fog had eyes (which in this part of London it often did) it would not only have noticed Mr Sharp leading Bill Ketch away into the narrow streets at the lower end of the square, it would have remarked that the knot of men who had been unloading boxes of candles into the Danish Church had finished their work, and that the carrier's cart had taken them off into the night, leaving only the burly red-bearded man with the pipe and a wiry underfed-looking young fellow in a tight fustian coat.

The bearded man locked the heavy doors and then followed the other across the street, heading for the dark carriage still standing outside the sugar refinery. If the fog's eyes had also been keen, they would have noticed that the red beard over-hung a white banded collar with two tell-tale tabs that marked him out as the pastor of the church whose barn-like doors he had just secured. There was a crunch underfoot as they reached the carriage and he looked down at the scattering of oyster shells with surprise. The wiry youth, unsurprised, reached up and rapped his bony knuckles on the polished black of the carriage door.

"Father," he said. "'Tis the Reverend Christensen. 'E wishes to thank you in person."

There was a pause as if the carriage itself was alive and considering what had been said to it. Then it seemed to shrug as something large moved within, the weight shifting it on its springs, and then the door cracked open.

The reverend's beard parted to reveal an open smile as the pastor leant into the carriage apologetically.

"So sorry to discommode you, Mr Templebane, but I could not let the opportunity of thanking you in person pass me by."

"No matter, no matter at all," said a deep voice from inside. "Think no more of it, my dear reverend sir. My pleasure indeed. Only sorry we had to deliver at so unholy an hour."

"All hours are holy, Mr Templebane," smiled the pastor, his English scarcely accented at all. "And any hour that contains such a welcome donation is all the more blessed."

"Please!" said the voice, whose owner remained hidden except for the appearance in the carriage window of a fleshy hand carefully holding an open oyster with the smallest finger extended politely away from all the others. The shell was full of plump grey oyster meat that bobbled and spilled a little of the shellfish's liquor as the hand airily waved the thanks away.

"You will embarrass me, sir, so you will. To be honest, the bit of business that resulted in me taking over the unwanted deadstock from the unfortunate, not to say imprudent, candle-maker left me with enough dips to gift all the churches in the parish."

The fleshy hand retreated into the shadows and a distinct slurping noise was heard.

"But a lesser spirit might still have sold them," said the pastor, working hard to make his thanks stick to their rightful target.

The fleshy hand reappeared as the carriage's occupant leant further forward to drop the now-empty oyster shell daintily on to the pavement, revealing for just an instant the face of Issachar Templebane.

It was a paradox of a face, a face both gaunt and yet pillowy, the skin hanging slack over the bones of the skull with the unhealthy toad's-belly pallor of a fat man who has lost weight too late in life for his skin to have retained the elasticity to shrink to fit the new, smaller version of himself.

He wiped a trickle of oyster juice from the edge of his mouth with the back of his thumb before reaching forward to grip the pastor's hand in a brisk, hearty farewell.

"I could, I could, but my brother and I are lawyers not tradesmen, and I assure you our fees in the matter were more than adequate. Besides, money isn't everything. Now, goodnight to you, sir, and safe home. Come, Coram, we must be going."

And with that he released the hand and retreated back into the carriage as the wiry young man sprang up to the driver's seat, gathered the reins and snapped the horses into motion with a farewell nod to the pastor, who was left standing among the debris of Templebane's oyster supper feeling strangely dismissed, rather than actually wished well.

As the carriage turned the corner a panel slid back in the front of the vehicle, next to Coram, and Templebane's face appeared.

"Did you draw the reverend gentleman's attention to the man Ketch and his suspicious bundle?" he asked, all the cheeriness in his voice now replaced by a business-like flatness.

"Yes, Father. I done it just as 'ow you said, casual-like."

If the fog had ears as well as eyes, it might by this time have noted a further paradox regarding Issachar Templebane, which was that the boy who called him Father did not have anything like the same deep, fluid – and above all cultured – voice as he. Coram's voice had been shaped by the rough dockside alleys of the East End: it dropped "h's" and played fast and loose with what had, with Victoria's recent accession to the throne, only just become the Queen's English. Issachar spoke with the smooth polished edges of the courtroom; Coram's voice was sharp as a docker's hook. If there seemed to be no familiar resemblance between them, this was because although Issachar Templebane had many children, he had no blood kin beyond his twin brother Zebulon, who was the other half of the house of Templebane & Templebane.

Issachar and Zebulon were prodigious adopters of unclaimed boys, all of whom grew up to work for them in the chambers and counting room that adjoined their house on Bishopsgate. It was their habit to name the boys for the London parishes from whose workhouses (or in Coram's case, the foundling hospital) they had been procured. This led to unwieldy but undoubtedly unusual names: there was an Undershaft, a Vintry, a Sherehog, a Bassetshaw and a Garlickhythe Templebane. The only exception was the youngest who had been taken from the parish of St Katherine Cree and he, it being too outlandish to call the boy Katherine, was called Amos, a name chosen at random by letting the Bible fall open and choosing the title of the book it opened at. If Amos had anything to say about the matter he might well have remarked that he had as well been called Job since, as the youngest member of the artificially assembled family, with brothers who shared no love between them, he got more than his share of grief and toil. He didn't remark on this because he spoke not at all, his particular affliction being that he was mute. Coram, by contrast, was garrulous and questioning, a characteristic that his adopted fathers encouraged and punished in equal measure depending on their whim and humour.

Coram cleared his throat by spitting onto the crupper of the horse in front of him and went on.

"And 'e remarked, the pastor did, that the 'ouse Ketch gone in was the Jew's 'ouse, and that she was a good woman, though not of his faith."

Templebane nodded approvingly, his hands busy with a short-bladed shucking knife as he opened another oyster.

"Quite, quite. He has no malice in him, none at all. As solid and upright and clean as a new mast of Baltic pine is the Danish reverend. Which will make his testimony all the more credible, should we require it."

Here he paused and slurped another oyster, tossing the shell out into the road. He chewed the unlucky bivalve once, to burst it, then swallowed with a shiver of satisfaction.

"Mark it, Coram: there is no better instrument of destruction than an honest man who has no axe to grind."

And with that the panel slapped shut and Coram Templebane was alone with the horses and the fog that thinned as he drove up towards the higher ground of Goodman's Fields.

# CHAPTER 4

## Hand in Glove

S ara Falk crouched in front of the trembling young woman and smiled
encouragingly at her.

"Lucy," she said.

Lucy Harker just stared at the door through which Mr Sharp had led Ketch, as if expecting them to walk back in at any moment.

"Lucy. May I?"

She reached for Lucy's neck, pushed away the hair, and then lifted the collar of the pinafore as if looking for something like a necklace. Finding nothing she sucked her teeth with a snap of disappointment and shook her head.

The eyes stayed locked on the outer door. Sara Falk moved into her field of vision.

"Lucy. You must believe the next three things I tell you with all your heart, for they are the truest things in the world: firstly, that man will never walk back through that door unbidden and he shall never, ever hurt you or anyone ever again. Mr Sharp is making sure of that right now."

Lucy's eyes flickered and she looked at the slender woman, her eyes making a question that her mouth could not, her body still tense and quivering like a wild deer on the point of flight.

"Secondly, I know you have visions," continued Sara Falk, reaching out to touch the pitch-plaster gently, as if stroking a hurt away. "It's the visions that make you scream. Visions you have when you touch things. Visions that make you wonder if you are perhaps mad?"

The eyes stared at her. Sara smiled and raised her own hands, showing the gloves and the two rings that she wore on top of them, one an odd-shaped piece of sea-glass rimmed with a band of gold, the other set with a bloodstone into which a crest of some sort had been carved.

"You are not mad, and you are not alone. As you see, others have reason to cover their hands too. And if you come with me into my house where there is a warm fire and pie and hot milk with honey, we shall sit with my glove box and find an old pair of mine and see if they fit you."

She removed the rings, reached for the buttons at the wrist of one glove, quickly opened them and peeled the thin black leather off, revealing the bare hand beneath. She freed the other hand even faster, and then reached gently for Lucy's bound hands.

"May I?"

Lucy's eyes stayed locked on hers as she gently began to unwrap one of the hands.

"I have something that will calm you, Lucy, a simple piece of sea-glass for you to touch, and I promise it will not harm you but give you a strength until we can find you one of your own—"

Lucy pulled her hand sharply away but Sara held onto it

firmly and smiled as she held out the sea-glass ring: the glass, worn smooth by constant tumbling back and forth on a beach matched Sara Falk's eyes perfectly.

"You need to touch this—"

Lucy goggled at it, then ripped her hand out of Sara Falk's, shaking her head with sudden agitation, emphatically miming "No!"

"Lucy—" began Sara, and then stopped.

Lucy was tearing at her own bandages, moaning excitedly from behind the tar and hessian gag. It was Sara's turn to watch with eyes that widened in surprise as the rags wound off and revealed their secret.

Lucy freed one hand and held out a fist, palm up, jabbing it insistently at the older woman.

Then she opened it.

Clenched in her hand was another piece of sea-glass, its light hazel colour like that of Lucy's own eyes.

Sara Falk's face split into a grin that matched and made even younger the youthful face she carried beneath the prematurely white hair. It was a proud and a mischievous grin.

"Oh," she gasped. "Oh, you clever girl. Clever, *clever* girl! You kept your own heart-stone. *That's* how you survived that awful man unbroken! Oh, you shall be *fine*, Lucy Harker, for you have sense and spirit. The visions that assault you when you touch things are a gift, and though it is not an easy one to bear, believe me that it *is* a gift and no lasting blight on your life."

A tear leaked out of one of Lucy's eyes and Sara caught it and wiped it away before it hit the black plaster.

"And this heart-stone, I mean your piece of sea-glass, does it glow when there is danger near?"

Lucy again looked startled and on edge, as if she was on the point of breaking for the door. Sara put a hand on her shoulder, gently.

"Did you know that only a true Glint can see the fire that blazes out of it when peril approaches?" said Sara. "Ordinary folk see nothing but the same dull piece of sea-glass. Why, even the estimable Mr Sharp who has abilities of his own cannot see the fire that guards the unique power that you and I have. It is not glowing now, is it?"

Lucy looked at the dull glass in her hand; it was like a cloudy gobbet of marmalade.

"Then if you trust it, trust me," said Sara. "And we shall find a way to soften that pitch and peel this wretched gag off without hurting you. Come to the kitchen and we shall see what we can do."

She smiled encouragingly at the gagged face. Her grandfather had indeed once sought out oddities like Lucy Harker and other people with even stranger abilities. The Rabbi Falk had been one of the great minds of his time, and though not born with any powers of his own, he not only believed in what he termed the "supranatural" but also toiled endlessly to increase his knowledge of it and so harness it. He had been a Freemason, a Kabbalist, an alchemist and a natural scientist, obsessively studying the threads of secret power that wove themselves beneath the everyday surface of things and underpinned what he called "The Great and Hidden History of the World".

It was perhaps proof that Fate had a sense of humour in that his granddaughter had been born with some of those very elusive powers which he had spent a lifetime searching for and trying to control.